Bonnets and Aprons: Fionna

Cover art by B. Williamson

To order additional copies, please contact us.
BookSurge, LLC
www.booksurge.com
1-866-308-6235
orders@booksurge.com

BONNETS & APRONS:
FIONNA

2006

KERRI BENNETT
WILLIAMSON

Bonnets and Aprons: Fionna

TABLE OF CONTENTS

ACKNOWLEDGMENTS:

Many thanks to my closest family and friends for believing in my work before it was shared beyond my immediate sphere, and to my online readers around the world for all their generously encouraging and supportive emails, and comments at www.bonnetsandaprons.com.

Dedicated to virtuous women the world over who seek and work to ennoble every spirit upwards; and to the gentle men who lovingly encourage and support them.

1
Mother and Benjamin

Her first was stillborn. She named him Adam. Not nearly beyond a year later her second son, whom they named Aaron, died the day he was born. I was the first to survive, but I was not the long awaited and hoped-for son. He would come later. I was their first daughter and five more girls came after me before our parents finally were blessed with Bertram, a son who lived.

I distinctly remember Mother as all things a woman ought to be: a wonderful example of an ideal and gracious lady to every one in her sphere of influence. She sacrificed all for her Husband and children and thought nothing of giving, working for and sincerely loving us from the moment she awoke to the moment she retired to her bed: exhausted and desperate for rest from her long day of work. Besides being a hard worker and dedicated to all those she loved, she was a very playful woman with a wonderful sense of humor and was adored by every one who truly knew her.

Beyond the two sons she lost, Mother brought forth four more sons, one after another; but within a few days after her fourth boy was born, the world we had known that included our dear sweet Mother, was shattered as tragedy took her away from us. Childbed fever, perhaps brought on partially by her years of laborious toil and giving life to so many children, sent her Heavenward where we trust and pray that she watches over us often. While it is truly something wondrous to believe that someone who dearly loves you watches over you from above, it is of course, somehow simply not quite *so* exceedingly comforting as being watched over by the living and we began to know life without Mother. That life as it was, was sadly lacking. We did not know how much she had done for us and truly *meant* to us until she was gone from the Earth.

The first thing Father did after Mother's body was laid to rest was to take sweet little Benjamin to a neighbor woman who had a young baby boy of her own and was therefore able to share her own mother's milk with our littlest brother. While we all saw this as indeed a necessity (for we had tried to feed little Benjamin milk from our goat as we understood that goat's milk is better for a baby than milk from a cow), it was still difficult to send our little brother away. I trekked over to visit him, to hold him and to help care for him as much as I possibly could between my chores on the farm. I made a special effort to mother Benjamin whenever I could, but I also felt compelled to do as much as I could, as Mother used to do for the rest of the family besides, so I was not able to go take care of Benjamin nearly as much as I desired to. Clara and Anna, my sisters just younger than I, took their turns helping with Benjamin whenever they could as well, for they were full old enough to help and cared to do so.

We all tried to carry on living as we always had, as we knew Mother would have wanted us to: each trying to live better than ever before, to do better in everything we did; but also to keep on laughing and sharing love one with another. I tried to encourage all my brothers and sisters to each take on something Mother used to do because I knew I could not accomplish it all as much as I might want to and try to, not just because I allotted time at the neighbors to be with and care for Benjamin daily when possible but also because I could only *hope* to be a fraction of the woman Mother was. I was training and practicing to become *like* her but was only aspiring as yet.

Our neighbors, the Blackwells, who took Benjamin in for us were indeed kind enough to him and we gave them gifts of food and such to repay them for their many kindnesses. As Benjamin approached one year of age, I began to believe it would not be too terribly long before we would be able to bring Benjamin home to us: for he was able to begin to eat foods and drink milk beyond what only a mother can give a baby. Just as I began to rejoice at the thoughts of bringing our cherished little brother home to live amongst us where he belonged, tragedy struck the Blackwells, and consequently also our family once again. Our neighbors' own baby suddenly took ill and then fairly promptly died. The mother, who's name was Blanch, was quite inconsolable about the loss of her own baby boy and thus clung all the tighter to Benjamin. We thought that we might leave her be a while and allow Benjamin to console her to a degree, and then soon she would be able to finish her grieving for her own son and therefore be ready and willing to give our Benjamin back to us: to be back with his own family. It was not to be. One day, the Blackwell's were suddenly and quite simply, gone. It was almost as if they had vanished without a trace. They had packed up and taken our dear little Benjamin without a word to us or any other. They were gone and there was none who knew where they had gone to.

It was as if a death once more: one more beloved family member was taken from our family. This time, though, we could not feel the peace of knowing our loved one was safely, securely and joyously in Heaven. While we knew the Blackwells to be good people who would love and raise Benjamin as their own (as long as he remained their very own, for what would come of their love for him if more of their own children were born to them?), now we also knew that they were both capable of doing such a thing as to take a child from his own family forever, as it would seem; and so a dark shadow was cast on our former beliefs in their goodness, integrity and honesty. I supposed they found their justifications and did not believe they had truly done so terribly wrong. I hoped for such at *least*, rather than something more sinister. We could not help but worry about Benjamin; and beyond that we missed him terribly. We feared he would grow up not knowing his own family and we would go on not knowing him, not watching him grow, not giving to him and loving him as it was our divine right to do as long as he lived.

It is true that for the first while we did hold out hopes that Clyde and Blanch would come to their senses and bring our Benjamin back to us. We understood that it was her grief for the loss of her son that was behind her willingness to take our boy. We hoped, thought and even *believed* that the Blackwells knew what they did was wrong, very wrong, and that they would want to right things: with the law, with us, even with themselves, but most especially with Heaven. I kept thinking, 'How could they do this? How could they do this to us and to Benjamin? How can they live with themselves? How can they *forget* who he belongs to and who belongs to him? Why can not they think of their own son in Heaven and hope for more sons and also daughters to mend the sadness and loss that they feel? How can taking what, no, *who*, belongs to others, feel *right* to anyone?' My questions were not to be answered and to this very day they are still ingrained in my heart and mind. One thought or hope I held onto was that when or if Blanch brought forth another child, or at least another son; that she would find it in her heart, and then find a way, to send our Benjamin back home to us.

I continued to hope that someday we would see our Benjamin again and each morning and night I prayed that God would bring him back to us as soon as He saw fit to do it, that angels above would watch over Benjamin in the meantime, that Mother could watch over her dear son as well and that the Blackwells would be good to him. I must confess I felt a great deal of hate and anger towards our former neighbors for what they had done to us all and to Benjamin, and I tried and prayed not to hate them and not to be angry because I knew such feelings were wrong under Heaven but it was very difficult to overcome those strong feelings which I felt against Clyde and Blanch. I kept telling myself that I must turn my prayers and thoughts and hopes to Benjamin's welfare, rather than against those who had taken him from us. I prayed to forgive the Blackwells, but that was a very difficult task for me to accomplish.

While I missed Mother as a great source of strength, nurturing, wisdom and such an exemplary model to follow; I felt immense peace in knowing that she was safely, happily and peacefully residing in

Heaven above: but Benjamin was somewhere in the lone and dreary world and I could *not* know how he truly was at any given moment. I did not worry over Mother and how she was for I felt assured of her joy in the afterlife. I did, however, worry continually over Benjamin, no matter how I tried to think consoling thoughts about him being loved and cared for as a substitute son, by the Blackwells. I only could ask the angels up above in prayers, to watch out for my littlest brother, since I had absolutely no power to do anything for him.

2
Mildred

Just when our family seemed to be able to go on without Benjamin, what could have been a wonderful addition of joy to our family turned out to be, at least to me, rather like another tragedy striking our family once again.

In the spring of 1840, Father met a woman in town. She was new to the area: a relation of the man who owned the general mercantile store and he had hired her to work there. I think all of us children had thought Father would live out his life alone, because what woman could ever replace Mother?

I was not necessarily against Father remarrying. As young as I was, I still understood that he was lonely in a certain way that a woman could fill for him as his children could not, although I certainly did not fathom the full scope of such things at that time. Some of my younger sisters and brothers did not understand Father's seeming need to marry again. There did seem to be an element of Father wanting to provide another mother for his children and perhaps another mistress for his home and land, but most of us believed that at least Clara, Anna and I could fulfill those roles sufficiently and thus those needs should be negated, but we could see that Father did not agree. What I did not understand most of all was Father considering someone less worthy of him, and even of us, than Mother. I thought that if he wanted to marry again, the least that he could do relative to the matter was to find a woman who measured up to Mother, even to some degree.

The woman Father fancied who worked in the general mercantile store was named Mildred. She *seemed* quite nice but I simply did not feel that she could at all compare to Mother. We all felt that way. We did not fully know how Father felt but he seemed to quite like Mildred and began to behave in a way that appeared oddly strange to us. I decided firmly that the word *silly* could only encapsulate his behavior. He would think me unkind if he had known I had thought such of him, but he could not see how he behaved from all our perspectives. It was truly like he was suddenly young again but not in ways that any of us liked. We needed and expected him to behave like a father: like a man; and not like a silly schoolboy chasing after a girl. Father began spending a great deal of time away from us, courting Mildred, as we of course presumed. When he would bring Mildred home to the farm or take us to see her in town, she would behave very cordially towards all of us: very cordially, to be sure.

I *tried* to like Mildred and to treat her as pleasantly as possible as I saw that she soon might become our Father's wife, and therefore in a very real sense a replacement of our mother to Father and apparently to us all. Many of my sisters and brothers were quite unhappy about this prospect and did not try very hard to make Mildred feel welcome on the farm or part of our family when we were in town to visit her. Father tried to scold and to force everyone to treat Mildred with as much delight as he was so inclined to do, but few beyond me made much effort to do so. I was trying to make the best of things because it seemed inevitable that Mildred would join our family but I think many of my brothers and sisters thought that if they made Mildred feel unwanted enough, she would think the better of joining Father in matrimony and therefore, of joining our family. The general family consensus among Father's children was that we all wished Mildred to go away: we wished her very far... *far* away, indeed.

Despite the misgivings and unwelcome treatment, Father and Mildred continued towards marriage and by the time the day was drawing nearer, some of my sisters and brothers began to give in and accept Mildred. Much of this acceptance was a credit to Mildred and her efforts to court Father's children as well as him. Mildred would treat us each to candies at the store: those of us who were willing and perhaps simply young enough to take her bribes. I tended to decline her offerings. She also brought candies and other treats out to the house when Father brought her to visit.

I tried not to think about Mother and what *she* would think of these entire goings on. I could not help but imagine Mother looking down upon all of us from Heaven and watching this other woman trying to take her husband and her children away from her in a very real sense, but then I would tell myself that Father was lonely and that perhaps Mother would understand Father not wanting to live out his life alone and also wanting a mother for most of his children who were not old enough yet to go through life without a mother. I decided not to worry about such things and simply hope that Mildred would make Father happy and that she would be a reasonably good replacement mother to us. I managed to think of her as some sort of an aunt and I hoped that she would continue to try to be a good one.

After Father and Mildred were wed, I could not stop thinking about Mother and wondering how she was doing, what she was thinking and if she was feeling any sadness about everything such as her husband marrying another woman and knowing her children were growing up without their true mother to guide and guard them, and were now looking at life ahead with a new substitute mother.

I found myself compelled to go to Mother's grave to spend some time talking to her: in case she could hear me and also just to make myself feel better. I stole myself away to the little family cemetery plot which sat quietly somewhat beyond the garden and some trees. On my way I gathered some roses from a bush that Mother had planted that were now in full bloom. I first paused at Adam and Aaron's little graves and put down a flower for each and then I flopped down with the rest of the bouquet at Mother's grave. I found my finger tracing over her first name as it was carved in the headstone: Sarah... Sarah...

Tears filled my eyes as they then glanced at the inscription of the year of her death: 1839. All at once I began to sob.

I cried out Heavenward, "I'm so *very* sorry Mother! Father has married another woman. It feels as if he has long since forgotten *all* about you; and his new wife wants all us children to forget you too. I am sure of it. Mildred is a nice woman I suppose, but she is not anywhere near the woman you are... the woman you were. She is not... you. I fear she is nothing like you. I truly fear how she will be as a mother. I wish you could come back to us. Why did you have to go away? Why did you have to die?! Can you hear me? Can you see us? Oh, *why* did you leave us?"

I fell to the ground shaking in sobs... uncontrollable sobs and flowing tears.

After a lengthy while I composed myself and sat up, wiping my tears away. I then continued my one-sided conversation, trying to be more sensible and logical while gazing at Mother's headstone as if to calm myself by fixating on it, tracing over and over her name: Sarah, "I know Father is lonely and wants a wife, and a mother for his children, but I wish he would have taken more time and care in choosing. I fear he has acted hastily, Mother. I simply think he could have made a better choice... in time. He should have waited longer... much longer. He should have taken much more time and thought, in choosing another wife. He should have chosen better, *far* better."

I started to cry again but then managed to compose myself once more, thinking of how Mother would want me to be brave and grown up, "I will try to make the best of it, Mother. I will try to get along with Mildred. If I think of her as an aunt who has come to live with us rather than Father's wife or more especially my own mother, I think I can bear it and be pleasant to her day to day. I just hope you are not sad about all this, Mother. I hope you are happy. I hope you are visiting all your old friends and family members who went heavenward before you and that you feel peace and joy and all those good things you told us are in Heaven always, for everyone there. If I know you are happy there... then perhaps I can do well here."

Soon determining to think along those lines that I had spoken into the air to my dear sweet mother, I tried to begin a new day with new feelings towards Father's new wife. Maybe Mildred *could* be good for our family, never to truly replace Mother, but to be a helping hand, a comforting voice and other good things that a family needs. Mildred could be a help to us.

It was astounding to me to see how Mildred had been accepted so much by so many of my sisters and brothers by the time Father and Mildred were settling in as man and wife. I supposed the boys were all young enough to begin to forget Mother and therefore easily make room for Mildred as their mother, and the younger girls seemed to do so as well.

Colin being only three years old, seemed quick to accept his new mother. Edward and Bertram were five and seven, respectively, and they too began to see Mildred as their mother figure. Victoria being only eight was growing more amiable towards Mildred as was Elizabeth who was nine. Charlotte at eleven seemed a little more hesitant to embrace Mildred as her new mother. Twelve year old Anna seemed quite doubtful about accepting Mildred and Clara who was thirteen was still not being very amiable towards Mildred at all. I still managed to be pleasant as I had throughout the entire affair. Not quite a mature woman at fifteen, I did indeed consider myself somewhat of a young lady.

In the beginning, Mildred seemed to be trying to fit in, to love all of us, to make us love her, to become our mother as well as wife to Father. I began to think that perhaps we could all find something together that was at least better than being completely, truly motherless. Now I did not have to worry so completely about all the responsibilities as I had for quite some time. I could think about myself a little and simply a few things I might like to do each day rather than being lost in doing so much for everyone else. I took to riding my favorite horse once more, escaping into the fields for long rides. I also took long walks and began to remember to drink in the sky, the fresh air and to feel the warmth of the sun on my clothing. My sun bonnet was in use again like it had not been in ever so long, for I had seemed long consigned and confined to the house, managing it and its inhabitants.

Everyone seemed to be settling into some semblance of family order, peace and happiness and then... Mildred began to try just a little less at pleasing all but Father. She began to complain that especially I was not helping as much as I should. She clearly resented taking on even the few household duties that I thought I could leave for her to be responsible for. I had still continued doing many things that Mother used to do but I thought that Father's new wife could take on some chores as well. Mildred soon continued and extended her complaints to include just about everyone. Even the little ones could seem to do no right. We had not seen this critical side of Mildred before and added unto such was also a frequent loss of temper, *particularly* when Father was not within earshot of her shouting. My attempts to reason with her only fanned the flames of her rage. When I saw her mistreating my younger sisters and brothers I could not stand by and would speak up only to be screamed at and told I had no such right to interfere with her mothering opinions, decisions and actions.

As this unpleasant situation with Mildred grew worse, I wondered how I could open the subject with Father. Mildred was beginning to make everyone miserable when Father was not near to hear and then seemed such a darling when he was there. Mildred's spirit of criticism, discord and contention soon permeated our home and most of the children began squabbling amongst each other without reason, like never before.

I knew I needed to talk to Father about Mildred but would he have ears to hear? Could he *listen*? He still was very much enamored with his new woman. I could see clearly that he thought he had found himself a wonderful wife and that his children could want for no better mother. I was sure that Father thought all was well, that his children were doing better by far with this new mother he had chosen for them than they were without. I could not see how things would or could get better with Mildred for the rest of us. It was certainly only going to get worse. It was getting worse already and steadily. I could not seem to talk to her. She would not listen. She did not seem to care to try to understand us. Talking to Father seemed increasingly imperative and yet I had never truly been able to talk to Father on a deep level or about sensitive issues. Mother was the one I had always been able to talk to. Mother was always our go-between with Father. But, Mother was gone.

One day I decided to go out into the field where I would be able to talk to Father alone and, more particularly, *far* away from any listening ears. I rode my dear horse out to where he was. I could have walked, and perhaps the strenuous exercise might have helped to calm my nerves but having my four-legged friend with me gave me the moral support I surely felt I needed. I brought some bread I had baked earlier; hoping this type of peace-offering would help me in this thorny type of situation. He seemed happy to see me and just *that* simply made my task all the more difficult to begin for I feared his smiling face would soon change into something quite possibly the opposite, when I introduced the subject of my visit.

Beginning extremely carefully, softly; saying very little, trying not to sound critical of his new beloved wife: trying not to sound as if I put all the blame on her but trying to take some sort of responsibility for my own misunderstanding; I thought that maybe one small beginning might begin to help the growing breach between Father's children and Father's wife. If he only knew but a little of what his children felt, perhaps he could start to help with some desperately needed mending. I tried not to speak for my sisters and brothers exactly, but simply verbalizing in a general sense to let Father know that it was not only *me* who was becoming distressed with the less than perfect associations with his new wife in our home when he was not there.

Happily surprised, I was indeed delighted to find that our talk together went rather well. Father seemed very understanding and was clearly willing to make a wholehearted effort to repair any damage and begin anew with a greater effort to please his children with the help of his new wife. My relieved feelings resulted in a generous hug given happily to Father before I mounted my horse and rode towards home with a renewed and hopeful spirit that with Father's guidance and suggestions, Mildred would be heartily encouraged to make a greater effort to understand and treat Father's children with tender care.

Back at the house I found myself somewhat avoiding Mildred, as if fearing that she would see written on my countenance that I had gone behind her back, in a sense, to talk to Father about her, and that she might confront me about what I had done to countermand her supposed usurped authority. I knew I had not done anything wrong to speak with my own father as regards to my new stepmother, but I also was sure that Mildred would not like what I had done. No matter. It had to be done. It *was* done. I also did not wish to get into any squabbles with her or cross her in any way before Father came home to talk to her about trying harder to get along with his children. I was hoping for peace between us and indeed between her and all of us. I ended up keeping my sisters and brothers outside playing games we used to love to play, but had all but forgotten the simple joy of in quite some time, while Mildred was inside in solitude to enjoy peace and quiet, free to work or not to work as she pleased.

Father came home. We supped. I scooted my siblings outside once more to enjoy the evening; to feed, pet and talk to the horses, dogs and cats, and even some of the other less favored animals: to await the coming sunset in the hopes that it would be a glorious one and to give Father a chance to talk to Mildred in seclusion, so that perhaps a *new* day would dawn and peace would prevail in our home once more.

At one point in that evening, I thought I heard voices raised from inside the house somewhat, but was not sure if this was so, since we were a generous distance from the house and being rather noisy ourselves: there was considerably happy chatter and laughter outside where I was trying to ease my tense nerves and my tendency to worry about the outcome of Father's talk to Mildred, by enjoying as much fun with my sisters and brothers as possible.

To my dismay, when Father called us in to prepare for bed, I was horribly sure that Mildred was looking at me with disdain but I could see that Father did not see what I thought I saw. He seemed all contentedness and happiness. I sensed in her a suppressed anger towards at least me and perhaps Clara and Anna if not all of us. I felt very distressed. I worried that Mildred was not going to do her part to make things better between she and us but that she was now even possibly more dreadfully determined in the other and opposing direction.

The next day seemed to prove my fears right. Once Father was off and gone into the fields, Mildred behaved her worst yet. She seemed to revel in contending with each one of us. I felt compelled to shoo my sisters and brothers outside to do chores and compelled some of the older ones to organize play with our youngest brothers. I was desperate to find important things to do outside simply to prevent our having to be inside anywhere near Mildred. Thank goodness and the Heavens above that the weather was conducive to being outdoors!

Now I surely did not know what to do. Should I talk to Father again? Might that make matters worse? Could he talk to Mildred again and find a better result? Could I try to manage Mildred on my own? Was there any way to get along with her peaceably? Why was she behaving so ill against us? I did not understand her, what she might be feeling, what her motives might be if any; why she found such difficulty in accepting Father's children mostly as they were: all whom seemed *especially* good-natured to me. I could not comprehend how Mildred could find so much fault with such as we. I had never thought of the lot of us as difficult in temper or difficult to like. We were all quite amiable indeed. It seemed Mildred saw something else, whether by choice or by happenstance it was all the same to us. I honestly supposed we were all annoyance and inconvenience to Mildred, more than anything. I believed that she certainly would have preferred to marry Father and his properties, without having to *include* his children in the bargain.

I decided to make the best of things with Mildred for a while to see if perhaps her angry or resentful feelings towards me particularly and my sisters and brothers in general would calm, if given some time. I could always try to talk to Father later, I surmised. I felt that his talking to Mildred about the difficulties between us, so soon after such poor results of doing so recently, would simply cause her anger and resentments to increase and all such would tend to fan the flames that seemed to already be blazing.

As some time passed, my sisters and brothers and I were learning a new mode of behavior. We were learning to manage: to manage Mildred. We found that we were required to tip toe around Mildred, to avoid her, to avoid confrontations and even conversations with her; to try to obey her more reasonable demands and just suffer through the parts of the days when Father was gone and Mildred commanded, complained, criticized and attacked us. I found it easier to keep my sisters, brothers and I outside a good portion of the days: doing our outside chores, entertaining and playing with the younger ones, taking our inside chores outside whenever possible and simply staying as far away from Mildred as we possibly could. Thankfully it was summer and the weather welcomed us outdoors day to day, despite the heat, for the summer sun did not press us with discomforts as much as Mildred's blistering temperament did. We did, thankfully, retreat to our places of shade and cool; and so enjoyed ourselves beyond and outside of the house that Mildred now ruled in.

Also thankfully for us, Mildred did not like the sun. She desired her skin as pale as it possibly could be and did not truly believe a bonnet was enough to protect her from acquiring a swarthy complexion. Even a generous sun bonnet or a prairie bonnet was not sufficient for Mildred. Her sun parasol was requisite whenever she ventured outside and even then she did not like the fact that we did not have enough shade trees on our farm for her liking. She insisted that her chores were all indoors. She did not seem all too happy alone in the house, but was happier alone than with our company and we were happiest separated from her whenever we could reasonably do so.

I began to wonder if maybe there was a way to have a family discussion to hopefully resolve some problems within the family. The more I pondered that possibility, the more I thought the better of it. I could see Mildred in my mind's eye: involved in attempts from my sisters, brothers and myself to talk to Father about our concerns and what we felt to be mistreatment, discord and injustices at her hand. But, then again, would Mildred show her most unpleasant self in front of Father as he had not yet seen to my knowledge? Or would she fain cooperation only to pour more misery down upon us later as revenge or punishment when Father was not there? *Either* result would be unpleasant. Neither would result in anything better.

Perhaps a few of us having a talk with Father again would be of some helpful possibility? Clara and Anna at least at my side to join in on a full report of Mildred's behavior and treatment of all of us in his absence might shock Father into laying down the law with his wife in his home relative to his children. Could that be possible? He was the man of the house after all! Was he not? He feared not to dare command his own children in *every* thing. Would he not then be capable of doing the same with his wife in defense and protection of his own children? He desired the happiness of his children, did he not? Yes, to be sure he desired the happiness of his still new wife, but not at the expense of the happiness of his own children? Surely, was it not possible for all to be happy with only a modicum of effort from everyone, *including* Mildred?

Taking Clara and Anna aside, I discussed the need for a long talk with Father and they were keen to help me in my next attempt. In point of fact, Clara was at odds far more with Mildred than I was, as Clara was not one to make nice with other people like it was clearly in my nature to try to do. Anna did not cross paths with Mildred as much as Clara did, but she still did so more than I. Clara and Anna were at the end of their tethers with Mildred more than I was and so were delighted to try something besides continually sparring with Mildred. We planned all that we should say and how we should say it, hoping in a way that would not create ire in Father but such that he would feel compassion and understanding for our troubled circumstances and sad situation *because* of the wife he had chosen and allowed to mother us just as she saw fit, to that point in time. We three agreed that those younger than us could remain ignorant of the plan and the execution thereof and so, therefore, hopefully be freed or spared somewhat from any possible wrath that might result in Mildred against her accusers.

First Clara, Anna and I organized a lengthy activity that was safe and fun for our younger siblings, far from the house where Mildred ruled; with Charlotte and Elizabeth in charge. Then Clara, Anna and I rode out to the field where Father was working. He seemed at first alarmed to see all three of us riding out to him in such a fashion and perhaps could see the concerned looks on our determined faces. He ran towards us to inquire of us what was the matter, possibly fearing the worst and so I quickly assured him that all was well at home but it was simply that we needed to talk to him about some things.

It all went better than I had expected. I was emboldened to speak my mind so much more than as was usual for me, with Clara and Anna there with me, and they were quite bold indeed as well. Their distress and dismay was translated *perfectly* succinctly. They were a credit to all of us and made clear what we had all been suffering under Mildred's roof so to speak. After initial resistance, Father was ultimately reasonable, understanding, amiable and willing to try to find a solution so that harmony would prevail in his home. He was concerned about our many negative reports regarding Mildred but I could see that he seemed sure it was all more misunderstandings than anything manipulative or malicious. I was not so confident and sure by this time, but was willing to wait and see what positive outcome might miraculously result after Father's next talk with Mildred about family.

Father was so very much moved by our discussion that he left the field that moment, determined to resolve everything with Mildred as soon as he could get home. Clara, Anna and I rode ahead at a bit of a gallop; even though we were not supposed to let the horses run so fast towards home. We all knew we must needs keep our siblings aside, outside and afar from the house, whilst Father spoke with Mildred about all our concerns inside the house. My heart was racing a fair clip faster than our horses. I was truly terrified at what would happen within the walls of our house in the next little while but even more concerned at what might transpire afterwards. Mildred's behavior had been far worse towards us since Father had last spoken to her concerning his children and more particularly my own concerns. Why would she feel better about this greater sack of complaints against her? Father, as the man and husband, could hold sway and his law would be the law. Mildred would have to change her ways towards us. She would have to change. Surely, she *must* change. Truly Father could compel her.

Mildred would have to treat Father's children far, far better than she had been doing for quite some time. Father would make sure of it now that he knew what his children had been going through. I believed he could. I *hoped* he would.

Above the noises of delight of my youngest siblings, I could hear them. No, it was that I could hear *her*. As far away from the house as we were, I could still hear the din coming from inside the house. I could not make out any words or phrases; but only a shrill noise of an angry female voice as it flew and sliced through the air. I supposed that in a very real sense I was in great part responsible for their first major quarrel. I was terribly upset but did not truly feel bad about what I had partially seemed to have started. Mildred had been a very large thorn in the sides of most of us, if only a small thorn to others, and *something* had to be done. If a fight between the relative newlyweds was what it would take for Father to *finally* lay down the law and establish a home of harmony once more, so be it. Hearing Mildred's livid shouts, knowing she was discomfited at least, had *no* effect on my compassions towards her. I could not care as she suffered. My cares were *only* for my brothers and sisters.

Enough time had passed whereby I had suffered the wrongs of my Father's wife that at this point in time it did not really matter to me if Mildred liked me or if she would *ever* like me. I simply wanted her to be civil to my siblings and me, to give our family a chance at the continual days of delight and peace we once knew. I had been uncomfortable enough for long enough. Perhaps it was time for Mildred to be uncomfortable. She had caused enough discomfort for so many for so terribly long that she had earned her own fair share of it.

Obviously Mildred had a strong constitution. Her ability to endure was sure. The sounds of her shrill voice permeated the air as it turned from later afternoon, to early evening and then even into the coming night. There we all were: outside. The sky was growing darker. We were trying to find things to do and diversions from our growing hunger at having missed our dinner. As we waited for the quarrel to be complete, Clara, Anna and I faced moments when we had to begin to explain to our younger sisters and brothers what seemed to be transpiring in the house and why. We were fast running out of reasons why we could not simply go inside the house and forage out something to eat.

In an almost type of desperation, I decided to take everyone to the garden where there were a few things we could find to eat. I tried to explain that soon Father would have settled everything with Mildred and then we could go in, eat and get ready for and then go to bed. Charlotte and Elizabeth began to whisper to each other. Then they started giggling. Somehow the screaming and yelling from inside the house, struck them as quite hilarious. Edward and Colin seemed fairly frightened. Clara, Anna and I did our best to calm everyone about what was happening; to change the subject, to promote more pleasing thoughts and to believe that soon we would be able to go into the house and that Mildred would have calmed down, whether by Father's command or her own accord.

Some semblance of calm was finally arrived at. We were all summarily called into the house by Father, told to prepare and serve ourselves a quick morsel to eat and then to go to bed. Mildred was not to be seen as she was clearly holed up in their bedroom. Father was abrupt and cool with us. We all quietly and obediently ate and went promptly to bed.

BONNETS AND APRONS: FIONNA

The days that followed were almost beyond description. It was as if we children were suddenly almost complete strangers to our father and he behaved as a stranger to us: his coldness and curtness with us that infamous night continued but with added vigor and firmness. Mildred became her worst: even in front of Father now, and he did nothing nor said anything in our defense, giving her full sway to say and do as she pleased with us. If any of us would try to speak back, to reason for justice on our side or to state our case in any way, to Mildred or to Father, he would lay down the law with us and tell us to mind our *mother.* We were clearly under her charge now and he had washed his hands of us *except* to back her up and discipline us as well. Father had made a choice between his wife and children and all nine of us had lost. Mildred had won. The battle *and* the war went to Mildred.

To this day I know not what things Mildred said to Father to convince him to allow her to treat us any way she pleased. I cannot fathom how a man who seemed reasonable and kind and good enough for all those years could be persuaded to turn his back on his own children in that dramatic way. Mother would have been mortified if she had known. Did she know? Indeed I sometimes wondered if Mother did know and if so, would or could be compelled to find a way to leave Heaven and come down to speak to Father and bring him to his senses and then to his knees, and to ultimately beg our forgiveness and then to set things right after all: and so thus could I imagine, but only in vain.

The family cemetery plot became my refuge. I almost daily went there to cry to Mother about Mildred's offences against us and Father's co-conspiracy with his new wife, against *his* own children. I did all I could to protect all my younger sisters and brothers from Mildred. I also began to pray more than once a day. I prayed fervently for help in knowing what I could do to find peace in this situation that seemed to be devoid of solutions and also how I could help my siblings as best I could.

As cold days replaced warm ones life became all the more difficult in Mildred's house, as such we began to call our former home. We began to become accustomed to the screaming, the shrill criticisms, the demands and commands and indeed all the unkind things that Mildred chose to heap upon each and all of us.

My heart ached for my youngest siblings because I thought they began to forget what life was like with Mother. At least those of us who were older could hold dearly on to memories of Mother and a once harmonious home where Father was almost as beloved to us as Mother.

I began to accept our lot with Mildred. I did my best to fight her criticisms with compliments. I praised my younger siblings to the skies. I battled Mildred's shrill screams with gentle kind words to all my sisters and brothers. I tried to be to my younger siblings what Mother had been to us. I hoped, prayed and labored to make up for *all* the unkindnesses, the stark coldness, the mistreatment and the injustice that Mildred, and now also Father through his duplicity, committed against us. I determined to hold my little family together, for this is how I began to see my Father's children. It was as if we were not his anymore and were orphaned. He had orphaned us by bowing to Mildred's demands: exactly what they were I did not know. Our stepmother had taken our Father and turned him also into a stepfather. They were not even as benevolent Uncle and Aunt to us. Were they like a reluctant neighbor to us? Perhaps that was what they had become. That was the kindest way I could think of Mildred. I forgave Father more easily, even though I nigh could understand why he had done what he had and why he was doing as he was to his own children. Father was more culpable than Mildred in allowing his own flesh and blood to be so terribly mistreated, but still, somehow, I could quite easily love and forgive him. My feelings towards Mildred were not so tolerant and generous, for I fought a violent hatred against her almost continually.

Clara fought with Mildred and with Father when he came to Mildred's defense. Anna followed in Clara's stead. Clara would not let Mildred forget that she was a replacement and a supremely ill one at that. Anna would join in. Clara would routinely speak of Mother and her beauty, goodness, talents, good humor and soft speech. Even when it meant harsh punishments from Father upon Mildred's insistences, Clara would still dig in and insult Mildred regularly. She felt the forthcoming punishments were worth reminding Mildred of how she felt about her. Anna was far more subtle in her insults but would covertly let Mildred know she agreed with Clara.

Charlotte, Elizabeth and Victoria felt similarly to Clara and Anna. They did not respect Mildred. They only obeyed her insofar as not to bring Father's wrath upon them. They tended to find ways to avoid the wrath of Mildred. Bertram seemed to be coping similarly to Charlotte, Elizabeth and Victoria. It was difficult to tell if or how Edward and Colin were coping. Mildred seemed to be bonding to some degree to Colin. She treated him far better than the rest of us. He was becoming her baby boy I supposed. She seemed to see him that way and what choice did *he* really have in the matter?

3

Dances

Four years later in early 1844 we had all still managed to stay close as sisters and brothers, despite the ill help from Mildred and also Father. Our little family was intact to a great degree in spite of Mildred and Father. Sadly, though, Colin was not as much our brother, for Mildred clung to him as hers: spoiled him, gave him far better treatment than the rest of us, and in a dreadfully real sense, constantly pitted him against us. She taught him not to be ours, but hers and Father's. It was most unfortunate, but these manipulations of Mildred's did cause Colin to behave badly towards the rest of us and it was difficult especially for Edward and Bertram to understand or to feel like Colin was their brother anymore. Edward and Bertram bonded together and learned to stay away from Colin – but Colin was doted on so terribly much by Mildred that he seemed content to be without his siblings. Colin was fast becoming exceedingly spoiled.

Clara was determined to find a husband who could take her away from the family farm that had become all but Mildred's place: as our stepmother ruled like a Queen over it, with Father being a doting servant; and we all as under classed subjects, or more accurately, subjugated slaves. In truth, Clara and Anna both were planning to get themselves husbands very, very soon. They were already teasing me for becoming an old maid as I had not considered any thoughts of marriage nor did I entertain advances from fellows in town, who were oft left with my cold shoulder when they attempted their flirtations with me.

While Clara and Anna saw marriage and men as their way

out and off of Mildred's farm, *I* feared marriage: or at least I feared marrying the wrong man. Marrying in a hurry seemed to me a gamble or even perhaps a sure bet towards unhappiness. I had seen a good marriage working, closely and at length in what Mother and Father had had together but then I had seen Father scurry towards Mildred and even though he seemed to think himself happy with her, I could not judge their marriage as a good one: no indeed, not at all. I had long since made the decision to hold out for a man who was the best of men: one I could adore, depend upon and be best of friends with: or never to marry at all. My current consideration was also that as long as my younger sisters and brothers needed me to stay on what had become Mildred's farm: until they grew up, married and moved away to their own homes; I could not abandon my siblings by marrying and running off for my own happiness. How could I be happy knowing what I had left my siblings to cope with, without me there to help them? Of course there was the fairly distinct possibility of bringing my siblings with me upon a marriage, but that was surely not a realistic option. How could I ask a new young husband to take on eight younger sisters and brothers as his own in the bargain of gaining me?

No, at age nineteen I could *wait* for marriage. I fully believed God could save the right man until the right time for me if it was His will that I marry. Clara, Anna and the others could marry. I would stay home to defend my sisters and brothers until not a one needed me there. I felt *quite* determined in the matter and no amount of teasing from my sisters could induce me to dream of marrying prematurely.

Sometimes Clara and Anna would drag Charlotte and I to dances in town. Elizabeth wanted to go as well, but Father drew the line at her, thinking her still somewhat too young at thirteen to be associating so familiarly with young men. I thought at least Charlotte perhaps full young as well, even though she was two years older than Elizabeth and my opinion was not typical. I went along to dances more to watch out for at least Charlotte while I also kept an eye on Anna and Clara. Perhaps more precisely, my eye was firmly fixed on the young men who fancied my just younger sisters. I could also see those men, many young but some older, who seemed to fancy me but I did my best to let them know through my cool behavior towards them that I was not interested in any one of them.

Something I began to notice that I thought odd or at least ironic was this: the young ladies who through their flirtations with the young men showed themselves to obviously desire something towards marriage, were the young ladies that the young men seemed *less* interested in. Those like me, who remained aloof, seemed desired *most* of all. There were few like me who seemed disinterested in approaches and efforts towards marriage. Indeed, I was the most stubborn in this attitude of all. I was quite certain of *that*. Those females, who most wanted attentions of fellows, were surely the least likely to get it. Although I saw this behavior among men towards women to be fact, over and over, I could not see that I should pretend to desire the attentions of men when I did not wish for them; even as a most unusual way to defend myself against their approaches and flirtations.

I felt like telling these men that I was only there to watch over my sisters and thus to leave me be as I preferred, but worried that by divulging such I might receive all the more attentions; so I resisted indulging in that honesty. I managed as best as I could. It became easier and easier to say no, to ignore, to avoid and to busy myself among other young ladies: my sisters and beyond, and thus have no time for the attentions of men: young or older.

One night, Clara and Anna came bustling over to Charlotte and me to tell us that there was a particular young gentleman who fancied me, but that he thought me a terrible snob who must think myself far above and beyond all the men at this dance. I could have let this revelation ruffle my feathers but found it rather easy to choose not to care one way or the other. After all, Mildred was a thorn in my side so large as to merit being named a new noxious tree and I had learned to ignore *her*, her opinion of me and her ill treatment. I needed not let some stranger bother me or my feelings. It truly did not matter to me one whit or jot that any young man thought me snobbish when I knew that I was nothing of the kind.

I knew who I was and why I had no time for young men, or more accurately: that it was not time for me to pay heed to the attentions of men. I had more important things to do; important family members to care for, first. I had chosen the order of things for me and was determined to focus on that or rather, to focus on the needs of my younger sisters and brothers until their needs were not so much my concern anymore.

Clara carefully pointed out the young man to me from afar. At first I could not see who she meant amongst the many young men who were standing in the general area she alluded to. I would have just carried on without knowing who he was, but then Anna began to describe him to me.

"He is the tall one. You see? The one who stands taller than all the rest around him there? He has dark hair and is *so* handsome. You should see him at a closer distance. He is *all* the more handsome, up close. Can you not see him?"

As my eyes found him amid and indeed atop all the other young men around him, his gaze met mine and I abruptly looked away, blushing. I tried desperately to suppress the color in my cheeks.

I answered, "I see him. But please, stop this. I do *not* want to make a spectacle of myself nor do I want him to know that we are looking at or talking about him. Indeed, I am not interested in the *least* degree and I do not wish him to think that I might be."

"Well!" said Clara, "Then Anna and I are free to quarrel over which one of us will pursue him first, if *you* have no interest in him!"

Anna agreed, nodding animatedly and then said to Clara with a small frown creasing her forehead, "But you have more than enough names on your list. Leave a few for me!"

"Oh, but Winston is *far* too handsome to be handed off to a younger sister!" replied Clara, adding, "I say Fionna is crazy not to think of meeting Winston and changing his opinion of her: that she is a snob! As for me, I am excessively glad of it, for then he will forget Fionna and begin to think of *me*!"

"He is just as likely to begin to think of me as of *you*!" smiled Anna with an air of confidence.

I glanced over at Winston as the girls were tugging over him in their thoughts and words and I saw that he was staring at me. I quickly turned and looked the other way, with almost a frightened feeling in my heart and a certain crimson flushing in my face once more.

At the next dance that the girls and I went to, Winston was there as were many of the other young gentlemen who were fast being added to Clara and Anna's lists. Charlotte did not speak of such a list but I could see that she noticed several of the young men and I suspected that indeed she did have a list of her own. I did feel that she was full young to be thinking seriously of marriage but hoped that her somewhat shy and demure nature would protect her from getting to know any of these young men as quickly as Clara and Anna seemed to be doing.

Clara and Anna were almost like a team of sorts. Perhaps they were like a duet. They certainly had no want of an audience. There were fair shares of young gentlemen gathered around about them most of the time. Indeed Clara and Anna almost seemed like a hive of honey with bees buzzing delightedly around them. Charlotte stood by me most of the time: this was more by my design than hers, perhaps. I did not want Charlotte *entrenched* in the hive.

While the young females who seemed *desperate* for male attention did not seem to get so much of it, those like Clara and Anna who were bubbly in personality, full of confidence and showed no apparent preference for any one young man over another: in them there was a certain attraction to many gentlemen. Clara, Anna and those like them seemed fun, amiable and available without being in the pining way. This seemed attractive to men.

Every now and again, Clara and Anna would leave their hive of bees and come over to report to Charlotte and me. Charlotte seemed delighted with their reporting to us. While I was not entirely entertained by these retold conversations, complete with this or that look, sigh and so on; I was glad of them. I wanted to know about these potential partners for my younger sisters. If Clara and Anna were to catch themselves husbands, I would like to know at least a *little* about their prospective companions before it was too late to give any advice or warning that might needs be given from an older, and hopefully just a little wiser, sister.

I was glad that Clara and Anna each liked every, or at least their most attentive suitors and had not begun to yearn or pine for any single one as yet. I felt a certain safety in knowing that both their heads were easily turned this way and that, for no one young man had stolen either heart as yet. Charlotte's heart was surely safe as she stood by my side much of the time. All their hearts were safe, for now and I was at rest because of it.

From time to time a young man would approach Charlotte to ask her for a dance. Some approached me as well, but I was good at making excuses or simply saying 'no thank-you'. Charlotte always seemed to look to me for approval and I would gently nod my head that she might go have a dance. I thought no harm in letting her dance, a little. I could easily say no for myself but could not seem to bring myself to say no for, or to her. And what could one little dance here or there do? I could see her the entire time and she was always brought back to my side when the song and dance was finished.

There were a few young men who seemed to become frequent and recurring dance partners to Charlotte. They seemed nice enough and somewhat reserved and so I did not worry about their characters or designs on Charlotte. They were also very polite and cordial to me, which fairly swayed me their way. There was so little in the way of conversations, that I could see no danger in Charlotte's dancing partners. Charlotte did not seem to talk terribly much during her time spent with any of the young men who engaged her for dances and so I thought that at least she was having some fun, which was hard to find consistently at home, so this was a very good thing for her: a respite from the unhappy storms on the farm.

Clara and Anna danced quite regularly with young men who often circulated around them and also with young men who were not part of that hive of activity. Sometimes I wondered if they would have any energies left for the next day of chores. Most of the dances were held on Saturday nights and since our family had always observed the Sabbath Day as a day of rest, there was no worry about this most of the time; but when the dances were held on other nights, I wondered at what energy could be left for the following day. Clara and Anna proved themselves full of vigor and with strong constitutions as they were always able to do their chores the day after a dance, but did seem to relish in the resting when the day after a dance was on the Sabbath as usual.

One lively song, when Clara, Anna and Charlotte were all occupied on the dance floor, each with a pleasant young man, and I was engrossed in enjoying watching them kick up their heels and smile or giggle with delight, there came a tap on my shoulder. Just a *little* astonished to see a young man before me as I turned to see who had tapped me (for I thought my reputation as a snob or a bore or something of that ilk that made me somewhat un-approachable, was secure), I managed to muster, "Yes? May I help you?" with some decorum in my manner and composure in my face and voice. I recognized him: he seemed a pleasant enough fellow. He had danced with Charlotte at least once or twice before and maybe Clara and Anna as well.

"Would you consent to just one dance, Miss? Your sisters have left you without conversation so you must allow me to fill that void and what better way to do so than to join in on the dance floor with your sisters? What do you say? Please say yes."

I smiled and paused before speaking. I quickly wondered if I should perhaps relax my determination towards avoiding gentlemen completely and just consider enjoying a little fun myself. Dancing was not necessarily courting or even on the road to it, I decided. I could enjoy a dance, could I not?

"Why not?" I answered with a smile and a twinkle in my eye, and then gave the young man my arm. He seemed very pleased: very pleased indeed.

The fact that I was on the dance floor prancing and leaping about with a young man did not escape Clara, Anna and Charlotte's notice. Each one of their smiles brightened as their steps lightened. It was plain to see that they could not be happier than to see their older sister *finally* falling prey to the lures of a man or at least to the lures of a dance; or this is how I thought they might see it when we eventually conversed about it afterwards.

When brought back off the dance floor when the song was done, I thanked the young man as he was thanking me. Charlotte was soon brought back by my side and then Clara and Anna converged on us in delighted chatter.

"I *can't* believe you *finally* said yes to a young man, Fionna!" were Clara's first words on the subject, and then, "Do you fancy him? Is not he a sweet dear? Could you fall for him?"

Before I could answer, Anna put in, "Of course you *must* fancy him! I wager you might fall for him, Fionna! He is a dear to be sure!"

I quickly tried to halt any and all of their speculations, "No! I do *not* fancy him or any *other*. I simply decided it was time for me to try having a little dance for I thought it might be fun. That is *all*."

Charlotte was of some help to me, "Well, at least you are willing to have a *little* fun at these dances, now Fionna. Isn't that what we come for? To dance and have some *fun*?"

Clara boldly answered, "I come to find a husband! Don't you, Anna?"

"Yes, but there is fun to be had in the meantime, is there not, now?" replied Anna with glee.

Before I could think to say anything more to either or all of my three sisters, Winston was standing before me. Anna was quite right. He was all the more handsome up close. This did not mean my heart would be all aflutter like Clara and Anna's or any other woman who is easily swayed by looks. Indeed, I was entirely determined to keep my heart quite still. I knew he had misjudged me snobbish and other such things and I also knew that a book cannot be judged by its cover. However enticing from the outside, it may turn out to be of less worth inside. Still, despite my efforts to repress such, my face felt full flush and my heart was secretly stirred.

He inquired of me, "Would you care for this next dance?"

I almost determined to say no to him *instantly* because he had judged me so completely harshly and wrongly before. I quickly decided that he must not still feel that way about me, or why would he ask me to dance? I also knew that I had built for myself a wall of protection against suitors and so I was partly to blame for misconceptions of me by any man who had spent time around me. And to say no would be to prove his earlier prejudice right.

Clara, Anna and Charlotte all seemed to be holding their breath. They knew me well enough to know me capable of saying no, of course, but they all seemed anxious to see me say yes, I supposed.

"All right." I said with a little smile.

Soon Winston and I were on the floor dancing and my three sisters followed with partners shortly thereafter.

I had to admit to myself that I enjoyed a great deal of fun that night. We all did. I likely could not have counted all the partners we each enjoyed throughout the night's dance. I was truly glad that it was a Saturday night. I did not have to worry about much in the way of chores tomorrow as it was the Sabbath. I do not know that I could have suffered myself to do a regular day of chores after dancing so much the night before. My legs were exhausted, my feet truly tired.

I did not get to know Winston well, nor any of the other young men that I danced with that night. I simply enjoyed a night of dancing. I was used to enjoying the music, and watching my sisters while they danced, but it was indeed nice to finally join in the dancing with these three of my sisters: and the greatest joy of it was to see their delight in seeing me up on the dance floor with them.

4

Graveside

There were many times when I would think of Mother and Benjamin. My grieving over the loss of each of them was unique and varied.

I missed Mother *terribly* oft times, but I never grieved for her well being. I grieved for *my* loss: for *our* loss. I grieved that she was *missing* from our family and that there was such a void with her gone from us. I was always sure that Mother was enjoying peace and joy in Heaven, surrounded by loved ones she had known before and who had gone before her.

As to Benjamin, I still prayed for him always, more than once a day: that he would be kept safe and happy in the life he had been *stolen* and taken to, that he would grow up safe and strong and that someday, the sooner the better, he would be returned and reunited with his true family. We all prayed for him. Of course Mildred did not, and Father did not seem to like being reminded of our little Benjamin, even through our prayers, but the rest of us never stopped praying for Benjamin. We heard nothing of Benjamin, nor Clyde and Blanch Blackwell, who had taken him. We knew not where they had gone. Nothing of their swift disappearance seemed known. We did not know if he was alive but of course we hoped he was healthy and happy and that somehow Clyde and Blanch might feel their consciences being pricked for what they had done against Benjamin and us and gain the courage to make things right after all this time and bring him back to us. I knew, or at least truly *believed* that after this life, Benjamin would be reunited with us; but I still held out hope that in this life he would know us again.

The family cemetery plot had become a favorite safe haven of refuge to me. It was a sanctuary of solitude and solace. It was off and away and I could pour out my heart and soul: I could cry out loud and not typically be heard by anyone. The trees between me and the house held the sound back like a heavy curtain and I never worried that Mildred or Father would hear me. I would go to the graveside to talk to Mother. I would complain about Mildred, lament about Father, hope for Benjamin's return to the family and secretly wish in vain for Mother's return as well. I knew Mother's return was an *impossible* miracle but somehow holding onto the wish comforted me. Mostly I would share my burdens with Mother and ask her advice and then I would imagine her consoling words and then her suggestions, solutions and words of wisdom to help me cope in the situation that Mother's poor children were suffering under. Sometimes it seemed that Mother's advice and consoling to me was beyond my imaginings. It seemed that she was actually near and was truly communicating to me.

From time to time it was as if we all had forgotten Mother and Benjamin. Life would go on. Life *had* to go on oft times. There were daily chores to do: indoors and outdoors. There were fields to prepare, to plant, to weed, to water and then there were the many crops to bring in. There was livestock to tend to: to feed, to shelter, to nurse when sick and ultimately to slaughter and prepare for our food. We had to feed ourselves day to day, month to month, season to season and year to year.

There was enough work to do and work to spare for *all*. Even the littlest ones would be given tasks and chores to do: anything they could do to help, from feeding chickens to carding wool. We all worked hard enough most of the time that when it came time to do our studies at night, for Mother had schooled us all and we all were continuing our schooling (the older ones teaching younger ones): our schooling work at night was very much a rest from all the work of the day. Indeed, our schooling did habitually feel like play and we did find respite and fun in it. I delighted in teaching my younger brothers and sisters to read, to write and to add, subtract, multiply and divide. Indeed, sharing both the Bible and all other manner of good books at our disposal, with my younger siblings, was a joy. I thrilled to see the young ones learn. My heart was warmed to see them so incredibly attentive, as I told them stories and taught them facts, history, good principles and morals. Thanks to the Heavens that Mildred wanted none of it. This was one of *our* wonderful worlds away from her.

Through all the toil it was easy to get lost in life: lost in the work of life. And yet there was *also* play, rest, laughter and joy: even on Mildred's farm; even in *Mildred's* house; as it all had become. She could not bring us all down at all times. There were too many of us to keep down. Sometimes there were moments when I saw good old Father: Mother's Father. In fact, Father was his old loving self to us many times. This gave me hope: that perhaps Mildred would not prevail in taking our Father completely away from us nor be able to entirely turn him against us. Indeed, I hoped the Father we had known in such happier times past would come back to us in all ways and in all things. Some day, perhaps he would.

Other times, my hopes for our father to truly once again become the Father we knew *before* would fade due to the circumstances we usually lived under. These were the times I missed Mother the most. I kept imagining Father doing as I thought he should: *forcing* Mildred to treat his children as I thought she should. I knew he could do it. I knew she would behave far better towards us if Father had manned the house as it was within his power to do.

Sometimes some of us would seem to unconsciously find a quiet place to talk about missing Mother and Benjamin: in the cemetery, in the hay loft of the barn, tucked up in the attic whispering or just off in a field somewhere. Indeed, even when we were well beyond Mildred's hearing, we would still find ourselves speaking in whispers and hushed tones: as if our stepmother would find some way to find us out and punish us. These times were rarely planned but generally spontaneous amongst us. Our talks together would reveal that we all missed Mother mostly for what she used to give to us and Benjamin for what we could not give him. We felt orphaned by Mother and somehow felt partially responsible for *allowing* our Benjamin to be orphaned.

At least we could all feel a certain sense of peace about our loss of Mother since we knew or at least believed that she was safely, securely and happily in Heaven: reunited with many loved ones including her first two sons who had gone on before her. We were sure that she received plenty of joy spending time with Adam and Aaron and also with her parents, siblings, grandparents, cousins, aunts, uncles and friends.

We did wonder how much Mother might know of us and if she sorrowed and was troubled over Mildred's mistreatment of us. I was sure that if she knew what we knew, she must abhor Mildred as much as we did, or at least Mother would abhor the *behavior* of, if not the woman; and that she was equally disappointed in Father for letting his own children be treated in such a way when he surely had the power to prevent it. Why *did* he not prevent such?

Our feelings about Benjamin were similar to our feelings about Mother, but oh so different, since we knew not *if* he was happy and safe from day to day. I worried about Benjamin often and so did most of my just younger sisters by varying degrees. Of course Colin did not remember Benjamin while Edward and Bertram barely remembered our little brother. Us girls all remembered and missed Benjamin the most, particularly us older ones. Our hearts ached all the more for him because we had loved and cared for him more, when we had the short chance of it: before the Blackwells took him away.

Not only did I wonder and worry over Benjamin but even my best hopes for him still meant that he was growing up without us and we grew older without him. Sometimes my worrying about Benjamin would engulf me in such a way that I thought I could go crazy about it. These were the times that began to teach me to turn my worry towards prayer. I would pray with all my heart for Benjamin and beg for multitudes of angels to watch over him and to guide, protect, comfort and direct him in his life since we were all completely and utterly powerless to do anything at all for him. We all prayed for his welfare and well-being and although our hopes had faded towards very dim, we still prayed for his return to us.

Oft times when we were tucked away from Mildred, speaking of Mother and Benjamin, we would take turns imagining what Benjamin looked like, what his interests were and even exactly what he might be doing at that exact moment. There were times I specifically led my siblings to the graveside for a memorial time of remembering Mother and especially to focus on our lost Benjamin. Sometimes we would shed a few tears for him, have a little prayer for him, and when it was my turn to pray, I would always ask that at that moment in time, he would or could somehow feel at least some of all our united love for him; and that somewhere deep down, he would know he was loved and missed by so many.

5
Town Fair

Before Mother was taken from us, we thought ourselves rich; not simply in family things but also in material things. Mother and Father were quite generous with us and they could truly afford such because the farm had long been doing so especially well. Father could trade or sell the many things our family farm produced: from eggs of the chickens and vegetables from the garden to livestock: we had prospered for a goodly length of time. My favorite crop, so to speak, were the horses Father raised and yet I hated to see many of them go to new owners. I was thankful though, to be able to keep our favorite horses: our very best in health and temper.

Oft times Mother and Father would take us all to town to choose a treat or a toy or some other such luxurious thing. These indulgences were afforded for us not only as incentives to help out with the work on the farm but also as a joyously given gift from our parents. These events were looked forward to whenever we knew they were approaching, and remembered long after they were passed.

Once our family farm fell into the controlling hands of the implacable Mildred, we promptly felt a severe pinch and so began to think ourselves poor. Suddenly, we apparently could not afford many supposed luxuries we had grown somewhat accustomed to expecting. We girls had to make do with our old dresses, even for Sundays, dances and other such events. Of course we had always been accustomed to far less than perhaps many of the girls in town, and were happy to take hand-me-downs from each other. Since I had not an older sister to hand down her dresses to me, I was wearing

Mother's clothes by then, but I had had to alter them to fit me since they were all somewhat large and roomy on me. Thankfully a dress can be made smaller easily, for if I had needed larger dresses, it would have been much more difficult, if not quite impossible, to alter Mother's dresses to fit me. I knew Mildred would never have allowed me new fabric to make new dresses. Even our aprons all seemed to be turning to rags and yet there was no monetary allowance to purchase even small amounts of fabric to make new ones.

Yes, we were now far too poor for new clothes but there was certainly enough money for Mildred to go to town for her luxuries. Truly, Mildred seemed not to want for much. There was enough and to spare for her. It was for us that there was not enough. While Mildred indulged herself in what seemed to be the latest fashions for dresses, ornately ornamented bonnets and sparkling jewelry, Father's children were wearing their old clothes and each others' clothes as best they could, with occasional alterations by me, for the most part. Our shoes were also becoming a difficulty. Sadly, those of us who approached Father for new things would be sent to Mildred and she always simply refused.

My own *most* missed luxury was perhaps pencils and paper. Beyond many things I enjoyed pursuing, my favorite pastime in times of leisure was to draw and my most treasured thing to sketch was my beloved horses. I had a trunk that was all but full of my horse sketches but now since I had all but run out of pencil and paper, I could not fulfill my creative need to continue to fill that trunk with my drawings of horses. Many a free hour of mine had been spent near the horses trying to capture their seemingly countless wonderful movements and their true natural beauty.

With a coming town fair later in the summer, I suddenly was inspired with an idea. Father had long since required that we older girls attend to his table with vegetables, eggs and such from the farm to sell. I realized that perhaps we girls could sell a few things of our own as we sold things for Father from the farm. In this way, we could raise our own money to buy a few needful things for ourselves. I could hopefully sell a few sketches of horses and the others could find their own things that they might sell. Clara was our wild-flower collector and presser. Her own trunk was partially filled with pressed flowers that I thought she could think up some way to make them into something townsfolk would like to buy. Anna was a tremendous needle-worker and had gathered many of those sorts of lovely things in her trunk over time. Charlotte had long-since collected many trinkets that could be sellable. In fact, I realized we all had many things from times past that we could perhaps part with and in a sense trade for new more needed things.

I decided to encourage each one of my sisters and brothers to consider trading some of their old treasures or anything they could make or gather, for some new spending money. Clara, Anna and Charlotte were delighted with the idea and Elizabeth, Victoria and even Bertram and Edward also thought they could come up with some things that they could exchange into money for their desires for just a few new things. I dared not involve Colin in my scheme as I knew he would tell Mildred and then she would surely choose to put a stop to it all. We had learned to *never* include Colin in anything that we wanted kept from Mildred. I swore everyone to secrecy.

Suddenly it was as if we each were taking every opportunity to prepare for this event in the hopes that we each could translate some of our old treasures and some of our new efforts into a glorious day of indulgences and luxuries of our choice, very much like the days Mother and Father would take us to town to be spoiled. I was determined to *prevent* Mildred from preventing us.

I knew that if Mildred suspected what we were planning she would surely try to stop us: for why would she not say no as she seemed to relish in doing whenever our hearts' desires could be smothered? I also knew I would not be able to stop myself from locking horns with her in a way I had never contemplated before. I was quite determined. Mildred was simply *not* going to be allowed to spoil our plans for a little deserved indulgence, to be sure. If it meant war with her, I was ready for war. I was well beyond my tether in so many things pertaining to Mildred that I actually feared what

I might do or say to her if pushed against one more wall by her. There was so *very* much unsaid by me where Mildred was concerned. I was the kind of person who could suffer in patience for a dreadfully long time but once completely roused, I was not unlike a mighty volcano. I feared my temper because of the few times it had erupted in the past. I feared myself in this way also because I was just like Mother in the case of temperament and I had seen Mother explode in rage when provoked long and severely enough.

I impressed upon my younger siblings of the absolute necessity of keeping Mildred from knowing what we were about in this matter. I made certain they knew what a profound disappointment we would *all* suffer if Mildred was allowed to discover and then halt our plans.

There was soon a certain joy and true delight amongst us in keeping this secret together as well as finding things we could prepare for the town fair.

I did lament somewhat within myself that I could not share our industrious plans and works with Father. I also struggled with hate towards Mildred. It was in times like these that my hate for her could fester. I knew it was neither right, *nor* good for me to let my hate build against Mildred but when I let myself imagine things she might say or do upon discovering our happy plans; I would then seethe in frustration and contempt to think of her and her selfish, greedy, manipulating and controlling ways.

Each of my siblings chose things from their treasure trunks that they could bring themselves to trade for money, which would then offer the power to purchase a new treat, treasure or toy. Thankfully, Mother had taught us to care well for our things, and so there were many wonderful trinkets and toys that could bring money to our table at the fair. We each also chose things we could gather or make that could be sold as well. I suggested to the boys to go out and about and gather certain berries that we could dry. Dried berries were like candies to some. They also gathered rare and pretty stones that some might like to add to their collections. More wild flowers were also gathered and pressed.

It was a thrill and a joy to see my younger siblings busily intent on our special goal. Such purposeful happiness had not been on their countenances in an extremely long time. I thought not perhaps, since Mother was with us.

As the first day of the fair approached, the bustle of activity and excitement amongst us grew, even as the secret between us deepened. I wondered if Mildred or Father suspected anything, but it did not seem that either did.

Colin, who still seemed fairly firmly attached to Mildred's skirt, and was surely tightly tied up into her apron strings, was obviously oblivious to the rest of us, which was unfortunately, quite usual. Luckily for all of the rest of us, Mildred was usually fairly attentive to Colin. She seemed to like to dote on him and to play with him like he was her one and only beloved doll. She even dressed him in a rather feminine way, even despite his years. Happily for him, he was still full young to notice and none of us were going to tease him in any way for it. She loved to spoil him openly and shamelessly in front of the rest of us. It was as if she pleasured in trying to make us all feel orphaned and also to revel in her success in stealing our remaining youngest brother from us. Edward, and also Bertram, suffered the worst from these efforts of Mildred's. As always, I did my utmost to make it up to the brothers I had, who were at this point in time, in effect, as if my own sons. Through it all, I also tried to continue loving Colin, which was not always easy since he was spoiled and would sometimes play Mildred and Father against us, which is oft in a child's nature to do in even less strangely advantageous circumstances.

Suddenly I became apprised of an upcoming and especially surprising secret event. Late one night I inadvertently heard Father and Mildred discussing her condition. She was with child.

Of course my mind became all abuzz with the ramifications of Father and Mildred starting a new family and how that was going to make life even more miserable for the rest of us on Mildred's farm and in Mildred's house; but I could not help but only be delighted that Mildred's mind was so occupied even more than usual, on herself rather than on the rest of us.

Neither Father nor Mildred told us of her expectant condition but more and more she kept to her bed and expected all to be done by any other than her. This made hiding our fair preparations all the more easily done and I could not have been happier about that. We could now go about our business with relative calm in knowing that Mildred was not going to notice what was going on around her.

The day of the Town Fair came. Father was busy getting his livestock into town while Clara, Anna and I manned the wagons loaded with the farm products to sell for Father. All but Colin, amongst my younger siblings, loaded themselves and their precious things onto the wagons. Mildred kept to her bed. Colin was not afar off from it. And so it was that we were easily able to go to town to sell more than that which Father had intended us to sell, and *all* without Mildred knowing, or even suspecting a single thing.

Perhaps never had my siblings and I been so full of energy and anticipation for the rest of the day's events and outcomes. By the end of the morning, we could see that there were wonderful fruits for our labors. We each had made profits beyond our hopes and there was still more to be sold. With Mildred back on her farm and Father busy showing and selling his livestock, we were selling freely at our tables; and with all this delight, we still had our upcoming luxuries to look forward to.

Each of my younger siblings behaved far beyond his or her years as they each joyously sold their items to passers' by. Never had anyone seen tables full of lively young ladies and happier youngsters selling their wares. I do think that the exuberance, delight and total amiability of my siblings in this their grand adventure in marketing and finance; was in *great* part a measure of their final financial successes.

I found no troubles in selling my sketches of horses. In fact, I received tremendous response from many customers. I had known I did have some talent, but never, since Mother's personal praises to me in the past, had I received such accolades for my work. I knew that as that morning had worn on, my face beamed all the brighter hour by hour with the wonderful comments from delighted customers buying my drawings of horses. I knew that my heart was in those sketches as it was my beloved horses that modeled for me, and perhaps that spirit translated in my drawings even more than any skill or talent. Yes, I thought my works perhaps more showing of soul than of ability.

It was around noon or perhaps the early afternoon when suddenly, as I was reaching down behind and below my table to fetch some more of my sketches, since so many on the table had already sold; I heard a familiar voice above me and over from the other side of my table.

"Are these *yours*, Fionna? Why have you been hiding such talent?"

I promptly stood up with more sketches in hand and saw Winston before me.

I felt my face quickly turn somewhere on its way towards crimson and tried to fight the flushing feeling, not knowing how to accomplish it. I hoped that between the sun and my fallen bonnet that my reddened face would be somewhat hidden and if not, not seem out of the ordinary on such a sunny and warm day.

I tried to smile with an ease of spirit to reply, "Yes. I like to draw and sketch, especially our horses." I took a long deep breath whilst trying to relax and calm myself hoping it would fade the color in my cheeks. I could not tell as yet if my valiant efforts were working.

Winston returned my smile, and with an apparent relaxed ease, "These are truly marvelous. But, I say again, why have you been hiding such talent before this? Why did you never speak of being an artist before?"

"I'm no artist, really. I simply like to spend free time drawing, when I get the chance of it. I was not hiding anything. You and I had never conversed enough for the subject of my sketching to have come up, is all, I suppose."

Winston smiled teasingly, "It was for no want of wishing and trying on *my* part to have longer conversations and *many* more of them with you. If I had had *my* way, we would have conversed all the way through *all* your drawings and horses and *quite* far beyond them. I would know *all* about you by now... if it had been up to me."

This time my face was surely completely crimson. Oh how I fought that hot sensation with calm breaths and every attempt at composure, but it was not the sort of thing that is so easily controlled. I was sure Winston could see the intense coloring in my cheeks and on the rest of my face. He seemed to smile all the more mischievously, clearly seeing what his bold comment had done to me. I tried all the more to calm myself even as it seemed I became more flushed, into a deeper and deeper hue than the complete crimson I had already arrived at.

As I was trying to calm myself enough to offer a reply, Winston continued, "I do not know why you do not proclaim yourself an artist, as such talent and ability surely warrants it."

All I could muster in that moment was a, "Thank you."

Winston seemed to take pity on me in my uncomfortably red condition, "Can you show me what you have left? I am quite determined to purchase one from you."

I proceeded to spread the rest of my sketches before him, wondering if he was sincere about my talents or his desire to acquire one of my drawings.

He seemed to truly enjoy looking over all my sketches and *even* studied them closely and discussed them at some length; and after quite some time, settled on one that he said was his favorite. By the time Winston bought that horse sketch from me, there were already many more people milling about asking me about my drawings and talents. I was too busy serving my customers to worry about letting Winston redden my face further, if indeed, that might be possible. He stood somewhat back, watching, smiling and holding his horse drawing of mine.

I was extremely grateful that Clara, Anna and Charlotte were far too busy selling their trinkets, treasures, handicrafts and wares to notice Winston anywhere near me nor that he had been at my portion of our family tables for quite some length of time: noticing my talents and buying one portion of them. Indeed, Clara, Anna and Charlotte were happily greeting many of the young men whom they knew as their dancing partners. I was relieved that my sisters should be kept so busy by their apparent suitors. I did not fancy the thought of being teased by Clara nor any of them, nor whisperings from any of my sisters to me about Winston: that which he might notice from his present position aside my table. In the bustle, I was spared.

In between serving my delighted customers, and even fending off a few apparent suitors of my own, I glanced around at our tables to see how each one of my siblings was doing in their own business ventures. Every one seemed extremely pleased as did their customers. Every now and again I would sneak a peek to see if Winston was still near and if he was still watching me. He was, and it was quite unnerving to me. He seemed to definitely delight in catching my eye and seemed quite desirous of holding it, eye to eye, as long as possible. Where he seemed quite bold to me in this way, the more he seemed to attempt to hold my glance and turn it into a gaze, the more nervous and shy I became. I was *quite* vexed, truly I was.

I did my best to keep from feeling flushed, even while knowing Winston was watching me, and to focus my total attentions on selling my sketches and also the things Father had entrusted us to sell for him from the farm. I was careful to keep Father's money and my money separate as I had also instructed the rest of my siblings to do. Every now and again I would gather up Father's money from my younger siblings. Finally, I glanced where Winston had been and he was there no longer. He had moved on. I was relieved, indeed I was, but I did find myself looking for him further, although I told myself *not* to. Why should I care if he were near or not?

With the afternoon not yet done and the dinner hour not quite impending, our tables were clear of all our products and wares. We were done selling. I gathered up Father's money and tucked it safely away in one of my trusted deep pockets of my dress which was well hidden beneath my apron. I carefully put away my money in the same fashion but in another pocket. I made sure each of my younger siblings took especial care of their own monies and then we were on our way. A night of delights was before us.

Before we could begin our grand adventure of indulgences and luxuries in town, we first had to take the makeshift tables and such to be put away in the wagons and then we could set out to enjoy an evening of whatever things would delight each of us. I also decided that we should find Father straight away and give him his money so that I would not be burdened with carrying it around with me throughout any portion of the evening.

When I handed Father his money, he asked me if we were to now go straight home to the farm and I told him we desired to stay and just look around a while and the older girls wanted to remain for some dancing. He gave me a small amount of the money for us to buy an evening meal for ourselves and I thanked him. He thanked us all for selling his things for him that day. We all smiled and were on our way.

On a *usual* night, the town would boast little open beyond the hotel and the saloon, but on such a night of a fair like this, all the shops were to stay open. There was simply so much business to be had, owners of stores would dare not close up shop and miss out on all the profits. The town was as if bursting. Farmers and folks from all around had come to sell, to buy, to trade and even just to see everyone and every thing that was to be there. There were also plenty of tables still open selling *every* kind of food and thing we could ever imagine. As was during the day, the sights, sounds and smells were excitingly scintillating to us that night. My younger siblings were all amazement. The bustle of the town was bursting over with every folk from far and wide. It was not often that one could see such crowds in our town. Bustling people were everywhere.

I told my younger siblings that they could spend every penny they had just made tonight if they liked or they could save some or most of it for later. Some of us had made so much money that we could not seem to fathom spending it all that night. I also told my sisters and brothers that we should do our best not to let Mildred see the spoils of our accomplishments, lest she should make trouble with Father against us. I told them there was no harm in hiding our trinkets or toys in our trunks or, indeed, our leftover monies, once we got home that night. I knew that some of what we had done that day would inevitably be *revealed* in time if not sooner, but was entirely prepared to face the consequences.

First we bought a nice modest dinner to share together with the money Father had given us for that purpose. Then we all began to go about town, looking at everything, from the tables at the fair which included the outer reaches of town, to the shops in the middle of town.

The boys tended towards treats and toys and our youngest sisters towards the same with a few trinkets added. I could not recall ever seeing Bertram and Edward so excited as they were that night, choosing new favorite things and using their hard-earned money to purchase them. The boys and also Elizabeth and Victoria each delighted in buying and sampling treats of many kinds. All their stomachs quickly became quite full of deliciously decadent food fare as did their pockets of their newfound treasures. I kept thinking how *deserved* this all was, with or without their having worked so hard to earn it. It had been *so* terribly long since there had been any indulgences for any of them. It was extremely long ago that Father and Mother used to take us to town just to spoil us, even if only a little.

Clara, Anna, Charlotte and I were bent on finding just the right fabrics to make ourselves new dresses, bonnets and aprons; plus I was set on getting myself a store of pencils and paper. After my successes, I felt that I could perhaps someday provide somewhat for myself through my drawings. I thought I could perhaps see a way off of Mildred's farm that did not depend on catching a man. I truly liked *that* idea.

Having indulged the younger four first, we older four could thoroughly concentrate on looking over fabrics while the younger four played with their toys in the corner of the general store. And should it become necessary to keep them entertained, we could also toss them each another treat or a candy or such from time to time to keep them busy while we planned a few new long-since needed clothes for ourselves. Thankfully, it seemed our younger brothers and sisters were too much engrossed in their new treasures and too full of recent treats, to need any bribery to keep them quietly entertained off to the side whilst we older four could do our shopping.

Clara had about settled on her fabrics and Anna and Charlotte on theirs. As I was looking over some beautiful bright blue calico fabric, and discussing it intently with my sisters; a voice from behind turned my head towards him. There was Winston again just as I had about forgotten him.

"That would look lovely on you. Are you going to make something new for yourself, I hope: a new dress for the next dance, perhaps?"

At first I thought it a total compliment but then without even pondering it over I wondered out loud, feeling somewhat resentful but trying to appear more playful, "I hope you are not insinuating that I have none but old dresses, sir?"

He returned with a broad, bold smile, "No, no! Not at all! I mean to say that you would look lovely in that blue like none other I can imagine and that I hope to see you in that in the form of a new dress at the next dance. To be clear, I would just as happily see you at the next dance in any dress you currently have and would be happy to wear."

There I was, blushing again. Why did he keep *doing* this to me? Why could I not retain my complete composure? All I could bring myself to say as I was trying to breathe calmly, deeply and slowly, was, "Thank you."

Clara, Anna and Charlotte's faces were beaming with delight. Clara quickly put in, "Fionna does look wonderful in blue: any shade, and I am always telling her she does not wear that color enough."

Winston turned to Clara and her address to him, "You are quite right. Now you must make sure Fionna buys this blue and makes herself a new dress for the next dance." Then he turned and grinned at me with a bit of a wink.

She instantly responded, "I will! Don't worry! I will. If I have to buy it myself and make it, I will make sure she wears it and you shall see her at the next dance in that blue and so you will have to dance with her... more than once I would think."

"Oh, most assuredly: I think I would try to dance the whole night with your older sister if she would *ever* consent to it. But we all know she is not *inclined* that way, at least not towards *me*, as yet." Again he turned to me with a mischievous smile.

Clara then shared, "She thinks she must marry us all off first, before she can entertain anything of the sort herself. That is why Fionna is so reserved."

I instantly whacked Clara's leg, "Clara! Don't say such things."

"It is the *truth*, Fionna! It *is*, Winston. She *does*! She is. So why should I not *say* it? Why should I not *tell* you that?" Clara smiled defensively.

Winston just smiled, looking at me, then Clara and then me once more.

I did not know *what* to say and so I stayed silent. Once again Winston took pity on me and took his leave of us with a few niceties. I was thoroughly and entirely grateful to him for *that*.

I truly *wanted* the blue calico but now I feared buy it. Because Winston had made such a point of wanting to see me in that blue as a new dress at the next dance, within myself I refused to cater to him. I did not want to seem desperate for his attentions. I was *not* desperate. I would simply not arrive at the next dance in that blue. There was also some green calico that I quite liked almost as well and was considering. Between Clara, Anna and Charlotte, there was *no* possible way for me to leave that store that night without the blue calico. I was glad of it anyway, since I *did* want it, Winston or no Winston; but I left with the green also, with plans to make the green dress *first*, so that the green would be the dress I showed up wearing at the next dance, instead of the blue.

We stayed for some dancing at the end of that day at the town fair. We could not stay throughout the entire dance which was to continue until far too late into the night for our younger ones, whom we needed to take home and get into their beds. I chose to bow out of most dances that young men asked me for, claiming the need to watch over my younger sisters and brothers. Clara, Anna and Charlotte were happy to dance many dances while I stood as Mother over our youngsters.

Later on, when Clara was just back from dancing, we both saw Winston making his way towards us. I told her to watch her tongue, feeling I had been embarrassed enough for one day. She promised to be good.

Winston asked me to dance, I said yes and we proceeded onto the dance floor. He said nothing of the blue calico as we danced; and neither did I, of course. He said nothing of my horse drawing and I wondered why he had bought it from me. We spoke very little, simply dancing around. Truly, it was pleasant to me. Winston was especially pleasant.

When that dance was over, Clara and Anna caught my eye as they were waving me to stay on the floor for more dances. I decided to stay for two more dances with Winston if he so desired. It turned out that he did. After that third dance was over, I let him know that I should go back and he escorted me to my sisters and brothers, leaving me there with good wishes and a hope to see me at the next dance if not in town before.

It was exceedingly late when we arrived home that night. We girls tucked our two younger brothers into their beds and their treasures into their trunks; for they had fallen quite asleep on the way home; and then we chattered animatedly, though quietly, before we did the same with ourselves. Deep sleep welcomed each of our exhausted bodies absolutely to be sure and offered pleasant dreams to our thoroughly exercised minds as well.

6
Mildred's Condition

It was not but a few days before Mildred had sniffed us out, at least to some degree and in some form. Bertram and Edward were playing with their new toys as were Elizabeth and Victoria. Perhaps we could have explained those away as if coming from one of our trunks but Clara, Anna, Charlotte and I were *flagrantly* sewing our new dresses. I knew we could not do that without questions as to where the fabric had come from, but I felt beyond caring. Mildred was long used to seeing me and the older girls remaking old things and knew there was no fabric left to be had in the house. Mildred was the only one entitled to new fabric, in her mind, and what entered her mind became her word and the law with her and sadly with Father as well: for so Mildred said, so it was done.

I thought Mildred would confront us and I would need to face that challenge when the time came, but she surprised me by waiting until mealtime to directly speak with Father about it in front of us all. Soon we were all being accused by Mildred of stealing from Father and his farm. Father actually quickly assured Mildred that all his money was accounted for that day at the fair as he knew what had been taken to be sold and *exactly* what the values amounted to. It was all tallied up, he said, and all other monies were, as always, accounted for. Mildred became somewhat irate.

Mildred screamed to Father, pointing her fingers at us, but mostly at *me*, "The boys and younger girls have new *toys*! The older girls have new *fabric*! *Where* did they get the money for *all* that, if they did not *steal* it from you?!"

I wondered if Mildred's condition would mean more screaming.

Father was somewhat speechless. His incredulous look turned my way so I took the opportunity to explain and managed to do so with rather an air of calm, cool and a casual look; even while my heart was pounding rapidly with attendant and combined justifiable anger and fear, "While we were selling the farm goods, the other children and I sold some of our own old things at the fair so that we could purchase a few new things. It has been an especially long time since we got *anything* new for ourselves."

This explanation seemed to satisfy Father completely and I also sensed that my last sentence might have dug *somewhat* at his conscience, but *not* Mildred's. Mildred turned on me with, "How dare you! How *dare* you sneak behind our backs selling and buying things!"

I calmly responded, "We have *every* right to trade our own *old* things for something *new*. Why would we need to ask your permission to do *that*?"

"How dare you speak to me that way! Of course you need your parents' permission to buy or sell *anything*! You were supposed to be selling for your *father*: not for *yourselves*!" Mildred seethed loudly.

I *felt* like screeching back at her. What right did *she* have? I wanted to tell her with fervor that she was not our mother, parent or anything but a nasty usurper and horrible hag, but I did my best to calmly respond once more, "We *did* sell for Father and we sold *every thing* he wanted us to sell, even *while* we were selling a few things for *ourselves* so we could have a little of our *own* spending money to get a *few* new things."

Father sat silently, listening, watching.

Mildred was red with anger. She was not quite sure what to say in retort it seemed. She paused, shifting in her seat, spurting somewhat with her pursed mouth and then she came up with something she thought would do, "Well, and just how much money did you make for yourselves, then?"

I quickly returned very casually, "Oh, just little enough each to get the few things we wanted or needed."

"How *much*?!" Mildred screeched at me and then glared around the table at everyone.

"Not much." I answered.

Mildred shrieked at me, "You will account for everything you all sold and *every* single penny you made to your father and me, and you will do it this *very* night!"

I quickly thought of the best I could come up with and said it as measured as possible, "I kept account of Father's goods and Father's money because I knew it was expected, but I did not worry about accounting for our own things and what money we made from them, nor how much we spent here and there that night. I did not think I should or would *have* to. I *thought* our personal things were *ours* to trade or sell or give away."

"We will begin right here and now to account for *every* single thing and what you each were paid for each and every thing you sold!" She scanned around the room with a determined look into each set of young eyes. All eyes were still. All sat motionless. Each was all trepidation.

Thankfully, Father finally interjected, "Mildred, dear, there is no harm in their trading a few *old* things for some *new* things or finding their own way to make a little pocket change."

"*Pocket* change?!" Mildred yelled at Father and then she lowered the volume and deepened the sound of her voice, "Pocket change does not buy yards and yards of fabric!"

Father answered, "Well, I think it fine that they could buy themselves some new things this way. They will *each* have to make their own way in the world someday and this was a good start, I think."

Mildred seemed somewhat dumbfounded. She seemed to know that Father had spoken and this was the end of the matter. She turned a scowl towards *me* and then glanced disapprovingly around the table. Some of us tried to stifle a smile, but not all were successful at it and this displeased Mildred exceedingly to see.

I felt a glimmer of hope within my spirit. Perhaps Father was coming back to his children in spite of Mildred's attempts to keep him far in the other direction: maybe the father we *once* knew was returning to us? I hoped and prayed that Father would come to his senses like this more often.

The next days were filled with more happiness than usual in our home and on our farm. Chickens and other farmyard fowl were fed with glee and their eggs were gathered with delight. All indoor and outdoor chores were done with a whistle and a song. Mildred kept to her room.

Clara, Anna, Charlotte and I were busily sewing up our new dresses as well as some much needed new aprons and sun bonnets. A dance was coming up soon and I had my new green dress ready. My blue dress was done as well, but I was planning to save that one until *later*: maybe for a special occasion of some sort. Each of the girls had new dresses ready as well.

As was becoming a pattern, Mildred was holed up in her room and that afforded us many pleasures without her company: our next trip into town yielded shoes, boots and many other needful things. With some of the monies I had made from my sketches, I treated my younger sisters and brothers to some things they needed that they could not afford; including some fabric which I later sewed into some needed and nice things for them as well.

With Mildred spending so much time in her room, Colin was becoming often quite unhappy for he was not welcome in Mildred's room when she desired her solitude there. Colin had become accustomed to being spoiled and doted on by Mildred but now she was making a habit of ignoring him. Colin had also become accustomed to behaving rather badly, especially towards his older brothers and sisters. Bertram and Edward began to take advantage of this situation wherein Mildred was not out and about to protect and defend Colin. As Bertram and Edward began to tease and torment Colin, I did my best to help Colin learn to fit in with his older brothers and to help them to have patience while Colin adjusted to relating with them as their brother once more.

I tried to help Colin desire to get involved with family chores; after all, he certainly was now old enough to help out a little. Since

Mildred was not interested in him at present, I could and should be. I also organized some fun things for us all to do together so that Colin could learn to fit in with us far better than Mildred had taught or allowed him to do.

Strongly assured as to why Mildred was shutting herself away from us, I wondered when Father and Mildred would announce the news of their upcoming child to the rest of us. I wondered how this event between them would affect the family. It seemed that Father had softened towards the rest of us and that Mildred was not able to control him so much as she had in the past. *Perhaps* Father would take control and take the lead now. Perhaps family relations would improve at least between us and him if not with Mildred. I hoped for better relations with Father and thought it imperative that this might be so with the new baby coming.

Colin did begin to adjust and fit in with his older siblings better than ever. He stopped moping about not being able to be with Mildred much anymore and seemed to revel in his renewed acquaintances with his brothers and sisters. Colin's behavior improved tremendously and he seemed all the more mature and grown up to me. Colin was far more agreeable easier to love.

I felt grateful to Mildred for finally shutting herself away and for pushing Colin away from herself as well. Not since Mother's passing had we known such joy one with another: our home was filled with peace, contentment, cooperation, happiness and lightheartedness. Even *Father* seemed changed towards us and more his old self once more.

All was delightful, except when Mildred would command from her room.

From time to time, one of us would have to take something to Mildred. I took it upon myself to do as much of this servitude as possible so as not to allow Mildred to distress my younger siblings if she should take to screaming.

Sometimes Mildred would come out for this or that thing, but she seemed always to want to promptly retreat back into her room. The rest of us could not have been happier with the change in circumstances. I suspected Mildred was not feeling especially well and I felt sincerely regretful that I did not feel any compassion for *any* discomforts of her condition. I seemed only to feel relieved that Mildred was bowing out of our lives for a time.

Father and Mildred had not made their announcement as yet but I assumed that would come in time: when Mildred began to show outward signs of being with child.

My younger sisters and brothers suspected nothing except that perhaps some of the older siblings thought that Mildred was sulking since she had *lost* the fight with me over our fair money because Father had sided with us all instead of with Mildred. I let them think as they may for perhaps that was a truth in part, but I chose not to divulge Father and Mildred's secret about her condition, to even Clara or Anna, for fear of the news being passed down and being spilled out. I did not want to plant a seed that could grow into discord. Our present peace was too precious a gift to risk its loss.

7

The Green Dress

When Clara, Anna, Charlotte and I began to speak of the next dance in town, Elizabeth began to beg Father for her to be able to go as well. Of course, then Victoria thought she should be able to go as well, and then the boys followed suite in their desires. Thankfully Father put a stop to it all.

When Clara saw me in my new green dress, she chided me, "What are you doing in *that*?! You *know* Winston wants to see you in the new *blue* one!"

"And that is *precisely* why I am wearing the green one." I winked.

Clara could see I wanted that subject closed and she kindly obliged me.

My sisters and I seemed more spirited and happy than we had ever before been on our way to a town dance. I thought that maybe it was our new dresses and shoes. Perhaps it was also that life at home had been so much more peaceful of late.

My sisters were *all* on the lookout for Winston. I tried not to be. With all my might and strength I tried to resist watching for him.

Soon we were all dancing near each other. I noticed a particular young man amongst us. The one who was dancing with Charlotte had danced with her quite a few times before. Charlotte truly seemed to enjoy his company and conversation. He seemed quite delighted with her. I wondered who he was. I was not the kind of person who openly inquired about everyone like some seemed inclined or able to. I tended to take a great deal of time to get to know others. I was reserved and rarely knew much about other folks in and around town. I wished for that moment that I was otherwise.

Realizing that Clara was more forward than I by far, I determined to ask Clara to inquire after Charlotte's young man. If this pairing were becoming of a serious nature, I wanted and indeed needed to know more about Charlotte's frequent dance partner. I worried. I thought Charlotte full young even to be approaching a serious attraction.

At a delightfully decorated refreshment table, I quenched my thirst as my three sisters were on the floor dancing with new partners. I felt like bowing out for the moment. I turned to enjoy watching my younger sisters enjoying themselves when Winston appeared from the same direction, closely approaching me. I composed myself. I stopped myself from watching him walk towards me. I as much as pretended not to have seen him approaching: I felt him draw nearer. He soon stood before me.

"Hello." I said, smiling somewhat coyly. I supposed I could not help myself.

"Hello!" he returned, cheerfully. He seemed *always* cheerful. He continued, "I was *hoping* to see that blue on you. Did you not choose it?" Winston inquired eagerly.

"I *did* choose that blue and this *green* as well. I felt like wearing the green tonight. I shall wear the blue some other time." I smiled again, wondering what he thought of my decision to go against his request, fearing that he took it as a personal insult, but also knowing that I did not want to give him the wrong impression of my intentions towards him by wearing the blue.

"Soon, I hope. I still maintain that you would look good in the blue." He smiled broadly.

"And do I not look *good* in the green?" I could not resist teasing.

"Some might say you look as good or *better* in the green as you would have in the blue." He recovered and then continued, "As for *me*, any shade of blue is my favorite color, and that one in particular was especially a nice shade so you could understand my *preferring* that blue on you, could you not?" Winston's smile was as broad as ever.

All I could think to say, also smiling, was, "Oh, yes, I understand."

"Would you care to join me in the next dance?"

I did not hesitate, "Yes, yes, I would."

As Winston and I proceeded onto the dance floor, Anna and Charlotte were escorted off and passed by us waving delightedly. They were headed straight for the refreshments. Clara was still busy with one of her many beaus. I could not keep a tally of them all, nor near begin to remember their names. I was never one to remember names anyway. A face I would always know if I had seen it before, but a name I had to work hard to master the remembering of.

It did not surprise me that my sisters were well attended at every dance, at other social gatherings such as at church and also whenever we went to town to shop for goods. They were each in their *own* ways especially beautiful. I could not own that I was *ugly*, although I had often thought myself *perhaps* a little plain and wondered at the many attentions I received from gentlemen myself. My sisters *assured* me that I was as lovely as any of them, but I could not see that comparison when I viewed myself in the mirror. The more I looked at myself in the mirror, the more flaws I could see. I had learned over time, and I shared my understanding with my sisters, that the less time spent in front of a mirror the better one seems to look to oneself. I tended to use mirrors as a useful tool rather than a trusted friend. A mirror can be a poor friend indeed.

As I danced with my tall and handsome partner, I wondered at Winston's attentions towards me. Could he be as fond of me as Clara was certain of? And what was I to do about it *then*? I could *not* contemplate marriage any time soon. I was needed on the farm. I was *needed* by my younger siblings. If Mildred were a gracious new mother to us all, all would be *very* different. If Mildred were a woman even remotely like unto Mother, I could begin to think about myself and my future. If only Father had exercised his authority over his wife as he had always seemed to know how to do with his children. I could not encourage Winston's attentions no matter how tempting it was to me to do. I had to think of more than myself. I could not forget my family.

8
Still a Secret

Mildred's condition began to show, but still she and Father had not made any announcement. I thought it odd that their secret was still remaining such. Why not announce to the family at least, if not the neighbors? Well, it mattered not to me how long Mildred wanted to hide in her room and not explain why she did so. Our respite without her was peace and rest indeed.

Autumn was busy with preparations for winter as always. All crops were brought in. Preserves were set aside as were dried foods. The pantry and root cellar were full. Father went to town a number of times to sell, to trade and purchase anything needed to hold us through winter. We tended not to go to town nearly as much in the winter. This flurry of activity escaped Mildred's notice it seemed, as she rested in her room much of the time, but then, Mildred had always been *for* herself: she was a queen to be waited on.

My store of paper and pencils were ready for a long winter of drawing. When I was not attending to family and household duties I would have time to do my sketches, if only a little. While I had always preferred to draw my beloved horses to anything, I had begun trying my hand at portraiture. While the older children did not mind posing for me, the youngest children were ill models to be sure. My best chance at capturing my youngest brothers especially was to catch them napping and as they drifted off to a land of dreams earlier than I. Some evenings found me sketching at their bedsides by candlelight. What angelic creatures they were when sleeping. The older girls actually seemed to enjoy the attention and importance of being an artist's model. Of course they each wanted to keep every drawing I did of them but I had to keep some samples, for I had plans for them.

I thought that perhaps I could find folks in town who would like their portraits done. My sketches of horses had been well-received, but would not people enjoy a portrait of themselves or a loved-one all that much more than drawings of horses? I found that portraiture came naturally to me and I was exceedingly pleased with much of the results. I determined to try to make a small business of my talents the following spring with the knowledge that if one can provide *somewhat* for oneself, so much the better. Indeed, sometimes, or perhaps, often times, it was truly a necessity.

Another project idea for us to earn some money had come to my mind. We each of us girls had more than one beautiful beloved doll that Mother had lovingly sewn for us from time to time, and the last few darling dolls that Mother had made for my younger sisters had been created with my assistance. I knew how to make dolls. Not all country dolls were created equal to be sure and I was certain that prettier faces and lovelier details would entice some buyers that might otherwise be content with their own home-fashioned dolls. With another town fair on the distant horizon as inducement, I solicited crucial help from Clara, Anna and Charlotte, and even our younger sisters and brothers, in assembling some dolls for sale. It was a good winter family project that we could all enjoy working on together, and a good use for fabric and other scraps that would otherwise tend to be used in making patchwork quilts anyway. Yes, we could also make some quilts to sell, but, somehow I fancied the idea of producing dolls as a better one. Every one of us was to share in the profits of our little doll venture.

We had always tended to do more of our schooling throughout the winter when there was more time for such things. Since Mother passed away, the task of schooling our family was mostly mine but Clara had been helpful in teaching the younger ones and now Anna and Charlotte helped a great deal as well. For us, winter offered a rest from many chores and much time for reading and other such enjoyments. Not living near enough to the town school to go to it, our home had always been our school. Mother had always offered a well-rounded education to us and I tried to carry on where she had left off.

Thankfully, Mildred had never inserted herself into our schoolwork beyond criticizing this or that from time to time. I did my best to counteract Mildred's criticisms in all things by complimenting, praising, encouraging and cheering my younger siblings on, in every good thing, including every aspect of our home education. We had all long since learned to ignore much of what Mildred said, for Mildred was *full* of negatives.

But *now*, with Mildred at rest in her room and away from us all for the most part, days and evenings passed in good humor and positive relations.

One night in our room, Clara, Anna and Charlotte were discussing Mildred's expanding girth in animated whispers. I thought it good that Elizabeth and Victoria were asleep.

Giggling, Clara burst, "Laying around all day eating is what's done it to her! And what does her precious mirror think of her now?!"

"I'm sure her mirror lies to her and tells her she looks as young and slim as ever!" added Anna with a snort.

"She has earned every roll of fat she carries now. She is lazy and doesn't help with any chores or work. What a wife Father got himself! What a useless hag she is." Clara sneered.

Anna and Charlotte nodded, smiling with some sense of satisfaction.

I could not let this continue. I decided I *must* explain, but without divulging that I had overheard a secret discussed between Father and Mildred.

"Perhaps she is simply with child."

"Oh *my*, that could *be*." exclaimed Clara, still in a whisper.

Again, Anna and Charlotte nodded, this time with eyes as wide as Clara's.

We all looked at each other in silence.

Clara broke the quiet slightly, "Well, if *that* is why she keeps to her room, we can *all* thank the baby for it. At least we have had this time of peace and there will be a little more yet to come I wager."

The winter passed quietly, peacefully, happily and mostly *without* Mildred. My sisters, brothers and I spent time joyously, like unto times past with Mother. Even Father enjoyed some time spent with us, like he had not since Mother was taken from us.

Still, Father had not announced Mildred's condition. I was sure it was *Mildred* who wished to keep her secret. Why would Father? What I had at first thought odd now seemed even silly: why keep such a secret, for such a length of time? I wondered if perhaps she felt a certain feeling of vulnerability. She behaved almost like an injured animal in its cave. There were occasional snarls and snaps coming from Mildred's cave and poor Father received the brunt of them. He seemed to dote on her, though and I did not doubt that he was looking forward to his new addition.

As early spring of 1845 began to delight the world around us, Father and Mildred suddenly took a trip into town. When he came back without her, his only explanation to us was that she wanted to spend some time at her cousin's home. I was sure she wanted to be near the town midwife when her moment of travail came and that was why she had gone to stay in town awhile. Perhaps she was staying at her cousin's or perhaps she was staying at the midwife's. I knew some women did stay at the midwife's house in their last weeks. Mother had always preferred to stay on the farm, but Mother was a special breed of woman. Not every woman was as brave and full of faith as Mother. There was a friend from town who had come out and stayed awhile to help out, though and I remember my services being enlisted to some degree for at least the three youngest boys.

Well, it was as if spring had brought a breath of fresh air even as Mildred's spirit had *left* the house. No longer was there an over-riding sense of tension in our home that accompanied Mildred's presence there. Our home was *ours* once more and joyful laughter filled it again. Father was not there to join in on the joy very much as he was spending much time in town when he was not at work in the fields and such. I did not wonder why. Neither did Clara, Anna and Charlotte. Our younger sisters and brothers only seemed to notice that life was good: very good indeed. Nobody even seemed to mind the many mounting chores that spring brought us, indoors and out. There was much work to be done and many happy hands willing to do it. Never had I seen such a spirit of cooperation and willingness to perform hard work among my siblings. It was a joy to behold. Mother would have been delighted and proud: proud in the *best* sense of the word. I wondered if her watchful eye was upon us all with a smile and also upon Benjamin, wherever and however he was.

As I often did, I stopped to say a word of prayer for Benjamin, and then wiped my tears. Nary had a word been heard of Benjamin or of the Blackwells. Every now and then I would ask someone in town if they had heard or knew of anything as to what might have become of our former neighbors and always the answer was similar, bringing similar sympathetic looks. Not one person knew anything of our neighbors' departure, travel plans or destination. Still I kept up hope that someday Heaven would grant my wish and reunite our little brother Benjamin to our family.

An early spring dance took Clara, Anna, Charlotte and I into town one lovely evening. I wore the blue dress and no amount of denying my expectations of hoping to see Winston and his pleased reaction to the new blue calico would stop my dance-loving sisters from teasing me about it. I finally threatened to change into the green dress. Their wagging tongues were all silenced and I was all relief.

Father was in town with no promise of a return at any specific time that night. I almost was persuaded by Elizabeth that she should come with us but then of course Victoria insisted that she would have to come too and so the boys would then have been left at home all alone. Bertram happily tried to convince me that he could play man of the house well enough and though I did not doubt it, I simply could not in good conscience go along with the pressured pleas of Elizabeth, Victoria and Bertram. I put my foot firmly down with a smile and commanded that they all have a lovely time, knowing that their day and undeniably their nights would come soon enough; and reminding them that Father would not necessarily approve and that I did not wish to stir trouble with him on their accounts.

At length acceptance by my younger siblings was achieved and we older girls left our younger sisters and brothers sufficiently bribed with treats and hugs before we happily embarked, knowing we were leaving younger siblings happily behind.

Our coats just off, and once in the assembly hall, I felt a tap on my shoulder. I turned, beaming, fully expecting to see my old faithful friend, Winston. I knew not why I reacted and thought thusly, but there before me was a young woman I barely knew.

"Hello. Yes, may I help you?" I spoke first.

"The whole town is *buzzing* with the news!" she announced.

I tried with great effort to remember her name but for the life of me I could not recall it. I hoped Clara or Anna would jump in with this young lady's name soon since they were always far better in such matters than I.

"*What* news?" I returned.

"Why, about your *Mother.*" She responded almost curtly.

"Our *Mother?*" I was stunned, and must have looked at least that, not knowing what supposed news she could possibly have within any good taste regarding our dear beloved and long since passed Mother.

"Why, Mildred, of course!"

"Oh! *Mildred.*" Now I understood.

"Well, everyone knows she is staying at the midwife's house and we all know what that means. Your father visits there almost every day or at least in the evenings he does."

"Yes." What else could I say?

"Well, when is the expected day of arrival?"

"Oh, I'm not sure. Who knows for certain about these things? Soon, though I would think." I grasped, trying to remain vague without appearing ignorant of details.

"Well, of course it's *soon*. So, is everyone hoping for a boy or a girl?"

"Yes."

"Yes?" she looked incredulous.

I had to smile a little, "Yes. We hope for a boy or a girl. As long as a child is born healthy, what does it matter whether it's a boy or a girl, wouldn't you say?"

"Oh, well, yes."

Clara, Anna and Charlotte were giggling a little off to the side.

"Well, congratulations then."

"Thank you."

Then the young miss was off and away, and my sisters and I took to a huddle.

"Well, the whole town knows *now*." I stated.

"How could Father *do* this to us? He hasn't even *told* us yet and now the whole *town* knows." Clara seemed quite distressed.

"I'm sure it's all *Mildred's* doing for some odd reason of her own. Well, who cares anyway? We can pretend we have known all along." I smiled reassuringly.

"More likely a *cruel* reason." Clara frowned.

"Who *cares*?!" Anna put in.

"I know *I* don't." added Charlotte.

Out of the corner of my eye I saw some prospective dancing partners coming our way and changed the subject promptly, "Get ready to dance and put on your smiles, sisters."

Mildred's odd or cruel reasons for making our family the last to know about her coming child were instantly forgotten and the dancing began.

Back at the refreshment table I finally was somewhat alone with Clara and therefore able to ask her about the young man who was once again Charlotte's frequent dance partner.

His name was Joseph. He was nice enough. What more was there to say, thought Clara. He was just one of many nice fellows who were vying for the attentions of my sisters.

I could not help but look for Winston. I told myself not to seek him out with my eyes, but then I told myself 'what was the harm?' My first glimpse of him was near the refreshment table. He was talking animatedly to a somewhat attractive young lady. I felt my heart thunder and my cheeks flush. How silly of me. I felt angry at myself.

Then I saw them dancing together. I felt angry at him, and I did not like her. I thought her odd looking. Suddenly, I felt excessively uncomfortable in my blue dress. Oh, I wished I had worn the green or anything else instead. I turned my attentions elsewhere. My eyes found my happy sisters dancing around the floor and I was calmed.

Soon Clara was at my side, out of breath and with eyes alight.

"Did you see her? The girl Winston was dancing with? Who is she, do you know?"

"I don't care." I *tried* to appear apathetic.

"Oh, you don't, don't you?" she breathed, not believing me of course and then continued, "Well, I think her funny looking. Maybe she is good looking in a certain sense but it seems to me that she is her best from far away. It is her fancy dress that makes her attractive. In a plain dress she would seem nothing. She is nothing to you. You shine in a plain dress."

"It's a good thing, then."

"What? What's a good thing?"

"That I *shine* in a plain dress, for that is all I have or can afford."

Clara burst out laughing. I had to laugh myself.

Clara was right. The girl Winston was paying attentions to seemed only attractive because she was dressed in finery. I supposed she must have a rich father who spoiled her terribly. And now I began to wonder if Winston's head was turned by money.

When Anna and Charlotte returned from dancing, they were all abuzz with speculations about Winston and the girl. I tried to make light of it but they would not let me, and neither would Clara. It was as if my three sisters believed I had a prior *claim* on Winston. As if they felt they had claimed Winston for me *themselves* and seeing him so attentive to someone else *vexed* them greatly. They seemed disgruntled to be sure.

Once more I had to change the subject with them by pointing their attentions towards prospective dance partners advancing in their immediate direction.

Soon my sisters were all happily dancing around as if they had long since forgotten me, Winston, and his apparent new girl. I contented myself in watching my sisters' smiles as they danced.

My turn finally came and I was up and dancing myself.

I decided to take the liberty of dancing with as many young men as I could that night. I secretly did not want Winston to think that seeing him with that other girl rattled me, even if it *did* a little. To own the truth, I felt heartbroken to a great degree, but I took hold of myself firmly; to move on from Winston, since he so apparently had moved on beyond me. I also wanted my sisters to put Winston out of their heads where I was concerned. If they saw me having a wonderful time with many different partners, they would forget that it seemed I had held a partiality towards Winston, or fancied him in any way beyond what I had felt for anyone else.

The dance was nearing an end. My feet were feeling rather worn out. My boots were holding out well and I was glad of it. I did not really have the money to buy another pair quite yet. I thought that a good pair of boots should last for a good ten years or so. I was thinking I might like to begin to pass on a few dances or bow out for the rest of what was left of the evening when I was *completely* surprised to see Winston abruptly directly in front of me.

"Would you care for the next dance?" his smile was relaxed and confident.

I wanted to say no. I really *did* want to say no to him. How dare he spend most of the evening with that girl and then come ask me to dance after all this time and the dance almost over. It seemed insulting to me. I felt like second skimmings, or something of that ilk. I almost looked around to see where that other girl was. I almost asked him the same.

"Please?" he smiled wider and held out his hand for me to take it.

What *nerve* he has, I thought. Who does he think he is? Does he think me *beyond* feeling? I felt like stomping on his foot and screaming, 'No!'

"That blue looks wonderful on you, to me." he diverted.

"Thank you." I softened.

He was still smiling with his hand out, but beginning to look a little unsure of himself. He looked like he might begin to feel embarrassed if I did not take his hand: so I took pity on him, and I did.

We danced the last several dances before the band quit for the night. I had to *admit* to myself that I surely did have a lovely time. I *did* prefer Winston to all others as much as I tried to stop myself. There was something about him that I could not help but fancy. From time to time I had looked around to catch a glimpse of where that girl was, but I could not see her anywhere: it was as if she had simply disappeared.

9
Lena

It was a girl. Mildred named her Lena. We all thought it a pretty name. Father did finally announce to us all about the baby, but not until after she was born: I was sure this was in keeping with Mildred's desires and it all seemed so very odd, silly and even, yes, cruel, to me.

Mildred had spent a number of weeks at the midwife's house before Father brought his wife and daughter home to the farm. I wondered how Mildred behaved towards the midwife's family, but suspected she was on her *best* behavior there. Mildred knew how to be *pleasant* when it was in her best interests to do so. After all, she had done so especially well at securing Father.

We all did our best to welcome Mildred back with warm well wishes and also showed delight in meeting our new youngest sister. She was a sweet baby and I could not hold *anything* Mildred had ever done against us all, *against* this newest Heavenly arrival. All babies are angels. I hoped Lena could remain an angel on earth throughout life, but wondered how that could be possible with a mother such as Mildred.

Mildred and her little Lena kept to Mildred's room for the most part. We all did a great deal to help Mildred out whenever she was in need, which was often. It was not but days before Mildred was commanding, demanding, complaining and yelling from her room. Most of us responded with patience as usual. We were all still delighted that she was not truly among us, but shut away, as we had come to enjoy in the recent many months past.

Days and weeks continued in a similar fashion. Mildred kept

to her room with her new baby girl, always reminding us all that Lena was *only* our half sister, half blood; and behaving as if Lena was not even sister to us at all. The rest of us served Mildred as well as worked on all the indoor and outdoor chores.

One afternoon, whilst hanging out the wash, three of my sisters and I had fallen into a hushed and secretive conversation regarding some recent frustrations with the unpleasant Mildred. The sentiments continued.

Clara frowned, "I detest Queen Mildred."

Anna and Charlotte nodded vigorously in communicatory unison, while I stoically tried to resist such an inviting temptation in an attempt to show a modicum of sisterly maturity.

Clara continued, "She is as evil a queen as I can imagine."

"Take heart. I can imagine even worse, and thus perhaps we should count some of our blessings." I teasingly tried to teach some perspective.

"The way she lazes around and commands us!" Clara complained.

"As if we were her personal slaves!" Anna added.

Charlotte emphasized, "Screeching at us to do this and do that... while she does nothing."

As an attempt to soften the mood I put in, "Well, she does have the baby now."

Clara contested, "Lena is Mildred's excuse to be lazy now, but, what was her excuse long before? She is a horrid, horrid hag."

Anna and Charlotte nodded energetically once again. I hung another shirt.

Clara thoughtfully grinned, "Hmm... mill dread... our dreaded stepmother is nothing more than a millstone around Father's neck!"

There was a prolonged hiccup in time before the meaning sank into our minds, and some chuckles and laughter escaped all our lips.

"What an epiphany you've discovered, Clara!" giggled Anna.

Chuckles ensued all around.

With some exertion, I suppressed enjoyment and quickly cautioned, "Take care to check yourselves, girls. Words spoken in some places may ultimately reach Father or Mildred's ears... and then we will all pay the horrible price of our own follies."

"Oh dread!" chortled Clara.

Anna held her stomach as her laughter ruptured almost painfully.

"Take heed." I disciplined with a smile.

"I confess I've never liked the name." expressed Anna.

Clara added, "And I confess that I've never known any other dreaded Mildred."

I reasoned, "I'm certain that there are many lovely ladies the world over who share the name. Let us not curse nor despise the name. The name is not to blame. Mildred called by any other name would still not be sweet."

Giggles cascaded.

Clara sneered, "The name of Mildred shall never be anything more than dread and millstones to me."

"Dreaded millstones about all our necks." nodded Anna.

Chuckles erupted once more.

Changing course, I lamented, "It is strange that Mildred would not encourage all our love for Lena by allowing us to embrace her fully as our sister. Would not Lena be the better for being loved all the more?"

Clara sniggered, "Mildred is strange."

"I hoped Lena could change Mildred for the better." I half dreamed.

"You hoped for too much by far." Anna concluded.

***

Clara, Anna, Charlotte and I were able to escape to town now and then to pick up supplies or to go to a dance. Clara and Anna continued to be courted by many beaus. I saw Winston from time to time and began to know and like him better. Charlotte began to prefer her Joseph. I watched him closely. I tried to observe all his friends and family to try to ferret out his character. He seemed a good fellow from a good family.

There was a late spring fair in town that brought many profits to our family. Once again my younger siblings and I sold our own things whilst selling Father's. Our many little uniquely darling dolls sold well, to the mutual delight of the little girls who chose them and to those of us who created them. I saved one special doll for Lena. I enjoyed some generous profits from my drawings and sketches again. After showing my sample portraiture, I began to receive requests for commissioned works. There were quite a few who wanted me to draw them or members of their family.

When Mildred regained her strength she came out again amongst us and began to settle back completely in to her old unpleasant ways. Lena was a little darling to be sure, but of course Mildred began spoiling her terribly. I could see that Lena may not seem as sweet as time went on because of this. I had seen what Mildred had done with Colin in such a negative sense and her adoration of her own baby girl was all the greater than it had been for our little brother.

It was difficult to bond well with our youngest sister since Mildred was *loath* to let any one of us hold her or have anything to do with her, for that matter, except when she deemed it *absolutely* necessary. When Mildred needed us to care for Lena, she would always reluctantly hand her over only to retrieve her as soon as she possibly could, shortly thereafter; and when she retrieved her baby from any one of us, there was always a great many things she would criticize us for, relative to our caring for Lena. Each of us had always done any number of things wrong.

Mildred was overly protective of Lena whilst being overly critical of the rest of us as always. She began shooing us all out of the house so she could be alone in there with Lena, unless there were inside chores and work to be done in which case she wanted everyone working inside rather than taking on *any* of it herself. Her work and her chores all revolved around herself and Lena's needs and desires. *We* were expected to handle all the rest.

One day when Mildred had scolded us all out of the house, we all ended up sharing our woes on the other side of a haystack beyond the barn.

"She yelled at me and hit me and all I did was kiss Lena on the cheek!" lamented Colin.

Victoria counseled, "None of us are supposed to kiss or hug Lena. Mildred said so."

"Well, she is our sister and so I cannot see why we shouldn't give her a little love too." shared Elizabeth.

Clara advised, "Well, kiss and hug her all you want when Mildred isn't looking: you know, when we are taking care of Lena; but when Mildred is there, just stay out of the way of the both of them."

"Poor Lena." said Charlotte, adding, "How will she turn out all right?"

Bertram thought out loud, "Well... Colin's turning out all right and Mildred did the same with him when he was little. She spoiled him rotten!"

Most of us could not help but nod, at least a little.

"I wasn't spoiled *that* much." defended Colin.

"*Yes* you were!" declared Edward.

As I smiled at Colin I put in, "Colin is turning out quite nicely now and hopefully so will Lena if we try to love her in spite of Mildred spoiling her."

Edward could not help contesting, "But Mildred stopped spoiling Colin and *that* is when he got better. What if she *never* stops spoiling Lena?"

Anna agreed, "That is true. Mildred will spoil Lena more and more and she will become spoiled no matter what we try to do to help her. Mildred won't let us do much of anything for Lena anyway. It is as if she is not even our sister."

"She is only our half-sister." reminded Clara with a slight groan.

"I think we should just do our best to treat Lena with love and maybe Lena will turn out alright even though Mildred will spoil her rotten *forever*." I said.

"I think we should all start marrying and moving away as soon as we can, that's what I think. I want to get away from Mildred forever." proclaimed Clara.

Anna nodded. Charlotte blushed. I wondered and worried about Charlotte.

Bertram whined, looking from Clara, to Anna, to Charlotte and then to me, "Don't you girls go off and get married and leave the rest of us alone to Mildred! What will we do then?"

"Don't worry. I have no intentions of running off and getting married and leaving any of you alone to Mildred." I consoled.

"That's right, Fionna. *You* stay on the farm under Mildred's rule and the *rest* of us girls will start getting married *instead* of you. Don't you think the boys would be okay without a *few* of us? They have to grow up." stated Clara.

10
Weddings

Father was livid. It seemed he would refuse his consent. He began proclaiming such things as that he should have never let Charlotte go to dances so young, that I did not chaperone her well enough, that he did not know anything about the boy or his family and that she was much too young to consider any marriage anyway.

Charlotte gently pleaded otherwise on all counts. She spoke highly of Joseph and his family.

Clara openly and loudly defended Charlotte and her beau. Anna joined in defending Charlotte. Mildred surprised us all by telling Father that he should let her do it. At first I thought Mildred was showing a sudden sense of caring for Charlotte but then I began to think that perhaps Mildred saw this as the beginning of getting rid of us all.

With Charlotte, Clara, Anna and *even* Mildred all working on Father, he gradually began to give in. The rest of us remained silent on the matter, likely for some similar reasons. Most of us did not want to see Charlotte leave us. I truly worried about her being full too young to marry and beyond that exactly, far too young to make the best choice in a marriage partner. It was true that many Charlotte's age did marry, more particularly in the country than in cities, perhaps; but, I feared for anyone marrying young.

Father finally relented. Charlotte was to wed.

My worries over Charlotte's upcoming marriage were calmed somewhat after my few conversations with Charlotte about Joseph and his family. She assured me that Joseph was a true dear and that his family was truly wonderful. It was good to know that his family was completely capable of providing quite for themselves and that Joseph would be gifted a portion of his father's land upon the wedding date. Indeed, Joseph's family was more well-to-do than ours and since Joseph only had one brother; his parents need not worry over dividing their property between their two sons.

I still worried about Charlotte, despite her assurances, since I thought her still full young to be running a home by herself and looking forward to having and caring for babies in the very near future. But at least she, and any children she would have, would be *well* provided for and not have to worry about a difficult life in that way.

The church was full to brimming over on the day of Joseph and Charlotte's wedding. Clara, Anna, Elizabeth, Victoria and I all cried.

It seemed strange to work on the farm, in and out of the house, day to day, without Charlotte there. She was sadly missed, especially by all of us girls. It was not long before Clara, Anna, Elizabeth, Victoria and I were all descending upon Charlotte in her new little home. Joseph, his brother and father, with a little help from their friends, had put together a lovely little home for Joseph and his lovely little bride to start out with.

Since Joseph was most often out in the fields working with his father and brother, Charlotte was quite happy to have her loneliness brightened by visits from her sisters. Sometimes we would all sit around sewing little things for her new home. Mostly there was chatter and laughter, though. Clara and Anna teased Charlotte a great deal for being the first to marry. It was clear that Clara was perhaps jealous or at least put out that her younger sister should marry before she did. She had thought herself to be the first to marry since she knew I had no immediate plans for marriage, myself.

One such afternoon when we were visiting Charlotte, Joseph's mother came especially to invite us all to supper that night. We obliged and thanked her kindly for the offer. After Charlotte's mother-in-law was well on her way back to her house, Charlotte joked that Joseph's brother Jacob was in need of a wife as well and she was sure we were all invited to be looked over for that precise purpose.

I laughed aloud thinking the idea preposterous. The others giggled for reasons each their own. I thought that if it were true at all, it must be a great compliment to Charlotte, for I surmised that no mother-in-law would seek out the sisters of her daughter in law to wed another one of her sons, in fact, her one remaining son, if she did *not* approve of her new daughter.

It was a lovely meal. A generous assortment of wonderful foods filled the table. Our appetites were overwhelmed to say the least. It *did* seem that this was somewhat of an interview of us all as Joseph's mother was continuously asking each of us many questions about ourselves. It was clear to me that Jacob was incredibly shy. He quietly watched. Jacob rarely spoke unless spoken to and then he seldom had much to say. His cheeks would color often when spoken to by one of us girls. Now I understood that it was quite possibly true that Charlotte's new mother was intent on helping her shy unmarried son choose himself a wife, as he was the older of the two brothers and already at least of marrying age. What *better* place to choose a good wife than from among the sisters of a delightful new wife of the younger brother?

My sisters delighted in flirting with Jacob. Each time we ventured to visit Charlotte, inevitably, Joseph and Jacob's mother would invite us all to her home for a meal when her oldest son would at least be present. Even if Joseph and his father were in town, we would all be invited to dine with Jacob and his mother. It was completely clear that Jacob's mother wished him to choose a wife from among us. I could not tell who his mother favored and indeed it seemed it did not matter much, if at all, to *her* as long as he chose one of *us*. Clara especially loved to bring Jacob out of his shell of shyness. Anna was equally friendly and fun with him and he certainly did respond to these attentions.

I thought that perhaps Jacob would be drawn to Clara *or* Anna as they were so overtly friendly with him. I was convinced that Clara or Anna would have been delighted to be the one to be chosen; although I wondered if Clara could ever be satisfied with a husband such as Jacob. I thought him far too reserved for her and wondered if she would rule over a man like that in time.

Although Jacob seemed to enjoy Clara and Anna's lively conversations with him, he seemed to glance over at Elizabeth a great deal. I hoped I was imagining this because I believed Elizabeth far too young for Jacob and indeed a great deal too young for marriage. It was true she was not much younger than Charlotte, but in my own estimation she was quite too young to be allowed to consider marriage any time soon. I knew it was common enough for girls her age to be getting married, but I thought it unwise for at least a few reasons. I did not wish marriage for her as yet.

Jacob's mother encouraged him in *every* direction. She delighted in his conversing with each of us and was always trying to spur conversations on between any one of us and her oldest son. Sometimes she would make efforts to start conversations between each of us and Jacob. It seemed she started doing this very thing between Jacob and Elizabeth quite often. I began to suspect that she knew of Jacob's possible partiality towards Elizabeth. I hoped Elizabeth was too young to be cognizant of this and that she would simply think of him in a friendly way and not beyond that sort of thinking. Elizabeth did seem to enjoy Jacob's apparent interest in her. I thought at her age she might be flattered by the attentions of almost any young man who was amusing enough to look at and benevolent in behavior.

I wondered if I should speak to Charlotte about Jacob and whether or not he favored Elizabeth and also to request that she warn him away from Elizabeth at least for quite some time for she was far too young in my opinion. To assume the least, I did not think Father would approve of Elizabeth marrying *anyone*, including Jacob.

***

BONNETS AND APRONS: FIONNA

Mildred had become entirely unbearable once more. Father looked the other way as much or perhaps more than ever. Each of us coped as best we could with the situation such as it was. Thankfully the agreeable weather allowed us to take many inside chores outdoors once more in order to avoid being around Mildred any more than was required. She kept Lena indoors with her but fortunately for Lena, although unfortunately for the rest of us, Mildred rarely kept to her room with Lena anymore.

Clara and Anna's chore time chatter turned to speculations about their possible future husbands on a more and more frequent basis. They seemed to want to reach a point of choosing. I knew they wanted off the farm. They wanted out of Mildred's house. Marriage would be a way out. I entirely understood their motivations although I hoped they would choose carefully and not let their rush to get out from under Mildred lead them into an unhappy situation in marriage. It would be *no* solution to go from bad to possibly worse.

Sometimes Clara and Anna would enter into a lively conversation about Jacob. They each thought him sweet and him sweet on them. They would sometimes playfully fight over him. I could not help but watch for Elizabeth's reaction whenever Clara and Anna would speak of or spar over Jacob, trying to detect if Elizabeth might feel a clear preference or serious interest in Jacob. Of course I worried that Elizabeth might be allowing her romantic notions to run away with her about the *first* young man who paid her attentions before she had given time or opportunity to think in a rational manner about what marriage would mean. I by no means thought that Jacob would be the source of a bad marriage: quite the contrary, for I felt and thought well of him; but I wanted Elizabeth to be mature enough to choose well for herself and to set the scene for her own happy marriage future. I hoped her to be able to love her partner in life with all her heart.

I decided I had better take Elizabeth to the next dance to give her a chance to realize other young men were available to her for future serious considerations. I thought this would serve as a form of protection to her. In *this* way she could see other young men, receive their attentions and her mind could be steered away from Jacob and into other directions. I determined to convince Father that Elizabeth should be allowed to go out with us older girls to the next dance we went to.

Father thought the better of it. When I requested that he allow Elizabeth to go to the next dance, he said that even if Elizabeth were old enough to go to a dance, Victoria was not quite mature enough and where Elizabeth went Victoria could not be kept from going. They were so close in age and it was true, as two little peas together in a pod, they had always been together. Father insisted it was too cruel to keep Victoria home while Elizabeth went out to a dance.

Some weeks later, there was news to digest.

I was sure that Father would lay down the law in a severe and determined way. When Elizabeth coyly told me about Jacob's proposal to her, I feared very little: feeling a strong confidence and a certainty of Father's objections to the match at this point in time, Elizabeth being so especially young.

Notwithstanding my objections because of her young age, I thought it slightly odd but endearingly sweet how Jacob had asked for Elizabeth's hand. Rather than ask her himself, for there had been no opportunity: they had never been alone together and there seemed no near future likelihood of them ever being alone together; Jacob went straightway to his brother to ask, Joseph went to his wife with the question and then Charlotte asked Elizabeth. I suppose it was more of an inquiry as to the possibility instead of a true proposal at first, but once Charlotte had her answer in the form of a positive from Elizabeth, the match was settled, only awaiting Father's approval.

Charlotte and Joseph made a special trip out to the farm to ask Father on behalf of Jacob and Elizabeth. I suppose it was worded as more speculation than a direct question, the whole event now only depending upon Father's answer. I was sure Charlotte *carefully* broached the subject and gently moved Father's mind in the direction of the possibilities for Jacob and Elizabeth should they perhaps marry. Perhaps, at first, it was worded in more of a future tense.

I know not how it was accomplished for I was not there or near to hear the conversation and discussion but by the time I was privy to anything, Elizabeth was engaged to marry Jacob. Father had approved. Perhaps Mildred saw one less mouth to feed or one less child to put up with and had encouraged him to push ahead rather than making them wait until Elizabeth was older.

I was *quite* shocked at the ease of which Charlotte and Joseph (perhaps with Mildred's generous helping) had convinced Father to consent. He barely had met Jacob and now he was giving one of his youngest daughters to him. I surmised that he had many reasons to think it a good match, if not perfect timing for Elizabeth. After all, Jacob was entitled to as much as or more wealth and land than Joseph was, and Elizabeth would be well taken care of. Father would not have to worry about providing for Elizabeth in any way, any more. Elizabeth would be all grown up and gone, albeit perhaps somewhat prematurely, but I supposed Father thought that it better to marry off Elizabeth a fraction early, than taking a chance on waiting for a less ideal match. Jacob was simply *too* good a catch to toss aside.

Jacob and Elizabeth's little home was built very near Joseph and Charlotte's house on the Jones family farm, of course. Elizabeth's wedding was just as well attended as Charlotte's had been. This time, Clara, Anna, Victoria and I cried. Victoria was deeply saddened for she was losing her dearest, closest sister. Charlotte seemed extremely delighted and shed no tears at all. Clara and Anna seemed to feel somewhat incredulous that such a young sister would be marrying before them: another younger sister well-married, and neither of them anywhere near to even an engagement. I did think Clara and Anna jealous and unhappy just a *little*, if not more.

The two couples became fast friends promptly. Of course Charlotte and Elizabeth had always been close sisters in many ways and it seemed the same was true for Joseph and Jacob. Soon Charlotte and Elizabeth were quite the fashionable young married ladies. Joseph and Jacob delighted in adorning their wives with the prettiest of things and also in seeing their wives thrill at the frequent gifts and surprises. Of course Charlotte and Elizabeth had never been dressed so exceptionally fine.

It became rare over time for either or both of the young Mr. and Mrs. Jones to come visit our farm. They feigned being busy or faulted business affairs but I was sure Mildred was an embarrassment to both Charlotte and Elizabeth as Mildred made no attempt to treat them any better than she did before they were married. Mildred did not care to be on her best behavior when Joseph or Jacob came: on the contrary, she was just as horrible as ever. I also suspected that Charlotte and Elizabeth's husbands did not appreciate Mildred's bad treatment of their wives.

The solution was that we would all go out to the Jones farm to visit as much as possible or sometimes we would meet Charlotte and Elizabeth in town. Even though Charlotte and Elizabeth gave the impression by all *appearances* of being far and above us all, they did not let their newest fashions and finery puff up their pride where being our sisters was concerned. Victoria and I did not envy Charlotte and Elizabeth's good fortune in marriage at all but I could see that Clara and Anna did. They each had much difficulty in seeing younger sisters do so well in marriage and the prosperity thereof, since they were still no closer to marriage themselves and had desired it so passionately for so *exceedingly* long.

Sometimes Clara would behave too familiarly or even flirt with Joseph or more especially Jacob, and I could clearly see that this did not sit well with either Charlotte or Elizabeth. I worried that Clara's improprieties might make us less welcome on the Jones' land or even with our own sisters, but there was simply *no* talking to her about it. She did not want to hear nor heed my counsel on the matter.

I began to think that perhaps allowing a little time and distance between my *married* sisters and my sisters who still only *wished* to be married, might be wise and I determined to keep Clara and Anna busy going to town rather than to Charlotte and Elizabeth's homes. The newlyweds were busy enough anyway and did not necessarily desire our constant company.

Clara and Anna were happy enough to go to town any time I suggested, whether to look at new fabrics and other such things that a young lady desires to keep herself fashionable, even if only somewhat; or whether to go to *every* dance and social event where young men may be.

Victoria insisted on accompanying us no matter where we were going; since the boys oft kept themselves busy out of doors: whether working with Father, doing their chores or playing; and had become adept at avoiding and ignoring Mildred whereas Victoria was not. Of course I abhorred the idea of poor Victoria being stuck at home with Mildred so I felt compelled to let her come along with us. Father made no objections, surprisingly and thankfully. Even though I thought Victoria truly too young at thirteen to socialize much with young men, I thought I could keep her close under my wing at dances and fend off any attentions that might come her way from any young man. I was determined to keep Victoria from marrying, at least for a small while. Even though Charlotte and even Elizabeth seemed happy in their circumstances I thought it wise to help Victoria grow at least a *little* older before letting her take that giant leap into womanhood.

At the next dance, Clara and Anna kept pairing off with two young men who seemed genteel enough. Rayner and Thomas were the best of friends. This suited Clara and Anna perfectly as they tended to always be together and fancied themselves marrying two brothers or two friends that were as if brothers. In point of fact, Clara and Anna had been joking that they wanted to find a pair of brothers to marry, just like Charlotte and Elizabeth had.

It was soon apparent that both Clara and Anna were focusing their attentions entirely on Rayner and Thomas. Clara favored Rayner, and Anna, Thomas. It was also clear that these attractions were exactly reciprocated by both young men, so that both matches seemed fixed, and happily so.

As both Clara and Anna were up and dancing with Rayner and Thomas almost constantly, I chose to decline all offers for dancing so that I could stay by Victoria's side as her guardian. We kept off and away where we would not be noticed too much and so remain spectators.

Victoria was simply delighted to be out socially and away from Mildred, and did not mind or perhaps she did not notice that I was obviously keeping her from meeting young men and dancing with them. I was happy to engage in lively conversation with my little sister and she seemed quite happy to have the close association with and attentions from me. She had felt lonely in missing her favored sister, Elizabeth. As we were busily and almost endlessly talking, I gradually realized that I did not know my sweet little sister as well as I might and perhaps should have, so I began encouraging her to talk about herself, her feelings and her desires in life.

As Victoria was quite young when Mother died, I could begin to see that Mother did not have the great impact and influence upon Victoria that I had felt and appreciated. I could also see that Victoria had few positive memories of Father as he had been before, when Mother was also with us; and that Mildred had made a more severe mark upon my little sister than upon me. The *loss* of Mother, the *decline* of Father and the *curse* of Mildred had harmed my little sister *far* beyond what I had ever imagined.

As Victoria and I chatted, fully engrossed in our intimate conversation, the world around us seemed to fade away and all I could see and hear was my little sister. I felt a swelling in my heart, a deep compassion and an intense sadness. As I fought to keep my tears from flowing and to remain composed with a pleasant enough expression on my face, I promised within myself from that day forward to take extra special care over my dear little sister. I would protect her, keep harm from her and provide all the good that I could for her; for she had been harmed *far* too much already. I realized I could have and should do more for my younger sisters and brothers. At that moment in time I wanted to curse Mildred quite *literally* for what she had done to my dearest youngest sister and to the rest of our family; but I knew there was a place being prepared for Mildred where she belonged and my energy would be better spent mothering my motherless sisters and brothers.

"Fionna?" never had Winston surprised me so, although he seemed to enjoy so doing. I tried to swiftly recover my shock and more especially my shocked appearance.

"Winston." I simply smiled as I turned towards him.

"And who is this lovely young lady with you tonight, pray tell?"

"This is my youngest sister, Victoria." I introduced.

Winston joined Victoria and me, away from the crowd, to converse about this and that subject. It seemed to me that he could see and seemed to quite understand that I did not desire to dance and in so doing, leave my little sister alone. I thought it a dear gesture on his side to visit with us apart from the dance and the dancing and sincerely appreciated listening to his lively chatter with Victoria. I occasionally pulled back and allowed the two of them to enjoy a conversation while I enjoyed being the silent audience.

It was not long before Clara and Anna were settled towards marriage. Clara claimed love for her Rayner and Anna for her Thomas. The double wedding was planned by the four of them long before Father was consulted about it, or his consent asked for. No matter, Father happily agreed. I hoped it was true love but feared it might be a quick settling, since they both wanted to follow in the footsteps of their younger sisters and let marriage take them off of Mildred's farm to somewhere where they could live side by side as married women.

Rayner and Thomas seemed good fellows with good families, prospects and ambitions, so at least Clara and Anna were not choosing badly, if perhaps a little hurriedly. Small homes on land were secured side by side and two more of my sisters were married and so began their new lives together with their new husbands.

***

The farm began to seem a little lonely. Four sisters were now gone from it and the loss was felt keenly. Visits to our sisters' homes were paid as frequently as possible and as much as young married couples will desire, but my brothers, sister and I almost felt like lost lambs with four of our vivacious sisters gone from us. Victoria and I bonded to each other in a very real sense. The boys clung to us, each other, and us to them as well.

KERRI BENNETT WILLIAMSON

With so seemingly few of us left on Mildred's farm, it almost seemed that Mildred's ill temper was emboldened against us. Clara and Anna had always somehow stood up to Mildred more than the rest of us and now they were no longer on the farm to keep Mildred in check, if at all. I had not thought Mildred able to become worse but I had thought wrongly. Mildred seemed bent on driving us all off the farm as quickly as she could send us; or at least to make life as miserable for us all as possible while we remained. I *still* marveled at Father. Why did he not see what Mildred was doing to his children? Why did he not care about or for his children? Was he not their father, *our* father? Did he not see that it was his *duty* to protect and provide for all his children? Could he not see the injustices? Did he not sense how wrong all this was? Why would he not see his very real sins of omission?

With Clara, Anna, Charlotte and Elizabeth all married off, and Victoria surely far too young by my estimations to be entertaining thoughts of engagements with young men, it did not seem needful to me to go to dances anymore. Victoria truly *might* have liked to, but she did not seem necessarily desirous of going to dances as yet, so I was happy to keep her away from them.

Instead, I took Victoria and our brothers off of Mildred's farm as often as I could: to visit our married sisters, to gather supplies in town or even simply for a special treat. We all did our best to stay as clear of Mildred and her beloved Lena as we possibly could. It was not that we were not fond of Lena, because we each were delighted with her in our own ways; but Mildred did not allow us to associate with our baby sister unless Mildred herself needed a respite from caring for her little daughter for whatever reason. We only were allowed to care for Lena when Mildred had something else to do. Beyond that relationship; which I was sure Mildred considered much more a relationship of servitude rather than of family relations; we were allowed *none*.

One day, in town, while just treating Victoria and my brothers to candy in the general store, I happened to bump into Winston. It seemed his habit to frequently surprise me or perhaps it was our fate to run into each other, but I seldom saw him coming, and was always grasping to compose myself when I did. Sometimes there was a mischievous glint in his eye when he seemed to clearly see me trying to pull myself together to respond to his greeting. He *enjoyed* that he discomposed me. He delighted in surprising me. This was clear.

I told no one, but I was indeed terribly drawn to this young man. Of course, most, if not all of my sisters knew of my preference for Winston as much as I tried to deny and hide it. Sometimes they would, in their turns, ask me what progress was being made between Winston and me. I always tried to divert the conversation or make light of my friendship with him. I rarely was successful at first but with dogged perseverance I would eventually turn all thoughts away from Winston and onto other, safer, surer ground.

I thought that if my family circumstances were more favorable, I might be married to him already, but *how* could I entertain such thoughts? I could not run off and marry, thinking only of myself: fostering only my own happiness. What would Victoria, Bertram, Edward and Colin *do* without me on Mildred's farm? Would they not likely wither away and die? Mildred would utterly destroy them and Father would look the other way as he had quickly learned to do under Mildred's manipulations and rule of ruination.

"Pray, why have I not seen you at the last several dances?" Winston inquired of me, almost in a concerned kind of earnestness.

"We have been much engaged elsewhere."

"But I thought you liked to dance."

"Well I do, but I tell you, I went to the dances much more for my sisters than for myself. And, as you know, they are all married now and so they are not dragging me off to the dances anymore. I also have much else to do, as I said."

"But what of *this* lovely sister? Does she not want to drag you to dances?" Winston waved towards Victoria with a grin.

"I know she does not look it, but she is still full young to be out socially and dancing with young men who are so much older than she is. And besides, you see I have these three young brothers who need my attentions as well. They do not like me to be always leaving them and going off to dances."

"But could they not *all* come to the dances to enjoy the music, even if you feel them too young to dance formally? Other youngsters come for the lively music and even to dance: a brother with a sister or some such relation or safe friend."

Oh, how could I explain how locked into mothering I was? Winston knew *not* my situation. He knew not our situation. Winston did not know Mildred or how our father neglected us at her behest. Winston did not realize how I needed to sacrifice my own desires for the benefit of my younger siblings.

"Could you not bring your sister and brothers to the next dance?" he continued.

"I… I suppose… perhaps I could." was all I could muster. But how could I do anything but stand off to the side with my younger siblings and offer Winston only conversation with me and my little family, while all the other young ladies would offer him every dance he wanted? I could not go to a dance with any intentions of dancing. I could not leave Victoria to the wolves that might be disguised as sheep; and it seemed uncivil to drag my brothers out to a dance and keep them up late simply on the hopes that I could engage in a little conversation with a young man I fancied.

I could not indulge myself so, without neglecting the needs of my younger sister and brothers. I could neither offer dances nor marriage, as yet, like other young ladies could.

No. I could not go to dances. I could not *dance.* I could not *court.* I dared not wish for marriage as yet. I already had a family to nurture and raise: *Mother's* family. I kept Victoria and my brothers busy. We visited our married sisters oft. I steered clear of town for a while: quite a long while. I simply could not *face* Winston and his charms. I could not explain to him fully why I should leave dancing to others for now. He would not likely understand why I must choose to leave marriage to others as well.

The next time I saw Winston in town there was a young lady on his arm.

I hoped he had not seen me. I hoped he had not seen me see *him*. I hoped he had not seen the smallest fraction on my face, of the ache that was instantly in my heart.

That same night, after Victoria and my brothers were tucked in bed with a little story as I often still offered; I stealthily went out near Mother's grave.

I felt the need to talk to someone. I desperately needed to confide what I had not allowed myself to speak of to anyone. Mother was the *only* one whom I could talk to about such matters and feelings and upon such subjects. She was still my only true confidante. I simply *knew* she would hear me, "I *love* him, Mother. I *do*. I think maybe he loved *me*, but I pushed him away; and *now* he has found another."

I began to cry. Through my tears I continued, "I pushed him away because I dared not allow myself the luxury of encouraging him. How could I have married him, Mother? How could I have *abandoned* Victoria, Bertram, Edward and Colin? How could I *leave* them to Mildred? Oh, Mother. If only *you* could talk to Father. If only he would *listen*. If only he would take *control* instead of allowing himself to *be* controlled. Why does Father accept her manipulations? He does not *master* his wife and home and so thus he and his home are mastered by *her*. He has not been a father to us since he married her!"

My tears turned to shuddered sobbing, "I feel *so* terribly alone. I feel so *incredibly* abandoned. This is too much for me, Mother. How can I measure up to *you*? Why did you *leave* them? Life is *far* too difficult without you here. Why did you leave *us*?"

I could not say more. I simply cried. I sobbed and sobbed as if I could never stop. I felt limp, barely able to stay sitting up as I was. I fell to the ground, laying there sobbing. I kept wiping the tears from my face and yet I could not dry it. The floodgates had opened and I could not seem to shut them off. I cried until I had used up every last tear and the well was dry.

***

I heard they were getting married. She had gone back to wherever she had come from and Winston had gone there to marry her.

Every now and then I would feel sad for my loss. Sometimes I cried again. And yet, I told myself that Winston was not *meant* to be for me. If he was *mine*, he would *not* be marrying another. How silly of me to cry. How could I cry over a man? A man who loved *another*? Somehow I came to know that my tears were as much or more for a general loss than just for the loss of one young man. I grieved over my self-imposed nunnery I supposed. It was not my time to marry. I had others to consider.

I often wished I had never met Winston. I was glad he had moved away. I was relieved that I did not have to avoid going to town and running into them. I was extremely grateful for that. Seeing them together over and over again would have been exceedingly painful to me.

At first, my married sisters chattered on about my missing out on Winston but they soon took pity on me and buried that subject forever. Our frequent visits could continue without continued pains to me. Victoria and my brothers seemed to truly look forward with delight, our visits with our married sisters. Time and places away from Mildred and her house were always a much needed refuge for all of us.

Life went on. In spite of Mildred, we found ways to laugh and chatter in her house. We kept finding new ways to cope I suppose. We each became better at ignoring her if we could not avoid her: I supposed we developed thick skins of armor against her. We took advantage of our small moments with Lena. We watched Lena grow up, more and more spoiled, less and less loveable; and yet I still held out some hope for her. Perhaps we could give her a few memories of something other than Mildred and her ways.

As to my married sisters, they were suddenly moving away. Joseph and Jacob had begun a business together that was taking them to greener pastures so they were taking our sisters Charlotte and Elizabeth away from us. Clara's Rayner and Anna's Thomas were doing much the same for similar reasons. Victoria and I were devastated. The boys were incredibly sad as well; but our married sisters had their husbands and at least Clara would still have Anna and Charlotte would still have Elizabeth.

I felt all the more needed by Victoria and my brothers now that our four sisters were going away, for perhaps forever, it seemed.

11
Letters

Aletter from Anna soon arrived, and I most joyously received it.

My Dearest Fionna,

I thought I should write and tell you a little of how we are doing here. Clara and I spend much time together while our husbands are busy in their business. It is a very good thing I have Clara as I would become very lonely without her. Clara's Rayner and my Thomas have high hopes that this move will profit us greatly. Clara seems as convinced as they are that all will go well for us but I have my doubts and fears as I try to hold onto faith and hope. I hope this is a venture that reveals itself worth all the efforts and upheaval.

We miss you terribly. I miss you all terribly. I did not near realize how I would miss my dear sisters and brothers that I left behind and I hope for a letter from Charlotte. I hope you have heard from Charlotte or Elizabeth and that they are both doing well. Charlotte's Joseph and Elizabeth's Jacob are so fortunate to have their father's fortune to back them in their ventures. They will likely succeed beyond their dreams. I am sure that they will. But if all does not go well or even if it all comes to naught, they can go back to their homes and land, near you all, and still live well. Do you expect occasional visits from them? I hope at least you will be able to see Charlotte and Elizabeth from time to time.

I long for a visit with you. I long to come visit and wish you could come visit here. I hope you, Victoria and the boys are all well. I hope that life on the farm is tolerable. I hope you are all able to go to town for a treat or some amusement sometimes to keep your spirits up. When will you take Victoria to the dances? You truly should. I hope you will do that for her sake and yours. The boys can do very well without you from time to time.

Oh, I wish we did not have to move away from you all. Thank Heavens Clara is with me. But I miss you, Fionna. I miss you all. I begin to think a girl should never have to leave her family. Oh, I knew not how I would miss you all. Clara misses you all as well but does not feel the loss as keenly as I do. You know our individual dispositions and how I feel these sorts of things more deeply than she does. Please write to me and do tell all.

Give all our love to Victoria, Bertram, Edward, Colin and Lena also.

All my love and affection to you all, always,
Your younger sister,
Anna

Before long, another letter came to me, from Charlotte.
Dearest Fionna,

I hope and trust this letter finds you well. I hope you have heard from Clara and Anna and that they are doing well in their new location. Elizabeth and I are quite fine here. We are enjoying spending much time together and seeing many new sights. People here are the same as anywhere I suppose, for they are very much like those we knew in our own home town. Of course, a big city offers so much more than a small town like ours does.

Joseph and Jacob keep very busy with their business and we are all sure it will be worth the many efforts and long hours.

Elizabeth and I have amused ourselves a great deal shopping for new dresses, bonnets, fancy hats and jewelry and such. I suppose we really should sew our own things, but, you know I was never as handy as you, Fionna and besides, our husbands like us to wear the latest fashions and do not mind us spending extra to purchase ready-made things that we could not make very well ourselves.

Oh, some of the bejeweled hair combs and jewels we have found and secured for ourselves! You would delight to see them. Well, hopefully you will see them sooner if not later when you see us all again. We hope and plan for a visit sometime in the near future. Joseph and Jacob's mother could not abide not seeing them for very long, and so their father will surely spend the money to bring us for a visit in not too very long. I am sure of it.

BONNETS AND APRONS: FIONNA

My Joseph and Elizabeth's Jacob talk of having sons someday but there has not been a sign of any such thing. We each feel somewhat sad from time to time about having no hints of children and this is why we have treated ourselves so much and our husbands do not complain about the expenses. Perhaps us girls are like Mother and will take a while and a few tries to finally begin a family. Our mother-in-law does want grandchildren ever so desperately and we hope we won't disappoint her too very long, but I don't mind the wait so much and I fear I am not quite ready for all that work anyway. I quite like my life of leisure, indulgences and frivolity.

Much love and best regards from Elizabeth and me to you, Victoria, Bertram, Edward and Colin,

Charlotte

There were more letters from Anna that revealed her distresses. I feared that she was not doing so well. I wondered how well things were going for her, Clara, and their husbands' business ventures. I could easily sense Anna's worries and wondered what troubles she might not be sharing. In letters, I sent her and Clara love from all of us and from Charlotte and Elizabeth as well.

Further letters from Charlotte spoke of fun and delights. She and Elizabeth found many things to amuse themselves and seemed to be enjoying a time of lengthy respite and pleasure. It seemed to me that Joseph and Jacob must be doing very well in their business and their wives seemed to benefit greatly because of it.

The contrast in tone of letters from Anna compared to letters from Charlotte were vivid to me. Anna was always concerned over a difficult time of life as it was, and continually worried over worse possible things to come; while Charlotte spoke of little more than what treasures were gathered on shopping trips, what delights were enjoyed while sight-seeing, what entertainments were found and what interesting new friends were made here and there.

In her situation that seemed far less than ideal, Anna seemed to miss her sisters and brothers greatly. Her heart pined for family. It became clearer and clearer that Anna hoped for better conditions but feared they would elude her. She worried that success would elude their husbands. Clara never wrote to me but Anna sent occasional greetings and love from her to us all.

Charlotte and Elizabeth seemed too busy to be missing their family. Letters from Charlotte came less frequently. Despite Joseph and Jacob's mother and her pleadings to bring them all home for a visit, the two young men were still far too busy with their new business endeavors to take time out to go to their family home for quite some time.

I tried to write consoling letters to Anna, hoping I could help her feel better. I also prayed intensely for especially her, and also for Clara and for their husbands to know what to do to find success in their business. Sometimes I would gather Victoria and our brothers together to say special prayers for our sisters, but especially for Anna since she was so troubled and seemed to be living in such a distressing situation. I also let Anna know we were continually praying for them, in the hopes that somehow that might help her feel better as well. I wondered how Clara was coping. Clara was one to talk but not one to write. At least Anna was writing for both of them.

12
Striking Out

It seemed but a moment before Victoria and Bertram were old enough to go to the dances. Edward and Colin were especially grown up too. In fact, my brothers were standing up to Mildred in a way that she would have *never* allowed any of us girls to do. She seemed to back away in a kind of respect for or of them, as they were quite becoming young men.

Joseph and Jacob's mother did finally find success in sending for her sons and their wives (as she could not go any longer without seeing her sons) and easily convinced her husband to spend the money that they might be able to easily afford to come for a visit. I felt grateful to her for wanting to see her sons for therefore I could see two of my sisters. Joseph and Jacob managed to put business details aside in order to make a trip to their family farm. Charlotte and Elizabeth were excited to come home particularly to show Victoria and I all their new fashions and to tell us in far greater detail about all their adventuresome experiences.

Every chance I got of it, I took Victoria, Bertram, Edward and Colin out to see Charlotte and Elizabeth whilst they were visiting Joseph and Jacob's family home. Thanks to such a gracious family, we were welcomed in, as much as we would or could come for visits. I always coached my younger sister and brothers to be on their very best behavior lest we wear out our welcome, and it was not difficult to achieve this model behavior since they all desperately wanted to visit with our beloved sisters.

As if true members of the Jones family, Mrs. Jones would lavish us with her wonderful baking and cooking. She also delighted in sharing stories from town or in and around her neighborhood. Mr. Jones took to our brothers as if they were his own sons. We always left late as none of us wanted to part company from our sisters nor their husbands and wonderful parents.

One evening after dinner, Mr. Jones was joking with Joseph and Jacob and complaining about them being gone from the family land, and how he was having difficulty keeping up with chores and work with them gone. Suddenly, like a miracle from Heaven above, Jacob suggested in all seriousness that our brothers could come to stay and work on the farm in his and his brother's stead. He spoke of how mature and beyond their years they were, and how they each could contribute much. Heads began nodding all around, and indeed I may say that my younger brothers' heads were bobbing furiously. Their smiles were a sublime delight to behold. I feared to be of any influence in the matter and remained silent and still.

Mr. and Mrs. Jones had always treated us each kindly and with respect. Compared to how Mildred treated us all and how Father allowed her to do so (and even backed her up in much of her unrighteous rule and reign), life on this farm seemed Heaven on Earth compared. I could imagine that my brothers would do well to work here.

I knew that Mr. and Mrs. Jones had been apprised of *conditions* on our family farm. I knew that they knew about Mildred and our father's cooperation in her cruel rule. Charlotte and Elizabeth had told me of some of the Jones family conversations relative to our family and more particularly Mildred's ruination of it. While I felt embarrassment over this, it was somewhat consoling to know that my sisters' in-laws felt compassion for us and the discomfiting situation that we had been living under.

Mr. Jones seemed intrigued with Jacob's proposal, but then expressed his concern about what our father would have to say about losing his boys. He seemed hesitant to follow through with such a proposal. Bertram quickly defended that Father would just as soon hire a man to help when need be, and also that our land was smaller and our father could take care of so much of it himself anyway.

Some thoughts struck me. Father did like us each to learn self-sufficiency and wanted us to be able to make our own ways in the world. Perhaps if my brothers were offered to work as apprentices, *surely* Father would likely agree to it? I turned my thoughts aloud to share a way as to how our father might be keen on the idea of my brothers working on the Jones' farm, and offered to share these ideas with Father on behalf of everyone. All agreed to let me at least try it, for what did we have to lose? I would be spokeswoman.

Soon Mrs. Jones added to such ideas, turning to Victoria and especially seemingly to me with a broad smile, "This puts me to mind of something that might interest *you* girls. I heard tell of a small school not afar off where they will soon be needing a teacher. I know well some of the folks who will be influential in the decision as to *who* they will hire and I should think you would be quite able to get the position. You could be the teacher, Fionna and Victoria, you could be her helper. You are so amiable, good with children, so well-read and possess so many talents and abilities, Fionna, that I cannot imagine they could find anyone *better* qualified nor better *suited* to be their teacher. You have *much* experience teaching your younger siblings and therefore you are just right to become a teacher. I will speak with my friends and tell them *all* about you, if you wish to consider becoming a teacher."

Of *course* I agreed. While I waited to see if Mrs. Jones could convince her friends to hire me as a teacher and allow Victoria to come along with me to help out, and also to keep me company whilst keeping Victoria away from Mildred's kingdom; I began to approach Father with ideas of us children getting out into the world to work on our own. I told him of Mrs. Jones' efforts to secure me a fine teaching position in a nearby town and how Victoria would come with me to apprentice as a teacher under my guidance. Father was especially amiable to the idea so I *began* to hope the professional adventure would come to pass for Victoria and me.

Then I broached the subject of Father's young sons perhaps also becoming apprentices at the Jones farm. I knew at least Colin and also Edward were full young to become apprentices, but considering the situation of Mr. Jones being almost our family, the fact that Edward and Colin would not take kindly to Bertram going without them, the reality that Mildred was becoming quite discomfited about the boys standing up to her more and more: all these things told me that Father would be prepared to entertain thoughts of letting the boys go out into the world, if only to the Jones' family farm. To my surprise, Father seemed delighted and more than welcomed these turns of events. Without as much as *consulting* Mildred, Father gave us *all* permission to do as we desired. I supposed Father knew that Mildred would be ecstatic to be rid of us all.

Soon Bertram, Edward and Colin, young as they still were, were off to make their way in the world, beginning on the Jones' family farm.

Shortly thereafter, Victoria and I were on our way to becoming teachers not far from our birthplace, many thanks to Mrs. Jones and her influence amongst her influential friends.

Charlotte and Elizabeth and their husbands were done visiting and gone back to where their business had taken them away from us all in the first place.

As Victoria and I began our new lives together as teachers, I felt a sure and certain confidence that our brothers would be *well* looked after and that I need not worry much over their welfare. Mr. and Mrs. Jones had sons on their farm once more, so to speak, and I felt quite sure that our brothers would be well fed, taught well and would do quite well, also having each other to depend on for familiarity and family of origin.

Victoria and I were made to feel quite welcome in our new situation and were given ample hospitality our first days and weeks there. We began to settle into our situation and positions, in that autumn of 1846.

I found teaching as a profession easy and the children were easy for me to handle. Victoria had no troubles assisting me in the classroom. We related well with our students and soon developed a rapport with them and a fondness for them. Indeed, I was assured of their fondness for us as well.

My only lament was our living quarters plus our salary compared to our expenses. I had felt sure that as a teacher, even with my salary being shared with my younger sister (and therefore a salary for one being shared amidst two), that we would be able to save monies towards our future. I had not known how *little* a teacher earned and how *expensive* many necessities could be. I also had pictured a more comfortable living situation. Our room was quite small and in the rafters of the small and, sadly, rather drafty school. Amenities were few and far between. As the weather became colder, especially during the nights, Victoria and I found it more and more difficult to stay warm.

We were allotted only so much firewood to keep the school somewhat warm during the days and were required to pay for our own personal firewood to try to keep us warm during the nights. It became not uncommon for Victoria, the children and I to wear our coats in the classroom. I wondered why the parents of these children would not offer more wood for the warmth of their children, but firewood burns quickly and is not always easily and cheaply acquired.

Victoria and I began rationing our firewood in the evenings. We needed the wood to cook our last meal of the day and would have a short space of time when we would feel reasonably warm but then soon we would rush to our bed and *try* to stay warm throughout the night. The morning fire was always a welcome treat to us, but was a hard-earned thing since we were so especially cold until its heat finally penetrated our beings.

I began to realize that I had grown up with a certain level of wealth. The family home I was born to was neither drafty nor so devoid of firewood. I wondered how many of our students were so chilled in the nights as we were. I also wished that the town hospitality had not waned such as it had. I wished to be invited out for a meal from time to time, but instead, I cooked meager offerings for Victoria and I, and we began to feel quite forgotten in our lonely existence in and above the school. The children brought a certain warmth and hospitality to us during the days to be sure, but sometimes the nights seemed extraordinarily long.

***

Another letter arrived from Anna.

Dearest Fionna,

Clara and I do far better. Thomas and Rayner have had a bit of luck of late, finally, and my spirits have lifted a great deal because of their successes. I am actually doing quite well and hoping my life's upward turn at the moment will stay up a while for we had more than our share of down turns for far too long. Of course I wish for continual ups but know that life always has its downs and so we must prepare for worse things to come.

My health is quite fine and luckily so, for Clara has not been feeling well recently and so I have been taking care of her and every household duty she would normally share. She sends her love to all. We believe she is with child early on, though her constitution is taking it very hard for some reason. Hopefully her current illness will pass quickly and she will feel stronger and better despite her apparent condition.

It seems very exciting to us that the boys are working on the Jones' farm, and that you and Victoria are working as teachers. How wonderful for all of you to be far away from Mildred! I was so happy to know that you all got away from her and off of our farm that is quite hers now. Who does she scream at now? Oh, poor, poor Father, although I dread to say that he brings so much of his wife's ills upon himself for not leading her. Poor little Lena too; how will she chance to turn out well? Oh, I still oft wish that Father would bring his wife into line and under a yoke. Why has he never troubled to check her so that life could be good for us all? Well, we are all rid of her now. Or should I say that she is finally rid of us?

I dare say you are well and happily teaching your students. I'm sure you find this work a welcome respite from working for Mildred! You must surely have much leisure time in the evenings? I hope you and Victoria are getting to dances in town and meeting many new young men there.

I shall continue to take care of Clara and I know you always watch over Victoria. Tell me any news of our brothers or Charlotte and Elizabeth, for I hunger to know of them and how they are. You are the only one who writes to me so I quite depend upon news from you.

Please write me very, very soon as I long to read from you.
Farewell my dear, dear sister.
Your younger sister,
Anna

Later on, another letter also came from Charlotte.

Dear Fionna,

Elizabeth and I do well here and hope you and Victoria are well there. It is good to know that Anna is happier and that she, Clara and their husbands are finding more luck and prosperity there. What happy news that Clara may be with child! Elizabeth may also be with child and she and Jacob are very happy. Joseph fears he will never become a father. I also fear it might be so. Sometimes I become somewhat despondent and despairing about the fact that I have not conceived as yet but then I take a lesson from mother and I pray that we will be blessed eventually. I still hope, and having that hope helps me feel better while I wait to see if I will be so lucky.

As I suspect the boys do not write you, I will apprise you of all their news. Mother Jones tells us they are doing well and not so skinny as they were. They work hard to be sure, but Mother feeds them so well that they have put on weight and are looking very healthy. It seems that Father Jones gives them much time for fun and they are very, very happy. Father Jones also says they are willing workers who are only too happy to learn new skills and he is delighted to teach them.

Elizabeth and I hope that you and Victoria are enjoying teaching, and also taking great pleasure in the time of rest that you enjoy in-between. I assume you must be taking Victoria to dances in town so she can meet young men there. She is old enough now, do not you think? I hope you are ready to entertain the advances of young men yourself as you are not getting any younger my dear, sweet older sister. I do not mean to say that you are too old to marry nor that you do not still have a while yet left of good courting years. I just cannot help but worry that you are giving your life to others too much and there will be little or none left for you if you wait too much longer. You must think of yourself more, Fionna. You always think of others and forget to think of yourself. Take this little lesson from your younger sister if you will. I know how to think of myself and am happier for it, I think. I fear that you are not as happy as you could be. Indulge yourself a little.

We hope to go back home for a visit someday soon and hope you will be able to be there as well, for we miss you terribly.
Elizabeth and I both send our love to you and Victoria and all.
Don't forget to dance,
Charlotte

Truth be told, I had not taken Victoria to any dance at all. She didn't seem to desire them necessarily and we seemed too busy with our teaching, and just trying to care for ourselves and stay warm. Victoria had also become ill numerous times. I feared it was the chill that did it to her.

This time for us was quite difficult in the survival sense and *especially* worrisome since Victoria had been ill quite oft but in another way it was a very *wonderful* time. Victoria and I had become incredibly close as sisters and I had grown to feel a love for her like I thought perhaps I had never known. I felt so protective of her and when she became sick I was so afraid she could be taken from me at any time: perhaps any night.

While I knew it was far more likely for someone to be taken from this Earth by illness while very young or when old, it was still possible for anyone in the prime of life to leave this sphere because of sickness. Perhaps my fears of losing Victoria were all the greater because we had grown so close to each other as sisters and had become such good friends beyond that, than because Victoria was ever truly terribly ill. It seemed she was often somewhat sick and it seemed it was due to us so rarely being able to feel *truly* warm. The other part of it was, I knew deep down that Victoria was the *only* sister I still had with me. Victoria seemed the only sister I had *left*. Anna had Clara, Charlotte had Elizabeth, and I had Victoria. I was determined to be close to her *forever*: to be as best of friends.

If Victoria had asked me to take her to dances, I would have made a special effort to do so for her sake I suppose; but I was not in any hurry to rid myself of my last sister. She was full young to marry anyway and *why* take her to dances while she was still truly too young to marry? Why let any courtship *begin* for her? And somehow,

I did not feel ready to entertain the advances of gentlemen myself *either*. I was surely old enough to marry, perhaps more than old enough, but perhaps the little heartbreak I had suffered because of Winston had turned me a little cold towards the thoughts of loving again; at least loving again so soon. I did not know *if* I wanted to marry as yet. I always thought I would want to, but for now, I was not quite so sure anymore.

I was immensely content to spend our quiet hours talking to my little sister of this or that dream or idea. I also enjoyed drawing again since I had not done it in so especially long. Victoria loved to read and our little school did have many interesting books for her pleasure. When we had enough light, I would often draw Victoria in her various positions as she read. It was good practice for me and indeed I quite liked the results. Victoria thought I drew her more beautiful than she truly was, but I truly drew Victoria just as she was: beautiful.

Life amongst our school children was quite interesting and sometimes even very entertaining. I thought it intriguing to see strong personality traits evident in individuals even at very young ages. Even our youngest students showed propensities in one direction or another. Some of our students were shy, some exceedingly gregarious, some dreadfully loud, some incredibly quiet, some exceptionally funny, some so terribly serious, some obviously highly intelligent, while others seemed to bloom later cerebrally; but all in all we enjoyed passing the daily hours with our dear children who were each unique from the other.

I *instantly* connected with the shy and quiet children as my kindred spirits because this seemed to always be my own nature even though I had long tried to overcome being too much this way; but I also learned to love even the most overt students as I saw their opposing ways as having obvious value as well. I supposed that any extreme can be negative in nature and something we all must learn to pull the reigns in on, and so a happy balance should be strived for by all. I saw that I could help our students learn to ease back from any extreme, towards a healthier balanced condition.

Not only did we try to impart portions of knowledge to our students, but also good behavior that included consideration of others and simply trying to *do* one's best and *be* one's best in *every* thing. I also wanted our children to know that we cared about and for them and tried not to criticize but rather compliment and encourage. I had seen what Mildred's harsh criticisms could do to hurt myself and my sisters and brothers, and so had also seen that generous doses of praise and friendship were a balm to the downtrodden in spirit.

It was somewhat amusing but perhaps even more flattering to see how many of the girls adored and wanted to emulate us, while some of the boys seemed to entertain schoolboy attractions to us. Sometimes an older boy would border on flirtation and *that* we did *not* encourage. I also found that we could not be too much as friends, or then lose all control of the classroom. We had to always remember we were the teachers and we were *charged* to take command and be *in* charge. But, it was not difficult to maintain order and yet not need to *order* anyone around. Our classroom tended to be a happy and peaceful place, even when there was lively noise and chatter. We knew they each loved us as we them.

We always graciously accepted such offerings as baked goods, fruits or candies from their homes and hearts. It made us feel incredibly good to receive their gifts, but I could also see how they were delighted to see our delight in the receipt of their contributions.

Charlotte wrote us again. She told us that Elizabeth was indeed with child as she had believed herself to be, although not feeling awfully well at all. She also relayed from letters from their mother-in-law of how the boys were doing. They were growing up in every way: taller, stockier, stronger, wiser and learning more and more the many tasks and skills necessary to run a farm, and make a piece of land flourish. I thought it entirely wonderful that Mr. Jones was so generously guiding our brothers such as he was, but also felt a certain deep sadness that our own father was not raising his own boys as he could and *should* be. Oh, but Mildred had spoiled *so* much for our family!

Charlotte did also say that the boys missed all of us girls. I realized that I missed them too; truly Victoria and I missed all our brothers and sisters. I grew tired of our living conditions in the school and in the rafters of it, and worried that the almost constant cold would be the very *literal* death of Victoria. She still was oft sick: indeed it was as if she could simply not get completely better. Full health seemed always beyond her reach. I wondered if perhaps we or I could get a teaching position closer to home, but more especially with *warmer* conditions so that we could see the boys now and then, as well as Charlotte and Elizabeth when they might go home for a visit.

Charlotte did say it was their every intention that they would be home for a visit soon and hoped upon hopes that Victoria and I would also be able to make it there for a visit at the same time. I knew we could not get away in the middle of the school year, nor could we afford the trip and would therefore miss out on visiting with our sisters. I tried to explain as much in my last letter but Charlotte did not seem to comprehend our situation.

Charlotte and Elizabeth's visit home went on without Victoria and me. We were especially sad that we could not be there to enjoy in all the delights and reunions, but could find no way to accomplish it. Charlotte wrote to us with lectures and lamentations that we did not come when they were there, and all my explanations seemed to be seen as excuses.

I decided it an appropriate opportunity to write Charlotte to ask for her influence over her mother-in-law to see if Mrs. Jones could exercise any influence over anyone who could help Victoria and I find a teaching position in town nearer to home. I mentioned our hopes of better living conditions as well, as I told Charlotte of Victoria's health troubles due to the perpetual cold we lived under, and my worries about her continued illness. I also lamented as well about missing the boys, our home town and especially missing our dear sisters, as in herself and Elizabeth, all the more particularly whenever they were able to come to town for a visit.

***

A letter arrived from Mother Jones.

My Dearest Fionna,

I am both shocked and grieved to have learned somewhat of the conditions you have been living under, in the situation I helped to attain for you. Had I been apprised of the full scope of the harshness of the conditions of that school, I would never have helped arranged your moving there to work and to live.

After Charlotte's most recent letter to me, and her having revealed to me of what you communicated to her relative to the drafty and cold conditions of the school, and Victoria's continued illness due to constant chill; I investigated further through my many friends only to discover with great dismay that you were not housed properly nor were you paid sufficiently for your service to that community's children.

I regret deeply that you have lived under these conditions and only wish that you had told Charlotte, or even more appropriately myself, of what situation you had moved to from the very beginning, so that I might have used my influence to have had the sorry conditions of school and your living quarters rectified, or to have had you moved into a far more comfortable working and living situation.

I am writing to you to express my sincerest apologies for what you have suffered these past far too many months and to tell you that you may proceed back home forthwith. I have already arranged a lovely little room in town for both you and Victoria. In reality, I have personally gone and checked out the room and the building therein myself to be sure it will be comfortable to you both. I have also arranged a teaching position for you if you should be happy to take it and if not, perhaps we can find some other work more suitable for you. If all else fails, you are welcome to a room in my own house if you would like, but I know you to be a mature young lady of independence and ability, and I am quite sure you would rather be in town and making your own way there rather than becoming a farm girl again, and be beholding to farmers such as us.

Besides which, Charlotte tells me that you and Victoria need to be in town so as to take advantage of every dance and social event possible. I hope this new situation and position will show itself a worthy reward and consolation to begin to help to make up for the months and months you both

*have suffered; far too much due to my negligence I fear and am loath to
say.*

   *Please promptly write back to me to tell me you are both on your way
home. I have taken care of the finalizing of your teaching position where you
are now for you so you need not worry over any of that. Just come home to
us my dears.*

   Yours very truly and most sincerely,
   Mother Jones

What an *angel* on earth Mother Jones was to us! I was overcome
with emotions and tears for what seemed hours because of her letter.
Just when I was beginning to feel that *no* person on earth truly cared
for us and our well being, family to my sisters stepped in to care
with *full* feeling.

   As soon as I could compose myself enough to write something
coherent, I responded to Mother Jones to tell her that we would be
on our way the moment we could get packed and ready to go.

   It was difficult to feel like we were deserting our students who
had almost become as our own children in many ways. I knew our
boys and girls did not want to see us leave and we did not truly want
to leave them. It was the chilly *condition* we wished to leave, and it
was also that we missed our brothers and the chance of seeing our
sisters as well. I took many of our students aside to explain to each of
them that we wished with all our hearts to stay with them but that
Victoria's health had suffered greatly because of the cold, and that
we missed our family and home town immensely too. It was not
difficult to gain their understanding and with promises to write and
perhaps even to visit in the coming years, their hearts were satisfied
enough to let us go, with peace in their hearts.

13
Returning to a New Home

At first light the next morning we were bound for home: a new home to be sure, but near the home we had always known. It was early spring in 1847 and every thing *felt* spring to me.

Victoria's coughing spells came and went throughout the trip but her spirits were high: the highest they had been and undeniably higher than when we traveled this road going in the other direction. My heart was full of hope and I daresay it had been devoid of most hope for many months to be sure. I felt delight, joy, excitement and gratitude: *gratitude* to Mother Jones for her firm hand in delivering us from the evils we had suffered, but also heavenward because I knew *His* hand was in this event as well. I *knew* He loved us.

As we traveled along, I realized I had not prayed *nearly* as I *should* have. I knew I had been focused on my work in teaching our students, absorbed by the work of trying to keep Victoria and myself warm and properly fed, and each night I would drop into bed, exhausted, cold, worried and forlorn, and intensely fearing the future. I did not take much time to pray. I had thought or at least felt us to be forsaken. I thought and felt us to be unloved. I wondered where Mother was and what she was doing. I wondered why Father did not seem to care about how we were.

Was *anyone* in Heaven aware of our difficulties? Did anyone up there *care*?

I did pray for Victoria when she was dreadfully sick, but so much of the time I became lost in the day to day business of work and mere survival. Much of my days were about tending to the needs of our students, and the rest of the time I was trying to make our ramshackle living quarters more livable, comfortable, warm and cozy. I would many times intend to pray before falling asleep but oft times sleep would take me before I would think to pray. When morning would come, prayer was truly the furthest thing from my mind as I would be rushing about trying to create a little warmth: a fire to warm ourselves by, and a place to cook a little hot breakfast to warm us inside.

On Sundays, when we went to the town church, it was a time of warmth for us, whether or not we felt inspired in any way by the sermon. Physically, we basked in the heat of that building. Sundays held out the warmest hours of the week for us. For especially practical reasons, we relished Sundays.

Just as I was beginning to give up hope of anyone *ever* loving and caring for me and for us, I believed that Mother Jones must have been reminded by angels to reach *out* to us, to defend us, to care for us and to care *about* us. Yes, I had given a nudge and a hint, but, this could easily have been ignored. It was not.

I felt so much gratitude and happiness that songs and hymns began bursting forth in my mind. As we rode along I could not help but hum. It occurred to me that I had not hummed in an exceptionally long time. I found myself looking around: at the blue sky, at the clouds in the sky, at the trees, at birds and all around us. Everything seemed to light up and glow just for me. I could not remember when I had seen all around me as if a painting. The world suddenly seemed a glorious place: a *little* of Heaven on earth. I began to imagine what Heaven might be like and wondered which wonderful, glorious part of it Mother preferred to spend her time in. I wondered what color the skies of Heaven are: perhaps like a glorious shifting sunset, always. What color are the trees there: how many different colors are the trees? And I wondered what of the flowers and butterflies and birds there in Heaven? Are there *more* colors than we can see here on earth? It mattered not to me as I decided that the colors we have and already enjoy here on earth are more than enough *and* to spare! I likely bored Victoria with all my relative chatter as I drove us towards home, but she was clearly equally as cheery as me.

***

Mother Jones welcomed us home with open arms, warm and delicious foods and almost *endlessly* repeated sincere and humble apologies. Victoria and I were treated like honored guests of royal blood. In between hugs and chatter from our brothers who had indeed truly grown in all ways imaginable, Mother Jones spent her every energy trying to make us both feel at home in her home: comfortable, warm and pampered. It was almost as if she wanted to make up for our past many months' discomforts in that very first night we arrived.

Victoria seemed to sleep quite soundly despite some coughing. Sadly enough, we had grown accustomed to her coughing. I had not realized how her coughing had become quite a normal every day and night occurrence to us. How could I have not lamented to Charlotte sooner for Victoria's sake? Why did I not have the courage to complain or at least *hint* of discomforts to Mother Jones? Why was I so afraid to bother people with my troubles? Could I have not (if not for myself, surely for Victoria), lodged a complaint with our employers? *Why* had I not done so? Why did I not try *something* to protect and provide for my Victoria? Was this not something where shyness must by *imperative* be overcome? Why was I so fearful and shy so excessively? Should not the well-being of my little sister *supersede* my fear to confront, to complain and to demand?

Although I lay awake a fair while chastising myself for having failed my poor little and now sickly sister, I *did* take time to say my prayers: to beg forgiveness for all my follies, to beseech for my own improvements, to banish my sister's illness and to restore her to full strength, and to thank fervently for being delivered and brought safely to a warm and loving place. When I finally fell asleep, I slept deeper and longer than I could ever remember doing. The crackling fire was a lullaby to me.

It was well nigh unto noon when I was finally fully awake and had gathered up Victoria and myself; cleaned, groomed and dressed ourselves to where we were fit to greet our generous hostess: Mother Jones, in her welcoming and happy kitchen.

Once again she was all warmth and smiles, serving up wonderful foods and hugs in abundance as she offered her *utmost* apologies to us over and *over* again. A funny thought occurred to me in those moments: I wondered if she wished she had had two more wonderful sons to bestow upon us to make us into two more of her daughters. I would not have minded *that*. Indeed not.

***

Our room in town was certainly comfortable and even somewhat spacious. It was actually so much more than I had hoped for. It seemed *positively* opulent. Mother Jones had surely made an especial effort to redeem herself from her feelings of responsibility and guilt pertaining to our less than comfortable situation of past months. I felt so much gratitude to Mother Jones that I knew not how to fully and completely thank her for her blessing upon us. I did exert my best efforts to show forth my thanks whenever I saw her but she would *not* have it. She would meet each of my attempts to thank her with her insistence of continuing her apologies. I just hoped she would know and understand at least a *fraction* of my gratitude and prayed that Heaven above would bless her for her generosity and caring towards us: we who were truly not her own but whom she had *made* her own. What a blessed and angelic woman our Mother Jones was to us.

I soon learned that the school I was to be employed by was quite small: not in *size* but in *numbers* of students I was to teach. It was a private school in town for somewhat privileged children. I felt quite inadequate to the task for I knew that parents of greater means often held far higher standards for what they placed their monies on. I feared I might be placed under some sort of scrutiny or held up to a standard that I may not be able to rise to. I argued within myself that I had been born into *some* means myself and my own

Mother had raised me in such a way that I always felt rich, worthy and worthwhile; but since Mother had been taken from us and Mildred had come to replace her I had come to *feel* poor, worthless and unworthy. Could this be part and parcel of why I succumbed to being subjected to poor conditions at our prior teaching post? Could Mildred, and her legacy regarding me, be *why* I had come to think myself happy for crumbs? I determined to try to overcome these feelings of being worth *less* and reminded myself that *all* children of Heaven are worthy and worthwhile. Besides, I told myself, even rich children have things to learn and could benefit from the kind of education I could offer. I reminded myself that I was quite well-read, particularly for a country farm girl, but even for a town girl. I was not devoid of talents and ability. I had found myself capable of bringing out the best in my students and I knew I could win them over, at least some of them.

Victoria would accompany me to the school when she felt well enough to do so. As for now, I wished for and insisted that Victoria stay home in our little abode, and repose with one of the good books I had gathered around her. I charged her with pampering herself while I was gone, and being pampered by me while I was home. Victoria's *work* was to *fully* recover. *My* work was to take care of *everything* else so that she could focus on healing herself.

After the initial discomfort of introducing myself to my new students and begging them to fully introduce themselves to me, I found that they were very much like my other school children. To be sure, a *few* were somewhat spoiled: the ample pocketbooks of their parents showed in their indulged attitudes and behaviors. More than that, perhaps a few of the children seemed naïve about much of the world around them, having been raised to be focused alone on their desires, appetites, wants and activities. I could see that few of these children had learned to work, since work to be done around them seemed done by others. Indulgences on their parents' parts had crippled or at least hampered some of them in those particular ways.

Worrying not that I might not be able to offer them opportunities to reform and rebuild themselves, I settled in to do my best to share what I could to help them each learn what they may, or what they *would* or *could*.

Victoria did better. The weather did better. Warmth was all around us more and more with each passing day as spring bloomed more and more. When I was not at the school, Victoria and I had time to do many enjoyable things.

We took time out to go to the Jones' family farm to visit Mother and Father Jones but more especially to visit our brothers. How Bertram, Edward and Colin had each grown! They were blossoming in this environ like they had not in so incredibly long. They were each growing and learning towards manhood. Again I felt so thoroughly grateful to Mother and Father Jones for taking my brothers under their wings to nurture and guide them. It was true the boys had to work for their keep, but Father Jones was a gracious and generous master and Mother Jones was always giving, and forever kind.

As always, I could not help but stare at the glaring contrast of Mildred and what she had done to Father to make him into so much less of a father to his many children. I wondered how little Lena was doing, growing up being so extraordinarily spoiled. I wondered if Father loved Lena more than any of the rest of us. Father had turned his back on his first children, the children of his original wife, while Father and Mother Jones had welcomed us all in to their family and home with open arms.

Like a revelation, the thought occurred to me that Father did not even *know* that Victoria and I were moved back home. Father did not know where we now lived. Did Father *care*? Whether or not he did care, I supposed I should let him know where we now were residing and what we were doing. Although he had never written us while we were away, I was sure or at least I hoped that he did care on some level and would like to know we were home again.

Victoria and I did enjoy some time spent in town, just looking around and visiting somewhat. I also took some time to sew us up a few new things. We had great fun in choosing some new fabrics. In all our time away, I had not the time, means or energy to make us anything new and it was an especially nice thing to be able to do that once more.

Much of our leisure time was spent quietly in our little apartment: a place of peace and warmth. Victoria would often read and I would often draw. Victoria was continually my subject but I would also peer out the window and try to quickly sketch passersby and capture the many horses as they rode by or stood around waiting or resting. Luckily for me there was a stable nearby and so there were always an abundance of horses coming or going. Watching the horses of varying sizes, shapes and color, a little here or there day to day, was like a bit of tailor-made Heaven to me.

Before I let life busy me too terribly much, I took time out to write to Charlotte to thank her *immensely* for her part in taking us from our cold school and rafters to this comfortable and pleasurable situation. I let her know how much her efforts had meant to us and how grateful we were now, to be where we were. I also asked her how she and Elizabeth were fairing and then wrote to Anna to see how she and Clara were as well.

I wrote to Father to let him know that we were now living in town and what our situation was, lest he should hear of our return first and possibly be embarrassed or even insulted otherwise. He could come seek us out in town if he wished but Victoria and I did not wish to go out to the farm to be mistreated by Mildred. Oh, if only Father knew how he had estranged us all from himself because of his disagreeable wife! *Why* did he continue to bow down to her?

Victoria had reached a point of increased health such that she was ready to come to school with me from time to time: most days in reality. I did not wish for her to over-exert herself if she did not feel entirely well and sometimes felt the need to insist that she stay home to make a day of respite for herself so that she could be fully rested for the next day.

Our students seemed quite instantly taken with Victoria from the first day: *especially* the older boys. It was amusing to me to see these very young men lavishing their attentions on my little, but oh so lovely sister. I had to remind myself that she was of their age or perhaps even younger than some. Victoria looked far older than her years and her behavior was of such grace and class that she seemed to outshine any of the girls around her.

14
A Dance for Victoria

Was it her first chance to dance? I was sure it was the first dance I really took Victoria to, at least officially, and I would not have thought of it on my own since dances seemed such a thing of the past to me by that time; but Victoria began to let her desire for a dance and dancing be known to me and I simply could not say no to her. Perhaps it was her close connections with young men of around her age at the school that spurred her on. Perhaps it was simply time for her to begin that time of life. She was certainly old enough now to entertain the advances of young men and to begin to think of marriage. I hoped she would not marry as yet, being still quite young, but it was full time for her to begin to entertain at least some thoughts of young men and matrimony.

Oh, how old I seemed to be now. I began to imagine Victoria married and me possibly able to begin to think of marriage for myself. Now that the boys were being well taken care of and raised by Mother and Father Jones, if Victoria were to marry I would feel free enough to consider it myself. But I felt too old now. I knew it was silly of me to think such, but I simply felt beyond my prime and feared my days of attentions from young men behind me. I knew I did not look too old to be considered worthy of marriage by men, young or older. The mirror told me I looked much the same as I had for quite some time. My birthdays told me I was still full young: at least *not* too old to marry as yet!

For me, perhaps it was that I *felt* like my one true chance was gone. Winston was the only young man I danced with or talked to whose *name* I even seemed to remember. It seemed as if Winston was as close to the right man for me as any could be and yet he had come to me at the wrong time in my life. I could not let myself consider *him* when he was considering *me*. I pushed him away and he found another. And now I was entering a phase of my life when perhaps I *could* consider marriage but there was no man in view at present that I desired to consider.

I could certainly be content to guard over my sweet sister as she entertained entertainments from young men. Mature and lovely beyond her years, Victoria was of mind, manners and modesty so as to shine above the commonplace of silliness and vanity in those other such females around her.

Victoria was like a flower surrounded by bees. I could not but think that it must be overwhelming to be in that position; but Victoria possessed a way to handle them gracefully. She managed to offer pleasant attentions to all, and all the young men seemed simply satisfied to be within her shining presence. I marveled at how every gentleman gladly took his turn around the dance floor with her. The young men were so well-behaved. Victoria danced with one and then another and then one after another until they each had had their own turn dancing at least once with her.

I knew there must be rivalries in their hearts for her attentions but each young man managed to compose himself and his desires or jealousies so that Victoria enjoyed equal attentions from each of her many suitors. She spent that first dance, dancing every dance that she wanted to, with every partner she desired to dance with. To say that she was the Belle of the Ball was to *understate* the supremely obvious. It was as if a Princess had been locked in a tower for a goodly long time and now the King had finally let her out to her first Ball. All the princes in surrounding kingdoms (and even all the knights as well) had all gathered because of her and were all vying for her attentions and desiring her hand in marriage, but there could be only one winner.

The jousting and fighting for Victoria's attentions were all peaceful enough on the surface but I wondered what violence might be brewing just below. I could see how passionate many of them were feeling about Victoria: each vying for a glance from her, a conversation with her, and a dance with her; for her attention and for her desire in their direction. Of course they each wanted her for their very own.

But Victoria was delighted to spread her attentions and affections all around about her, for she did not see one gentleman who stood out to her as more desirous than another, nor did she feel partial to any one individual young man. I was extremely glad of it. It was better for her at her still young age to dabble in flirtation, conversation, attentions and affections while dancing or not; rather than to settle too soon on just one suitor. Yes, this was just as I would wish for her.

While Victoria was well taken care of by these many young men, I could relax and think of myself a little. There were still a few attractions left for me. I was not devoid of attentions from gentlemen. Indeed, I felt renewed in spirit insofar as knowing I still was blessed with some blush of youth and some sort of beauty in the eyes of a few of my beholders. My own suitors were not all so young as many of Victoria's, and I could see that none were too old for me. I enjoyed my share of conversations and dances that night. I was intrigued by some especially pleasant fellows.

The night was finished off by Victoria and I being walked home by what seemed a multitude of young men, many handsome: very handsome to be sure. What *prospects* we had discovered that night! Or perhaps I should say that *we* were discovered that night.

With exhausted bodies and soaring spirits, Victoria and I retired to our beds that evening. Only after extensive chatter relative to the night's events and our new acquaintances, did we finally manage to find our ways to sleep.

15
Spring 1847

Elizabeth lost her child. Charlotte's letter sadly revealed that our little Elizabeth was quite devastated with the loss of her baby: the little one passed on long before he or she could even begin to look forward to life. Jacob was quite distressed. Elizabeth and Jacob were both somewhat sick with wondering if Elizabeth could ever carry a child to term. Charlotte and Joseph were sad for their brother and sister but were also wrapped up in their own disappointment. Charlotte still had not conceived and they began to think she could never do so.

In my letter response to Charlotte I tried to cheer them all up with hopes towards successes in that family way. I reminded my sisters that our own mother had similar troubles just in case they were beginning to forget. I happily reminded them of how many children Mother did eventually bring forth and that this was likely for them as well. I told them not to give up hope for each other or themselves. I suggested they pray. I begged them not to despair.

I did not write all my feelings relative to their woes and situations. I did not wish to preach. I dared not counsel. I feared to share all my feelings and thoughts, but I could not help but ponder within myself that Charlotte and Elizabeth were surely blessed in many ways. To be sure neither had yet been blessed with a child who lived, but they were still young with plenty of time, health and life left to look forward with hope for possibilities likely beyond their imaginings. Charlotte and Elizabeth were each blessed abundantly: they each enjoyed the love of a good man who was their very own husband; they both were adored as true daughters by Mother and

Father Jones; they had sisters and brothers who loved them; they did not want for much nor even remember much want. Prosperity had smiled constantly upon them since their marriages. Yes, Charlotte and Elizabeth were truly exceedingly blessed and yet I thought all they could see is that which they did not yet have.

I could not help but think of what I did not have. It was true that Mother and Father Jones had spread a wing over all Charlotte and Elizabeth's brothers and sisters, but I still knew that *they* were not truly my own. It was as if they were lent to me for a season or a partial parcel. I knew I did not truly have claim on them. They were my sisters' new parents. They were not truly *mine*. I could not necessarily call on them for help. I had to wait until they offered charity my way. I was sincerely thankful though, for the immense help that Mother Jones had given Victoria and me, and for what Father Jones was giving our brothers still.

Yet there was a lacking. I sometimes wondered how far or for how long the Jones' charity would or could last. I hoped and prayed it would last long and far enough to benefit the boys completely. I desperately desired that my brothers could reach manhood, ready to meet the world and its challenges. I sincerely desired each of my brothers to marry well: to find true happiness with a good woman. I wished with all my heart that they would follow our father's first choice in marriage and *not* his second.

My heart began to ache for my own man. I did not *want* to do it. I told myself I could continue along *without* a man; and indeed I would far rather be alone than be partnered badly. I did not desire anything like unto what our father had chosen his second time around. Oh, Heaven forbid I should *fall* into something terrible like that!

I did not want to settle for someone who might simply satisfy to some degree, if perhaps someone nearly wonderfully perfect was around the corner for me. But how does one know? How does one know when one has found the right one: one's soul mate? Winston had come closer for me than anyone I thought, I *felt*, and yet Winston chose another.

Each time I conversed or danced with a pleasant young man I could not help but let my mind wander; let myself imagine this gentleman as my own. I would picture this young man in a future with me and try to see if he would *do* for me. Could *he* make me truly happy? Would he help me to forget all others? Would he be a good father to our children? Could he provide for us? Would he be a devoted and loving husband to me? Could I always love him and be glad to be with him? Such were the questions I let myself entertain as I entertained the attentions of men.

I often laughed to myself to think of how *serious* my thoughts could be in the midst of *casual* conversation and while dancing animatedly. I laughed aloud inside to think of what a shock my inner thoughts and questions would be to my dance and conversation partners! I could laugh at myself but what would they *think* of me? Would they wonder at such serious considerations at so soon a beginning? Surely they would think me silly *if* they knew. I thought myself silly.

And yet courtship was such a tremendously serious thing. Choosing a mate for life was a terribly solemn business. I did not think such should be taken too lightly: indeed and in fact, not lightly at *all*. Of all the decisions and choices in life, was not marriage the most *serious* of all? Should not everyone think in seriousness about those they danced and conversed with?

Beyond dances and school, I was equipped with time and energy to parlay my talents towards my future provisions. My name was becoming somewhat known locally for my artistic pursuits and abilities, and there were those who began seeking me out to do drawings and sketches for their walls: mostly portraits. Sometimes people would sit for their portrait at Victoria's and my little place and other times I would go to their homes for the sitting.

It was obvious to me that my growing success as a portrait artist was more than *partially* due to my teaching position of somewhat privileged youth. My students would no doubt praise my talents to their parents, and parents oft want portraits of their children. *That* was where it mostly began: portraits of my students and then of their parents. Neighbors would see my work and hear of me and then there would be more requests.

Victoria was happy to read as I drew at home and when I would go out to the portrait sitting, I often would have Victoria come with me as I did not wish to leave her at home much. She always seemed a welcome guest wherever we went, especially if there was young man there. Victoria also was well liked by young ladies her age or thereabouts; as was true at our school. Moreover, she was very good with young children: always amiable and pleasant. Who did *not* like Victoria? I could think of none who did not respond positively and sometimes even profoundly to her. Victoria seemed one of those born to be loved by all. She was indeed truly and completely loveable.

Well, of course Victoria was not loved by *Mildred*. None of us were. It was easy to think that perhaps we were not loved by our father *either*. It was strange to me that although Victoria and I had been back at home and living in town all this time, Father had not sought us out as yet. There had been *no* attempt by him to see us. I also had no knowledge of our father having visited his sons: even in *all* the time they had been on the Jones' farm. I also knew that when Charlotte and Elizabeth last visited, our father did not visit them; even though they had apprised him of their upcoming visit, when they would arrive and approximately how long they would be staying.

None of us had ventured to our family farm, our home of origin, in an extremely long time. Father had not made any effort to see any of us. I supposed he was very busy working on the farm and also doting on Mildred and Lena. I had from time to time heard that he or they had been in town, but I had not seen or run into them as yet. I began to wonder if a chance meeting sometime would seem quite awkward: perhaps terribly awkward indeed.

***

"I adore them *all*, Fionna." Victoria expressed with delight.

"What? *No* preference at all?" I was relieved, in actuality.

"No. *Truly*! They are all sweet tempered and doting and there is something handsome about *each* of them. How can I choose just *one?*" she frowned.

"Well, there is no need for you to choose one any time soon. Enjoy them all, enjoy them each, have fun: for you are still full young to settle, I dare say." I advised.

"Yes, but even if I were older, I cannot *imagine* sending all but one away." Victoria sighed.

"I suppose no matter what your age, if you feel that way, perhaps you have not met the one. You know: your soul mate."

"I suppose. But how does one *know?* How can you *recognize* a soul mate?"

"You know, I do not know if you *can* know for sure, but I do think you would feel a definite preference towards one if he was *the* one."

"So, do you believe in true love, Fionna?" Victoria inquired sincerely.

"I do. I think so. Well, I do believe that two people can be happy together throughout life if they are *basically* good people with similar goals and beliefs; but I also sense that for *some* there is one special someone."

"Are you waiting for that *one* special someone?" she grinned.

"Yes. I think so. Well, I hope so. I hope I can meet a man who I can feel assured is the very best choice for me, that I could ever make for this life. I never want to look back and think I could have done better for myself."

"What about the next life? Do you think love goes on, then?" Victoria was all seriousness now.

"Well, I am sure Mother is up there feeling love for us; that she shares love with our brothers who are there with her, and her parents and all her family and friends who are there; so, I tend to think... *no*... I *believe*... that the love between a man and a woman must go on too. I do."

"Me too." she wiped a tear.

I thought to hug her and perhaps talk more about Mother for I suspected that thoughts of Mother were where her tear came from, but I did not know if she wanted to linger on those thoughts and break into complete sobbing; so I felt to change the direction of her thoughts, if only just a little, and hopefully not in any contrived way, "We both believe in true love and soul mates, or so it seems, then?" I ventured.

"Yes. I do." she firmly stated.

"And so, you should keep enjoying the attentions of all your handsome suitors until *just* the right one comes along to make you forget all others!"

"Yes. I think I shall." she smiled now.

"And yet not *toy* with any one of them, you know, not play with and then possibly break any of their hearts, of course?" I queried and advised all at once.

"Of course not." she assured me.

"But I think it would be easy for someone like you to break many hearts without even trying to or realizing it, before you were done and had settled."

"No." she seemed certain it was not really possible for her to do this.

"No... truly... I am sure of it. You could easily break hearts; far more easily than you know." I was quite serious now.

"But I am only enjoying attentions. How could I break any of their hearts?"

"From my vantage point, I see many of these young men truly beginning to fall in love with you, to become sincerely attached to you, and when men or women fall with their hearts, their hearts can easily be broken. It is very true, I assure you." I spoke from some secret experience.

"But I do not *want* to break any hearts. I simply want to enjoy friendships and that is all. Since I am not falling in love with any one of them, though, I feel in my heart that I love them all in *some* way." Victoria lamented.

"Then just take care not to make them love you so much and do not love them *all* too deeply. *Save* your deep love for only one."

"But how can you *keep* someone from falling in love with you? You say you already see young men beginning to love me and yet I have not tried to do that to any of them… truly." Victoria looked even worried.

"I suppose you cannot prevent love. You cannot prevent someone from falling. It does not surprise me to see gentlemen falling for you, for you are so loveable. I suppose you simply must take care not to lead them along, you know, to make them believe that you love them if you do not." I thought aloud, trying to find the right advice or perhaps some truth.

"But, if I do feel some love for many, can I not show that love?"

"Well, friendship is love, so I am sure it is fine to show that. Maybe it is simply that you should not show a certain seriousness if it is not there, you know, just be sincere. But I suppose it is all right to flirt a little as long as you do not do it too much, because you have the power to break hearts. You do." I smiled, thinking I was truly far too serious, as was often the case.

Victoria sat pondering.

"But, I am too *serious*! Do not listen to me *too* much. You are young and *should* have fun! I think I am becoming an old maid and have forgotten how to just have fun! You must teach me how to be young again my dear, sweet, lovely little sister!" I grabbed her hand and squeezed it, "Let us go out!"

We decided to go choose some new fabric to make ourselves new dresses for the next dance we were to go to.

Soon we were at the General Store mulling over beautiful blues, greens and even reds.

"You would look wonderful in that red," I said to Victoria.

"Dare I?" said she.

"I wonder if we should tread carefully and stay with blue or green as we always seem to." I smiled.

"If only we could afford silk." Victoria sighed with a lengthy breath.

"Well, the better, softer, smoother cottons are silk enough for me, but maybe one of these days you and I should do as Charlotte and Elizabeth have been so fortunate to be able to do *so* many times. Perhaps you and I should purchase some silk to sew up a couple of *very* special dresses for us. We would have to order our very favorite colors, though. Maybe we should think about what color our one and only silk dress should be done in."

Victoria smiled at me dreamily, "Do you *really* think we could each have a silk dress someday?"

"I think so. Of course we deserve it, as all good, kind ladies do, but few can afford to... but maybe if I sell a few more portraits we could afford just one each." I gave my little sister an affectionate hug.

Just then Victoria's face turned visibly paler. She truly looked as if she was fixedly staring at a ghost. I swiftly glanced in the direction that her gaze was fixed upon and saw Father! As I saw him, he saw us (if he had not seen us before that moment). My heart was suddenly in my throat and tears welled up behind my eyes, but I fought them back. I wanted to rush over and embrace him (but was that what he would want, I wondered). Did he love or care for us at all anymore? Did he prefer to avoid us? Did he want to forget that we were once his? He had not tried to contact us since we had moved back. Was this severe separation all his choice, or was it simply Mildred's command and he was complying with her?

Father looked as awkward as I felt and I was sure Victoria felt the same discomfort. It was as if time stood still while we three stood and stared: Victoria and I at Father and Father at us. I wondered if I should wait for him to approach us or possibly leave, but decided to take a chance and first move towards him.

I urged my legs to take me promptly over to greet my father and, all amazement to me: they complied obediently. Thank Heavens they did not buckle or shake! Without thinking further, I simply gave my father a hug and a pleasant greeting, trying to hide several tears that appeared by quickly wiping them away. When Victoria saw that Father hugged me in return and offered his greeting to me, she followed my lead and came over to give him a hug too. We each did not say much, but Victoria and I asked Father how he was doing and he asked us the same. We stood in the store ignoring those around us, trying to catch up with one another.

The unplanned visit with Father that began so awkwardly, ended pleasantly enough. He seemed genuinely interested in how we were and what we were now doing, and also in our life of the past months to almost a year since he had last seen us. I apprised him of all news pertaining to his children that I thought pertinent, and could see that he was very much out in the wilderness where his first family was concerned. He did seem pleased to hear of each of them and their progress, though. I then asked him how little Lena was doing and he happily told us of her and how she had grown. It took some effort to remain pleasantly composed as I spoke it, but I then asked him how Mildred was. He told us she was fine, as always. I suggested to Father that he truly should visit the boys and that they would love to see him. He said that he thought that such a visit to his sons was long overdue and that he would surely try to do so before long. We said our goodbyes with warm and somewhat prolonged hugs.

Victoria and I walked home without our new fabric. We had forgotten all about purchasing our materials for new dresses. We left Father in the store after we parted company with him. Father had been our focus that afternoon. We could choose and buy our fabric another day.

After arriving home I quickly wrote letters to Clara and Anna as well as to Charlotte and Elizabeth, telling them all about our impromptu visit with Father. I also told Victoria that she and I should ride or drive out to see the boys as soon as possible to let them in on the news about Father, and perhaps somewhat prepare them for seeing him again, given that it had been so long since they had visited with him. I wondered if perhaps Father could visit the boys when Charlotte and Elizabeth would next come home for a visit. My last letter from Charlotte suggested that they would soon be home for a time and I thought she and Elizabeth would like to know that they could hopefully see Father. I also thought that Clara and Anna would at least like to know that Father was happy to hear of them and how they were doing. It was good to know he cared, if only somewhat, and I thought all my sisters and brothers should surely know of it.

When Victoria and I went out to see the boys, Mother Jones and I planned how it should be. We decided that if Charlotte and I both wrote Father letters to tell him when she and Elizabeth would come, and that they wished for him to visit them and the boys while they were on the Jones' farm, perhaps he would come to visit the boys and all of us then, whether or not he came out to see the boys prior to Charlotte and Elizabeth's arrival there. Mother Jones and I both truly wondered if Father would indeed come sooner.

Between my teaching salary and my portrait work, after I imparted a fair portion to Victoria for her work assisting in teaching, and after our basic expenses for our room and for food and such necessaries, both Victoria and I had been able to lay up some generous amounts of savings. Although our monies were growing nicely, I was trying to teach Victoria that we should think of our extra money as mostly not our own at present to spend *now*, or rather, that we should think of such money as something to provide for us in our *future*, for who does know what the future will hold.

Victoria had taken to heart what I had impressed upon her: that although we had money enough saved to adorn ourselves with jewelry and order liberal lengths of silk and lace yardage for many glorious dresses, we should realize that our prosperous times and full pocketbooks *now*, did not mean we could truly afford to indulge ourselves when taking our future into account. We should take care *not* to spend all monies that we had set aside for our *needs* in the future, for *wants* in the present day.

And yet, I thought it good to treat ourselves every now and then with something special. Mother used to do it and I thought it a worthwhile thing to do. Mother never spent all the money she could have done, to keep up with every fashion nor to impress anyone with what wealth she and Father had, as Mildred had been tending to do, nor did Mother choose to go to an extreme in the other direction and wear her clothes until they were rags, as we had been forced to do when Mildred held tightly to Father's purse strings.

One thing Mother taught me about fashion was that just because something was all the rage in fashionable places and among fashionable folks, it did not mean that we should feel compelled to comply with those fashions, whether or not we could afford to. She always said our fashions should be comfortable, practical and of our own choosing and mostly of our own making: not dictated by anyone else. And so, although muslin, silk and all manner of finery were all the rage in England for the longest time and some ladies wanted to measure up to that ideal, we did not need to do so too and could be *just* as happy in cotton. But, this did not mean that to save for and make a special dress in silk was *wrong*, either.

So, Victoria and I spent many hours planning our future silk dresses. We wanted to choose just the right colors and styles that would please us immensely for many years to come. We each wanted to make ourselves dresses that would be worthy of wearing for many special occasions and also something that maybe could be passed down to a daughter some day.

Neither one of us was in any hurry to create and wear our special silk dresses but we were enjoying the planning of them. It became a shared treat to talk of, to draw pictures of and imagine ourselves with our special silk dresses. Sometimes I marveled at the hours we could spend just simply talking about our future silk dresses, and it seemed as if the *anticipation* of someday making and wearing them was as much or *more* exciting than actually having them would eventually be. I thought how imagination was like a *food* we should treasure.

In the meantime, we both still had our new cotton dresses to think of, for there was soon to be another dance and the time to sew our new dresses was becoming quite limited. The next time we went to the general store, it was past time to mull over the many colors, patterns and general choices before us. As we were thus engaged, something sparkly caught my eye and gave me an idea. There was a most bewitching new amethyst broach in the display case of such treasures, and I determined to surprise Victoria with a special such gift before the next dance. Nearby the beautiful purple jewel there was also a new cameo that caught my eye and transfixed it upon the lovely face of a woman who seemed adorned and surrounded by flowing curls and fresh flowers. I also saw a garnet broach that almost matched the amethyst one in size and beauty, and wondered if Victoria would prefer that. Victoria and I both raged over amethysts and garnets, which were more affordable than some of the finer gems we might liked to have dreamt about: yet I did not know her preference of the two lovely, if not royal, purple and red gems.

Purposely, I chose to point out these new treasures to Victoria to try to discover which she might prefer of all in the case. Victoria and I were oft in the habit of window-shopping whilst not buying, and it was not unusual for us to enjoy dreaming about owning such things and yet not be tempted to reach into our savings to do so. I thought I had taught Victoria well. I believed Mother would be pleased. Victoria seemed to be most attracted to my first choice for her, and I impulsively divulged my secret preference and dreamlike wish to her for the cameo, of all things there.

Coming up with what seemed an ingenious plan, I suggested to Victoria, "Since you love that glorious amethyst broach, why not choose purple fabric for your next dress and it will be as a sort of consolation for you since you cannot get the jewel." and I handed her a bolt of amethyst colored cotton to consider.

To my delight, Victoria thought my idea perfect and chose the deep rich purple to become her next dress for the upcoming dance. She had formerly been swaying towards a deep crimson but now purple was settled on. We each thought it a bold but beautiful choice, and she could wear red another time.

Now, Victoria and I did already each own a couple of special items of jewelry that we had chosen from among Mother's collection, as had our other sisters. We had all divided Mother's jewels evenly amongst us; and we always wore these few things; but as is likely true for many women, young or old, there is a certain want for a few more such sparkling or bejeweled things as the years go by. Beyond their wedding rings, I did not know for sure about Clara and Anna these days, but I did know that Charlotte and Elizabeth had been fortunate enough to be able to indulge in these sorts of treasures in recent years; while Victoria and I had never chosen such a thing, nor had we felt justified or able to.

As I thought the matter over, I decided that not only would I give Victoria the amethyst broach but I would secure the cameo for me since I adored it so very much: indeed I could not seem to stop thinking about and picturing it on any given dress of mine and the flowing lady amid flowers was as if *haunting* me more and more since leaving the store.

As soon as I possibly could, for I feared the amethyst broach and the cameo lady might be snatched up by another treasure hunter, I went to the store by myself, making some excuse of some business I had to attend to, when Victoria was happily busy in a book at home. I felt a thankful heart when I saw that the amethyst broach was still there but my heart sunk to see my lady was nowhere to be seen. I hoped she was simply hiding. I inquired after the cameo and was told she had already been sold. Alas, but I decided that perhaps it was meant to be: she was not to be mine but only to haunt me in my dreams. She was now but a ghost to me. I consoled myself that I could certainly wait for another cameo that would call to me someday like that lady had; whilst knowing all the while that not just *any* cameo could do nor would speak to me as she had amongst her flowers, since the face and all else must exude beauty, just as that lost lady cameo had done.

The night before we were to go to the dance, when I had just finished the final details on Victoria's new royal purple dress, I pinned the amethyst broach onto it when she would not see me do it, and then I asked her to try on her dress now that it was done. I hoped she would not see the broach until the dress was on her and she was checking herself over in the mirror, but, she at once saw the glorious jewel and began to cry. Happy tears they were, of course. She kept hugging me and sniffing and thanking me for the surprise gift. I was crying too. We were both so happy in that moment and I knew such times were indeed more treasured and rare than the broach itself was. I wanted Victoria to know how much I loved her and what a *treasure* she was to me: that she was worthy of wonderful things and though our lives had not always given us such, now was a time to tell her this in an unspoken way.

Soon we were both composed and peacefully basking in the warmth of the wonderful feelings between us on that evening: Victoria was back at a book as I was steadily (but not frantically) trying to make needed headway on my new dress for tomorrow night's dance. I knew that if I did not finish this new dress in time, I had a couple of other lovely dresses I could wear that would be perfectly wonderfully suitable. Nevertheless, I did so want to finish and be able to wear this new one. I had chosen a fabric in a fabulously greenish-blue turquoise that was truly my favorite color and not a color that was always easily come by, so it was exceptionally special to me.

As I was bent over my fabric in full concentrated focus, sewing swiftly, stitch by tiny stitch; Victoria shocked me out of my trance: she called my name in a way I had *never* quite heard before; in a way that caused me to drop the dress from my hands. There she was before me: crying openly, sobbing actually; holding a fancy little box in her beautiful slender hands and motioning for me to take it from her. In curious amazement I did so and followed her silent signals to open it, for she was sobbing so much that she could not speak for trying. Inside the special treasure box I was shocked to find my beloved lady: the hand-carved shell cameo I *thought* I had lost forever. The lady that had haunted me was now a dream come true, to be my very own. As a gift from my dearest little sister and closest beloved friend, my own little Victoria, this cameo would mean one hundred, no perhaps one *thousand* times more to me than it ever could have as a special purchase for and from myself.

Well, there we were: a puddle of tears, heaped on the floor in hug upon hug upon hug; like one endless embrace, it truly seemed. We were as if two crumpled dresses trying *desperately* to compose ourselves and yet cherishing this fraction of time in eternity as one to remember with the *deepest* fondness and blazing warmth *forever.* Neither one of us could speak for the longest time: unbelievably, for what *seemed* perhaps as much as at least a half an hour. Each time either of us tried to speak, to say something, anything, we would succumb to our tears again. My tears would trigger her tears and hers mine: a *crescendo* of tears and sobbing that was combined with intermittent laughter and giggles. What a pair we were!

Finally, Victoria was able to tell me that as soon as she saw that I loved the cameo, she knew she had to get it for me *right* away before it was gone. She almost immediately snuck out to get it, risking the chance that I might be upset with her for being frivolous: spending any of her savings on such a luxurious thing for me, but she said she simply knew she *must* do it and was willing to suffer *any* lecture I might preach in heaps upon her because of her bold and expensive purchase.

I thought the contrast of the peachy colored cameo against the turquoise fabric of my new dress a *wonder.* I had not thought the two colors an *obvious* match but the marriage of the two was so extraordinarily complimentary that I marveled in splendid surprise. I had never recalled seeing these two colors placed together before, but I was instantly a believer in the combination, and now considered my cameo color another favorite color indeed. As an honor to Victoria, the generous giver of the gift, I knew I had to wear my lady cameo soon, often and of course with my new dress; since I was sure it was the most lovingly given gift I had ever received in my life. Although, I was not instantly certain if my new turquoise dress was the very best background for the peachy color, so I had begun holding my new glorious cameo up against my other dresses. When my 'Lady Victoria', as I was now calling her, was finally once again placed against my nearly done turquoise dress, it was obvious that *this* splendid favorite color of mine was her ladyship's most wonderful backdrop.

Victoria seemed a royal dream in her purple dress and although her new amethyst broach did not contrast against her fabric like my combination of broach and dress did, it was a perfect match and looked extraordinarily regal indeed. When she was all ready to go to the dance, I dubbed her 'Princess Victoria'.

If it were *possible*, Victoria seemed adored by a greater throng of young men than usual. My poor Princess seemed in danger of dying of thirst since she was kept on the dance floor so constantly, and found her way to the refreshment table so seldom. Sometimes I felt *forced* to steal her away from her many admirers just to make sure that she had a quick drink and a little bite to eat, and any other rest or respite she needed before accepting *another* invitation to dance with another handsome young fellow. Oh, how I protected my fair princess, Victoria.

I too danced a great deal that evening. I was genuinely enjoying myself, but confess that my eyes and mind were more oft on my little sister than on any partner I was paired up with. I knew not if my suitors realized I barely noticed they were there, but I did not care one whit. My heart felt no interest in any one of them.

My heart was filled with love and admiration for my dearest little sister and my mind was filled with thoughts of the very brightest future for her. I *fervently* hoped and prayed secretly within myself (even while on the dance floor) for one very special specimen of the very *best* of men, for the very best *life*, for *every* good thing for my dearest, darling, wonderful, beautiful little Victoria. She knew not well herself what a caring, sweet, amiable, intelligent and extremely worthy young lady she was. My amazingly beautiful and uniquely special cameo was only a *semblance* of the goodness, grace, and wonder that its benefactor, my Victoria, was.

16
Crossing Mildred

While gathering a few needed things at the general store one lovely day, Victoria and I suddenly spied Father. Victoria and I both expected another relatively nice reunion with him, but on this occasion when we approached him, his manner was rather cold and he seemed somewhat uncomfortable about speaking with us. Victoria and I were a little taken aback and became instantly uncomfortable ourselves, not knowing why Father should behave so differently than he had done during our last meeting.

As I saw Mildred enter the store with Lena in her arms, I realized the source of Father's discomfiture. Mildred's gaze met mine. Her pleasant composure dissipated like water droplets on a hot griddle. Mildred's glare at us was amazingly sudden and it was for all of us: not just for me, or for Victoria and me, but also for Father. I chose to pretend not to notice her furrowed scowl for Father and Lena's sake, and exercised my greatest effort to be amiable towards Mildred so that Victoria and I could especially reunite with our little half sister at least for a few moments after all this time apart, and also with our father once more. I thought that maybe with Herculean exertions on Victoria's and my side, our family could be held together even by a few threads, despite Mildred's unvarying efforts to tear it all asunder forever.

Victoria and I managed to excite some delight out of Lena in seeing us, but the more Lena was happy to see her much older half sisters and showed this pleasure openly, the more Mildred became somewhat livid with the unwanted connection. At first, I wondered at Mildred's public display of anger and ill-treatment of us, but then it *occurred* to me that this was somewhat Mildred's territory as she had not so long ago worked here for a relative of hers, and it still belonged to those who were her family. Thus, Mildred felt the General Mercantile Store her first home, still her home and not only were we intruding there, where she felt it her own place, but we were also reaching out to her husband and her daughter, and I could clearly see that we were not welcome in any way with Mildred, to do either of the three.

A little bit of rebellion surged up inside me and I refused to recognize Mildred's overt display against Victoria and me. Please Mildred by leaving we would *not*! Going against my nature to a great degree, I could not but seem to help reveling in Mildred's discomfort, as I coyly persisted in playing with little Lena, and drawing Father into a conversation with Victoria and me. Beyond that unusual boldness for me, I even found the audacity to smilingly offer conversation to Mildred, which truly seemed to enrage her all the more. I could see that it was a mighty effort for her to hold in much of her anger against me, but I did not care one whit. I wondered why I should always bend to Mildred's pleasures, whims and ill nature. Let her be vexed. I could have my fun and delight in making my little half sister smile and giggle, as well as engaging my own father in conversation.

"Lena has grown so very much since we last saw her, Mildred!" I smiled.

With pursed lips and in a scoffing manner, Mildred answered, "Yes, of *course* she has grown. *That* is what children do."

"And she is so *beautiful*!" I next offered.

Seemingly sparring for a fight, she responded, "Did you think she would be *otherwise*?"

"Oh no, Lena has *always* been the most delightfully beautiful girl and now she is even *more* so! Just as I think her as lovely as she possibly could be, she grows even lovelier after all. I mean it only as the *most* sincere and heartfelt compliment."

Mildred grumbled.

I turned back to entertain Lena, along with Victoria. Ignoring Mildred seemed the only option, as had always been the case, for getting on with her *never* worked because she absolutely *chose* not to cooperate.

Quite suddenly, Mildred seemed to show some interest and drew me in with a grin of some sort, "*So,* I have heard about town that you have a *prime* teaching spot and have also made a *name* for yourself with your portraiture."

"Yes. It is quite wonderful for us, really and Victoria is a teaching assistant at our little school. We could not be happier with our situation here and now."

"Well, I cannot imagine why or how you both got *that* position or why anyone would want to hire *you* to do portraits for them when there must be far greater ability and talent to choose from elsewhere. You certainly have *luck* on your side at the moment but it will *not* last forever, mark my words on that. I *do* know that Mrs. Jones had a part to play in connecting you to these *coveted* opportunities but do not count on *her* good graces benefiting you *forever* for I have heard that she has a *horribly* weak constitution and has been *excessively* ill often enough of late to worry her husband such that he will soon be a widower. Mrs. Jones will likely not last all that long to be sure and then your luck in these pleasant and easy things will be *gone*. And, as you are fast approaching what *most* would consider an old maid now, Fionna, with what bloom you *have* remaining fading swiftly, marriage may not save you from a most unpleasant fate."

I was aghast. I could see similar thoughts and feelings emanating from Victoria and Father as well. All three of us were perfectly silent and still. I was sure our shock was evident from afar.

Mildred perceptibly reveled in her achievement and even seemed to blush with some sort of excitement to have wounded me in such a vicious manner.

Could there be a more unpleasant sort of woman the world over?! Why had she said such horrible things to me? Why did she revile against my sisters, brothers and me so vehemently? Why could she not simply make at least some effort to be gracious towards any of us, rather than to focus so much of her energies to do so much the opposite? Why did she hate us so? Was it not enough of a victory for her to have taken our father from us, and to have also secured all his land and monies for herself forevermore?

I did not know what to say in answer to Mildred. I could not feel that her ill words deserved any response. I could not even look at her anymore. I found it even too difficult to look at Father or Victoria. The floor was my only respite to gaze at, as I stood wondering what to say or do.

Suddenly Victoria exploded at Mildred, "Why must you always be so terribly hateful?! Your heart must truly be entirely black. Of all the things to say to Fionna! Well, I believe you are wrong on all counts. It is not only Mrs. Jones who thinks well of Fionna's abilities and talents, but many others justly do as well. Mrs. Jones is quite well and robust of health and I say it is a *cursed* thing for you to say that she is *all* but dying. I've *never* heard anyone say *anything* so horrible. *And,* I will have you know that *many* eligible men fancy Fionna greatly. *Contrary* to your insulting assertion, I am *entirely* convinced that Fionna's bloom will last *another* ten years at *least* and she will have her leisurely pick of many men! It has been her *choice* to wait for just the right man, for there have been many who have wanted to court her and it is her *own* particularity that keeps her single even *now.*"

Victoria continued at a pace and with a fervency that seemed to dizzy Mildred, "Do not *forget* that *you* made your living in this very store because of *family* connections. Where would you have been without *those*? And as to the *fate* of either Fionna or *any* of Father's children, *none* of us would have *anything* to worry about as to what would become of us if *you* had not swept in like a *vulture,* and taken *everything* that was rightfully *ours.* It was not *you* who built that farm into what it is. It was our *mother* and *us,* who helped and not you. *You* never lifted a *finger* to contribute!"

Victoria gulped in a generous breath and persisted, "And do not *think* you are worth so much as the fingernail snippings of our mother. You have *usurped* her throne and *taken* her kingdom whilst doing *everything* you could to cast out *all* her children into the wilderness, but we all *know* you have taken what you are not *remotely* worthy of. Our mother was a woman of *great* worth and respectability, and Heaven was only *too* delighted to take her back when she passed beyond this realm. As to you, the depths of a black and flaming abyss are waiting with open arms for you, for you *truly* do belong there with *every* kind of devil!"

Victoria was finished. Before I could look beyond the shocked faces of Father and Mildred to see who else in the store may have witnessed what had just transpired, Victoria had grabbed my arm with a strength of might that shocked me with her unexpected physical power, and she took me promptly out of the store and well beyond it, in mere seconds.

It had all happened *so* excessively fast that my head was justly spinning. I could not help but feel a certain pride in Victoria for her boldness, bravery and quickness of mind and exemplary wit in such a moment. I did indeed feel quite grateful for her defense of me *and* of Mother. I also felt a great feeling of satisfaction to have seen Mildred put down in such a passionate and truthful manner. Beyond all my fulfilled feelings and thoughts pertaining to the dramatic event, I began to wonder if we could show our faces in the general store *ever* again.

As Victoria pulled me along towards our little abode she spoke, "*Ooh*! I was so *very* angry at her! Please forgive me for bursting out in that *wrongful* manner but I could *not* let her get away with saying such things to *you* and *about* Mother Jones. Mildred has been far *too* terrible for *far* too long and I simply could not help myself."

I smiled, "It is *more* than understandable, my dear sweet sister. I have *long* wanted to say some such things to her myself, but never dared."

"Well, if she had only insulted me, I could have born it with far more patience, but she insulted you so very severely and as much as cursed Mother Jones to death. How could I stay *silent*?" a lengthy breath escaped Victoria's lips.

"I know what you mean to say. I would have not been able to stop myself from defending you with similar vehemence if she had said *anything* like that against you. To own the truth, I was wondering *what* or *if* I should say anything in retort, or if perhaps we should just walk away."

"A *part* of me wanted to walk away but something else *compelled* me to speak honestly about such things to Mildred, for *once*." Victoria expelled.

"I dare say you have certainly given her some things to think about but I doubt she will ponder them long beyond simply being angry. Nor will she change her person or opinion because of what you have confronted her with, for she is determined to be as awful as she is and will always continue against us, pulling Father along with her. If only Father would ponder at least *some* of your words."

"There is too much truth in that." Victoria answered with a few nods.

I continued my mounting thoughts aloud to my dear sweet youngest sister, "I *do* worry though that we will have to find a neighboring town to gather all our supplies or perhaps beg Mother Jones to make our needed purchases *for* us, as I doubt Mildred's relatives will be pleased to serve us in their store, for a while, at least."

"Oh, dear, I had not *thought* of all that!" Victoria lamented.

"Worry not much my little sister. We will find a way to manage somehow."

"I suppose we will, but it will be most inconvenient if we cannot go to the general store anymore."

I mulled a moment and then, "Yes, it will, and you can be sure Mildred will do all she can to convince her relatives not to serve us should we be bold enough to try to enter their store any time soon, if ever again."

Victoria nodded.

"Well, I do not know, but I *do* think any inconvenience, or even lacking in our basic needs being met, are *well* worth the look you were able to create on Mildred's face!" I said with delight and a broad smile.

Victoria ruptured into laughter so loud that people on the other side of the street were startled, and it seemed everyone around us looked our way in that initial instant.

As I broke into laughter myself, in unplanned unison, Victoria and I both tried to muffle our guffaws, with our hands placed quite firmly over our mouths. We scurried along hoping our audience of gazers would go about their own business once more.

Our little home soon welcomed and protected us.

***

Mother Jones was all vivacity. She had driven all the way from her farm on her own, *just* to find and talk to us.

She began breathlessly, "I have such news of great import that I was absolutely *forced* to make my way to town myself to tell you *straight* away! You will *not* believe the buzz that is stirred because of you! You *know* how I prefer for Father Jones to take me into town whenever I need come, but I could not wait for him today! No! For he was far too busy in the fields to take me any time soon and I could *surely* not wait until the morrow or even more, to speak with you both!"

Oh, no! I was *all* dread. I was *sure* she spoke of Mildred and how our reputations were now *ruined* because of Mildred's renewed and expanded efforts *against* us.

Mother Jones continued, "I just heard from *very* good friends that Mildred's relations who own and run the general store are *all* aflutter about you!"

I *knew* it! I *feared* this would happen. Of *course* it would happen. Without a doubt, Mildred's relatives would not stand by and let her be insulted, as she so surely *had* been by Victoria, and they meant to punish us severely because of it. Indeed the very town might now gather *against* us and we would be ruined in *all* this land and be forced to once again go to another!

"Of course I have heard about you, and what you said against Mildred to her face in the store that day, Victoria. People were *all* about in earshot at the time and unquestionably you *knew* the news would spread. As you might have well guessed, Mildred did her *utmost* to cause her relations to *close* the store against you." she paused after delivering us the dreadful but not so unexpected news.

I feared there was *more*. Victoria and I braced ourselves for *worse*.

"But what you do *not* realize, nor did *any* of us realize *before*, but Mildred's relatives are no longer so *fond* of her, if ever they were!" she said with a completely incredulous and beaming expression to her motherly face.

Mother Jones continued with complete delight and exuberance, "Not *only* are you both still very welcome in their store as you have heretofore been, but they will likely treat you with more graciousness than *ever* before. It seems, Victoria, that *you* have put Mildred in a place where many others might liked to have done and you have commanded a *good* deal of respect round about! And to think that one so very *young*, was the very one to do it!"

Victoria and I were all bewilderment.

Mother Jones enthusiastically shared, "It seems many folks suspected a hint of how horribly Mildred had been treating all of you all this time, and *many* do not like her: they see through her usual polite façade. And her relations who know her *best* like her *least* of all! Can you *believe* it girls?!"

Vindication was felt by at least me. In reality, I thought that perhaps Victoria felt vindicated most keenly, as well she should.

Mother Jones continued her lively visit with us and told us other related details that had been circulating about town. There were many who preferred to choose our side over Mildred's, and so it was that she had far fewer friends than either she or we could have imagined possible. It was not as if Mildred would be turned out from her relations store or any other place of business, for she had Father's money to spend and people generally liked to get along with other people for many reasons. It seemed human nature for most folks to prefer to keep up appearances of acquaintance rather than not, in any case. *But*, there seemed silent smiling universal thoughts of comeuppance in the town and round about it.

Quite relieved that Victoria and I could continue to gather our needs in town rather than having to venture afar off to do so, I suddenly felt a relaxation and satisfaction that was exceptionally mending to my previously somewhat vexed person.

Once done with all this local news, Mother Jones proceeded to enlighten us with the happy news that a visit by Charlotte and Elizabeth was extremely imminent.

Victoria and I enjoyed delightful conversation with our dear Mother Jones before she was done and ready to leave us. I could not help but allow my mind to wander off to Heaven where I thought I felt our own dear mother looking down upon us. I thought that Mother might be watching over us all and feeling a gratitude to Mother Jones for watching out for us in such a loving way, as she had been doing for quite some time. I too felt such a deep sense of gratitude to Mother Jones for adopting us, for mothering us, for loving us and for doing what she could to make up for the fact that we had lost our earthly mother and were left orphaned, particularly since our father had chosen a bride who turned out to be the epitome of the evil stepmothers we had too often read of in old children's fables. I supposed that most stepmothers would be benevolent: indeed I hoped it was so, but my own personal and familial experience sadly spoke otherwise.

17
Visiting

I felt very badly that it had been so terribly long since we had gone to the Jones' farm to see our brothers and to visit there. Victoria and I had been quite busy with school and many other details in town, and everything beyond town simply seemed so especially far away to us now. We had begun to count on seeing our brothers when they occasionally came into town with Father Jones or with both Father and Mother Jones, and it was true we had enjoyed less visits with them that way than hoped for.

Now that Charlotte and Elizabeth were coming for a visit, Victoria and I were planning as many lengthy visits to the Jones' farm as possible so that we could reconnect completely with our brothers and Charlotte and Elizabeth, and also with their husbands while they were visiting. We also never seemed to tire of associations with Father and more especially Mother Jones.

With our dearest Mother Jones fairly regularly keeping Victoria and me current on how Charlotte and Elizabeth were doing, and what messages they passed along, I found that I was not writing to them nearly as much as I had been in the past.

Mother Jones was still terribly sad about Elizabeth having lost her baby and was quite despondent about it. She longed to become a grandmother. I knew she did not want to make Charlotte and Elizabeth feel bad that neither one of them had been able to add to the Jones' family numbers as yet, but she was an open and vocal woman who could not hide the fact that she dearly wanted grandchildren. I sometimes wondered if Mother Jones ever said anything to exacerbate the grief of both Charlotte and Elizabeth for not having had any children to date. I knew this could be done easily enough and hoped I never would say anything that would add any hurt to either of my sisters.

I had been better at writing to Anna, since my correspondence with her was her only connection to our family and she quite depended upon me to keep her and Clara current of everything regarding everyone. Anna's letters to me were also the only news we ever had of Clara and Anna. I tried to tell them all that I thought would interest them, and I begged for every morsel of news from Anna about how she and Clara were doing.

I had some difficulty breaking the news of Elizabeth's lost baby to Anna and therefore Clara for a variety of reasons. Sending bad news is *always* unpleasant, but I also hoped that Clara would not worry more over her growing child because she knew Elizabeth had lost hers.

Every time I saw my brothers they seemed *so* much taller, more robust and increasingly mature. They were growing nicely under Father and Mother Jones' care and I was so eternally grateful to them both for stepping in for my brothers' sakes, and being the mother and even father that had been lost. Such a weight of responsibility had been lifted from my somewhat burdened shoulders, and I had been able to worry mostly only over Victoria and myself. Worries for my brothers were melted away for me while being taken care of by a generous benevolent couple, such as they were.

What would I have done if Father and Mother Jones had not invited my brothers to live with them? How could I have gone on living under Mildred's roof and on her farm? I could not have abandoned my brothers to a fate alone with Mildred knowing there was no protection from Father. I would have had to stay on Mildred's farm to do my best to protect and provide for my brothers and Victoria as I had done before, but it had become more and more difficult. Mildred had become more and more difficult. Thank Heavens our dear Mother and Father Jones chose to help get us all off of Mildred's farm. They were as saviors of sorts to us all.

BONNETS AND APRONS: FIONNA

Victoria and I had just arrived on the Jones' farm, the evening prior to Charlotte and Elizabeth's expected arrival. Victoria and I wanted to be there to greet them the moment they drove up that next day: we did not want to miss out on any visiting moments that we possibly could share in. Victoria had instantly and happily gone in to visit with Mother Jones, for Victoria's bond with our somewhat adopted Mother was truly genuine. I begged forgiveness that I wanted to first seek and find my brothers whom I had not seen in so exceedingly long. They were not difficult to find since they had seen or heard us drive up, and had raced towards the house posthaste.

"Bertram! You are almost a *man*!" I declared to him as I grabbed him for a hug.

"I think perhaps I *am*." he smiled.

"I dare say you are certainly a *young* man now." I settled.

"What about *me*?" Edward was fishing as he trotted up with Colin.

"You *too*! You too, of *course*! Bertram, *you* and Colin *all* grow taller, stronger and more mature every time we see you!" I hugged both my youngest brothers at once, at length, and they each had to struggle to get out of my firm and steady grip.

Edward and Colin fairly beamed once they were free from my fond grasp.

Colin held up his arm, rolling up his sleeve, "Want to see my muscle?"

"Oh, yes! Show me how it has grown since the *last* time you flexed it for me!" I suppressed an inward giggle at the prospect of seeing and squeezing a tiny whelk of a thing that was to masquerade as a massive manly muscle.

"Me too! Look at *my* muscle!" Edward begged.

"Okay! Show me your muscles, the *both* of you!"

Colin's young muscle was not truly perceptively, but just possibly, *slightly* larger than the last time I was witness to it, but Edward's upper arm sinew did seem somewhat more impressive.

"Wow! They are *really* getting bigger!" I pronounced to both of them.

"Now, Bertram, don't you want to show me *your* muscle?" I asked of him.

Bertram was a little less eager to share his growing bicep but sheepishly rolled up his sleeve and flexed it for me. *Now* I saw *obvious* improvement.

"Wow! That is *definitely* bigger than the last time! Good for you!" I praised Bertram and then to all of them, "You three must be working very hard because your muscles really show it!"

I could see that they each were proud of growing stronger and I was also sure that they all felt a satisfaction in working hard. While I was so happy that Father Jones helped immensely in their growth and happiness, it did sadden me to think that their own father, our father, was missing out on all of this growth and joy with his sons. The boys were missing out on what Father could have given them too. Father Jones was a truly wonderful substitute father, but I was sure that deep inside themselves the boys still felt a longing and a loss for our own true father, as Victoria and I did. Father was still *so* near and yet so very, *very* far.

Father Jones brought up the rear and brought us all inside to where Mother Jones was busily preparing and presenting all manner of good eats for us to delight in. Never had I been in a warmer kitchen or a warmer home: not since Mother had died had I enjoyed the love and generosity that only a mother seemed to give to those she considered her children. Oh, what a joy and a *comfort* it was to be considered *her* children!

Victoria and I helped prepare for Charlotte and Elizabeth's arrival. Beyond preparing rooms and beds, Mother Jones' kitchen was all abuzz with our preparations. Feelings of true excitement and eager anticipation filled our souls. Wonderful smells filled the air. Father Jones and the boys zipped in many a time to sample delicious morsels in between much work all farms demand.

When Charlotte and Elizabeth finally arrived the next day, somewhat late in the day, in fact; there was jubilation and joy heard and felt throughout the Jones' house and beyond.

BONNETS AND APRONS: FIONNA

Our tongues were all soon quite fatigued with wagging to catch up on any and all news we each could think of relating one with another. Charlotte and Elizabeth always had their special brand of far away big town and city news that those of us who had never lived, nor even traveled far beyond our small town sphere of birth, were certainly excited to hear all about. Victoria and I had our own unique news relative to living on our own, and all the experiences we were having together. The boys had plenty of farm stories to tell. Of course, Joseph and Jacob had much to relate to their parents, and it was always obvious how close they were as a family.

I could not help but miss and think about Mother intensely, and also feel such a profound sense of loss as far as our Father was concerned as well. Feelings of anger and resentment towards especially Mildred, but also towards Father would often bubble up at times like these when my mind pondered upon our father and his wife, our stepmother, but I always did my best to overcome those negative sentiments, no matter how strongly and easily they tended to grow in me. I *tried* to focus on the fact that the Lord had blessed my siblings and I with surrogate parents who were doing a good deal to fill the obvious void that was left by the loss of our mother, but also the unnecessary void that our father had allowed to happen to us, his children, due to the nature of his replacement wife. Numerous doors had closed to us all because of Mildred, and also because of Father; but through Mother and Father Jones, new doors, replacement paths, had opened for each of us.

It was indeed late by the time we all turned in for the night, exhausted but gleefully satisfied to have bonded again together as a type of family unit. My belly all but ached, filled with far too many delights. Victoria was still exuding chatter in the room we were sharing together, as I felt myself truly ready to drift off to sleep in order to rest and prepare for the fun-filled next day. I tried to stay awake as Victoria rambled on happily about all Charlotte and Elizabeth had told us, and the happiness she felt about us all being together again, but I thought I must have entered dreamland even as Victoria buzzed delightedly.

18

In Danger

The next day was one of much activity. Beyond avid eating and visiting, and helping Mother Jones with all manner of kitchen preparations and cleaning up, some of us accepted Father Jones' generous offer to allow us to enjoy his best riding horses. Oh, but it had been so excessively long since I rode a beautiful horse, and I immensely missed my favored horses that I had been forced to say goodbye to. Mildred would not have lived with me taking any but one or two of the oldest most valueless horses that Father owned, and so it was, along with the oldest most dilapidated wagon on the farm.

Father Jones presented Victoria with the beautiful strawberry roan which was her first choice and I was delighted with my selection of a darling palomino, while Charlotte favored a black and Elizabeth a beautiful buckskin horse. I was no horsewoman in my own estimation, nor had I ever been one; but I had long been fairly comfortable on and around horses, for I had grown up depending upon them and adoring them as well. At first I was somewhat nervous about riding as I had not been on a horse in quite some time. Indeed, I may say we sisters each were quite nervous since we had all been in the wagon, coach or buggy way, and well beyond riding horses for such a great length of time. I had always wondered why I never saw Mother riding upon any horse, but had never thought to ask her that question as it just seemed the way it had always been. I had wondered if she had ever ridden, but now I wondered if perhaps she had graduated off of horses and into buggies, as we girls had done quite naturally as part of entering womanhood, and trying to relate to feminine things, ways and means. I was thinking, as I tried to get my horse legs back, that perhaps if I had stayed off of a horse long enough, that I would truly be afraid to climb up on one again. I surmised that must have been what had happened to Mother. She *must* have ridden once upon a time. How could she *not* have?

I also knew that an older woman would certainly prefer the relative comfort of a buggy or wagon to jostling on a horse, and even more importantly, the safety was or at least seemed surely more secure above wheels than above a creature that continually kept a mind of its own, and at least a little of the wild within. It seemed to me that no matter how good a horse was, no matter how well behaved, no matter how in tune with and respectful of its master; a horse could *still* be unpredictable and could choose to toss its rider off as it pleased. I never truly or fully realized it while growing up on horses, but I had come to comprehend in getting older and hopefully somewhat wiser, that when it came right to the facts, a horse could be a dangerous method of conveyance. I had heard too many stories to doubt the danger that was inherent with horses. And yet, to me, they were still the most beautiful of God's creatures, and as many of nature's wonders, grandeur is oft if not always somewhere near danger. Fire and water can be so very beautiful, and useful, as well as quite absolutely necessary to existence, but yet so very perilous: and so it was with all in nature, I supposed.

Three of my dear sisters and I spent a good part of that day scampering about on our glorious mounts, soon forgetting our fears of riding, and remembering years of being as one with horses as any girls could be: indeed, both the years and fears melted away in unison. The spirit we shared of that moment in time was of pure delight and childlike abandon. It was as if we were all sent back to a beloved time when Mother was back at our family home, preparing a delicious meal as Father was out in the fields working with fervor, and our other siblings were either riding alongside us or playing near Mother while she worked, baked and cooked with a tender love in her heart for those she loved so dearly. As I thought these thoughts I tried to suppress several tears but they overpowered me and I succumbed to some very raw and tender feelings before I was able to swiftly wipe away the wet evidence of my swollen heart and throat. I was happy not to have been discovered as I did not want to spoil the joy being shared by my sweet younger sisters.

It was fast becoming late in the day and we all began to concur that it was surely time to give the horses and ourselves a rest, and the sustenance we all so surely had earned. I had forgotten what work a horse-ride could be for the rider. I knew my legs were going to be scolding me at least tonight and tomorrow, and perhaps beyond a day or two. Victoria determined to take just one last ride through a wooded path, while Charlotte, Elizabeth and I began slowly sauntering towards home.

Some time elapsed before I felt a growing concern begin to swell within me. Victoria should have caught up with us by now, or at least come out of the woods to where we could see her, and yet she was not within sight nor could we hear a sound from her. Without speaking a word, instinctively I turned my horse around and began traveling back towards where we had parted company from Victoria. Charlotte and Elizabeth called after me but I was too focused to find a way to open my mouth to answer their queries of me even though my mind rushed with things to say. I was as if in a dream where even a scream cannot be brought forth.

As I drew nearer to the woods, Victoria's mount came trotting out: quite alone, and without my youngest sister atop. I felt a sense of sheer panic and demanded that my horse gallop, as tired as she might already be, in after Victoria to see what had happened and where my dearest sister was. Into the woods on the path a short way, I discovered my beloved Victoria lying in a heap on the ground: motionless, *lifeless* and yet strangely peaceful. In complete and utter horror, I dismounted instantly, dropping down from my horse to the ground with a hard and fast thud, while calling Victoria's name in terror and dread. As I tried quickly to assess Victoria's condition, Charlotte and Elizabeth's voices were calling closer and closer behind me.

I soon sent Charlotte for help while I cradled Victoria's motionless body in my arms. At least I now knew that she was not dead, and there was very little blood so my concerns were alleviated to a great degree. Victoria had obviously taken a fall from the horse and her head showed the results of it. I had high hopes that she would soon awake with only a severe headache as punishment for not holding fast to her horse during whatever event had taken place to remove her so promptly and harshly to the ground.

Some hours later, Victoria was still deep in some sort of sleep in her bed in her and my guest room. Father Jones determined that he should go for the town doctor, who, when finally arrived, could see no help he could offer beyond treating Victoria's slight wound to the head, and recommending we just care for her in every way we possibly could. All hopes and prayers were that she would awake sooner rather than later, but not the *unspeakable*: never.

Days passed and I was at Victoria's side as constantly as I could be: praying, hoping, crying and trying my best to stay calm while I spoke softly to my precious little dear, hoping my voice would bring her back to me. Charlotte, Elizabeth and Mother Jones also sat by Victoria in their turns, feeling and behaving much as I did while on watch with our sweet invalid. Father was notified, but he *never* came, nor sent word. This astonished and saddened me. We were all incredulous.

Almost as suddenly as we had lost her to wherever her mind or spirit traversed, Victoria awoke while I was in attendance at her bedside. I was lost in prayer with my eyes firmly shut even as I held her hand, when her hand squeezed mine *just* a little and then she croaked out a soft moan. With a heart *full* of thanksgiving, I answered my little dear's somewhat feeble noise with questions as to how she felt. She explained that her head ached and was obviously trying to remember anything: where she was, what had happened and where she last had held onto consciousness. I quickly but gently explained all I knew, wondering if her mind would recall exactly the event that could have cost her life itself. Victoria could not recall her fall and barely could even remember her solitary ride through the woods that day.

BONNETS AND APRONS: FIONNA

It was extremely difficult for me to look at Victoria without shedding tears, for her face was quite lopsided: swollen and bruised darkly on the one side of her head that had been injured. I tried to look beyond her wounded and somewhat sickly appearance and *into* her eyes, deep into her soul. I did not want my overwhelmed feelings of compassion to make her feel unpleasing to gaze upon, or any such thing. I tried to behave as normally as possible as I talked to Victoria while she still came around fully. I kept mirrors far from her. Thankfully, she never asked for one. I feared the sight of her own face would be more than a fright to her.

None of us felt assured that Victoria's full recovery was certain as she was surely not herself and was in a great deal of pain. Her head ached *immensely* and her appetite was barely there as she was often overcome by nausea: I assumed it was the pain which was making her stomach decline food. I tried to entice Victoria to eat whatever and whenever she could, such as someone with a sickness of the stomach would. I offered her dry bread, broths and such, which she was amiable to attempt and thankfully able to keep down. I also encouraged her to drink as much water as she felt comfortable with, in between her small, simple, plain and humble meals.

Another thing that I persuaded Victoria to do was to sleep as much as she could. It pained me to see her suffer from the severe aching in her head, believing also that sleep was a welcome respite from that pain and would afford faster and surer healing from her injuries. I also noticed that the *more* rested she was, the *less* the pain of her injured head seemed to bother her. Sleep was indeed somewhat of a cure for her pain.

Victoria could not even read in bed as her head hurt too much to do so, and so I would read to her as she closed her eyes often and laid back in relative comfort. As I read, when I saw her eyelids heavy and a land of dreams seeming to beckon her, I would read softer and softer in my most gentle and soothing voice possible, that she would be lulled into sleep and drift off to a place of greater comfort where there was no pain for her. I *desperately* wanted to remove the pain from her. I would have gladly taken it unto myself. Indeed, I prayed to the Heavens above that Victoria's pain could be given to me, that she could finally be free from it. I took care not to pray for her *total* relief from pain, as I feared it might mean her removal from our sphere. Death surely is a welcome relief from all pain, but I was not ready to give Victoria up to the Heavens where she would be reunited with Mother and all others who await us there. No. I was a selfish being and wanted to keep my little Victoria with me, even if Heaven wanted her there now. I wanted and needed her more. I prayed for her to stay with me. I prayed harder than I had ever done in my life before. Undeniably, I *begged*.

Still, Father did not come, *nor* inquire. This was a horror to me. Not only had Father *not* bothered to visit Charlotte and Elizabeth while they were in the area, but he did not even *attempt* to see Victoria nor seek to find out how she was.

A *good* deal of praying was exercised throughout the house by all of us, and in the fields where Father Jones and the boys were working, most of the better part of the days that followed; as had been done during Victoria's lengthy slumber. We all tried to keep our worried expressions from Victoria's gaze as we wanted her to think that we thought all was well, even though we feared she still might take a turn for the worse. At least the swelling on one side of Victoria's face was mostly subsided and was beginning to take a normal shape, and the coloration had gone from deathly blackened to unpleasant greens and yellows. This was reason for relief but there was *still* reason to fear for her. My greatest worry was fed by the fact that Victoria seemed quite lethargic and was certainly not her usual cheery and chatty self. I had never thought that a bump on the head could make someone so entirely ill. It was true she had suffered a *severe* bump and so the headaches, bruising and swelling did not surprise me so much, but it was Victoria's lethargy that concerned me *most* of all. I worried for her memory and so began to test her to see if her mind was truly all right, by reminiscing from happy recent memories to past ones.

The more we talked together about past events, the more I believed that Victoria's mind and memory were *quite* sound. I also found that revisiting happy moments seemed to help her forget her painful head, and also revitalize her spirits and health. Over the next many days, I spent a good deal of time in Victoria's sick room: our guest room at Father and Mother Jones' home. Charlotte and Elizabeth took short turns watching over Victoria as did Mother Jones, which gave me some respite from drawing from my own well for my little sister. And of course Father Jones, Joseph, Jacob, Bertram, Edward and Colin all stopped in to cheer her up more than once each day as well. The men folk were out in the fields much of the days while Charlotte and Elizabeth helped and entertained Mother Jones in her kitchen most of that time. I was happy to sit with Victoria whenever she was awake, and catch up on some visiting with the two of my other sisters, whilst Victoria slept, during those days.

It was not too terribly long before we saw vast improvements in Victoria: in her appearance as well as in her spirits and vitality. The swelling and bruising on the side of her face and head were gone in relatively short order, all things considered, and her headaches were not nearly as severe which also seemed in tandem with her appetite which improved substantially, although I still felt she was not eating all that well, as yet.

Victoria began to get up and around much more, including joining the family for meals. She was no longer an invalid in a sick room, but she still lived with a chronic and distracting pain in her head. I could see it on her face even while I could see her trying to hide the fact that she was *still* suffering. Victoria tried her best to put on her old familiar cheery face and to chatter amongst us as she used to do, but I could see the twinges of pain on her face from time to time as her aching head *obviously* overcame her efforts to ignore it. When I spoke to her of this, she did admit she was still living with a steady pain, which sometimes became sharp and more difficult to bear.

By the time Charlotte, Joseph, Elizabeth and Jacob had to say their farewells to all their kin, we had enjoyed much time visiting together, and felt ready to give our last hugs and fond wishes for each other, for a long while. Of course all of us women folk shed tears during the lengthy goodbyes and then the final waves as they faded out of sight. We did not know how long it would be before we were together again. I still wondered why the Jones boys had to take my sisters away. Why could they not come back home and work the farm with their father? Mother Jones was so exceedingly wonderful enough that Charlotte and Elizabeth would be quite content to live with or near her. Indeed, Charlotte and Elizabeth's new little homes sat empty on these visits, for the many guest rooms in the main Jones' home were so very welcoming, comfortable, ample and warm.

The Jones farm was exceedingly large and productive, and could provide well for Joseph and Jacob, but they both had dreams of greater and more exciting wealth than that which is found on or from a farm. Charlotte and Elizabeth seemed content to venture out into the world with their husbands, and I thought that their having each other for certain female socializing and comforts did make up for their being taken away from their first sphere and land of origin. At least Charlotte and Elizabeth, who had always been close, had each other. I took great comfort in *that* and it helped me worry about and miss them less, knowing they were happy in each others' company.

I realized I felt much the same, relative to my brothers. Father and Mother Jones were so good to them, but so much beyond that was the fact that they each had each other and were growing steadily closer as they worked the Jones farm *together*. I did not have to worry about them nor miss them when I could not see them very often. Clara and Anna were also close and together and that *also* gave me steady comfort to know.

Mother Jones tried to convince me that Victoria needed to stay where she was and continue healing. With summer ending, I soon had to go back to my teaching duties at the town school. If I had buckled under to Mother Jones' demands, I would have left Victoria with her on the Jones' farm and gone back to town to resume life as a school teacher, and try learning to live *alone* for the first time in my life. Victoria claimed she was well enough to go back to work at the school with me, but I knew she was still plagued by headaches and I could not agree to *that*. I came up with a compromise that Victoria finally agreed with, and Mother Jones reluctantly relented to. Victoria and I would go back to our little home: Victoria to convalesce during the days while I was teaching at the nearby school, and of course we would be together the rest of the time. Victoria could now read without exacerbating her headaches and thus I planned to provide her with every book she needed to lift her spirits and fill her soul, while she finished her last remnants of healing. I also was to insist that she rest and sleep as much as she could between books, that her healing could speed towards entire completion. I also would provide her with plenty of nourishing and favored foods to make sure she was eating enough. Her appetite was still not up to my standard as I saw that she was wasting away into a waif. I did not know how long Victoria would have to live with her headaches, but I believed they would eventually completely disappear, since they were very slowly and steadily subsiding almost day by day.

19
Back to School

In very short order, Victoria and I settled in to our daily and weekly routines. On most days, when I left to teach our beloved students, my young sister was left with her books and good foods comfortably nestled into our little abode, and I would leave her with hugs, counsel, encouragement, well-wishes and all *other* things and advice that a Mother Hen prattles on about to her young, when she must leave them to fend for themselves for a while. Victoria was doing exceedingly well with this arrangement, for she was quite content to read many hours away each day, being transported to another time or place, or just reveling in learning new and interesting things. Sleeping a little here and there, Victoria kept showing improvement and I was more and *more* relieved. Oft times I gathered a few foods and things on my way home from school, but other times when I needed to go out to shop for a few necessaries, Victoria would accompany me as long as we would not be out for too long. We tried to guard against increasing her headaches in intensity or in frequency. Indeed, if Victoria was left house-bound for too many days on end, she became quite anxious to find any reason to go out for a little while. If there was nothing needed to be shopped for or gathered, sometimes we would just take a small and gentle stroll together.

Some of our shopping adventures and strolls became ample sources of delight for Victoria, because from time to time we would meet with young men of our acquaintance who fancied Victoria, and perhaps some even thought of me. I tended towards thinking that most if not all of the flirtatious male attentions were for Victoria, though she believed more often than not that they were meant more for my benefit. Many a night after having enjoyed gentlemanly conversations on the street, in the General Store or elsewhere; we enjoyed teasingly arguing with each other about who these young men were intrigued by: she or me. It was quite clear that *my* great delight was in seeing a dear young man interested in my little sister, and it was *hers* to see a good man giving me attentions.

Soon these young men were inquiring after the both of us as to why we had not been to a dance in ages on end. When we told them of Victoria's accident as reasons for our absence, most seemed to think us making excuses, and vocally desired our presence at dances all the more. The plain and simple truth that was quite clear to us was that the loud music and the lively dancing would have been far too much for Victoria's poor little sore head, causing much more pain to her at that time and also possibly halting or at least stalling her healing process. Victoria did not want to fully confess of her continual uncomfortable and occasional intense headaches publicly, particularly to her prospective suitors, because she thought it might make her seem less healthy and desirable, and so we let these young men believe that we were just too busy or disinterested to go to dances for the time being. Our disinterestedness about going to dances seemed to simultaneously vex and peak the interests of such fellows all the more. Victoria and I found it great fun to be so sought after and yet all we did to deserve and earn such attentions was to stay away from dances, and instead go out for strolls or venture to the store.

There were times that some young men seemed to take to the streets looking for us rather than to go to the dances! In point of fact, there were nights when the dances took place while Victoria and I were taking a nighttime stroll elsewhere in town, where we were met with many a young man whom we would have thought to have been at the dance seeking out young ladies. Instead, they seemed to be seeking after us. We could never have imagined something so unexpected and strange, and yet so enchantingly charming and amusing to have happened to the two of us. Well, Victoria and I made a habit of taking nighttime strolls on nights when dances were taking place, and many suitors made habits of missing out on dances to meet up with us.

I later heard from Mother Jones that there were many young ladies who had somehow come to understand the unusual *strolling* dance that was being quietly danced by Victoria and I, and our numerous gentlemen, beyond the social events of the boisterous dances, and that these young ladies were completely vexed with us for taking their young men *away* from the dances and thus depriving them of dancing.

While I could understand the feelings of these young women, having their numbers of eligible dance partners thinned so greatly, what was I to do about it? What could Victoria and I do to aid and comfort our competition so to speak? Why were we to blame? Of course we *could* have shut ourselves up in our humble abode. We could have stayed at home, but Victoria and I both fervently agreed that we preferred to go out and enjoy a quiet walk, arm in arm with the night air, the stars, the moon and any gentle young man who might prefer our company and conversation, to dancing with the other young women who were available for their consideration and even serious courting pleasures.

***

Clara was blessed with a boy. Anna was overjoyed to relay the message in her letter. Rayner was so proud to have fathered a son and *so* Anna delightedly told me. Of course I knew that Anna and Thomas also desired children and so I wondered if there might be some slight pangs of yearning for one of their own, but was sure most of what they were feeling was a shared joy and happiness for her sister and his dear friend.

Anna told of a long and hard labor for Clara and a slight worry for her and the baby for a while, but all turned out well in the end. Both new mother and babe were fine, healthy and strong. Clara desired to name her boy Benjamin, after our long lost little brother, and Rayner saw no reason to object. So thus it was. Benjamin was his name: Benjamin and then Thomas, as an ode also to Rayner's best friend and to Anna's husband.

Most of Anna's letter was filled with happy reports of Clara's new baby boy. Clara and Anna thought he looked like many on our side of the family whilst Rayner was sure that little Ben looked just like his father. Thomas was apparently pulled from both sides, desiring to please his best friend by agreeing with him, but also needing to agree with his wife. It sounded to me as if Thomas was swaying to and fro as if in a breeze agreeing on both sides, trying to keep the peace with both of whom he loved. The debate raged on about whom little Ben looked like, but all agreed he was a little darling.

Anna described little Ben's hands and fingers, feet and toes to me as she knew these were somewhat my favorite details of little babies. She shared how enamored both new mother and father were with their baby.

The remainder of Anna's letter spoke of challenges, many quite severe. Rayner and Thomas's business pursuits were not amounting to much and their money was growing very, very thin. Their best horse had dropped dead one day for no apparent reason while another was getting too old to be of much worth, and there seemed no way to buy any new horses since they were having difficulty just paying the rent of their humble rooms and providing food for their tables. The four of them had indeed struggled financially from the beginning and now the challenges were growing greater. Anna said that Clara now showed worry that was not usual for her. Clara worried for her little boy. How could they be *sure* to always provide shelter and food for him in the future?

I wondered if I should or could help. I wished I could request of Father to send them a little gift of money. I had shared of my sustenance a time or two already, but I could only afford to do that *so* often, keeping Victoria and my futures in mind. And yet, sending gifts of money would only last a small while and then what? They needed to find a way to make their *own* way. How could I help long term and with that? What advice or help could I give that would enable Rayner and Thomas to become successful in some sort of business, or way of making a living? Of course my mind always traveled *back* to our family farm. I often would wish that Rayner and Thomas could work on Father's farm, and make a living that way, there. But Mildred would have none of that and we all knew it. Even Father's *own* sons seemed unwelcome there.

I decided to send what I could afford to part with at that time, keeping in mind my need to be capable of caring for Victoria and myself continually, and to be prepared somewhat for our future; especially in case one or both of us should never marry. I sent a little more money their way in the hopes that it would help at least a little, and then I determined to pray all the more for them. I was not *always* the best at praying. I tried to pray every night for all these kinds of important things, for those that I loved, and of course some for me as well; but sometimes I would just feel sad and wonder if Heaven was truly listening or cared, and would answer my heart's desires in any way. It was true that many of my prayers in life had surely been answered but many were *not*, and it was sometimes those unanswered prayers and the seeming *lack* of their power and influence above, that found me feeling down in spirit when praying, or sad *about* praying when I was not so doing.

I knew that to focus on the bad or sad things, was not a helpful thing to do but I still found myself doing it oft times. This was a *great* weakness in me I thought. I could *easily* tend towards despair and sorrow. I always *tried* to remind myself of the good in order to lift my spirits. I tried to feel thanks for all the good that my family and I had enjoyed over the years. I truly worked at having a grateful and happy heart despite sad or difficult times, but I was never all that good at such. I knew many others were far better than me at that talent, or ability or gift as it might be.

Well, what were we here on this earth *for*, but to exercise faith in Heaven and its ways, to improve ourselves in *every* way we could, to learn of our own *follies* and try to *repent* of them, to care for and love others around us, and I did not know what else but I was trying to understand it all. I often wondered if Mother could have helped me out in these things, for she was truly wise.

***

Victoria was almost herself again but her headaches did persist, albeit less bothersome and not as excruciating or frequent. I still felt that she should stay at home when I went to the school, for I feared that the occasional happy and boisterous noise of our students could have brought on the worst kinds of headache for Victoria. I knew she could cope with the constant drone of a dull ache in the head, but to allow a painful episode to be triggered was simply not something I was going to tolerate for my little sister. Victoria desired to be of use and tried to convince me she could try to go to school to work with me on occasion, but I stood my ground exceedingly firmly on that point. I suggested to Victoria that she could make herself useful instead, by accomplishing some needed work in our home from time to time, as she felt compelled and able to do.

Victoria continued to spend many hours reading in our cozy dwelling, interspersed with a few light household chores, while I made a living for us. Our other hours together were spent in enchanting and animated conversation or strolling beyond our comfortable domicile. Victoria thrilled to tell me about what she had been reading each day and of course I was delighted to hear it. I also enjoyed telling Victoria about the entire goings on at the school and how each of the students was progressing. There were always plenty of jovial details to report, and messages and notes sent home for her from our dear students.

Sometimes I would allow very small groups of our students to come visit Victoria at our home. At times, they would meet up with us in the street when we were out and about to shop, to eat or to enjoy the outside air. There were also occasions when Victoria and I would enjoy a special meal at the hotel dining room, and there we would see and greet a student who was out with his or her family.

As to seeming suitors, it was quite especially enjoyable to visit one or two kindly young men who were interested in Victoria or myself, but when three, four or even more accosted us at the same time it quite embarrassed me. I could not help but wonder what onlookers might be thinking of the display. Victoria seemed to bask in the light of these attentions, as if to be surrounded by young men who were each vying for her heart to have unto himself, was a *very* normal and everyday thing. To me it seemed most unusual and I shrank quite away from it, but then, all I ever wanted was one man to call my own. I still could not seem to forget Winston as one I would have liked to have as mine. Victoria, on the other hand, had never really preferred one young man above another, so to her, to be surrounded by many loves was quite a comfortable thing for the time being.

I had to admit amongst all the fellows who lavished attentions on Victoria, I was also hard-pressed to choose just one for her either. Each was handsome enough, reasonably capable and so very nice in his own way, and each had some sort of prospect that could provide for a wife and children. While neither Victoria nor I were the kind to marry for money, a man's ambition and ability to provide for his future family was of course *one* consideration that had to be weighed into the entire picture of the man. But from among those young men who were attending to Victoria's any whim, every chance they got to do it, those few who were wealthy to *any* degree did not excite her passions any more forcefully than those who were *less* financially able. I too did not hope for the rich gentlemen to win with Victoria any more than I did the more poor, for a rich man can lose his money soon enough and a poor man can gain his own gold if he is willing to work, and has perhaps a little luck or some of Heaven's blessings on his side.

As I often said to Victoria, she was still full young and there was certainly no hurry for her to set her sights on one young man over another. Was it not better that she take her time since she had an abundance of it? She could choose the best young man for herself in due time, and in the meantime she could enjoy getting to know many young men. I had come to think her time spent in somewhat flirtatious conversation good for her health and spirits to be sure, and there could truly be no harm in it, since she and each gentlemen she conversed so playfully with, were quite unattached and each was not necessarily in search of immediate attachment.

While Victoria was getting out much more now and feeling so much better most of the time, I was still the protective Mother Hen to her and still did not feel she was ready for dances or dancing, even though her numerous young men were trying their very best to persuade her to attend such events, and she herself certainly wished to. I felt even more strongly that she should not partake in dancing nor subject herself to the loud music at the dances, than I did about her going to school where there was occasional noise, for fear of inciting one of her severe headaches, which almost pained me more to see her suffer through, than they pained her to be in the throes of.

Victoria still did not wish to be considered an invalid even in a slight way, so we chose to continue the ruse that we did not wish to dance, and that we had other things we preferred doing to dancing. It was humorously clear to us that many of Victoria's suitors were stupefied and bewildered that two attractive young ladies would continually choose not to dance, nor partake in such social delights at the town dances.

It seemed that the more Victoria and I stayed aloof and stayed away from the dances, the more desirable we each seemed to become, to many of the young men in the territory. Many a young lady could not discern how it was that two young women who did so little or even perhaps *nothing* to gain attentions from young men, and who were not in any seemingly measurable way more attractive than themselves, could be tossed to the *top* of the loft for so many gentlemen. Victoria and I set no traps to catch men, but oft found them following and fawning over us as if purposely ensnared.

From my perspective, I thought Victoria the center of most of the male attentions, but Victoria kept reminding me, and I had to admit at least to some degree, that I certainly received my own share of attentions as well. Oft times I felt I was becoming too old for many of the young men who paid their addresses to me. I truly only desired to receive attentions from the men who were at least my age or older, but I soon decided that who is to say what is attractive to whom, and what is the difference of a few years when you begin to get on a little in years? It had been so long that I had *not* allowed myself any serious considerations where men were concerned, that I had begun to think myself already an old maid and destined to always be alone in that way: that I would *never* marry. Tending not to take any attentions from men seriously, I enjoyed attentions on a superficial level: it was little more than play for me. My genuine focus was always on who might be right for *Victoria*. I fancied myself much more a cupid or matchmaker than desirous of my own match. I do think the heart of the matter was that I dearly wanted Victoria safely married before I entertained the prospect for myself. I knew it a silly notion since I could of course continue to care for Victoria if I married, but somehow I felt selfish about entertaining thoughts towards marriage for myself, and could not seem to see beyond the idea that I should see to it that Victoria married well before I made any efforts or allowances on my own behalf.

Whether or not I could see clear to a close match for Victoria, it truly mattered not but little to me at present: since all the attentions she received were surely good medicine to her. Victoria's appetite grew healthier, her face glowed peachier, and her soul seemed lifted far and above her remaining headaches. I was overjoyed to see my little Victoria daily being restored more and more towards full health and strength.

20
Worrisome News

Another letter from Anna revealed that little Benjamin was dreadfully ill. Beyond that great worry, money was terribly thin. The greater part of Anna's letter focused on fretting over little Benjamin and begging for our prayers for him; and though she said little about their provisions being low and being desperate for prosperity, I could clearly see that these material matters and considerations had only become worse for them.

I determined not only to encourage the rest of our family to pray for Clara's little Benjamin Thomas, but I sensed that perhaps it was time to try to prick Father's conscience a little by at least *hinting* to him that he could surely use a little of his wealth to help out one of his daughters in her time of greatest need. I had previously sent word to Father that Clara had brought forth a son but at that time I could not seem to find a way to let Father know that Clara and Anna were still and continually falling on hard times, for I feared my pleas would fall on deaf ears (or that if he did indeed have ears to hear, his wife would drive away any desire he might have to help one of his own). I chose to press with a sense of double urgency this time, and so in my letter to Father asking for prayers for Clara's little Ben, I also suggested that any charitable financial help was also very much in order as the distressed situation of these of my two sisters was only growing more desperate over time. I emphasized my suggestion to Father for donations to Clara and Anna with my *own* declaration of having been doing such myself.

I wanted also to suggest that Father invite them back to his land so that Clara and Anna's husbands could work for him and make better livings that way, but Mildred stood firmly in the way of that notion. She would rather hire out to strangers than offer the same help to our family. She was no doubt very pleased with herself that she had driven all of us so completely away, so successfully, and also to have secured all Father's land and wealth for herself and her daughter. If Father Jones did not continually hold out hope that his sons would soon return to work his land with him, I thought it quite likely that he would have offered a place to live and to work for Clara and Anna's husbands, and in reality Mother Jones sometimes hinted of that, but I was not so very bold as to push or presume in that direction even though my own feelings were so strong in hoping for any sort of help for Clara and Anna.

As was typical, I did not receive any answer from Father. As was also typical, I half thought that Mildred might have intercepted my letter to Father. I never knew whether or not Father read any of my letters as he never responded to them, nor had he mentioned them the very few times I had run into him in town. I was too reluctant to inquire after those kinds of details in the hopes of discovering whether or not Mildred was halting my communications with Father, and so these mysteries would likely remain through my lifetime.

This was another time in my life when I prayed as fervently as I could, crying many tears as I poured out my heart. My prayers seemed to have become tears. Although I had never seen little Benjamin Thomas, I felt dearly and strongly for him from afar. I could imagine and empathize with Clara's, Anna's and their husband's worries and feelings, and I knew how beloved this little Heaven sent baby boy was to all of them, but especially of course to his earthly parents. With all that had gone wrong for these two of my sisters and their husbands, and with all the trials and difficulties they were experiencing now, I knew that little Ben's life was all-encompassing to them at this moment in time, and diminished their other worries insofar as they were not directly connected to Ben's health and livelihood. I sensed what a loss to each of them it would be if little Ben went back Heavenward.

In my prayers I begged that little Ben could be spared and thus they all could be spared one immense trial in this life. Not only did I pray privately a great deal on my own, but I also began a new habit between Victoria and me to pray together regularly: always at each meal and also nightly before we retired. Neither Victoria nor I were morning folk and so we did not always have the sharpness of mind to remember to pray together in the mornings, but tried to remember when we could. I feared at first perhaps that Victoria would think me silly for praying out loud so much, but that did not come to pass whatsoever. I also feared that Heaven would tire of my constant pestering and wailings, but decided that enough Biblical scriptures tell us to pray oft if not always, and so Heaven should not lament me fulfilling that directive, however imperfect my attempts might be.

It was not to be. Another set of prayers was to be left unanswered. Of course I wondered why this must be. I did not understand why one little boy in this world could not have stayed to bring joy to his parents while he grew up healthy, strong and abounding with abilities. Anna's letter was *full* of grief and sorrow. Little was said of the nature of the illness that took Clara's Benjamin Thomas back to his place in Heaven, and indeed little was written at all, but in those few lines, much was spoken of the overwhelming grief that smothered them all. There seemed to be such a severe sense of desolation and misery amongst these my two sisters and their husbands.

My next letter to Anna was *most* difficult to write. What could I say to help diminish the pain they were feeling? What could I do to help from here? What was there to say that could help promote a kind of healing? I did my best to communicate to Anna, Clara and their husbands, how much Victoria and I were feeling their loss, and were hoping and praying that they would be comforted. Such seemed so painfully inadequate to the task.

I almost did not write to Father to tell him of the sad news. I felt a certain kind of anger towards him for not seeming to care about any of us, his first and other children. A part of me knew that he still did have a right to know, that I had a responsibility to tell him, and that maybe this tragic event would be one more opportunity for him to wake up to the sorry fact that he was far from being the father he should be, to children he had been a party to bringing into the world. Oh, if Mother were here now! What things she would say to him! Her ire would be raised *beyond* measure! Oh, to hear her words of wrath! Father would surely *shrink* before her!

Ah, yes... Mother: she would be embracing Clara's Benjamin Thomas even now to be sure. I imagined Mother and all our other loved ones, known and unknown to us who resided in Heaven, now welcoming Clara's Ben into our family fold. This picture gave me great comfort for I believed it to be true.

I knew my own personal religious beliefs to be of my own kind sometimes, if not more often than not. I did not see God and Heaven as many others did. I had not been raised in one organized religion even though we did attend church from time to time. In fact, our town boasted several churches and so I grew up having the choice to go to one or another. Sometimes it seemed a requirement to choose one over the others: to join up with the one you believed to be true. I even thought it more popular amongst certain townsfolk to go to one church rather than the others, and some people seemed to choose their church according to where their friends went, or which preacher they liked best. Occasionally it seemed some sort of tug of war to me, with little or nothing to do with what was true under Heaven.

There was often contention between the pastors because each believed his own church to be true, and sometimes arguments would abound amongst the church leaders in town. I was sure that other towns had worse contentions between their churches than ours, because for the most part, the open disagreements were not as common or as confrontational as they could have been. It did seem that our town's pastors wanted to get along and enjoy harmony between them and throughout the town, so they did allow for many of us to feel free to go to whichever church we chose, week to week.

BONNETS AND APRONS: FIONNA

Mother had never felt inclined to choose one church over another and so we had grown up going to each of the three in town in no particular order or preference, but *most* of our religion was gleaned at home with the Bible and Mother's wise insights to many passages we perused through together by fireside and candlelight as a family at night. Indeed, much of our schooling included reading the Bible together. Mother was a spiritual woman and some would say, *quite* religious. Father was never truly religious in almost any way, but he never objected to Mother's spiritual pursuits, or to her teaching us in that realm nor all other subjects, as she wished. I supposed Father left the teaching of his youngsters to his wife, as he left religion to her.

I often did not agree with what ministers and pastors preached. Sometimes I wished not to go to church at all when some of the things taught there did not seem to me to be true. Many teachings simply *felt* wrong. I did believe that each of the pastors in our town were trying to teach what they believed to be true, and the people were trying to keep the Sabbath day holy by going to church to worship. In a certain sense, gathering as a flock together and singing hymns had its own rewards: even if the preaching seemed not quite right sometimes. I often thought some of the hymns more inspired than the preaching, and wondered why we could not simply *sing* more and listen to sermons less. *That* would have been my preference oft-times.

As my Mother had, I did decide that I should at least try to go to church with some regularity, and if there was something preached that I did not believe, I could overlook it, rather than embrace it or be vexed by it. Victoria once said half in jest that at least when we went to church, we did not get into other mischief that was not befitting the Sabbath. On Sundays, we did try to go to church when we could, and being in town, it was far easier to do than when we were growing up and living far out of town. Even though sometimes going to church seemed more a social rather than a spiritual event, Victoria and I could partake of something spiritual at home if we left church dissatisfied and hungry of spirit, just as Mother had taught us to do when we were young. But, at least most hymns offered a spiritual lift, if little else did.

21
Richer or Poorer

Aletter came from Charlotte. First there were lamentations and condolences regarding Clara's loss. I had hoped Charlotte would write to Clara directly, but it seemed she wanted me to send her love and shared sorrow to Clara and Anna, *for* her and Elizabeth. There had become a habit of my four sisters of making *me* the one Charlotte and Anna would write to, so that I would pass on all their communications for them. At first it seemed their way of only having to write the one letter rather than many, but then I began to wonder if it was just more comfortable for each of them to simply send word to me, and then I could send word onward.

There had grown a type of discomfort between Clara and Anna, and Charlotte and Elizabeth, I sensed. I was sure that *money* was the main factor, if not only one. The material lack on one side versus the material blessings on the other, made it difficult for both sides to feel at ease with each other. Clara and Anna knew misfortune while Charlotte and Elizabeth knew fortune. Anna's letters were replete with their troubles while Charlotte's were abounding with the pleasures that money can buy. I knew each had their joys and sorrows, but the contrast between their communications was glaring to me from my own middle ground.

From either side I thought the economic distance must seem vast, and *so* the relationship had become. Clara and Anna could *not* relate to Charlotte and Elizabeth's lives and so it was the *other* way as well. Neither side could really understand the other. And so, I had become the sister in the middle who could understand a little of each side, perhaps, and who certainly was a more comfortable place for *each* of their communications to be sent to.

Not rich and not poor, and also the oldest sister: I supposed these were reasons enough for Anna and Charlotte to choose to write to me rather than to each other. They each knew I would pass family news along, and they each still felt comfortable enough to write to me. Sometimes I supposed that maybe I was a substitute mother for them in some ways, since our dear Mother died, and so thus I had become a certain type of fundamental home for each, so to speak. I imagined that if Mother were still alive, all letters would go to her, and she would distribute the family news to all. Yes, I was certain of it. Mother would be receiving these letters instead of me. But, Mother was gone, and I was here to communicate to and through.

As I had grown to expect, Charlotte's letter was full of delights. After she had done with her sorrows over Clara's loss, she proceeded with all she and Elizabeth were about. It seemed somewhat unfeeling to me that a letter that *started* with grief over a death in the family could so soon turn into all the delights of the season. But, perhaps she wrote the sad beginning one day and then the report of happy times, days later. Yes, that *must* be it. She could *not* have moved from grief to gladness *so* quickly. It would seem unconscionable or, at the very least, unreasonable to me.

Charlotte treated me to descriptions of the latest fashions and styles, newly favorite fabrics, recently discovered gemstones, foreign pottery and other treasures, plus a whole host of other such things. Charlotte also spoke of pleasant people and the terribly rich folk they had been meeting at dinner parties, and other social gatherings that seemed vital to them. It was clear that Charlotte and Elizabeth's days were filled with much enjoyment in the shopping for and gathering of treasures, and that their evenings were filled with social events fit for the gentry of Europe.

This letter of Charlotte's, like others before it, seemed to weigh *heavily* on me somehow. I could truly own that I did not feel a personal jealousy or envy, but I surely did feel a certain sadness or emptiness. I could not help but feel the severe superficiality of it all. I could not stop thinking of how Charlotte and Elizabeth could share a little of their wealth with their older and poor sisters, with no obvious loss to themselves. Perhaps it was that they were younger that they felt no sense of obligation to their older sisters.

If destiny had played out in the opposite direction, I wondered if Clara and Anna would have stooped down to help their younger sisters up. I could not be too sure of it, knowing each of my sisters as I did. Perhaps it would have been exactly the same way, the *other* way. Anna very well might have been writing me the same sorts of letters: full of all the exciting, beautiful, delicious, impressive, rare, exotic and wonderful things they were partaking of. And all the while, Charlotte could also be writing me letters full of lamentations of hardships. I suspected that feelings would also run in the reverse directions, in accordance with what fate had dealt to each of them, if fate had chosen otherwise. Charlotte and Elizabeth would think how unfair it was that they were suffering and going without, whilst Clara and Anna would prefer not to be brought down from their wonderments: parties and treasure-hunting trips to the many shops that surrounded them. Yes, I did think it might have been exactly the same in a very real sense, if things had been the other way around. Clara and Anna would have traveled on the wealthy path in much the same fashion, indeed, worshipping fashion as Charlotte and Elizabeth had been doing.

I often found myself wondering why things happened the way they did on all counts for everyone. Why did the sun shine so brightly on some and not others? Why were some so well fed, while others hungered? Sometimes it seemed deservedly so, but *surely* not most of the time. Were Charlotte and Elizabeth more deserving or good than Clara and Anna? If it was possibly so that two of my sisters were somewhat better than another two, it was truly not anything beyond *incremental* to be sure. They were each basically good young women. They each seemed to me to deserve somewhat equally. The fates had not dealt deservedly in their cases, it seemed clear to me.

As to destiny and what is deserved, what of life or death? Clara did not deserve her loss in the death of little Ben. I also supposed women who could have children that grew up healthy and strong did not always deserve them, while many a childless woman did not deserve to go without motherly joys. Now to Mother and Mildred: Mother did not deserve to die and Mildred did not necessarily deserve to live. Mildred undoubtedly did not deserve Father and the farm that he and Mother had built together. We did not deserve to lose Mother and we certainly did not deserve to be cursed by Mildred. I knew that some of the details that seemed to be destiny or fate were in actuality cause and effect based on choices. Father chose to marry Mildred. Oh, how all our destinies could differ if not for *that* choice Father made! What if he had held out for a wonderful woman: a woman like Mother or Mother Jones instead of settling so badly so soon? Perhaps if he had not married at all: surely it would have been better for him to *never* marry, than to marry such a woman as Mildred. She was a curse on us, and even on him.

Beyond all that, of course, Father could have chosen to lead instead of to follow such a woman as Mildred. All of our fates would have been the better for it. Father *could* lead Mildred still. Father did still possess the power of dominion. Oh, but if *only* he would exercise that power over Mildred as it was his right and even his responsibility to do.

***

Victoria and I were quiet for quite some time. There was a sadness that seemed to follow and even hover over both of us. We each grieved for Clara especially, but also for Anna and both their husbands. We spoke little of the tragedy, for what can be said? We only really talked of Heaven and how we truly believed that Clara's Benjamin was especially happy there, and also that it is those who are left behind that feel sorrow in the passing of their loved ones. We each tried to write to Clara and Anna but felt that we fell short as far as what we could say. We did send money to help out with those more material troubles: more than I had *ever* sent before. Victoria and I had decided together that we could go without any frills for a time, and so then send what we would have spent to Clara and Anna so that they could meet their necessities better than they had been able to do recently.

Soon, Mother Jones went out of her way to come to town and invite us out to the farm. We began to visit there more often. In her own dear and wonderful way, Mother Jones was trying to help us feel better. In her kitchen we were surrounded by all manner of her delicious favorites, and in her parlor we were treated to her talents at the piano. Never had I known anyone who played like Mother Jones and what joy exuded from her when she played. Mother Jones was a jolly sort of woman and her ability to play anything on the piano was echoed by her abilities in the kitchen. She had a way of shining in the realm of music and food, and what delights both were to us.

It was indeed especially good for Victoria and I to spend greater amounts of time with our brothers again, and also to enjoy the hospitality, warmth and love from Father and Mother Jones. We truly felt like family. I often thought that Father and Mother Jones must be amassing blessings in Heaven and endless gratitude from Mother for their good deeds to my sisters, brothers and me. I tried to show my gratefulness but no sooner would I try to lavish praise than Father or Mother Jones would stop me, saying such as, 'No, no, none of that!' and then change the subject to something light and happy. What humble and wonderfully angelic people they were.

22

To Oregon Country

When a letter finally arrived from Anna, I was terribly anxious to read it, as it was long overdue. I worried to know how they were all doing. First Anna thanked Victoria and me for our generosity. I was thankful to know they had received our gift of help and that it had been gratefully received. She next communicated very little before she dropped an announcement that shocked me immensely. She, Clara and their husbands were to join a group going west: to the Oregon Country. They were to travel along what was known as the Oregon Trail. Anna spoke of the lush countryside they were to go to. It seemed their hopes were exceedingly high.

At first, my reaction was to instantly write back to Anna and talk her and Clara out of such a silly notion. How could they do something so extremely dangerous? How could they travel so horribly *far* away? I understood that prosperity had not shone on them where they were now but could they not simply come back *here*? Could they not come home? There *must* be a way for them to make a good living here. Surely they did not have to go *all* the way to the Oregon Territory. Did they have to travel to the *ends* of the Frontier to make their way in the world? In the least, Father and Mother Jones could be easily prevailed upon; to offer Rayner and Thomas work on the Jones' land, temporarily. Could not Rayner and Thomas overcome their pride to accept such an offering from what truly was family? I began to wonder if perhaps I should speak to Mother Jones on the matter before it was too late. I knew Father would not offer work on Mildred's farm, but surely Mother and Father Jones would make room on their land while their sons were away.

Victoria and I talked at length about it. We both agreed that night to fervently pray for help in knowing what we could perchance do or advise to help Anna and Clara as they faced this crossroads. We both feared they might be making a horrible mistake: possibly surely even a deadly one. I wondered if their grief was driving them away from *anywhere* that would remind them of little Ben being gone. I would never say it to anyone, not even to Victoria, but the thought that their grief had driven them mad was not afar off in the back of my mind.

After saying our prayers together and then some time spent in prayer on my own after Victoria settled in for the night, I began to feel comforted about Clara and Anna. It was as if my heart was being told that they were going to be all right and that this thing was right for them to do. Yes, they needed to go somewhere new. They needed to move on from their grief and this move was certainly a symbolic one of the greatest kind; but it was also likely a greater answer to their past and continuing difficulties. It seemed to be providence that nothing financial had worked well for them where they were and thus their hearts and minds were being told to travel to what would be greener pastures for them. My heart felt at peace about them and their plans.

The more I thought about Clara and Anna coming back home to stay, the more I thought it was wishful thinking on my part. Of course I would *want* us all together forever. Father and Mother Jones were so loving, gracious and generous that I knew if I begged for their help on behalf of Clara and Anna, our Jones parents would concede to allow their charitable efforts to go beyond what they were already doing for our family, and also encompass Clara, Anna and their husbands.

But what extended future would Rayner and Thomas truly have on land that was ultimately to belong to Joseph and Jacob? And if the land could or would be divided further beyond true kin, would it not be more likely that Bertram, Edward and Colin would benefit, having been raised in a great degree by Father and Mother Jones? Why would Rayner and Thomas want to take any of that land away from Joseph, Jacob and possibly our younger brothers? It was only a dream to me for us all to live side by side, and some dreams and wishes are not granted in this life, but are saved for the next. I knew that sometimes in this life, we are parted from loved ones one way or another; but as long as we could remain close in *spirit*, in feeling and in our hearts and minds, then at least it could be a comforting substitute.

I determined not to dissuade Anna and Clara from their quest, as much as my heart might want otherwise. I wrote a most supportive kind of letter wishing them all my very best wishes, hopes, dreams and prayers for their safe delivery to Oregon. I wanted to beg them to come to visit us first but I knew supplies and monies were thin enough that all had to be collected together for the great journey they were about to undertake. I did not know how quickly they were to go but knew they were joining a group that was going and so had to be there to join the wagon train when it was leaving. I *hoped* that the money Victoria and I had sent was going to be enough to help them make their journey without too much sacrifice or hunger of any kind. I did beg that Anna would write as often as she could, to let me know how they were doing along the way, so that I would not worry about them needlessly. I understood that there was some system of mail delivery that my sisters could make use of to let me know they were safe from point to point: from forts along the way at least.

Charlotte and Elizabeth were *far* more shocked by the news from Clara and Anna than Victoria and I were. I wondered if Mother Jones' fears and concerns (for she had many and had vocalized them instantly and intensely) had translated in her letter to Charlotte relaying the dreadful news and thus Charlotte and Elizabeth were more shocked than they might have been otherwise. Mother Jones was not *for* the plans at all. She was in fact worrying herself somewhat sick that our sisters would choose to embark on such a treacherous path. She agonized so, that I thought she might offer something relative to, or part of the farm to prevent them from going.

In the letter that I received from Charlotte, she was quite beside herself as to why anyone would want to trek off into the wilderness simply for some land to call their own. I sensed that she and Elizabeth took for granted all the land that was to be theirs, and also that their comforts and riches seemed to blind them to the very real troubles that a severe lack of money can bring.

It saddened me more than somewhat to sense a certain callousness from Charlotte if not Elizabeth. Charlotte's communications included some sarcastic remarks and unsympathetic criticisms of Clara and Anna and seemed to lay blame of their poverty and troubles on their bad choices. It seemed clear that at least Charlotte believed that she, Elizabeth and their husbands were prospering because *they* knew to do better than Clara, Anna and their husbands. Charlotte seemed to feel that neither luck, chance, fate, providence, destiny nor divine intervention had to do with outcomes on either side. She clearly thought *either* situation (good or bad) completely *earned* on either side.

Charlotte's subsequent reports of glorious events and treasures wearied me more than usual. It took me quite some time to respond to Charlotte's letter. I simply did not know quite what to say to most of her communications and was so grieved over some of them that I needed time to recover to the point that I could be more than biting and at least civil. In the end I chose to focus on the conjecture that Clara and Anna were likely already Oregon Territory bound. I shared that I too had been shocked and worried at first but that a sense of peace about their decision had finally brought me to the conclusion that perhaps they might be doing right, and that it *could* turn out to be a good thing for them after all. I also pointed out my thoughts relative to their need to move on from their grief at the loss of little Ben and that physically leaving the place of his death would do them all good in that way. I also surmised that perhaps they were never meant to be successful where they had gone to, and perchance Oregon Country would fulfill certain dreams for them in the end. Perhaps Oregon held their best destiny.

It was likely presumptuous of me to try to teach my sister something I thought I *might* understand more than she, but I could not help dropping in words like "providence" and "divine intervention" amongst suggestions that maybe better destinies awaited Clara and Anna in Oregon. I doubted Charlotte would take offense much or for long if she *did* realize I was scolding her in a most gentle manner, but it was more likely than not that she would not catch what I was inferring, at any rate.

As I worried about Clara and Anna from day to day, which was my nature to do, being so much of a fretter, I tried to turn my worries to prayers for them. I had realized that there was nothing I could do to help them from where I was and so calling upon angels to assist them was the best I could do, and it did afford me great peace. I often imagined Heavenly helpers surrounding my sisters on the western wilderness trails to a faraway frontier.

***

Since Victoria's headaches had all but vanished of late, she and I decided together to finally make an appearance at the next town dance assembly. I was delighted that Victoria agreed to my suggestion: I had wanted to cheer her up for she seemed rather melancholy since our received knowledge pertaining to our sisters embarking on their trek to the Oregon Territory.

We both knew without ever saying so, that it was quite likely that we might *never* see Clara and Anna again in this lifetime. Oregon Country was not a few towns away. It was a whole *world* away. We understood it would take months and months if not half a year for our sisters to make their way, all the way to the Oregon frontier. Of course it was possible they would choose to stake out land somewhere along the way and settle somewhere closer, but, even still, they would be far, far away and might never be able to afford a return trip to visit us, and how could we *ever* conceive of visiting them?

I did not confess to Victoria, but I was strangely thankful that she did not feel terribly close to Clara and Anna, and so she would not miss them even perhaps as much as I would, although I was not as close to them as I desired nor as I once was. I was now realizing that my sisters beyond Victoria had grown apart from me. What closeness we had before they married and moved away, was diminished markedly and *that* was a source of some lament for me. It was sadness itself to think that what closeness we had built together through our years of growing up had faded to such a degree, in such a relatively short space of time.

23
A Beau for Victoria

In preparation for an upcoming cheery event, I took it upon myself to sew up new dancing dresses, for both Victoria and me. I did have some fabrics to choose from: materials I had purchased before, but had never implemented the plans of to date; and so now was the time to create wonderful new things for my little sister and me to wear on that extra special night.

Victoria's dress was done in the palest creamy yellow and she looked an angelic dream in it. Mine was a pinkish peachy color and I fancied that my complexion looked its very best next to this glowing color. Indeed, who would not look rosy and full of healthy hue in such a color? Yards upon yards of cloth were gathered and ruffled into perfect place and I used up plenty of lace that I had gathered in shopping trips past, to create dresses that could not be outdone by any in the shop windows in town. Victoria's sighs and gasps were enough to make all my extensive labors worthwhile. As we walked towards the dance I feared us slightly guilty of vanity as we happily knew heads were turning our way.

We did not repent enjoying attentions and admiration, not knowing for certain whether or not we might be somewhere in the realm of sinning in the form of pride. Neither dignitary nor royalty from *any* land could have received a warmer or more glorious welcome than that which Victoria and I experienced that night.

We seemed encircled by handsome young men. I cannot say that the other young ladies in attendance at the dance were happy to see us, for none greeted us, save those we knew well from our school class room. Some older ladies did pay their addresses to us and I learned through the evening that some were mothers to some of the young men who were showing such interest in us. Oh yes, and there also was one young lady we did not previously know who introduced herself to us, and then began to speak of her brother who was admiring Victoria from afar.

Victoria and I both danced more dances than perhaps we should have, but with so many temptations at one's door, how can one resist? I did make an effort to bring Victoria off to the side often, so that she could catch her breath, partake of some refreshments and more particularly to make sure she was not beginning to suffer under any headache. She continually assured me that she was well, and so we continued to dance, number after dance number. It was good that I knew my little sister so well because to own the truth, we had little chance of private communication with young men surrounding us almost constantly, and so it was necessary for me to *interpret* Victoria's well-being to a great degree, rather than learning her thoughts through her direct vocalizations.

The young lady who had approached us in order to acquaint us with her brother, made their names known to us. She was Catherine and his name was Ethan. Catherine, a definite beauty to *my* eye, seemed a delightful girl in personality, a person of good character and seemed somewhere near Victoria's age. Ethan, who Catherine was happily telling us (or more particularly me) all about, was also attractive to look at and he seemed rather shy in nature. While some would not consider the trait of being reserved a positive one, I had always appreciated some such reticence in others. Indeed, I appreciated shyness over boldness: some of the *nicest* folks are reserved.

Poor Ethan could not gather the strength to come over and meet Victoria, let alone ask her to dance. Many much bolder young men had monopolized her attentions, but more than that, a great deal of courage was required in order to break through or at least *into* the group of gentlemen who were vying for Victoria's time. I could not help but smile, watching Ethan watch Victoria.

BONNETS AND APRONS: FIONNA

From afar, Ethan observed Victoria as she enjoyed conversing and dancing with her many suitors. In-between my own gentlemen enjoyments, I tried to make it easy for Catherine to become acquainted with me as she perceptibly wanted to, and I was even quite charmed when she persuaded me to go over with her to meet Ethan. Once introduced and begun in conversation, he *really* was quite amusingly talkative. Having gotten to know him a little better, I knew I really *must* make sure he was introduced to Victoria. I could *heartily* recommend him to her.

At some point later on, I found just the right moment and excuse to rescue Victoria from her throngs of admirers, so that she could be taken over to meet Ethan. As I suspected, Victoria was quickly attached to Ethan. I could see that she found him quite as witty as I did, as well as charming and *entirely* a darling who was *quite* handsome. Yet, his reserved nature kept him from being an obvious target for audacious young ladies.

Ethan soon had Victoria dancing. Victoria chose to continue many dances with Ethan. The disappointed youths around were visible. Many a young man could be seen sighing, frowning and lamenting that Victoria had discovered Ethan, because the instantaneous sparks between them were quite visibly perceptible.

While watching Victoria and Ethan dance number after number, I took the opportunity to get to know Catherine better, asking her about her and her family. As she delighted in telling me: she, her brother and their parents were quite new to the area. Her father had bought a great deal of land and they had settled on it for good. It seemed that at least her father wanted primarily to go into the cattle business.

The more Catherine spoke of herself and her family, the more pleased I became. It was not long before Catherine begged a promise of Victoria and me coming to dine at their home, and pledged to follow through with a formal invitation once she had settled it all with her mother.

The dance that night ended all too soon for Ethan and Victoria. I had felt ill-equipped to appease the young men who were dashed at seeing Victoria swept away by Ethan, but I did dance with many of them when they asked me to so do. I was sure these gentlemen were asking themselves who this young man was to have suddenly appeared from the shadows to steal away the heart of the young woman they had all been vying for. Ah well, we all knew Victoria could only belong to *one* young man in the end, and thus it was inevitable that *all* but one would be disappointed.

It was not but a few days before Victoria and I had received our formal invitation to dine with Catherine, Ethan and their parents.

"Well, Victoria. Pray, tell me your feelings. I would suppose that you are thrilled?" I ventured.

She simply smiled. I tried again, "Victoria. Don't tell me you are not elated that we are invited for dinner so soon?"

"I dare say," said she, "I do like him very much."

"Just very much, that is all?" I inquired further.

"He is more to my liking than any other young man I have known."

"Aha! I thought so!"

"Yes."

"You are saying so very little, it truly makes me wonder why. I want to hear every little thought and feeling you have about him, and you are being so very silent, which is horribly vexing for me!" I teased.

"Well, I do like him very much, but..."

"But... but what?"

"Well, we have only just met him and his sister, and we do not know them very well as yet... and we have not met his parents, so..."

"So you are reserving judgment just a little longer?" I smiled.

"There is no hurry to rush to judgment."

"True, very true. You are wiser than your years, my dear little sister: wiser than me to be sure."

She just smiled coyly.

"Well, I think his sister and him very sweet, but it is good that you are not falling as yet. It would be good to proceed cautiously, of course… not that there is any reason to doubt him or her that meets the eye."

"Well, we have not met their parents as yet." Victoria spoke thoughtfully.

"True. But are you worried that they might not be nice folk?"

"Oh, no, it is not that."

"Oh, you are worried that they will not think well of you?"

"Yes. I suppose."

"How could they *not* adore you?"

Smiling, Victoria answered, "I don't know, but… they wouldn't like Mildred."

"Ah… I think I know what you are feeling. You are thinking that Ethan and Catherine and their parents will have to meet Mildred sooner or later, and what will they all think of you once they have met her?"

"Something to that effect, yes."

"Well, here is my solution or plan, if you will: we will not allow them to meet Mildred for the longest while, until they completely know and therefore adore you, and then Mildred will be nothing to them but a thorn in their sides, as she is to everyone else! We will introduce them to Father and Mother Jones long before they are subjected to Mildred and indeed, perhaps we could just explain that as in so many fables of old, we have been cursed by the choice of our father to endure an evil stepmother as long as she lives!"

Victoria began giggling.

Then I had to add, somewhat playfully, "And what does our evil stepmother have to do with ourselves anyway? She did not raise us. She has little or nothing to do with us. She is not our blood relation. She cannot reflect badly on us because we do not choose to own her, and she has never chosen to own us as hers either. And, do not forget that our four other sisters married well in spite of our having a *most* vile and evil stepmother in the mix!"

We both laughed and at that moment I could not resist giving my little sister a big hug at which point we both lost our balance and fell onto the lounge together. We each roared in hilarity until we soon composed ourselves.

"But do you really think that they will like me?" Victoria was all seriousness again.

"But of course! Catherine seems to adore you already as does Ethan, and so why would not their parents *also* adore you?"

"I do not know, but it *is* possible."

"Well… I suppose it is *possible*, but, if they do not adore you then they are not worthy of you. Anyway, I cannot imagine any young man's parents not adoring you instantly. What family would not want to include you amongst them? *Everyone* who meets and knows you loves you." I insisted.

"Well… Mildred doesn't."

"But who does Mildred even *like*?" I protested.

"Few, I suppose."

"I think only *money* would attract Mildred to liking *anyone*. I do think that was her greatest attraction to Father."

"Do you think Mildred married Father for his *money* then?"

"I do think that was the greater part of her attraction to him. And, now that I think about it, I do suppose the fact that he is so generous with his money, on her behalf, and so amiable and so forgiving and tolerant… yes, those were *all* the kinds of qualities that suited her ways well. What *other* man can you imagine who would let such a woman walk into his life, to walk all over him and cause him to throw away everyone he loved, and give her all control of his property and monies?"

"I doubt *many* men would allow *any* woman to do all that."

"I would have *never* imagined that Father would have given Mildred *such* control over his life, lands and money. He is *not* the man we knew when Mother was with us. I will never know what possessed him to bow down to such a woman."

"Maybe he will go back to being himself *some* day?"

"It is possible. He *could* awake one day." I sighed.

"I hope so." Victoria looked rather sad.

"Me too... So, speaking of marrying for money... I believe *you* will marry for love." I winked with a smile.

"You too, of course; neither of us would marry for *money*!"

"And yet, *neither* of us would say no to a *little* money in the bargain, I dare say!"

"Of course not, but..."

"Do you fancy him rich?"

"Who?"

"Who do you think!?"

"Oh, Ethan."

"Of course, Ethan!"

"It is clear his father has some money." Victoria pondered.

"Yes, it does seem so."

"But does it follow that Ethan is entitled to much money: to *any* of his father's money?"

"Well, with only two children and no more in sight, I would think that Catherine and Ethan will be well taken care of."

"Likely so."

"Unless their mother dies and their father marries a Mildred." I joked.

"That is a *horrible* thing to say, Fionna, *even* in jest!" she looked thoroughly shocked.

"I know, I am *wicked* even to think of it, *very* wicked."

"You are not wicked... weak perhaps... where Mildred is concerned, but certainly not wicked." Victoria offered consolingly.

"Very weak where Mildred is concerned. I confess I fight thinking bad thoughts relative to her all too often!"

"It is very understandable."

I nodded, "And I joke about her far too much as well."

"Yes, but..."

"It helps to ease the pain and the anger somehow. I would *rather* laugh than frown about it." I smiled.

"True."

"Laughing at Mildred helps me to hate her less, and I know that I should *not* hate... so joking about her seems to help me.

KERRI BENNETT WILLIAMSON

Maybe it also helps me to feel sorry for her somehow. Well, at least it takes my mind off of being angry at her. A change of subject so to speak, I suppose."

"I know what you mean."

"And so, what should we wear to the all-important dinner?"

"Oh dear, I do not know." Victoria sighed.

"Let us go look through the wardrobe and find just the perfect thing for you." I gently grasped her arm to take her to choose something perfect, with fondness for my little sister filling my heart.

Victoria had great difficulty choosing between her favorite dresses and I thought it wonderful that I had been able to sew *so* many lovely things for her: so much so that she would experience such trouble choosing just one special dress to wear. I was of no help to her either, as I thought everything looked superb on her. *Every* color seemed her best color. Every style she tried to choose between seemed to suit the occasion. She reached a point of begging me to first decide what I would wear, and then she might be able to narrow down her choice based on coordinating with my own.

My desire for that night was to wear something subdued: something that would pale in comparison to my little sister who was, in my mind, to be the belle of the ball. I wanted to be a back-drop to her. I also wanted to appear mature: the older sister or mother figure. I chose a dress that soundly spoke of *decorum*. As Victoria chose, I encouraged her towards shining.

***

It was a beautiful house. Everything in and surrounding it was indeed perfection. The dinner was wonderful: all the food delicious and a good variety of it. I was taken in by many of the furnishings and décor details: luxurious fabrics and magnificently carved woods. It was all a treat to behold. Catherine and Ethan seemed beside themselves with delight that we were *their* company for the evening. Their father also seemed delighted with us being there. Their mother, on the *other* hand, seemed somewhat cold and standoffish, I thought.

I could not help but keep comparing this home to the Jones' household. This house was glamorous and impressive to be sure, but not quite so warm and inviting like the Jones' home. I began to think that as luscious as rich details are, without genuine feelings of friendship it can all amount to nothing.

At first, I gave Catherine and Ethan's mother the benefit of my doubts. I thought that perhaps she was simply a reserved standoffish person in general, and that this would account for her seemingly cool behavior towards us; but I soon could see that she was cool towards Victoria, more *especially*, as the evening wore on. It became clear to me that Ethan's mother opposed his interest in Victoria, inwardly if not openly.

Catherine and Ethan seemed somewhat oblivious to their mother's disregard for my beloved sister. I began to find it difficult to respond with genuine warmth to their mother because of her coolness towards Victoria, but at least I managed to remain quite civil with her. However, I knew it best if I focused my attentions more on Catherine, Ethan and their especially invitingly kind father. I was not sure if Victoria detected what I could see plainly about the mother, but I hoped my sweet little sister could not, as I knew it would hurt her to know.

That night when the evening event was all over and Victoria and I were alone, I did my best to hide my livid feelings towards our new friends' mother. If Victoria felt slighted by the woman, she did not show nor communicate that to me. I chose to remain silent on the matter. Victoria did not seem to see through to my true feelings. I supposed that I did well concealing my feelings about the mother, as I was concentrating on all the positives of the evening. We talked almost endlessly about how cordial Ethan and Catherine were, how dear their father seemed, and also of all the delectable details of the meal from the first course to the dessert; the furniture, the draperies, the lamps and candles, and even the fine delicacies of the tapestries, from the pillows to the paintings, and down to the seat cushions of some chairs.

As weeks and months followed, it became thoroughly obvious to me that Ethan's mother was trying to thwart his relationship with Victoria, and that she seemed to have higher expectations for her one and only son. I could not imagine why she could not accept Victoria as a worthy match for Ethan, or what kind of girl would or could satisfy her, save one attached to *money*. In reality, I wondered if any girl could truly measure up to whatever was this woman's ideal as a prospective wife for her son. Gentleness, sweetness, kindness, goodness, grace and class in behavior and beauty was surely not enough, as I knew Victoria had those qualities in abundance. I supposed that Ethan's mother indulged herself in fantasies about wealthy Princesses from afar as being the only match *worthy* of her darling only son.

Despite Ethan's mother's subtle but sure efforts against Victoria, Ethan continued to grow in his affections towards my sweet and dear little sister. It became so obvious to all that Ethan loved Victoria, and she him that all other suitors faded away from Victoria's realm. Victoria talked little of her feelings about Ethan: she did not need to speak aloud of such, for I could see what she was feeling, and was sure that I could see what he was feeling as well. Both Ethan and Victoria grew in shyness to all but each other. The match was tenderly sweet.

Catherine seemed enthralled with the new and close connection to both Victoria and I: in point of fact, Catherine was fast as another younger sister to me and a true friend to Victoria. Catherine spent more time visiting and conversing with Victoria and I than Ethan did, which meant that Catherine was a practical continual visitor almost always by our side, because Ethan was certainly near as much as could be considered respectful. Little was said of her mother by Catherine and none that I knew of by Ethan, but the little Catherine did say or hint to rather, was in as much as 'Do not worry about what she wants or thinks' and 'Ignore her'. Catherine intimated that their father's acceptance and happiness in the case was *more* than enough to make up for their mother's reticence and reluctance.

From the little which Catherine confided, I gathered that her mother was often unhappily accustomed to *not* getting her way, as her expectations were always far and beyond the mark. As to Ethan and his choice, he had always had quite a mind of his own, and to his mother's frustration, had always done as he pleased even though it was often against her wishes. Indeed, Catherine and her father also did much against the desires of the mother. They each were accustomed to doing as they felt best whether or not the mother approved. I supposed such *one* solution to managing a woman like that, and also thought that Father needed to take a much overdue lesson, and *if* he could learn likewise, he could manage Mildred *likewise.*

24

A Happy Match

Ethan's quiet determination in pursuing Victoria easily won all around. His father soundly and gleefully approved with all his heart while his wife reluctantly, but somewhat silently, accepted. Catherine could not have been happier in her brother's choice in adding to their family: Victoria was a friend and sister she seemed to have always wished for, and I was embraced by my new sister wholeheartedly as well. I was satisfied with the match. I adored the family, save the mother. Marriage plans began.

"You seem so very happy." I hugged my little Victoria, beaming.

"I am. I truly am... but..."

"But what? Pray tell me!" I feared I already knew the subject.

"It is... his mother."

Of course it is. What else could worry my little sister? "Yes? What of his mother?"

"She does not like me. She does not approve."

"I know... but I am quite sure she would not approve of anyone."

"I have tried so terribly hard to please her when I have been around her. I do not understand why I cannot make her like me, and accept me as good for Ethan."

"Victoria, I truly believe that there is no pleasing that woman where this subject is concerned. I doubt she would ever warm to anyone her son or daughter would choose. I cannot imagine who she could find and choose for either of them that could satisfy her dreams, wishes, ideals and indeed, her unrealistic expectations. I think you will simply have to look the other way when it comes to her, and completely focus your attention on especially Ethan, and also his sister and father who *do* adore you more than enough to make up for the dissatisfactions of the mother."

"I have been trying. I have tried. I cannot seem to forget that Ethan's mother does not want me to be a part of their family. It troubles me greatly. I know it should be enough that Ethan loves me as he does, and I am so happy that Catherine is such a dear and that she adores me. Their father is also wonderful to me... but the mother..."

"But you have not spoken of it before this. Why have you not confided these feelings to me before, Victoria? I was wondering if you sensed..."

"I was trying to ignore and forget their mother's misgivings, disapproval and displeasure as I knew Ethan and Catherine wanted me to. It is an embarrassment to them that their mother feels as she does. They want her to like me; to love me, like they do, but it is not to be. You and I both know it."

"Victoria, my dear, sweet Victoria. Their mother's disapproval has only to do with her own dreams. She seems to entertain fantasies of princesses and princes, of wealth and connections: these are what she wants for her son and daughter, and I tell you if she by chance could get them, I am sure she would *still* not be satisfied. She would find fault no matter the match. It is her way. There would still be something lacking for her because she looks to what she does not have, rather than counting her blessings. *You* are not unworthy: it is *she* who is unworthy of you. But, if the censuring mother does not seem to bother Ethan, Catherine or their father, do not allow her to bother *you*. And besides, in time I think she will warm to you. She will likely face reality and settle in, and accept you as much as she ever *could* accept anyone joining her family."

"But what if she *never* does?" there was such concern on Victoria's face. I hated to see such worry attend her.

"Well, Ethan adores you as do his sister and father, but even if only Ethan loved you while his whole family was against you, his devotion alone could be *enough*, could it not?"

"Yes, he is so sweet, so kind and so dear. He makes me so happy."

"So it is enough that *he* loves you!"

"Yes, I suppose it should be."

"And Catherine is a newfound best friend and sister for you!"

"Yes." she said, smiling.

"And their father will be a wonderful father to you!"

"Yes."

"And I do truly believe the mother will come around to you more some day: maybe sooner than we might think. Maybe once the marriage is over and done with, she will accept. I think she will have to. It only makes sense."

"But we both know what makes sense does not always happen, Fionna, and we both have learned by sad experience how horrible some women can be. Need I mention *Mildred?*"

"Yes. Well, Mildred is a one-of-a-kind, don't you think? We cannot compare Ethan and Catherine's mother to Mildred, can we? Not yet, anyway."

"Of course I do not *think* Ethan's mother could ever be as bad as Mildred has been, but…"

"We did not know how horrible Mildred was until after she married Father and moved in to move us all out!" I sighed with some sort of a smile.

"Yes." Victoria lamented with a look I could read so very well.

"Do you truly feel she may be as bad as Mildred? That she is anything like Mildred?" I asked with dread.

"No."

"But?"

"Well, I don't think she will be anywhere near as bad or anything like, but…" a sincere frown completely engulfed Victoria's face.

"But?"

"But I fear she will cause me sadness and heartache, nonetheless."

"I cannot say that I do not believe it very unpleasant that she has been so cool or even cold towards you, but I also believe that she will warm to you once you are her son's wife. She *must* surely warm markedly towards you once you give her grandchildren. Do you not think so?"

"And if she does *not*?"

"You will learn to cope, but you are not marrying *her*, so it matters little."

"I try not to allow it to trouble me, but it *does* matter to me."

"You will have to learn to *not* let it matter. You cannot let her matter to you if she chooses to be so unfair to you. I tend to think that only Ethan matters when it comes to the point. You are marrying Ethan: and perhaps he will need to learn to *shield* you and protect you from his mother."

"But he is so especially amiable. He, Catherine and their father are all so amiable. None of them ever crosses the mother. She always gets her way if it is possible, does she not? This is why I fear her becoming Mildred. Father is so amiable that a monster has been created in Mildred."

"Oh, I tend to think Mildred was *always* a monster, but you are right that Father could have prevented, or at least halted and corrected, much of her bad behavior if he would have been less accommodating."

"Yes and this is my *fear* for Ethan's mother!" Victoria's countenance was truly full of fear.

"But Ethan's mother does not get her own way in *many* things. Her family seems to often ignore her unreasonable wishes or demands as in *this* case." My spoken thoughts seemed of little help to my little sister and so without thinking further, I spontaneously offered, "You *poor*, dear thing!"

I embraced my worrying Victoria. As I held her she quivered and began to weep. Her tears and sobbing became quite uncontrollable, as if a dam had burst and now could not be stopped. I sat her down on the lounge with me and continued to hold her as she cried. I could see and feel that Victoria had been holding many of her trepidous feelings inside, and now that some were out, *all* were flooding out: her sadness, worry and many deep concerns.

Oh, but I wanted to grab hold of that mother-in-law to be and shake her! I had such feelings of anger and frustration towards that woman! How could she be so unfeeling? How could she be so... so... so dim-witted? How could she cause such hurt to my dear little sister? Victoria was as sweet and dear as I could ever imagine that any young woman could be. She was virtuous and beautiful. She was refined and intelligent. She was mature and amiable. What did Ethan's mother possess that was superior to my sister beyond a husband with money? Who was this woman that she thought herself loftier than my little sister?

I took a deep breath to calm myself. I took many deep breaths. I turned my focus away from the culprit and her sins, and focused back to my wronged sister. I did my best to wipe away Victoria's tears and tried to console her in her grief.

Once Victoria had composed herself, and had calmed down to a great degree, I thought I should breech a somewhat new line of the subject...

"Does Ethan know how you feel? Have you spoken to him about this?"

"No. I have not thought he would want to talk about it. His mother tires him because of it, and I do not wish to worry him further."

"But *surely* you should talk to him about it. He should know exactly how you feel. Truly... he should know how his mother pains you. You are to be his *wife*. Do not wait until you are married to begin to truly talk to him."

"But you know we are seldom alone enough to talk of such things. We are rarely but out of earshot of you or Catherine. We cannot explore such intimate subjects with either of you nearby."

"I can arrange for you to be alone in such a way that you could truly talk to him. I could make sure you could pour out your heart to him by being completely out of earshot. I can keep Catherine just as far away with me, as need be."

"But, like you said, perhaps his mother will warm to me after we are married. I would rather wait and see *if* I still need to talk to Ethan about it… about her… after I am his wife."

"Maybe you are right. Maybe that is best."

"Yes, I do think so. I hope so."

"Surely, it must be best." I tried to sound definitive and final as I pondered the matter in my own mind, thinking that Victoria would indeed have much more *power* in the situation as Ethan's *wife*, and that with all things considered, perhaps she *should* wait to climb that mountain until after the wedding.

"Anyway, they will be here soon. I must be completely composed. Do I look like I have been crying? Will they know I have been sobbing like a baby?"

"No, no, you look wonderful. Go to the mirror and see for yourself. You have recovered completely: your tears are all dried and gone, your cheeks are all rosy and your eyes are not red, nor are they puffed up for crying. Do not worry my little love; you look your wonderful self."

When Ethan and Catherine arrived, we all took a long evening stroll. Catherine and I walked ahead of Ethan and Victoria as usual, only this time I quickened our pace to give my sister and her beau ample space to talk out of our earshot.

The thought of the young betrothed pair not having enough privacy in conversation was to haunt me for a while, and so I determined to make a greater effort to give them the opportunity they needed to get to know each other better: on a more intimate level. I thought they should not enter the marriage date not feeling *completely* comfortable with each other being able to converse about *anything*, even if it was wise for Victoria to leave the unpleasant subject of her impending mother-in-law to a later date, when the full results were better known.

As I did my utmost to engage in lively conversation with Catherine about everything we passed by, and anything that seemed to enter our heads, I could not help but carry on my own personal thoughts in-between conversing with my newfound friend and sister. I kept thinking of how wonderful Father and Mother Jones were and how I thought that Catherine and Ethan's father was also this kind of dear person, but that I did not know how their mother would turn out to be. It was clear she was not to be a Mother Jones and this was very regrettable, but was she to be a Mildred in any way? She could not be that bad, *surely*.

It was possible that this woman could be another brand of Mildred: different, but similar. It seemed to me that she could never be as overt and shrill, nor as nasty and malicious as Mildred, but could she be as selfish and unfeeling? It *was* possible. She certainly possessed a cold side. Was this coolness a sign of an unfeeling spirit or something else entirely?

Whatever Ethan's mother was, the thought that there would always be a separation between her and Victoria did not seem *so* terribly problematic to me. It was the relationship between Ethan and Victoria that truly mattered in the end, and Ethan certainly seemed capable of giving Victoria all the necessary attentions and affection *despite* his mother. Had he not pursued Victoria against his mother's will? Had Ethan not already proven that he was not *entirely* subject to his mother's wishes? And Ethan had an ally in his father, and also of course in Catherine. Yes, Ethan could make Victoria happy *even* with a mother who could perhaps be something of Mildred's ilk; and yet I doubted she was anything near the likes of Mildred.

The few times I happened to catch suspended sight of Ethan and Victoria (for I did not allow myself to glance back, nor to stare or watch them for fear of appearing to eavesdrop, and of making them feel uncomfortable or on display), I saw two sweet young people steadfast in love and it was so alleviating to me to see that Victoria's worries about her future mother-in-law seemed chased miles away. Ethan possessed the power to end Victoria's worries and hurts, and it made me very, very happy. They were so exceptionally good together.

The joyous day grew nearer. Beyond Victoria's and my work at the school, our days were often filled with plans for the wedding, and just quiet contented time spent visiting and going for strolls. Victoria's nights were somewhat less than restful and therefore my nights held less rest for me as well, for I worried over the concerns and fears of my little sister. I knew she was fretting and fussing over Ethan's mother but there seemed little to be done about it. I thought to discuss the discomfiting subject with Victoria again, but decided to wait instead: allowing her to lead the way should she need me to consult with, or choose to use my listening ear.

Victoria and I finally took Ethan and Catherine out to meet Mother and Father Jones, and our brothers. The meeting had been long-since planned but somehow had been put off until this long overdue date. Victoria chose not to invite a meeting with Ethan's parents as she tried every way to avoid being around his mother. Luckily, as it happened, Ethan and Catherine's father was extremely active and preoccupied in his business, and thus there was ample excuse not to include him, and therefore his wife, in such a visit.

Father and Mother Jones were elated with the match, and lively hosts to our guests. Ethan and Catherine thought them wonderful adoptive parents. Between communications from both Victoria and I, Ethan and Catherine knew a fraction of the extent of the sad story that resulted from our father's remarriage. Victoria had not as yet sent word to Father of her upcoming wedding, and I respected her wish for Mildred not to have anything to do with it, and therefore Father could not know from us until afterwards. It seemed likely that he or they would hear of the event to be, but perhaps they would think they heard rumors and knowing them as I did, I doubted they would make any effort to be a part of any such event in Victoria's life anyway. Father never responded to any of the notes and letters I sent his way, and he never made any effort to seek us out. Chance encounters in town were seldom, and always somewhat awkward between us, and if Mildred were with him, communications were brief and cold to be sure. Yes, Father Jones seemed our only father now, as sadly, Father was ill-qualified to be recommended as our own father in any way.

Ethan's mother had inquired after our family many times, and I had always grabbed a firm hold of the reigns from Victoria to steer the topic to our far-off sisters, our beloved mother who resided in Heaven, and then to our brothers and Mother and Father Jones. I supposed my efforts to hide and evade were silliness, for there was *plenty* of information to be procured about Father and Mildred around about town. *No* doubt, Ethan's mother had uncovered much information to date; but I was somewhat confident that Victoria and I were cast in a *far* better light than Mildred was more often than not. Thus, any and all gossip would likely be clearly more to our *advantage* than against.

One night, very close to Victoria's wedding day, I awoke to the sounds of her intense sobbing.

"Dearest? What is wrong?" I spoke softly as I gently wrapped my arm around her huddled shuddering figure.

She tried to speak through her sobs but could not get a *single* word out and so I tried to help, "Is it your worries about Ethan's mother again?"

She nodded whilst still shaking amid her fountain of tears. I thought better of pursuing the subject just yet, and only hugged and cuddled her, stroking her back firmly, trying to calm her. Without thinking through the possible ramifications, I instinctively began humming a tune Mother used to sing to us. If it were possible, Victoria sobbed all the more, convulsively quaking.

"I am *so* sorry, sweetie! I did not mean to... I... I am *very* sorry."

She shook her head, weeping hysterically, trying to stop long enough to tell me something, or some things. I continued hugging her, stroking her back, saying nothing: I began rocking her as if she were an infant, and began to say a prayer in my heart that she would receive comfort from above. What else could I do? What else was there to do?

I wanted to ask her a myriad of questions. Had she and Ethan quarreled? Did Ethan or Catherine say something that hurt her, or had something else unsettling happened? I thought to make innumerable suggestions such as perhaps that she should confide at least some or all her feelings in Ethan, or that maybe we should even postpone the wedding, but, I stayed silent as we rocked. I turned my thoughts alone to prayer for my sister.

Finally Victoria became composed and began to spill all worrisome things that were on her mind, amid bubbles of some continued weeping, although she remained in a type of control, "It is Ethan's mother and her coldness towards me that bothers me most… but… it is… also… Father, and… Why does he not care about us? Why did he forsake us for Mildred's sake? Why did Mother have to die? Why are Charlotte and Elizabeth so far off? Why must Clara and Anna go so terribly far away? We shall never see them again!"

Victoria sobbed grievously a little more and then continued, "Our family has been all torn apart since Father married Mildred! If Mother were still here, or if at least Father had not remarried, or if he could have found and married a nice woman like Mother or Mother Jones, or any number of nice ladies, or even if he controlled Mildred to at least some degree rather than always being controlled *by* her… our family would still be together. Clara and Anna's husbands would be working Father's land with him, instead of going to their deaths!"

She burst forth with more tears and then I tried to help, "Sweetheart, Clara and Anna will be safe, I am sure of it. I do not believe they will die on their way to the Oregon Territory. Yes, they are taking a long and dangerous journey to a wild place far away on the frontier, but I truly feel all will be well with them. We do not know that we will never see them again: there is a chance we will."

"In the next life, yes, but I just know I will never see them again in this lifetime. Why could they not stop and visit us at least?"

"They could not afford to: in time or money, dearest."

"I know, I know, but…"

"Victoria, I do not know *why* our family has been so cursed by Mildred's entering it, but I do believe Father has made some *terribly* mistaken choices in first choosing Mildred for his bride, and *then* allowing her free reign to do as she pleased, even when it harmed his own children so horribly. *We* are suffering for *Father's* mistakes. Father will have to answer for his sins, as will Mildred, when they meet our maker: I am sure of it."

"But that does not make me feel better *now*. Why can Father not be the father he used to be in *spite* of Mildred?"

"Well, I wish he *would* as well, but... I tend to think that Heaven has blessed us in *other* ways that compensate somewhat. Father and Mother Jones have been wonderful to us."

"I know, I know... but... if only Father would never have met or married Mildred, or at least if he would make Mildred mind..."

"I know... but he *did* marry her and he does not stand up to her when she is wrong, and so he wrongs us all and himself as well. I am sure Mother is grieved if she knows of it. I am sure Heaven *grieves* for us, Victoria."

"And... poor Clara and her little Benjamin Thomas: why did he have to die? It is all so sad. Poor Clara must have suffered so and she must be suffering still. And now they are to travel all the way to a place far away in the corners of the frontier called Oregon. Oh, I hope they do not die. But why would they want to travel all the way to an unknown place like that? Why would they want to go so far from us? Why do they have to travel so far just for some land? There is land closer: there is land here. There is other land nearer. I just do *not* understand." Victoria's tears came faster once more.

"Victoria, try not to worry about Clara and Anna. I tend to feel they will do well. Perhaps it is their *destiny* to go out west. We cannot see as far as Heaven can. As to little Benjamin, you *know* I believe he is safely, peacefully and very happily in Heaven with Mother and other loved ones, and in time, Clara will be comforted more and more about missing him. Please do not worry yourself so." I began to worry as Victoria seemed almost in hysterics and was looking *horribly* ill to me, although all the light I had to see her with was the candle I had lit near the bedside when I had first awoke.

"I know... I know I should not worry as I am. You are right that maybe all will be well. I just feel so hopeless right now."

"Well, I think it is understandable for you to worry more than usual since you are embarking upon such a new and unknown course. I would also have fears entering marriage, even if my future mother-in-law had not made me feel as unwelcome as Ethan's mother has you. Her behavior has been *abominable* – truly it has. With all *that* and possible ramifications for the future to worry about, plus Clara and Anna joining a wagon train on the Oregon Trail, and little Benjamin dying, and us not being comfortable enough with Father to even contact him about you getting married... Well... All things put together are overwhelming you with worry I think... and who would not be worrying with *all* that weighing down upon them? If everyone and everything around us were perfect, I would think you would be overwhelmed with happiness, rather than worry, don't you think?"

"Yes, you are right." she said, and with vigor, wiped away her many tears.

"So simply focus on Ethan: you and Ethan. Do you not feel perfect happiness if you can just make all those other worries go away? Does not Ethan and thoughts of him, fill you with contentment and peace and calm?"

"Yes." She smiled and swabbed a few more tears.

"Then think of nothing but Ethan, and smile my love." I soothed.

25
Horribly Ill

The next morning, Victoria looked awfully ill. She thought perhaps at first that she was simply weary and muzzy because she had slept so little and cried so terribly much. Her head ached tremendously. I told her to stay in bed through the morning and that I would gently and kindly send Ethan and Catherine away for the time being, as they had planned to come to call fairly early that day for many hours of visiting and such other pleasures together.

By the time Ethan and Catherine had sadly said their farewells and given their condolences to Victoria through me, Victoria's forehead was very hot and I could see that she should remain in bed for at least that day and a night. I spent that day doing what I could for my little sister and cared for her needs that night as well. She obviously had taken ill with some sort of a fever. I thought that perhaps a night of crying and many weeks of worrying had weakened her constitution such that she was susceptible to sickness, and thus she had succumbed to whatever illness had floated by to snare her.

A kindly neighbor lady called on the doctor for us and when he came, his conclusion was as mine had been. He recommended as I would have done anyway and so I continued with all things I had learned to do for such sicknesses. I continued to do all I could for Victoria and between the help offered and given by a neighbor lady friend, and Ethan and Catherine stopping by with nourishments to give Victoria and me, I was able to focus entirely upon doing everything for my sister that I possibly could.

Each night I thought that *this* would be the last night of illness for Victoria. I expected each day to bring health back to my sister. Neither the doctor, nor our neighbor, nor Ethan and Catherine, nor I believed Victoria to be truly seriously ill. It seemed little more than a common feverous complaint we each tend to experience from time to time. Victoria did complain of terrible headaches and her neck and back were aching as well, but she and I had both experienced these discomforts before, and had recovered each time, and so thus I did not worry too terribly much.

The plans for the upcoming wedding were halted and postponed so that Victoria could recover from her sickness entirely, and gain enough strength to go ahead with the event with ease, comfort and joy. Ethan was truly saddened to have been restrained from seeing his beloved. Catherine did end up stepping in briefly only once to give a sisterly visit, but Victoria was truly not up to *any* company or visiting in any way, and truly preferred for me to hold them both back from attending her until she was better enough to make herself presentable, and to feel more comfortable. I kept assuring Ethan that when Victoria was recovered, he would have plenty of time to be at her side, and so to try to wait with patience.

One night, when Victoria was especially feverish, she spoke to me through her discomforts, "If I die, tell Ethan not to worry about me. Tell him I am with Mother and am happy."

"You will *not* die, darling." I stroked her hand in mine.

"But, I *might*, Fionna. I *feel* that I might."

"You simply need to *sleep*. You will feel better very, *very* soon if you get your rest."

"But if I die, *promise* to comfort Ethan for me? Tell him I was sorry not to have been able to visit with him since I have been sick."

"Victoria, *please* do not speak so. It frightens me to hear you speak about dying."

"I'm sorry. But promise to tell Ethan how I was feeling… if I *do* die."

"All right. I *promise*. But you are *not* going to die."

"And Father: tell Father that I *missed* him... that I missed having him as a father *all* this time... tell him how I have felt *without* my father."

I thought Victoria a little delirious perhaps. I continued to try to comfort her, "*Yes*, I can tell Father how you felt *if* you should die, but *please* do not think about dying now. Think about resting and sleeping, and getting *better*. Do you need another drink?"

"Yes. All right."

I helped her to another drink of water, wiped her brow and tucked her into her bed.

"Try to sleep now, my sweet little sister. Let me pray by your bedside that this is your last night of suffering through this illness, and tomorrow you will begin to feel much better. Promise me you will rest and try to sleep and think of getting *better*, my dear Victoria."

"All right... Goodnight."

I knelt beside Victoria as she rested quite peacefully. I began silently beseeching Heaven above to restore my sister to her full health as soon as she possibly could recover from the illness. I desired her better quickly that she could get back to life, and then onto a new life in marriage to Ethan. *Poor* Ethan: he had been *so* worried about his Victoria and so frustrated that he could not see her nor talk to her. I feared and felt certain that he tired of seeing my face each day instead of hers. I had begged Catherine to help keep Ethan's spirits up while he waited to see his darling once more. I hoped their mother was not delighting in this circumstance... nor hoping to begin thwarting any marriage plans. I prayed that Victoria would soon sleep soundly and have a goodly and lengthy night's rest that she could combat the sickness that fought to remain within or perhaps overcome her.

Sleep soon found my sister. I chose to stay on my knees a while and continue praying for Victoria and also for Clara and Anna, who were also in my thoughts and on my worried mind. We still had not heard word from them. I hoped and prayed that they were all right. I did not know if spending much time on my knees in prayer would make a great difference or not, where Heaven pertained to Victoria, but I decided to try my best to do my part to earn a miracle that night for my dear sister. I stayed on my knees praying fervently as long as I could muster, and then I took myself to my own bed to try to find a good night's sleep, so that I could be of service to my Victoria once again on the morrow. I would be of *no* use to her if I became ill as well.

The next morning, since Victoria was still and quiet, I took the opportunity to try to catch up on some cleaning and tidying around our little household, and then I readied myself for another day of being nursemaid to my sister. Whether or not she was to finally begin recovery today or not, I knew she would need a good deal of my tending and care. I hoped that she would feel much better today, but even still, I knew that she would continue to need my nurturing efforts to help her to complete her recovery promptly or no.

As the morning turned into the afternoon, I thought that it good that Victoria was gaining so much sleep. I thought surely that she would awake very well rested and well on the road to complete recovery; but as the afternoon wore on, I began to feel a sense of *dread*. I began to worry: wondering why Victoria was sleeping so *extremely* long. I did not want to wake her, thinking she must need the sleep, since she was sleeping at such length, but I decided to just check in on her to see how she was doing.

Victoria looked dreadfully still: too still. I could hear no heavy breathing: indeed, no breathing at all. I could see no signs of rising and falling with breaths of deep sleep. I felt *intense* fear as I moved one of my hands toward her. When my fingers gingerly touched her head it was *terribly* cold. Where a fever once heated up her forehead, now there was nothing to warm it at all. She was cold and *still*. I stood there staring at her, my hand suspended: my mind suspended in disbelief. My heart *raced*, a thick hard swallow *caught* me in the throat and one burning tear blinked from one of my eyes. I was still: as still as my little sister. My head began *spinning*. Suddenly dizziness overtook me and I dropped to the floor, both my knees thudding hard, as they hit the wood planks. I blinked away a few more searing tears, and determined I must wake my little sister.

"Victoria…" I said… "Victoria! *Victoria*!" I screamed.

I began shaking her by the shoulders to wake her, *screaming* her name over and over again.

And then I cried out, looking Heavenward, "No! *No*!"

I dropped my sister's lifeless form on to her bed and fell beside her, sobbing, screaming upwards, "*Send* her back! Give her *back*! Don't *take* her! Please! Please?! Oh, *please* give me a miracle… and bring her back to *life*! *Mother*… don't let them take her from me! I *need* her… I need her… *This* is *too* much. It is too much for me to *bear*. I cannot bear… *this*… I can't… Or let *me* die too. Just let me *die*. Mother? Mother? *Victoria*! Victoria…"

***

Smothered in my own tears, sobbing uncontrollably, I did not hear them enter. *Somehow*, they entered our home. Soon our dear neighbor friend was at my side with her husband in near attendance. She was stroking my back, hugging me, rocking me, telling me that everything would be all right… telling me that Victoria was at peace in Heaven with our mother now… and that she was an angel there also to watch over me now…

I lost all track of time and *everything* else. I did not know how Catherine or Ethan were told about Victoria's death, nor how they responded. I did not know who informed Father and Mother Jones, nor our brothers that our dear sweet young sister had gone to be with Mother. I did not know what kind of letter Mother Jones must have sent to Charlotte and Elizabeth. I knew not who did what for Victoria's funeral arrangements. The funeral was all a blur to me. *All* I *knew* were tears, an aching heart, time spent in bed sobbing and refusing food offered to me by our dear neighbor and Mother Jones.

Soon I was taken by Father and Mother Jones to their farm to recuperate as I had become rather ill. I felt certain that I was just simply sick with anguish, but others around me feared it could be more. Regardless, I was not so very able to care for myself in any event. I was all but delirious. I continued to decline food but Mother

Jones was so insistent that I eat, that I soon began eating a *little* here or there. I was all utter disbelief and shock. I could not believe Victoria had gone to Heaven to be with Mother. I kept thinking Victoria would suddenly appear before me. My sleep seemed intermittent a great deal, but when I *did* sleep I often dreamed. I would dream that Victoria and I were doing as we had done: day to day activities... and then I would awaken with a fresh realization that my sweet, dear, little sister Victoria was gone: that her lifeless body was buried beneath the soil and that her soul was with Mother now. This was a stark kind of torture to me: to believe she was still with me and then to apprehend that she was gone... over and over again.

I tried not to despair... or to spend my nights and days sobbing. I tried not to wonder why my dear beloved little sister was taken from me, or to continually wish for Victoria's return to earth to abide with me once more. I tried to accept Heaven's will. I *tried* to pray but would *always* end in tears upon tears so I *began* to fear to pray. I did not know what to pray for. I wondered who might be listening to my prayers. I did wonder why my fervent prayers on behalf of my sister were not answered. I felt as if so much that I had formerly believed and had felt I had known, was naught. Had I been so wrong about almost everything?

And *why* had I not seen Victoria's death coming? Why had I not sensed the *seriousness* of her illness? Why did I not feel that her life was *threatened*? Why did not the doctor or someone know that there was something very, very *wrong*? Was there *something* I could have done so that she was still with me now? Was I to *blame* in some way for Victoria's death? Why could she still not *live*? Why did she *leave* me? *Why*?

I tortured myself with many questions *even* as I tried not to do so. *One* part of me lamented and asked these questions *endlessly* while the other part of me told myself that it was *folly* to continue asking why. The part of me still maintaining sense and calm, told myself that I had done *all* that I could: all was done that *could* be done... and Victoria *still* died. I told myself that death was a *part* of life. Clara's little son died. Mother died. Mother lost her first two sons to death before I came along to stay. Where was the sense in death, and *so* much in life? Was it foolishness to try to find sense or fairness in any of it? I *craved* sense and fairness but could not find much of it, if any at all. I do not know how long I grieved Victoria's death, but it seemed a terribly long time.

Father Jones had contacted Father about Victoria's death promptly afterwards and it was Father's wish as well as everyone's assumption that Victoria be buried next to Mother. I know not what Mildred thought and I paid no heed to her at Victoria's funeral and all surrounding events. I was *far* too distraught, and so much in a sort of *despairing* dream world that I did not encompass the ability to pay any proper respects to such as Mildred, as if she deserved any. I remembered hugging Father and crying as I held onto him for a time. He cried as well.

26
Resuming

Once I was feeling somewhat more like myself and feeling like I could move on in life without my dear beloved Victoria, I determined that I would *not* let Mildred keep me from Victoria's graveside, as in a very real sense she had done with Mother's grave. I had felt so unwelcome on Mildred's farm that I had stayed away, which meant I had little or no relationship with Father, but also that I could not go to Mother's grave as I used to. I decided to go to the gravesites when I needed to, despite Mildred. I was *all* defiance.

My brothers did not take Victoria's death as dreadfully hard as I did, although they were very sad about her being gone. Charlotte and Elizabeth were sad and shaken over Victoria's passing but it was *I* who was *most* severely affected. Victoria and I had become so especially close in recent years and thus it was a great devastation to me to lose her. I thought it a supreme blessing that Bertram, Edward and Colin had each other, and also that they had Father and Mother Jones to look out for and finish raising them. I was so especially grateful to Father and Mother Jones for taking my three brothers unto themselves as their own.

Catherine was dreadfully distressed as was Ethan, although he seemed quite a great deal more devastated for a much longer period of time than even *I* would have imagined he would be. Ethan kept very much to himself for an awfully long time. As Catherine began visiting me quite often, she would tell me of how she, her father and especially her mother were worrying about Ethan and the time he was spending alone: mourning, grieving and not wishing to speak to *anyone*. It seemed even clearer, in Victoria's death, than in her life; how *much* Ethan had loved her. Catherine seemed to find respite in her visits with me for she did not have Ethan to spend many of her daily hours with as she had been accustomed to doing. I wondered if Ethan's mother felt any contentment in knowing her son would not be marrying Victoria. All her attitudes, resentments, prejudices and sentiments against Victoria were all for naught *now* and did not truly matter to me, but I *still* found myself wondering occasionally; for Catherine's visits seemed to remind me of how Victoria had *suffered* in her worries over not being accepted by Ethan's mother.

In time, I was back at my little home: the place that used to belong to Victoria as well as me. I was *terribly* lonely there much of the time and yet I *often* sensed what seemed to be Victoria's spirit reassuring me. I also resumed my teaching duties and as I tried to comfort my students in their mutual loss of Victoria, I found them comforting me so very much more than I could them. *Never* had a teacher been blessed with such obedient, sensitive and nurturing students! Never had students been *so* wonderful to their teacher: I was *quite* sure of that. I soon felt somewhat spoiled as they lavished me with attention, praise and *even* gifts and offers of meals at their homes, which I gladly accepted to offset my frequent feelings of loneliness.

When I was not at school, the homes of my students, out at the Jones farm or visiting Victoria's grave and Mother's as well; I was spending time with Catherine. In many ways she took the place of my Victoria for me: not that she could replace her, but she was like another little sister to me and was an enjoyable companion to pass time with.

As Catherine and I would take strolls in town and in and out of shops, suitors would pay their attentions to both of us. She seemed to *especially* enjoy trying to play cupid for me. I still carried a great deal of sadness with me and so, in my cloud of sorrow, I did not truly notice the attentions of men, but Catherine was fully aware of any young man who seemed to be interested in me and so she delighted in encouraging addresses my way. Indeed, she seemed more desirous of marrying *me* off than in finding a match for *herself.*

BONNETS AND APRONS: FIONNA

Time carried on and Catherine was my companion as much as I allowed or had time for, while her brother continued in his brooding and severe melancholy. Catherine seemed to wish to carry on in *happy* spirits and I thought perhaps that she did not know what to do for her brother, if there was indeed *anything* that anyone *could* do; and so she focused her energies on trying to cheer *me* up since I seemed so much easier to cheer than her brother was. At least I was a more pleasantly amiable companion.

Ethan continued in his own world of grief while Catherine tried to find as much happiness and cheer as possible. I began to see her attempts to find me a husband quite amusing. There was one young man who seemed certainly to be paying his attentions my way, and since I was not giving him the kinds of interest and conversation Catherine thought fitting, she began to make her very best efforts to do it *for* me: hoping to make a match on my behalf.

I tended to stand back and enjoy Catherine's many attempts at encouraging conversations between the young man and me, and yet I was quite still on the matter. I was not in the frame of mind to remotely consider marriage at that moment in time, nor was I supremely interested in the advances of the young man in question. The more time that passed with Catherine playing cupid for me, the more I could see the young man transferring his affections and attentions towards Catherine, if indeed his heart was *ever* turned towards mine in the first place. What was so exceedingly delightfully amusing was that Catherine could not *see* the transformation. She was so *incredibly* involved in telling him about me and getting to know him *for* me that she was securing his affections unto herself all the while thinking that she might be securing him for me. What folly! What fun. What entertainment for me.

In a short space of time I thought I began to see Catherine fighting her *own* attractions for this young man, fearing that she was encroaching upon *my* territory and so I realized that I must find a way to assure her that she was free to enjoy his attentions towards her, as *I* held no interest in him. Ah, what a *relief* I could see upon Catherine's countenance when she learned that the young man was hers if she so liked to pursue attentions in his direction, even as he was pursuing her. Soon, they were to be married. I did not inquire as to whether or not Catherine's mother approved of the young man but did wonder what kind of upheaval might exist in her mother's mind regarding this upcoming marriage.

Thus, with Catherine in the midst of planning her wedding, I was alone once more. Loneliness became a frequent companion of mine, but I tried my best to overcome it by busying myself with worthy pursuits. I went back to my drawing, which I had not done in an age; and so *many* quiet hours in my home were spent sketching.

It seemed that Catherine's upcoming marriage held its healing medicines for Ethan, somehow, for he began to be himself once more. Perhaps it was Catherine's new husband-to-be who was able to draw Ethan out, or perhaps it was simply time for him to go on living; but Ethan had a new brother and it seemed to suit him very well. I was happy to see this, as I did not wish Ethan to drown himself in his sorrows over Victoria forever: I thought that he was far too young not to consider the life he could enjoy, ahead of him.

With a doting sister and new brother at his side taking him everywhere that there were any social possibilities, particularly of the feminine kind, Ethan was soon considered an eligible bachelor once more and to my surprise, quite a pretty young lady set her sights and designs on him and soon secured him towards marriage. I did hear that Ethan's mother did not like this young woman and, ironically, thought her worth *far* below my own Victoria's.

Indeed, in time, a very real rift developed between Ethan and his mother over his new bride. It was *often* heard far and wide that Ethan's mother considered his *first* choice a far superior one, and that she now wished she had seen Victoria's true worth in the first place and if only Heaven had seen fit to let her remain to become Ethan's wife rather than the conniving and manipulating young woman who held that position now.

It was not long before I too saw that Ethan's mother was quite right to be less than satisfied with his wife, as I could see many unpleasant traits in her which reminded me greatly of some of

Mildred's faults. I was happy at least to know that Victoria was now highly esteemed by Ethan's mother, although I could not be happy for Ethan. I wondered at his second choice and how he could step down so far in her, compared to Victoria, but then I only had to think of Father and his choice in Mother and then in Mildred. Oh, what a contrast. Oh, what a fall. What a difference a marital choice can make in one's future.

Catherine was luckier in her choice of partner in that both her mother and father accepted him into their family readily, but far more than that, she had chosen well, for her husband seemed quite worthy of her.

From time to time I would run into Catherine and she would delight in telling me of her happiness in marriage, only to follow that good news with bad. She lamented for Ethan that he had *not* the likes of Victoria, but was downtrodden by a young woman who seemed come to destroy family felicity for them all. Catherine seemed to abide her sister-in-law little better than her mother could, and both women were relegated to attaining and keeping up the appearance of friendship, and ever-pressing efforts at politeness and civility towards their new family member in order to maintain any felicitous relationship with Ethan. Catherine and her mother did at least find some solace in each other and their common distaste and disgust for Ethan's wife.

From what I saw and heard, I supposed Ethan made the best of his marital situation, as Father continued to do with Mildred; although, Ethan made greater efforts to keep a sound relationship with his family. Ethan's wife also behaved better towards his family than Mildred did to ours, but then there was the matter of money: Ethan's wealth was quite dependant on his father and thus it was in his and his wife's best interests to stay within Ethan's family realm that they might partake of their riches. Ethan's wife would not *dare* to do as Mildred had done or anything like unto it, for fear of relinquishing one *possibly* probable object of her marriage in the first place.

Even as Ethan's wife was doing her best to get along with her husband's purse-strings (family), even on her best behavior, Catherine and her mother were truly far from content with the new addition to their family. It seemed that Ethan's father was more amiable to Ethan's wife or perhaps it was simply that he saw less faults in her. I have come to wonder if some men do not tend to see the subtle little things in behavior and conversation that most women can do, and as it may be fortuitous or not, negative or positive, men oft see less of character than women seem or tend to be able to. The little I had conversed with Ethan's wife, I could see why she was not well liked by her mother and sister-in-law. It seemed clear to me, as I was sure it was clear to Catherine and her mother that Ethan's wife was of the typical conniving and manipulating female variety. I had long detested that type; since I was old enough to see clear through those who were of that ilk, and of course, Mildred had taught me well of that sort.

When in the company of Ethan and his wife, which was *very* seldom (for it seemed that Ethan was uncomfortable having his wife around me, and tended to try to avoid me when out with his wife: indeed Ethan had been uncomfortable around me since Victoria's death as I supposed I reminded him of her), I did my best to behave pleasantly towards her more for Ethan's benefit than for that of his wife. I *truly* felt sad for Ethan. I did not think that he knew the long life of misery he was destined for with a wife like that. I also felt compassion for Catherine and *even* her mother. Adopting a young woman like *that* into one's family could not be a pleasant thing for them, and having had such as my angelic Victoria to constantly compare Ethan's wife to would only make the reality of the disagreeable situation all the more distasteful.

I supposed that some would be of the mind that this was only poetic justice for Ethan's mother: that she deserved to be saddled with a most objectionable daughter-in-law since she had rejected an angel in not accepting Victoria; but I could not stay in that frame of mind, even though I confess I had stopped briefly there. It was such an ironic twist of fate for Ethan's mother and surely she had learned something from the life's lesson in it, but I could not take *any* joy in it; for all I could feel was compassion for Catherine and her mother that their family would be forever altered in a dreadfully negative and disagreeable way because of Ethan's ill choice.

Only *too* well did I know how *much* one woman could bring of immense unhappiness into a family. To be sure, Mildred had more *power*, or was given more power by Father and the situation, to wreak havoc than did Ethan's wife, but even still, that young woman could still do much damage to all in her new sphere.

***

I was overjoyed to finally receive a letter from Anna telling me how they were progressing towards their final destination. I understood that letters could be sent from Forts or little settlements along the way and so letters could make their way home from the long trail to Oregon Country. In actuality, I would have to save my precious words and also my dreadfully *sad* news about Victoria, for my sisters until such time as they settled at a place long enough to receive a letter from me. I decided to write letters to them from time to time and when I finally knew I could send letters to them with confidence of being received, I would send my many letters all at once, at that later date.

Anna seemed to be in quite high spirits considering their living and traveling conditions. From all that she said in her letters, I could see that they were all focused forward with *full* hopes of a more prosperous life ahead of them.

As I understood it, the Oregon Trail began in Independence, Missouri and was some two thousand miles long, ending in the Oregon Territory with many alternate destinations in the midst of it and near its end. Clara, Anna and their husbands had joined up somewhere along the way: I was not exactly clear as to where they had begun their own journey.

Anna said little of their day to day struggles along the trail, but it was clear to me from what she *did* communicate that it was an arduous journey. I secretly hoped that they would soon choose a nice place to settle on, along the way, but they seemed quite determined to continue all the way to the end to a place called Williamette Valley in Oregon Country, for they had heard of its rich farmland and believed they would prosper greatly there. I truly hoped they would prosper wherever they settled, but truly did not wish them to settle so *extremely* far away for fear of never, ever seeing them again.

What mattered to me most, though, was that Clara and Anna were happy, healthy and well provided for. If this had to be accomplished alongside the possibility that I would not see them again in this life, I *could* live with that. It was better that they be far away but happy than near by and suffering. We would have letters. And I dare say that sometimes there can be a closeness in correspondence that even surpasses that which can be felt in person-to-person communications. I looked forward to being able to send Anna and Clara letters and consoled myself in the meantime by writing them: pouring out my heart to my sisters; expressing my deep love and concern for them and my hopes and prayers for their comforts and joy wherever they may be. I was happy that they had each other, and also that they each had a good husband.

***

Time for me passed quickly in many respects as I kept myself busy and yet as it is prone to be in life I suppose, time passed dreadfully slowly in other ways and at other times. There were times on my own when I could hear the clock ticking as if it were slowed down to a snail's pace and so much louder than usual, even and almost banging or drumming in my ears, and I would often be inclined at those moments to think of my many losses: I would lament and grieve at having lost Mother and especially Victoria of late, and I would sink into tears and agony as if virtually in a pit of despair.

Sometimes it was truly terribly difficult to pull myself up out of that pit of tears and to soften the aching in the very core of my soul; to lift myself up and out of those deeply gloomy feelings. But I knew that Mother and Victoria would not have me sink so low, to stay there and waste even a few hours of my precious time on earth doing nothing but crying and lamenting over losing them. Yes, I was lonely. Yes, I missed them terribly. But, my feelings of missing Mother were so tempered by time that *this* very thing taught me that my intense feelings of loss regarding Victoria would also soften over time. Indeed, my feelings of grief and sorrow had already abated to a great degree, if only I could stand still in reality and see clearly enough to realize what truly was.

I began to try to turn my feelings of loss into feelings of comfort by reminding myself that Mother and Victoria must truly be enjoying Heavenly peace and love together: such that I was certain I could not even imagine. In knowing or at the *very* least believing that my lost loved ones were truly happier than I might suppose, I could go on and live my life in honor and remembrance of them, realizing that it is the *missing* them that was my real hurt and that since my belief was also that I would surely see them again; feelings of missing them were truly only temporary and so I could take patience in waiting to see them again, and focus on life without them in the meantime. But, I also believed that they were near in a very real sense and so I was not truly without them, *even* still.

In fact, there was one night when I was lost deep in despair and as if drowning in my tears, when I cried out upwards to anyone who might hear or be willing to listen: it was if I was praying for comfort and begging for connection with Mother or Victoria all at the same time. I did not cry upwards long before I sensed a very real comfort, as if Mother and Victoria both wrapped their arms around my sobbing form in perfect love for me. The feeling of being hugged by my loved ones from beyond was so incredibly real that its intensity lasted with me for many days, and I believed the event was quite actually and possibly true.

As often as I could, I would go out to the Jones' farm where I was always comforted by the love of Father and Mother Jones and my associations with them as my adopted parents, but I was also prone to begin to focus my attentions on my brothers and their well-being more. I would spend my time and efforts in asking each of them how they were doing or feeling, and what they had been doing since I last saw them. This very simple act of sisterly care and concern likely did more for me than it did for my brothers, but it did seem to do a world of good for them as well.

Rather than my thoughts being focused upon myself and my feelings surrounding my own personal losses, I was thinking of my brothers, their incredibly intense losses and how they were progressing in life. They each seemed to delight in showing me their many accomplishments: things they had made, how their muscles had grown, how tall they were becoming, how broad their shoulders were, new things they could now do and all the work they had helped Father Jones in achieving. It was amazing to me to see what little efforts on my part in taking interest in my brothers resulted in such faces full of joy in being attended to and doted on in any way. Even with all that Father and Mother Jones did for my brothers, I could see that in a very real sense there was still hunger for adoration, attention and praise. It seemed to me that Father's complete lack in crucial caring and Mother being gone so long, and perhaps all the other losses of such as their sisters being gone in death or simply moving away; had left my brothers with empty spaces in their hearts and it did not take much in the way of efforts from me to begin to fill some of those voids for them.

I began to take the efforts, time and pains to travel out to see my brothers on the Jones' farm more than I had ever thought possible before. It was good for my brothers, good for me and good for my ongoing relationship with them. My first thoughts were that they needed their remaining sister more than ever before, but more of the truth was likely that I needed associations with them more than before since I now felt so alone *without* Victoria.

27

Bonnets and Aprons

Once somewhat over my grief and shock over my loss of Victoria, I finally found strength enough to look through some of her things. It was a painful process to be sure, but it did need to be done; and while I cried a great deal, I also sensed her near and I was comforted by that. Amid some of her more personal writings, I discovered a letter addressed to me: an apparently tear-stained letter. I thought surely that Victoria had planned to give it to me before she died, indeed I was quite certain she had no plans for this letter to come into my hands after her death: but who is to know whether or not she felt some sort of premonition prior to her passing, and perhaps wanted to be sure that she communicated certain things to me, in case she did not live long enough to express those thoughts in person.

Dear Fionna,

You are out: I am home. You are working for our livelihood while I am resting and relaxing. I know you think not twice about such, about all you do and have done for me, but I dearly want you to know that I notice your countless works on my behalf. I think of your every step for me, and appreciate you and all you do and have done for me. I know the sacrifices you make for me; or at least I recognize some of your sacrifices, for there are surely some I do not comprehend. I see your many gifts to me and I am most grateful for your generous efforts, my dear and beloved eldest sister.

I greatly esteem you. I desire to emulate you and indeed I place you high up on a pedestal with Mother, for you have been as much a mother to me as anybody ever could be: ever since she passed from us and left us alone without her.

It is difficult for me to say these sorts of things to you, partially because I feel much too shy to launch into such a subject, but more especially because I know I will cry and therefore have too great a difficulty in communicating my tender thoughts to you as I want to. In point of fact, I am crying as I write this; but no matter, for deep feelings of the heart often include the gushing forth of tears. I have been trying to write you a poem, as a gift from me, as a tribute to you: I know not what it is exactly, but when it is done, I will give this all to you...

Within the note I found this poem, I supposed perhaps unfinished, at least half finished or maybe simply unpolished, but there it was, as was the small note: a hidden treasure to me, to be sure...

Bonnets and Aprons

Bonnets and aprons you sewed for me,
Since the days of my earliest youth.
Treasures and trinkets you gave to me,
But the greatest of all was truth.

Yards upon yards of velvets and silks,
Adorned with fine trimmings and lace.
Hours of time, toil, labor and work,
Freely given, love shone on your face.

You took me to meet many young men,
To enjoy those nights at town dances.
Together we talked of my suitors,
Imagining love and romances.

You dreamt more dreams of me and my life,
And saved all life's dreams of yourself.
You placed your life so far behind mine,
Your own dreams lost on a shelf.

BONNETS AND APRONS: FIONNA

You chose for yourself to be last,
As you gave me position of first.
You took great heed to feed me well,
Even while you did hunger and thirst.

Bonnets and aprons created with care,
You also made blouses and dresses.
You carried my burdens as if your own,
And lifted them as if only tresses.

My heart you protected with tender care,
You were bound and determined to defend.
My sister, my greatest champion,
My closest, dearest lifelong friend.

You are to me someone to follow,
So much like our dear lost Mother.
You will always stay in my heart,
Forever cemented like no other.

Oh, but Victoria's words held fast to my soul and tore tears from my eyes for quite some time. All at once I felt intense pains of love and missing her, even whilst I felt joy in knowing how she had felt in appreciation, admiration and love for me.

28
Betrayal

One day when I was feeling quite alone in my home (confessedly somewhat in a wallowing way), unable to go to the Jones farm mostly because the weather was not permitting travel, for it was a dreadfully wet and soggy day and the roads were miserably muddy and difficult to traverse; Catherine surprised me greatly by coming to call. She was by herself. Once I had closed the door behind her, after inviting her inside (to her seemingly great relief), I could see her composed outward demeanor instantly vanish away as if washed clean by the rain: immense and intense distress was written all over her. I quickly offered her the lounge to sit on, for I feared she might faint away at that very moment.

"Catherine. What is *wrong*? I can see that something is *terribly* wrong."

She began sobbing even as I thought she was going to try to begin to tell me what was on her mind, or pressing upon her heart. I thought I would try to help her in communicating her distress by guessing the first most obvious possibility that came to my mind, "Is it Ethan's wife? Has she said or done something to injure you?"

Catherine shook her head vigorously. I tried to help more by grasping at straws, "Is it your father or mother, or Ethan? Has something happened to them?"

She shook her head emphatically once more so once more I tried, "Is it your husband? Have you and he quarreled?"

Catherine slowly shook her head just a little before she threw herself prostrate on the lounge, hiding her face from me and shaking bodily amid deep and strident sobs.

I thought that asking further would be folly, especially since I could think of no other thing or person that could distress Catherine enough to bring her to my door in search of my comfort, or perhaps even counsel, and I did not see the wisdom in asking questions of someone who was at that moment, obviously incapable of answering in any audible form.

One of my hands began stroking and rubbing her back quite instinctively in an effort to calm her down enough that she could begin to stop sobbing, and tell me what she surely wanted to. I confess my curiosity was peaked beyond measure, as I hoped it was nothing truly serious. I feared to say anything as it might be the absolute wrong thing to say at such a moment. Had I not yet stumbled and said enough already? I felt that anything I *had* said had not helped in any way and perhaps had hindered her, so I secured my lips together in complete silence, and determined to do nothing but stroke and rub her back or hug her as it seemed appropriate to do.

As minutes that *seemed* like hours passed with me doing my best to calm Catherine's anguish through what little physical contact I felt helpful, her loud and fervent sobbing began to subside, and she started to take hold of herself, being nearly to the point of finally being able to speak to me of that which was on her mind.

Catherine was finally able to sit up somewhat towards composure. I offered her a nearby handkerchief, as I did have many of them handy for myself and my frequent need of them since Victoria had died. She wiped her face clean of the layer of tears, and seemed to be trying to swallow any further weeping so that she could speak. I sat calmly, quietly; patiently waiting for her to be ready to communicate what she so dearly seemed to need to.

In time, she began, "My heart... has been... broken."

I nodded and took her hand, hoping to give her courage and composure to continue as I knew she truly wanted to.

"My *husband*... has broken... my heart." Her head dropped, her chin as if hitting hard against her upper chest.

She began to cry again, jerking the handkerchief up to her face. I let go of her other hand as she pulled it away, needing it to cover her face and wipe further tears. I continued to sit quietly in a sincere spirit of compassion.

Soon she began again, "With... that... *woman...* the one he's known so long..."

I took her hand again and held it lovingly to give her all the compassion, strength and courage that I could.

Catherine continued, "She wanted him for herself... and his marrying me... did *not* stop her designs."

Now Catherine's demeanor turned to more anger than hurt, "She *pursued* him behind my back. What is she *thinking*? What does she think she can *attain*? He is married to *me*!"

Catherine's weeping began again, "And he... *succumbed.* How *could* he?!"

Her face was thrown into her hands, into the handkerchief once more. I patted and stroked her knee, knowing not what else I could possibly do. She continued violently sobbing for quite some time.

She looked up at me with the most pitiful expression and burst, "How could he *love* me? How could he love me and do *that* to me? How could he do that *against* me? He must *not* love me! Why did he *marry* me? *Why*?!"

Catherine threw herself upon the lounge once more, deeply engulfed in her sorrow and tears. As she cried much time away, I sat there next to her pondering, confused, feeling that the situation was more than *quite* unfathomable. Catherine's husband seemed such a nice young man: a good man. What on earth could have *possessed* him to succumb to the wanton seductions of a conniving young woman who was not *nearly* as pretty, nice nor of good family as his own wife. Was there a previous attachment he had not confessed to Catherine before marrying her? If attached to this other young woman, why marry Catherine? There was no sign that he had married Catherine for any money or convenience. I could not understand nor comprehend it.

Soon Catherine said more, "He *says* that he loves me. He says that he was simply *not* thinking. He says that she *tempted* him and he *fell.* He insists he has no feelings for her."

She controlled her emotions and looked to me briefly before looking down. There was such intense pain written upon her face. It pained me deeply to see.

I exerted my voice for the *first* time in at least many numerous minutes and perhaps an hour, wondering if it might fail me, but proceeding nevertheless, "Did he... have a prior... intimate or... *improper...* relationship with her?"

Catherine eased a little, "No. He says he did not. And he says it was all a dreadful, stupid mistake. He says he fell the one time, and he is so horrified at himself that it would *never* happen again. He will never even *speak* to her again. He will not go *near* the temptation even though he is sure he could not fall with her again."

I did not know what to say in return and it sufficed for me to simply sit there silently, for Catherine had more to say, "I have seen her since it happened. She seems *so* haughty and satisfied with herself that she has done this against me, as if it makes her *superior* to me somehow. She thinks *she* owns my husband, even though he will not speak to her now. I want to scratch her eyes out! I think about *killing* her! I *know* that is evil to even think of such a thing, but I cannot help it. I feel such *hate* I cannot tell you how much it fills me. I *hate* that woman. I *hate* my husband. I wish I would have *never* married. Oh, *why* did I ever fall in love?"

"I don't know what to say that might be of any help, Catherine. It is *so* difficult to believe he could *do* this thing. I'm sure he *does* love you but why or *how* could he betray you *so* completely? It is all so *dreadfully* horrible. You *poor*, sweet dear." I took hold of and held her hand fast, "Have you told your mother? Will you tell your parents or Ethan? What will they *say*?"

"Oh, *no*! They must *never* know!" exclaimed Catherine to me. A look of fright filled her face and her eyes locked on mine, "What would they *think* of me?!"

I was shocked, "*You*?! You are the *innocent* in all this! They would think only *good* things of you and feel compassion for what you are suffering, because of the sins of others! I would think you would worry about what they would think of, or even *do* to your husband."

"Yes, yes, I know, I *know*. They would *hate* him. They would *never* forgive him. They would want me to *leave* him, forever. I am *certain* that they would."

"It seems that way now... but I think... over time... they *could* forgive him... as you will be able to... if he fully repents of what he has done."

"But I don't know if *I* can *ever* forgive him, Fionna. I don't know if I *can*."

I briefly hesitated but felt to say, "You may never *forget*, Catherine, but I believe you *must* forgive him. You must *try*. I *believe* you will be able to, *eventually*."

"I know. I am trying. Sometimes I think I *am* forgiving him already and that soon it will all be behind us, but then all the horrible thoughts and feelings come back, and I hate him with a *violent* passion once more."

"Of course: anyone would understand that."

Tears welled up in her eyes, "But I *love* him." She looked so very sad: truly completely pitiful.

"I only hope he will earn your love again. I would think that if he did *all* in his power to win you back, your heart will be eventually healed and you will be able to truly forgive him."

"I hope so, but..."

"Don't expect your heart to be healed very soon, for I do believe it will take a *great* deal of time." I spoke with conviction.

"Yes, of course... I know that." she sighed.

"And your husband must *win* back your heart."

"Yes, he is *trying* to." She looked down and then added, "He's being *especially* good to me. He is so *horribly* sorry. Sometimes I think his heart is aching more than mine for what he has done."

I simply nodded, but I doubted that the sinner could feel more pain than the sinned against.

"I have such strong emotions one way and *then* another. I love him, I hate him. I think and feel I can *never* forgive him but then I tell myself that I can. I *feel* it to be true, most of the time."

I stroked her hand.

"It is all so *terribly* difficult."

She broke down crying once more. I did my best to comfort her. I truly did not know what was best to say to help her feel better. Indeed, I did not know if it was within my power to help her feel better. I thought that a certain healing power rested with her husband, and perhaps more especially with Heaven. Nevertheless, I did my best to be of help and assistance. I held and stroked her hands. I put an arm around her. I rubbed and patted her back gently. I instinctively tried to do what I *could* to comfort her and to share her burden.

Finally I thought to say, "I can only *imagine* how difficult this must be for you, dear, *dear* Catherine. I can only imagine the heartbreak you *must* have felt, and *still* must be feeling."

Her sobbing seemed worse and I wondered at the wisdom in my having said *anything*. I worried that perhaps I should have remained silent.

Still, I felt I must add, "But... in time... I do believe you can be healed. With Heaven's help and with the help of your husband, this horrible thing can be in both your pasts. I truly do believe it can."

In the midst of her extreme sobbing, she managed to blurt out, "I know! I believe it too. That is what I am holding onto."

I held her hand firm even as I held her shoulder snuggly. I realized I was rocking her... like a baby. She calmed down somewhat.

Finally I could not help but put in, "But you truly do not wish to confide in your family at *all*? Not even in your mother? I would think that..."

"No! They would *not* understand. They would *never* forgive him. I must not tell them... *ever*!"

"Are you certain, Catherine?"

"Yes! I am *assured* of it! Promise you will *never* tell a living soul!"

"Of *course* I promise. Don't worry. I will never tell *anyone*."

I continued my efforts to comfort her as her tears continued to flow. I could see that my suggesting that she confide in her family regarding her husband's monstrous indiscretion was extremely distressing to her, and I felt badly that I had inquired of her thusly once more. I just felt that if my own mother was alive and I was in such a situation, I would surely wish to confide in her and seek comfort from her. But *Catherine's* mother was not *my* mother. I supposed Catherine's mother likely to hold a grudge for years to come if not a lifetime, and could see why Catherine preferred to confide in me, a friend, *over* confiding in her family.

Soon, she was calmer again and I chose to offer her some refreshments, as a change of topic in an effort to ease the strain of her poor red and swollen eyes. At first she declined, saying she was devoid of appetite, but soon I was able to convince her to start at least with a glass of water and then she eventually agreed to partake of some sustenance.

Catherine acquiesced to my favorite corn bread that I often made and had on hand. It was Mother's recipe and a favorite with at least Victoria and me.

I tried to speak of other things to keep Catherine's mind off of her grief over her husband's cruel betrayal.

Soon Catherine was much more composed with more color in her cheeks and less around her eyes, and she spoke of how hiding her sadness and despair was such a difficult but necessary thing to do around her family and all else, but me, now. She said that she had never intended to even tell me but her feelings were about to burst, and thus she had come to confide in me, knowing I could keep her secret and be of some comfort. She had felt such a strong need to tell *someone*.

I told her I feared I was of little comfort, particularly since I had no experience in marriage. I truly felt in the dark as to *that* realm, and greatly lacking in wisdom in the area of marital concerns. She assured me that simply having one ear that could listen was enough comfort to her. She said she felt that her burden was lifted a great deal just by being shared with me, and indeed that I had been of comfort to her. Just knowing that my heart also grieved with her in her pain, was of some comfort to her, she said.

At some length, Catherine was steadied and said she needed to leave, else her husband would worry over where and how she was. I walked her out to her carriage and hugged her goodbye. As she rode off I thought that no spectator seeing us could imagine what our visit had consisted of. She looked completely composed, and I dare say, even happy. Truly she did.

Despite being a mere confidant in Catherine's distressing situation, I felt my heart ache as my mind buzzed with chaotic confusion. *How* could this be? How could a decent man do something *so* indecent? How could a man who loved his wife fall with another woman? How could a good man harm so innocent and pure a lady? As much as I believed Catherine that her husband was suffering greatly for his sins, I could not help but think that her suffering must be so very much greater. She had done nothing whatsoever to deserve this suffering. The sin was all *his*. Why should *she* suffer so? What could his suffering be *compared* to hers? I doubted it could *near* compare.

I felt anger swell within me. I wished to seek him out and slap him violently for harming such a sweet girl. What *stupidity*! What a stupid, stupid man! And where was the *trollop* who tempted and then succeeded in snaring him? I would surely like to *tear* into both of them verbally and yes, even with some physical blows as well! What kind of woman could *do* this? Oh, but pits of the darkest depths await such!

My heart was racing with *fury*. I felt I could not contain my rage. I tried not to stomp into my home for fear of drawing attention to myself. It was with great difficulty that I walked seemingly calmly towards my abode, containing my resentments. Once there, I decided I must take an evening walk for I could not stay still nor within such a confined space, and remain completely sensible. I knew it would *not* be a stroll that I undertook, for my irritation would propel me much faster than *that* to be sure! Oh, if only I had Victoria to pace with. She would be a good marching partner, even if I could not tell her what vexed me so greatly.

It was a calm evening: a great contrast to the storms I felt inside. The more I thought everything over, the angrier I became, thus I tried not to think at all and just enjoy the evening air, and my vigorous walk within it. I wondered what a sight I might be and tried not to worry what people might think. There I was, walking so briskly many a man might have to huff and puff to keep up with me. I seemed as if in the midst of some sort of footrace. Ah, well... I was trying to escape my own anger, I supposed.

As I walked smartly along, I almost laughed at myself even as I fought feeling supremely angry at my young friend's betrayer who *should* have been her best and most loyal friend on earth. Her lover was her torturer. The walking did calm my nerves a great deal. Indeed, it surprised me how effective a balm setting foot in front of foot rapidly could be. It was a true relief, even to the calming of my soul.

29
Winston

I walked seemingly endlessly around town, from one end to the other. In no short time, I felt ready to set my direction homeward: calmed and more rational, I hoped.

Then from behind me, a familiar voice startled me with, "Fionna. Could that be you?"

I spun on my heels to see him, and then in severe shock blurted, "Winston!"

His smile was magical to me. I could not help but smile back.

"I have not seen you in far too long." His eyes held mine.

"Yes, it has been a very long time." I checked myself, *remembering* him surely a married man long since, stepped back a little and coolly spoke again, "and how have you been?"

"Oh, very busy... you know, trying to make my way in the world." He smiled.

I wanted to broach the subject of his wife but such a move felt *far* too bold to me and I could not do it: all I could seem to do was wonder about her, hoping he would mention her soon and ease my discomfort.

"Yes, yes... many of us are busy making what living we can." I stayed as composed and cool as I could, whilst I tried to fight the color rising in my cheeks.

"I understand you have been teaching the privileged youth of this fair town?" he inquired of me.

"Yes... and you? What do *you* do for your maintenance?"

"Well, well... I have been learning all about merchandising and such; that I may work towards owning and running my own shop some day."

I wondered when he was going to mention his wife as I said, "That would be a good business to have. I wish you *all* the best in it."

"And do *you* wish to remain a teacher for many years to come?"

"Well, it is a good living for me, for the time being. My students are good to me and I am exceedingly *grateful* for the position... but if I had my *true* wish, I would rather make a living by sketching and drawing: *that* would be very much to my liking."

"Well, you *do* have the talent for that and so I hope your dream *does* come true."

"Thank you and I hope you have a *splendid* shop some day soon as well."

He smiled in acknowledgment. I returned a smile, but it was especially reserved, by my design.

There was an awkward silence as neither one of us seemed to know quite what to say.

Winston offered his arm as he said, "I suppose you need to retire to your home? May I escort you there?"

I hesitated and then found that I must speak my mind plainly, and there was some attendant annoyance displayed in the tone of my voice, "But it would not be proper for me to accept such an offer from a *married* man and so I *must* decline, sir."

He burst forth laughing. Finally he spoke, "You thought me *married?*"

"But... you were... to be... married..."

"I suppose I was... but I *soon* thought the better of it."

"So... you are not... married, then?"

My heart *leapt* a little... with excitement. I held it back... steady.

He smiled, "No. And you? You are not married, I understand."

"No... You understand?"

"Yes. When I first came back I asked... around... about you."

"About me?"

"Yes." He smiled broadly. He looked at me with warmth and intensity.

I felt my cheeks flush hotly and I feared to smile too responsively. I took his arm so I would not have to look at him directly. We walked along towards my home.

"So you have been learning all about the intricacies of running a store, then?" I queried of him.

"Yes, and you have been learning the intricacies of educating children?"

"I suppose I have. But, it is no difficult task."

"Well, perhaps not for you. But *others* might find it difficult."

"Perhaps."

"I… I heard about your sister and I am so *terribly* sorry."

Sadness overtook my countenance but I was able to say, somewhat choking up, "Thank you."

"And your other sisters have married and moved away. I hope you are not *too* terribly lonely."

"Often I am… but I do have my brothers and the wonderful folks they live with. I also have my students… and a few friends."

"May *I* be your friend?"

I was a little taken aback and could only seem to say, "I suppose."

"You *suppose?* Is that *all* the response I can expect? I was hoping for a little more *enthusiasm!*" he teased.

"Yes. I would *like* to be friends with you." I smiled fondly.

"I have wanted to be your friend since the *first* time I saw you."

I blushed openly quite against my will. I was at least relieved that it was night and my glowing red cheeks were subdued in the relative darkness.

"I was drawn to *you* too." I feared I might have been too hasty to simply allow my first thought out to him like that, but it was said and I could not retrieve or erase it. My embarrassment was eased by the fact that we were now very near my home and it was past time for me to go in and retire for the night.

"Well, then… we are *friends*. Could I call on you tomorrow? We could enjoy an earlier evening stroll, perhaps?" he proposed.

"If the weather permits, yes, I would like that very much."

"And if the weather does not permit, is there anything else you might like to do?"

I felt flustered and knew not what to say and so made an effort to speedily excuse myself from his presence which agitated me, "We could discuss that tomorrow. It is so very late, I am so very tired and I really should retire."

"Yes… yes, of course. Tomorrow, then?"

"Yes. Tomorrow."

He kissed my hand. My heart fluttered. He smiled down at me as he still held my hand in his. My heart beat so loudly I feared he would hear it. I smiled, said a quick farewell and promptly took myself and my quivering hand inside.

Once safely inside my little home, I peeked out my window to watch him walk away. What *sensations* I was feeling! I wanted to suppress them but it was *impossible*. Oh, I liked him *very* much. I always had. But I *feared* allowing my heart out. If only I had my Victoria to share with. If only Mother could advise me.

A part of me wanted to talk to Mother Jones about Winston, but then, Mother Jones more than likely would let something slip out to somebody and the word would surely get around, and worse than all that, quite possibly back to Winston.

It was not that I considered Mother Jones a gossip, but she had many friends and she was a talkative sort. She did not always seem to see the wisdom in keeping certain things secret. While I would have loved to have been confident enough to confide in and get advice from her, I could by no means be assured that she would *not* tell her dear friends *any* information or feelings I shared with her, and then over no small space of time, I would feel like *everyone* knew my innermost feelings.

No, I must keep my feelings to myself and hope that I was wise enough to find my own advice within myself, and also from above. My heart told me to open up and forge ahead, while my mind told me to stand back and stay safe. I wondered what Mother would tell me. I was quite sure Victoria would be encouraging me, for she knew that there never was any one who stirred feelings within me like Winston did. And yet, Winston had broken my heart in some small way when he took up with that young woman, and moved away with the intention of marrying her. I could not blame him for losing interest in me for I was not encouraging him, but still I could not forget that his eyes, mind and heart had once completely left me for another.

As thoughts of Winston enticed me, I could not help but allow thoughts about Catherine's husband haunt me: thoughts of what he had just done and what it all was doing to her. Poor, poor Catherine: I kept wondering how her husband could have done what he had done and why. It was all so terribly unfair to Catherine. Oh, but I did not ever want to go through such! Give me a life alone, rather than a life with a man who could do that against me! What a deep and horrifying betrayal to have to face! And to live with!

Even as I had been encouraging Catherine to forgive her husband I wondered within myself if I could ever completely forgive a man for such a deep abomination and sinful betrayal. How long would it take me to accomplish such forgiveness? I thought that perhaps I would rather die than to have to go through that kind of pain, suffering and betrayal. I *certainly* would rather be without a man than have to live with one I could not trust nor feel safe with and loved by. How could one feel beloved entirely if one's man had been with another: if he had loved another even after promising himself faithful to one?

As I thought about my feelings for Winston and his apparent interest in and feelings for me, I wondered how deep his love for me could ever be. Perhaps it was immature and unwise of me to compare, but I could not help but think of that *other* young woman, and how Winston's attentions were for her, even after they had been for me. I thought of how quickly he had seemed to forget me.

I could imagine Victoria advising me, that it was pure folly in me to blame Winston for moving beyond me to that young lady, because I had not let Winston know a fraction of my true feelings for him. It *was* true that I had not *allowed* myself to consider Winston and even more, I had not allowed him to suspect how much I regarded and was attracted to him. I supposed that it was no small wonder that he had given up on me and pursued that other young lady. Indeed, as I recalled it, it was so much more her pursuing him, and of course it would have been easy for him to simply accept the attentions that came his way from her. I compared that to me: I was decidedly and purposefully cool and distant. I was no easy fish to catch. He *surely* thought me disinterested based on my behavior towards him.

And yet, I kept asking myself, if Winston's love for me was true or if he was *meant* to be mine, how could he have faltered and forgotten me? *I* had not truly thought about *any* other than him, but he had nearly *married* her. *That* fact disturbed me greatly. I could not seem to get *her* out of my mind.

Early the next evening when Winston came to call, I was on my guard. Truly, my behavior was quite guarded. I wondered if he noticed my slight coolness and reserve towards him as we walked and conversed. I supposed it was true that I had always been guarded with Winston and all other gentlemen. I had never been quick to allow my attractions to reveal themselves. I had always preferred to keep my heart *safely* tucked far away from all men, deep within me so that no man would know the inclinations and intimacies of my heart. I fancied that a heart that could *not* be reached could not be *broken*.

But then, I knew Mother and Victoria would both tell me that unless you share your heart, you can never know the joys of love; for how can a man love you and embrace your heart if he is never allowed to find it? I had known love of family and friends, but I had never truly permitted myself to know love *for* a man or to invite love *from* a man. I believed that perhaps I had always been somewhat afraid to fall in love, but now, knowing Catherine's plight, I feared love more deeply than I ever could have imagined doing before. I knew what Catherine's love for a man had brought her. Sadly, she now knew much misery.

Even while Winston's attentions and expressions seemed to be drawing me and my heart out, my misgivings and doubts were surely pulling me back to defend my heart. I was in a state of confusion to be sure. Yes, I liked Winston very much, but I could not forget my fears.

As we talked and walked along, and my memories of his former young lady were haunting me, I decided to make a bold move and in a way confront him about her, "Forgive me for so saying, but, it has been so very long since I thought you married that I find it quite difficult to see you as otherwise."

"Oh, please put that from your mind. That irrational inclination is so much in my past that it embarrasses me for you to remind me of it."

"I am sorry, but I cannot forget it as yet. Pray, tell me, how long after you left did you decide *not* to marry her?"

"Almost right away: I ended it very soon afterwards."

"So all this time I have thought you married; you have been the single man."

He struck me with his sudden glance, "Very much the single man."

Composing myself again, "And no other young lady pursued you."

"Ah, yes. You have struck the precise truth of the matter. She did pursue me, it is true. And I was ignorant enough to fall to flattery. I am thoroughly ashamed of myself."

"So no other lady..."

"No other lady."

"But in all this time, a man like you... and no other lady..."

"A man like *me?*"

I felt my face redden as his eyes pierced through into mine. I faltered and then was able to recover somewhat, "Well, I simply supposed perhaps there might have been *other* young ladies interested in you, or *you* in them."

He appeared to be trying to read my thoughts and then finally spoke, "Oh, I suppose there were *some* ladies interested in me, but none interested *me* enough to pay them much attention."

I did not quite know what to say to him in response and fortunately for me, he had more to say...

"But then, I was *very* busy, having set my mind on finding a business to practice throughout life. I thought that perhaps I should pursue a livelihood before pursuing a bride."

"That is very wise, I think."

"I hope so. And you? I would think many young men have pursued you?"

"Me?"

"Yes, you!"

"Well..."

"Oh, I am sure there have been many young men who have wanted to pay their attentions to you."

"Well... I..."

"And knowing you a *little* as I do, I am sure they were rebuffed and had their hearts broken."

"*No!*"

"Well... I have heard about town that there have been many young men who sought your attention only to be ignored by you. Yes, there have been broken hearts because of you." Winston said with a mischievous look.

"No indeed!"

"Truly! The word among the young men in town is that you are unreachable. They are all afraid of you."

"Afraid? Of me? But why...I..."

"You are beautiful, talented and intelligent. Most men would feel they could not hope to measure up to the kind of man that could charm the likes of *you* into marriage."

It all seemed incredulous to me. I had to protest, "You must be mistaken or inquiring after someone else!"

"You will not accept my compliment relative to your good qualities?" Winston almost winked.

"No... well... yes... thank you, I am honored, but..." I had to smile.

"But you cannot believe these young men feel beneath your standards."

"I am only reserved, that is all."

"Only *reserved?*"

"Mostly."

"Ah! It is more than reserve then, I think! Explain yourself, madam!" he was surely teasing as there was a twinkle in his eye.

"I do not know that I can fully explain beyond the fact that I am mostly, just *simply*, reserved."

"Can you *try* to explain?" he smiled with an assuring air.

"Well, perhaps it could suffice for me to simply say that I am not *inclined* to throw myself headlong towards love."

"Ah, well... I cannot argue with *that* attitude. Indeed I admire it." He smiled broadly.

"I tend to feel that falling in love is a serious business and should not be taken lightly."

"I do agree there as well. And to fall is to be hurt, perhaps?"

I felt he could see through me, "Well, oft times to fall, is to be hurt."

"And you do not wish to be hurt?"

"Well, of course I don't, but, but perhaps it is *more* that I want to put my energies in the right place."

"A wise practice, to be sure."

"It just seems to me that there is no point in wasting one's time chasing after the wrong things."

"Or chasing after the wrong men." He said, surely teasingly.

"Well, yes." I smiled and then clarified, "But it is not in my nature to *chase* after *any* man anyway."

"*That* is clear."

I desperately wanted to change the subject and so did my best, "So where do you want to open a shop?"

Winston hesitated a little, smiled broadly and then, "Hmm... well, I suppose it does not matter *where* so much, except that a growing co mmunity that is in need of a nice little shop, will do."

"Yes, true, and when do you think you will be ready to begin this venture?"

"Well, I have been learning the trade and saving my money, and soon I will be ready to begin, I think."

"And so you have simply to decide *where* to begin."

"Yes."

"I am sure you will do wonderfully at it. I would think having one's own shop could be quite delightful. It would be a good steady business with many advantages."

"And do you think you might not mind that kind of business? Could you *ever* leave your students to help run a shop?" he queried, in surprising seriousness.

"Well, teaching chose *me*: I did not choose *it*. I would love to have or work in a shop. It would be a perfectly charming livelihood, I would think."

Winston held my arm closer to him and I suddenly realized that his question meant more than just about business and shops. I blushed overtly.

Once again I desired a change of conversation. I looked around at the buildings, the people, the horses, hoping to find something to speak of and all I could find to say was, "I miss my horses."

"You miss your *horses*?!" He chuckled looking somewhat bewildered.

"*Yes*! I miss my horses!" I answered, a little irked at his chuckle.

"Oh, forgive me for laughing just then, but your thoughts of missing your horses were unexpected. My mind was… on us… running a shop together."

Oh, dear, but I did not want to *talk* about running a shop together just now! Such serious and intimate conversation frightened me and I felt I *must* avoid it! I determined to stay focused on my horses, "Well, seeing that palomino back there reminded me of my favorite horses back on my father's farm. I have not seen them in so long, and I do miss them terribly."

"I am so sorry you miss your favorite horses. I can certainly relate to missing a good horse. I have lost a few in my life."

For the rest of our evening together, thankfully I *successfully* managed to steer and keep our conversation towards more superficial matters, and we talked no more of a shop, working in it together or anything like unto it.

When we said our goodbyes, Winston pressed me for another walk or other such meeting within the next days and I feared to comply, and so made excuses that I was too busy with this or that. He then told me he was to leave town for a while and so would see me upon his return. At first I was relieved that I would not have to avoid him, and his talk of shops and running them with me, but then I felt vexed at myself for pushing him away and not accepting another engagement with him before he went away.

Oh, but I was a tangled mess. I could not stop thinking about Winston and our conversations; but more especially about what I believed to be his overtly obvious hints towards marriage, and yet I did not want to think of him. I was afraid of him: of loving him, of marrying him. I did not want to fall in love: to take a chance of getting hurt or of being betrayed. I feared being vulnerable. I did not want to give my heart to him. But, I did feel love for him: at least a strong attraction and sincere fondness. I also wished I had not pushed him away again, as before. Indeed, I was *so* troubled that I spent much time and many nights, in tears of confusion and frustration.

30
Early 1849

Catherine came back to me many times. My shoulder was hers to cry upon, my ears hers to confide in, while my hands were there to hold hers and to stroke her back. I encircled my arms around her in efforts to comfort and console her. I also did my utmost to find words that would *advise* her best, and *comfort* her most: to help relieve her suffering and calm her nerves, for she was often hysterical with grief.

As much of my time in many days and weeks were spent soothing Catherine in her heartache, I could not help but think of myself and my apprehensiveness and anxiousness about considering marriage with Winston, *or* anyone for that matter. Sometimes I thought myself silly in the way my mind would run away with imaginings about the possible pains of marriage, and would then stop to think of many good marriages I had known. I told myself that it was just as possible for me to make a good marriage as it was to fall into a bad one, and I supposed that it was not just the choice of a partner in marriage that could make all the difference, but the work afterwards that mattered greatly as well, if not more so.

As a young girl, I tended to think that you only needed to find a man who loved you, whom you also loved. But some years had taught me, I thought, that there were many kinds and levels of love, and just to fall in love was truly not enough. Had not Father fallen in love with Mildred? I could not fathom within myself that Mildred actually loved Father, but it was likely that she did, in her own way. Ethan had love with his wife and yet theirs was not the kind of marriage that I would ever desire. It also haunted me somewhat that Ethan had fallen in love again and married relatively soon after Victoria had died. What kind of love could he have had for Victoria to have forgotten her so completely? Oh, how *inconstant* can men be! I felt some despair for Victoria's sake. Catherine and her husband surely loved each other and even so, although a good man in many respects, he had fallen with another and Catherine was paying a severe price for his egregious sin. I knew not what he was paying for his own sin, but I did see a part of Catherine's suffering for her husband's recklessness.

No, I decided marriage was a tricky business. Love a dangerous affair. Choosing a mate was surely a life-altering decision that should be taken with the utmost seriousness, and painstakingly cautious and measured stages; and even if one *did* choose a perfect partner, that partner could always *choose* to stray from the correct path or might change into something *less* perfect. Indeed, we all changed through time and I surmised that it took constant vigilance to change oneself for the better as time progressed in this life. How could I be sure to choose a man who would choose to change for the better?! Climbing takes effort whilst falling is effortless, though to fall would mean injury. I did not want to attach myself to a man who might fall, for I did not welcome wounds.

Sometimes I thought I would rather never marry. But, then, I also could imagine myself years and years down the road of life: alone, a spinster, childless, lonely and wondering what might have been, if I had been brave enough to forge into marriage with a man. I almost wondered if choosing to remain single *or* saying yes to being married were almost choices between the lesser of two evils. If only Mother could hear me thinking! What a scolding she would have given me! I thought that even though Father had as much as forgotten her, that she would still defend her choice to marry and have children, for she had enjoyed much love, affection and happiness in that life; and she had learned much. Those years of being a wife and mother had taught her much wisdom. I did not know what her future in Heaven held, with Father particularly, but I was sure she had earned a place in Heaven as beloved mother to her children forevermore, and those relationships would bring her joy throughout eternity.

As time passed since Winston had gone away again, and I did not receive any letter from him, I thought less and less about marriage for me. I focused once again on my students and on my brothers: on being a good teacher and sister to them. I continued to occasionally correspond with Charlotte and Elizabeth, and also wrote letters to Clara and Anna, holding my notes for them until they settled in a place I could securely send all my letters to, all the while wondering how they were doing on their journey towards the Oregon Country. I prayed for them daily, indeed I prayed for all my sisters and also for my brothers. From time to time my thoughts would settle on our long lost brother Benjamin, wondering where he might be and how he was growing up, and also upon our half sister Lena, wondering if she would ever be a part of the rest of us, despite her mother. Yes, I hoped and prayed for all the best things for all my brothers and sisters.

Soon, Mother Jones was all abuzz with news. Her sons were coming *home*! They had closed up business and were bringing their wives home. I never saw a woman so beside herself with delight, and all her energies were spent in preparations for the joyful event. When my sisters and their husbands arrived, there was much jubilation. Mother Jones was floating, or indeed, almost flying with euphoria.

The day following the grand arrival, Mother Jones was devastated to discover that her sons planned to strike for California Country as soon as they could possibly do so. Rumors of gold on that western coast had recently begun to reach most of us, and indeed Charlotte and Anna's husbands were struck with the gold *fever* that *many* were being affected by. They had sold their business and were planning to earn a lifetime's worth of riches in a relatively short time, whilst their wives stayed on the farm with their parents. Mother Jones thought the idea *pure* folly and certainly said so.

In fact, Mother Jones *fervently* tried to convince her sons to entirely forget the idea of traveling all the way out to California territory in search of gold. She was very worried at the thoughts of such a scheme, but her sons were convinced that the trials would be worth the riches that they would bring home with them in a year or so. Surprisingly to me, Charlotte and Elizabeth were quite supportive of their husbands, believing that all would turn out very well, and they were happy to remain on the Jones' farm, while they waited for their husbands to hunt and then bring home the riches that they felt awaited them.

Father Jones was somewhat open-minded about his sons' plan, and chose to support them in it since they seemed so determined to do it. I supposed that men are always more inclined for adventure and that any hunting trip might tend to excite their natures, whereas women, especially mothers, always tend to worry more and resist such things. I truly felt for Mother Jones as she tried to dissuade her sons from planning and preparing for their California campaign. Of course I did not interfere nor intervene, but I could not help but silently tending towards *agreeing* with Mother Jones that perhaps her sons' energies and time might be better spent here or elsewhere nearer, rather than going off to a far off land in search of gold.

The pleadings of a mother were to no avail, and Joseph and Jacob set off for California in the early springtime. I understood that they were to join up with and travel partially along the Oregon trail on their way to the land of gold and my thoughts were suddenly with Clara and Anna: wondering how their travels were going, particularly because their destination was just somewhat north of where gold had recently been discovered. I wondered if perhaps they and their husbands would change their destination plans, and also strike for gold after hearing news or word of it. My only comfort in the entire goings on was that Charlotte and Elizabeth were to stay here. Within myself, I was *very* relieved that they were not going to California with their husbands. I was glad I would not have to worry about them, but truly felt deeply and sympathetically for poor Mother Jones, who I knew would worry greatly over her sons in their absence. The frontier was not assuredly safe.

I was delighted to have Charlotte and Elizabeth near me, especially knowing that they would be here for quite some time. I hoped that they would be of comfort to Mother Jones especially and also thought it nice that they would be around Bertram, Edward and Colin, on a daily basis. Having two more sisters near would be so especially good for my brothers.

As time passed, I was able to visit with Charlotte and Elizabeth a great deal, as well as spend much time together with our brothers. If not for Mother Jones' distress, we *would* have enjoyed many perfect moments.

Indeed, Mother Jones was beside herself with worry awaiting the first word from her sons. She seemed to imagine all the worst of what could happen to Joseph and Jacob and could expound at *length* regarding such. It was surely true that there were many real dangers and possible perils along the way. They would pass through plenty of Indian country and while many were peaceable, many were hostile. There would be all manner of weather to contend with as well as wild animals to worry about, and then there was always the need for shelter, food and, more especially, water. As much as I worried over my sisters who were on that trail, I reflected that I would quite unquestionably worry *more* if I were their mother, and so could understand and have compassion for Mother Jones and her travails relative to her sons and their trek.

Joseph and Jacob were at least well armed: they knew how to protect themselves in case of attack, they possessed survival skills and they were also well armed with money and so could afford to pay for certain needs along the way. I tried to remind Mother Jones of such positive details. It was for lack of money that I worried most about Clara and Anna; although they had said that they were well enough equipped and funded when they left. I *hoped* so. I *certainly* hoped so. I also *prayed* a great deal that all would be well with them. I knew that Clara and Anna's husbands were resourceful and capable, as the Jones brothers were; so that fact eased my worries a great deal. Still, I fervently and continually prayed that all would go well for all of them. What more *could* I do? Worry was of no comfort (indeed: quite the opposite) nor could worrying offer any help in the matter. Prayer was *truly* my only solace. I had long since learned this remedy for worry.

Charlotte and Elizabeth seemed quite calm considering all things, and were taking the loss of their husbands very well. They entertained themselves with reading, visiting, playing piano and singing. They oft came to town to shop a little and to visit with me. They loved catching up on all the events and people of the town and surrounding area. They seemed full of confidence that their husbands would come home in the next year, laden with gold and prepared to offer them lives filled with *all* the comforts and excitements great riches can buy. They continually assured their mother-in-law that all would be very well, but despite their reassurances, Mother Jones continually worried and fretted about her sons. Even as Charlotte and Elizabeth spent their time and energies enjoying themselves, as they waited for their husbands' triumphant returns, Mother Jones seemed to fret more and more, day by day. Indeed, the dear woman continued to worry herself sick, and ended up spending much of her time in bed, trying to recover.

As Mother Jones spent more of her time *truly* sick from worry and thus confined to her bed a great deal, Charlotte and Elizabeth took over much of the kitchen and household work, providing meals and most all else for our brothers and Father Jones. I went out to the Jones farm as often as I could to be of help, and to hopefully offer some comfort and encouragement to Mother Jones while there.

As I was trying to be of assistance at the Jones farm whenever possible, problems at the school began to arise. In actual fact, the problem lay with one of my new students: a dreadfully spoiled girl. An exceedingly wealthy family had moved into town and the parents of this one girl soon swayed much influence over many who had great means, and so they began to have a hold on the school where I held my increasingly tentative position. I cannot explain what went wrong between this girl and me, but perhaps it was just simply some sort of conflict of personality. More precisely, there was also certainly a conflict of *character*. I often caught this girl cheating or lying, and my attempts to speak with her or her parents about the need for character building only ended in their continual attacks against me. Soon, I was targeted for termination by these wealthy folks. I could see that my dismissal was imminent. The likelihood that I would soon be relieved of my livelihood seemed very clear to me.

I roused enough courage to speak with Mother Jones about my troubles, and although I knew she desired to get out and speak with all her friends on my behalf in order to gather influential forces to my side, she had only the energy to offer a room for me there in her home. I was glad to have it. I did not relish the idea of fighting against people of money and influence, nor of dealing with a troubled young lady further, and so tendered my resignation and moved onto the Jones farm. The change was a welcome one for me. I was glad to be near Charlotte, Elizabeth and my brothers. I was happy to help out with cleaning and cooking and to be there to support my dear old friend who had been as much a mother to me as any woman beyond my own mother ever *could* be.

With Mother Jones mostly confined to her room, in time, I became as mother to all: becoming the prime cook and caretaker of all household things. Charlotte and Elizabeth seemed quite content to hand most things off to me, and I supposed it seemed somewhat a natural pattern for us all to fall into: I being the oldest sister. I confess that somewhere deep down inside me, I *did* resent the fact that my sisters so easily shirked so many duties to fall upon me, *alone*. I did not know why Charlotte and Elizabeth seemed so content to rest and relax so thoroughly, as I worked constantly. Perhaps they felt they had earned a respite.

Maybe Charlotte and Elizabeth felt that I should earn my keep more than they, since I did not truly belong to the Jones family as they did. My sisters also had formerly become accustomed to somewhat royal treatment in their life away. Their husbands had made sure that they wanted for nothing and little work had ever been required of them. They had become as well accustomed to idly enjoying themselves as I was to working hard: and so, days and weeks went by with my working and serving in the Jones home whilst my sisters lived as if vacationing. I was still glad to be there, however. I was only too happy to be able to serve Father and Mother

Jones as well as my brothers if not my indolent and spoiled sisters quite so much.

Mother Jones began to concern me greatly in that she did not seem to improve in health: indeed her health seemed declining as her worries over her sons consumed her. I tried to encourage her to turn her worries towards prayer, but she could not seem to master the monster of fretting that nearly continually engulfed her. She was almost continually overcome by anxiety. Father Jones tried his best to help her as well, of course, but our concerns for her seemed to no avail, as her concerns for her sons far outweighed everything else in her mind.

The doctor was certainly called in enough times by Father Jones, but the good doctor could only recommend that which we were *already* doing. The only medicine that seemed a very necessary thing was for Mother Jones to hear from her sons and to be assured that they were well. *Finally*, that good medicine came. All was proceeding as planned: Joseph and Jacob were *well* and *quite* well on their way to the land of promised gold. This morsel of good news seemed to buoy Mother Jones' spirits up tremendously, and we were all overjoyed to see her in her kitchen once more. Her laughter filled the house again. What joy to finally see her up and around, and quite herself!

For a goodly length of time, Mother Jones settled into her old healthy and happy ways, but gradually, as no second letter arrived from her sons, she began to let her worries overtake her, and her concerns for her sons took precedence once more as her health took the blows because of her worries. Again she took to her room and her bed; again I became her primary nursemaid as I took over the running of her kitchen and whole household.

One day as I helped her to a little meal as she sat in her bed, she quite suddenly took a firm hold of one of my hands, looked deep into my eyes as if trying to see into my very soul and said, "My dear, dear Fionna. *Thank* you so much for coming to live with us."

"*No*, Mother Jones. Thank *you* for inviting me here... for sharing your home with me."

"No. It is such a *great* blessing to me that you needed to leave the school and come here. What would I do *without* you? What would I have *done*? You have been Heaven sent directly to me. You are as if my *own* daughter... indeed I think of you as the daughter I never had. I could *not* love you more, if you were my very own daughter."

"And you are the mother I *lost*. I love *you* as I love *her*."

Tears welled up in both our eyes. We both did our best to compose ourselves. We both swallowed hard several times. Then I just simply smiled and patted her hand as it held mine. She continued with her tender thoughts, "I do not want to say anything against your sisters... against my daughter-in-laws... but as much as I love them and think them good for my sons, they *cannot* comfort me as you can."

I could not speak. I could not return her stare into my soul. I looked down. I blinked a few tears away. She had more to say from her heart, "Oh, Fionna... if only I had another son for *you*. I *so* want to see you married and happy. You *deserve* so much. You *give* so much. You work so hard and ask so little of anyone. You have faced some very hard things in your life thus far and you have handled them *so* exceptionally well. You are an angel: a very living angel from Heaven sent to me to comfort and encourage me."

I looked down again, tears streaming down my face. Oh, but her kind words comforted me. Her tender speech washed away *so* much grief for me. It was so *good* to feel appreciated and loved. I felt completely welcome in her home and family. I felt as if I truly *was* her very daughter.

As I choked back my tears I tried to answer her, "And you have been an angel to me. You have blessed my life so very much. I am sure you do not know *how* much I have appreciated all you have done and all that you continue to do for me... and for my brothers and sisters."

For a small while we sat silently together, hearts as if communing without words. I knew I could not speak for fear of crying openly and I sensed it was the same for dear Mother Jones, and so we both sat quietly, hands holding and patting each others', tears being swallowed, feelings being held back and thoughts being hushed.

Soon she began lamenting about her sons and so I held her as she sobbed.

Even as Father and Mother Jones did all they could to make me feel that I belonged in their home and family, somehow Charlotte and Elizabeth made me feel that I could only earn my place of belonging there by continually laboring. My sisters seemed almost as strangers to me. They did not treat me much as a sister would expect to be treated. It almost seemed that no matter how hard I worked and how much I did to serve everyone, including and especially them, it was never enough to make up for the fact that I was living there *free* as they seemed to deem it. They felt entirely *entitled*, but I was to *serve*, to deserve to be there. Mother and Father Jones were not really privy to these little subtleties of my sisters, for Father Jones was almost always out working and Mother Jones almost always in her room.

I gave up asking Charlotte and Elizabeth to do the occasional chore to help out as they openly resented my doing so, the few times that I had. They obviously thought themselves much more guests rather than contributing members of a family, and all the while they made it clear that I must work to pay my way. They seemed to think that they had better things to do than to work in the kitchen, or in and around the house. I thought it unkind that they did not feel compelled to serve Mother Jones in any way, preferring to leave all that to me. They became pure ladies of pleasure when home, but seemed to prefer to be gone shopping or visiting in and around town. I tried not to let my sisters, or the situation because of their attitudes and behavior, cause me discomfort. I confess I felt somehow relieved when they were gone, but I did not let myself focus my attentions on their idleness and condescension towards me when they were home: instead I put my energies into working and serving.

In fact, when Charlotte and Elizabeth would go out, it was a time for me to relax a little. Much of my relaxing actually entailed visiting Mother Jones and tending to some of her needs; but partially due to *her* insistence, I did spend some time reading in my room and also began drawing again during my time *off*: or more precisely, the times when my *sisters* were off and gone. And since they seemed to prefer to be gone, I began to be able to enjoy some generous leisure time myself. I worked exceptionally and visibly hard when they were there at home, but when they would go out, I would take that opportunity to focus on some of my own needs that I knew I surely needed and deserved to take care of.

My brothers were also my focus. I did all I could to praise, encourage and love them in order to add to all that Father and Mother Jones had done for them.

***

A letter from Anna arrived. It was short but she communicated that she, Clara and their husbands were making their way along the trail and that they were doing quite well despite all the challenges. They had been detained from time to time, due to lack of funds and supplies, and their husbands had worked to further fortify them on their journey. Despite these delays, Oregon Country was imminent for them.

Anna's good news from the trail towards Oregon Territory lifted Mother Jones' spirits a great deal and she was soon working in her kitchen again. While I insisted on helping her, she insisted that I take some time to pursue my talents and pushed me towards my pencils and papers. I very much enjoyed the leisure time to draw and sketch, and all the while Charlotte and Elizabeth seemed to look the other way as I became almost as much a guest as they had made themselves for so long. It was wonderfully good to have Mother Jones looking out for me and showing my sisters that I was as much a welcome guest as they were. Some time passed, generally quite happily for all of us. Days were filled with various sorts of work and evenings were filled with music, chatter and laughter.

Catherine took occasion to come out to see me fairly often as she was *still* in need of my ears for her lamentations, shoulders for her tears and comforting hand to console her. She did not feel free to let her tears flow anywhere in the house for fear of being heard by others, but we did take rides in her carriage, and where we found secluded places she was then unencumbered and could speak and cry freely. From what she told me, her husband was on his best behavior and was truly trying to do all he could to heal the damage he had done against her and their union, that sin which he had committed that had shattered the sanctity of their bond, but despite all his noble and gentle efforts, her heart still ached and seemed still quite broken yet. I did my very best to comfort and advise her, and yet I felt ill qualified to do the *latter* as I was still an unmarried woman. What did *I* know of nuptial love and what it took to bind a man and woman in holy matrimony?

31
On Horses and Beyond

I rarely went to town. I truly enjoyed the quiet calm of the farm. It was actually a time of respite for me and thanks much to Mother Jones; I was spending much of my days sketching. I usually ended up where horses were at rest, eating, playing or doing other interesting things horses do, that gave me ample scenes to draw from. As always, I could sit for hours gazing at, studying, talking to, petting or drawing horses. Their structure always was so pleasing to me. Their musculature, their motions, their twitching ears and tails, their sleek coats and flowing manes; all called attention to my senses, while their large eyes drew me into their spirits.

Though I knew that any horse had the power to kill me, I always seemed to feel that they were my friends and I always tended to love them. Whether walking near or riding on them, I tended to feel at peace around horses. What magnificent creatures!

Sometimes, the sight of a horse made time stand still for me. Suddenly I was transported to the earlier days of my youth when it was pure joy simply just to climb up and sit upon a still horse. I remembered in days gone by, long ago, my enticing horses to a fence with some sort of treat so that I could climb onto their backs just to sit awhile. It did not matter to me if they were content to stand by the fence or to walk to a nearby spot to graze, as long as I was up sitting on them. I would often lay my face upon their necks and drink in their fragrance, petting and stroking them with my hands. I would speak to them and watch their ears take turns twitching back to hear me. I oft wondered if they could perhaps understand me: indeed I imagined that they could and that they were my dear loyal friends. Now, upon looking back, I supposed that they were just gauging the sound of my voice to judge whether my voice sounded friend or foe, but still, to be near a horse is and always was a way to find calm for me.

Such things of beauty are horses. While I always had my favorites, there was never a horse I did not think beautiful. Their form, their colors: it is all beauty to me. Yes, their tempers and personalities surely varied and there was many a horse I would never want to climb upon for fear of being thrown off, but I could still admire the beauty of even a horse I did not appreciate the temper of.

Thus, many days passed with me out with the horses that were not at work, enjoying their company, gazing at their beauty and drawing all that I could. Father and Mother Jones seemed to marvel at my sketches and at my talents in producing them. I shyly thanked them for their compliments and offered them as many sketches as seemed their favorites: the walls of their home soon seemed crowded with many of my drawings.

From time to time, it seemed that I could detect *some* jealous feelings from Charlotte and Elizabeth, that I would be singled out and adored by their parent-in-laws in such a way. I did my best to divert focus on me to my sisters' talents by begging them to play the piano and sing as often as possible. I would join in sometimes, but mostly, I encouraged them to display their abilities as I watched and applauded them encouragingly. The nightly entertainment seemed a welcome rest and diversion for both Mother and Father Jones.

Alas, but, for me to relate to and adore horses seemed far more easily accomplished than to be truly fond of my sisters oft times; and it was undeniably because of their attitudes and behaviors in general and more particularly towards me. Horses did not think and behave so.

Our brothers did not always join in with what they felt was more a tedium of evening society, and would find other things to do inside. More often they were outside, to amuse themselves during their evening rest hours when they were not obliged to work in the fields or otherwise.

Inside, Bertram would lead Edward and Colin in games with cards and such at the kitchen table. Outside, they would wrestle or play all manner of who knows what: the kinds of things boys and young men are want to do that many of us females never understand. I was so glad that they had each other, for I feared I could not offer them what they each needed beyond an older sister's praises, encouragements, hugs, foods, love and other such motherly things. I knew I would always be eternally grateful to Father and Mother Jones for their large part in parenting my brothers. Of course I also had much to thank them for, just for me… and also for my sisters.

***

One day, Catherine came out to see me again. I thought our time would be spent as it had so many times in the recent past; with me consoling and comforting her in her sorrows. However, as we drove away from the farm in her carriage, she surprised me greatly with a very curious announcement, "He's *back*!"

"Who's back?" I could not imagine who she might be referring to.

"Winston! And he's been *asking* about you!" she proclaimed with a gleeful grin.

This puzzled me greatly as I had not spoken of Winston to Catherine. Indeed, I thought my attraction and interest in him mostly my own secret, but somehow, it seemed, the secret might be partly out: from who or how I could not guess. I decided to inquire cautiously, "Indeed? Asking about me? And how do *you* know him, pray tell? I did not know that you knew him."

"Oh, please do *not* be so coy! The whole town knows you like each other! There is much talk of you and him. Everyone thinks he should hurry up and *ask* you!"

"*Ask* me? Ask me *what*?"

"Oh, but you can be so *exceedingly* tiresome sometimes! It is high time that he should ask you to *marry* him, of course!"

"Catherine... please tell me *who* is saying such things about me. I cannot imagine anyone in town who would..."

"Oh, Fionna! I know you think it a very great secret, but, there are *many* who love and care about you, who are only too delighted to pick up the hints from Winston as he *inquires* about you and why you are no longer living in town."

"Hints? What hints, pray, please *do* tell me?"

"Well, I just know that it is quite obvious that Winston has had his eyes and heart set on you for a very long time and now that he is back and asking all about you... well... everyone knows he will ask you."

My face felt terribly hot and I was sure that it must have turned crimson. I did not know what to say. I was quite aghast, really. My mouth *must* have been gaping open.

Catherine overlooked my blushing and ignored my silence, happily continuing, "It is true that I do not in fact know him as we have never been introduced, but I have friends in town who have pointed him out to me: oh, he is so *very* tall and handsome! You are *so* lucky! All my friends have told me the history of how he was after you and how you jilted him, and then another young women stole him away and he moved away to marry her but then..."

"I *jilted* him?!"

"Yes. You kept putting him off and pushing him away until he was sure that you did *not* love him like he loved *you*... so he took up with that *other* young lady because she was so *completely* taken with him and was throwing herself at him..."

"Who *told* you all this?"

"Oh, *everyone* knows."

I was speechless. How could all this be buzzing around about me without me knowing any of it? I felt... betrayed... somehow. I wondered aloud, "So, how much has Winston been *saying* of these things? Is it *him* who has spread these rumors and stories about me and him?"

"Oh, no, no... I believe he has *actually* said very little, but you know how people talk, and put things they see and hear together."

"But this is *incredible* to me. How could so many people be so busy buzzing about me like this?"

"Oh, what does that all matter?! He wants to *marry* you!"

Catherine was reveling in the romantic possibilities for me. It was at least good to see her grief and sorrows subdued well beneath her happy thoughts of Winston asking me to marry him. Oh, I did not like that the whole town was talking of me and Winston wanting to marry me! It was bad enough that I did not know what to think about the possible question, but to have an *audience* while I might be thinking it over was *ghastly*!

Catherine interrupted my thoughts and silence with, "And you will say yes. Will you not?"

"I don't know."

"You don't *know*?!"

"I am not *sure*."

"What do you mean?! Did you know that he has saved quite a heap of money? He means to set up a shop in town... or wherever you want to move to... I would imagine... from what he's been saying!"

"No... yes... What has he been *saying*?"

"Oh, very little, but enough that people can begin to see a clear picture of his plans. But I cannot believe you are not sure what you will say when he asks you. You really *must* say yes. Won't you just say *yes*?"

"Well, first, we don't know that he will *truly* ask me and secondly, I... I... would have to *think* about it."

"What is there to *think* about? A handsome and good man with money and ambition wants to marry *you*. And you have *never* really looked at anyone else since he went away the first time, so it is *obvious* you love him. You *must* say yes. You *simply* must."

"I have never looked at anyone else? Who told you that?"

"Oh, everyone knows. I have heard it from a few people. Don't think your attraction to him such a secret. It never really *has* been. I am *quite* sure."

My mouth fell wide open. My jaw dropped.

Oh, to be a horse, I thought. Surely *they* do not have such worries and cares. Horses do not chatter around, about each other. Horses do not spread rumors, and delight in uncovering secrets of strangers and friends alike. Horses could likely hide a private attraction without being uncovered.

In self-defense I began a protest, "I have considered him a friend and..."

"Yes, yes. You are a friend: his friend, but do you *deny* that you are attracted to him and always have been?"

"Of course he attracts me. Who would *not* be attracted to him?"

"Exactly!"

"But to be attracted and to be friends, does not necessarily mean marriage must follow."

"Why not? Well, maybe if he were terribly poor or lazy, or a bad man in some way, but he is a good man, and he can make you a comfortable home and offer you a secure life. Why would you dare say no to *all* that? *How* could you say no to him?"

"I do not know that I *would* say no, but..."

"But!? Oh, Fionna! How *long* do you think you would have to wait for a *better* man to come along and fall in love with you? Do you *think* you could ever receive a better offer? I do not think you would ever get a better chance than *this* one. You are *not* going to get younger, you know."

"And so you think me almost an old maid then?"

"Not *yet*, but... well..."

"I am not *desperate* to marry."

She sighed, "Well, *that* is obvious... but... you cannot wait until you are a spinster to decide you want to marry... finally... for then it will be too late for you. You are very lucky Winston wants you. Don't you *see* that?"

"Yes... I am sure Winston is the best I could hope to marry... if I want to marry... but..."

"Fionna, I do *not* understand you. Do you think you would have a better life, living it out alone... teaching the children of others...

growing old alone... fending for yourself... trying to survive in this world... *alone?*"

"I suppose not, but..."

"Of *course* not! Winston is the best chance at a happy life you will *ever* have and when he offers his hand, you *must* say yes!"

"But I can be happy *alone*. I do not know if I need a *man* to be happy."

"How happy can you be alone? There is *more* happiness in *marriage*."

Without thinking I challenged, "But how happy are you in *your* marriage?" I regretted my words instantly. Her countenance fell markedly and immediately. Catherine looked away and tears began to well up in her eyes.

I swiftly tried to begin to repair the hurt I knew that I had caused, "I am so sorry, Catherine. I did not mean that. It is simply that I am *afraid* of marriage. I am afraid of being betrayed and being hurt like *you* have been and I..."

She turned at me fiercely, her tears flowing freely down her cheeks, "So my wayward husband and my pains *because* of him are the reason you may *never* marry?!"

"No... well... I admit knowing how you have suffered plays a *part* in my thoughts against marriage but..."

"Well, not all marriages are *tainted* by sin like mine!" she said sharply and looked away.

"Catherine... I have *many* reasons for fearing marriage... many *other* bad examples... I..."

Still looking away, tears still flowing, Catherine cut in, "Well, I am sorry my horrid marriage is such a bad example to you."

"Catherine... I... I have seen many follies in *many* marriages and... it is me... it is just simply my own fears of being hurt... of being unhappy... of not being loved completely... Please do not take what I said so terribly hard. Do not take it to heart. *Forget* what I said. I am *so* horribly sorry. I should have *never* said..."

"I can *not* forget what you said. You don't think I'll ever really be happy in my marriage. Well, I'm happier than *you* will be as a lonely old *spinster*!"

Truly, I had become an old mare: easier among horses than with people and even dear old friends. I could not seem to mend the sudden breach between Catherine and me.

And with such a far from charming closing comment as she had just made, Catherine was up in her carriage and riding away, leaving me on a wayward roadside and so I began my long walk home. As I trod along, I mulled over our conversation, or our argument as it was, to be much more precise. I was grieved that Catherine would take my words and my fears so hard unto herself and her marriage: that she would feel so angry at me for what I had said. I did intensely regret my mention of her sorrows within marriage because of her husband's folly, but it *was* innocently done. I had meant no harm. I was somewhat astounded at her reaction. I was shaken. I kept wondering what I could have said to smooth it over. I hoped that in time I could heal the breach. I kept wishing I had never revealed my feelings about fearing marriage relative to the pains she had suffered in her marriage.

32
Questions of Marriage

Deep in concerned thought, I was nearly oblivious to the sounds of a horse cantering up behind me until it was very near, and I finally instinctively turned around to see who it was. My face must have turned ghostly white with the shock I felt at seeing Winston before me.

"I am sorry to have startled you!" he proclaimed from high above me upon his saddle.

Oh my, but he looked so very much taller than usual up there on his handsome horse. I was sure my countenance radiated as I enjoyed the sight of him on that magnificent creature. He did look incredibly, undeniably handsome. Of course, for me, there was nothing more appealing than the sight of an attractive man on a handsome horse. The very *sight* of Winston on his horse seemed to thrill me in a way I tried with intense effort to suppress, but with little success.

He hopped down off of his mare, tipped his hat briefly, added a small bow, and said, "Even'ng M'am."

"Good evening to you, as well." I smiled, still desperately attempting to suppress my flutterings.

"Well, I confess I did not expect to find you out walking so far from home."

"Yes... well... I am sometimes somewhat of a walker..."

"I was planning on asking you out for an evening stroll, but part of that plan was to tie up Daisy first, so I could walk with you... well... unencumbered... you know, without my horse... as we walked."

"As you well know, I adore horses, so Daisy is welcome to stroll with us."

Winston cleared his throat and spoke, "So... it has been a very long time since I have seen you."

"I know. How have you been all this time?"

"Well... and you?"

"Quite well."

"I was quite surprised to find that you had moved from town... from your teaching position..."

"Yes, well... that is a *very* long story... but suffice it to say that I chose to leave the school, and go to the Jones' farm where I was wanted and needed more."

"So you have been well, then?"

"Yes." I smiled.

"And life on the farm goes well."

"Yes... I have been enjoying some relaxing of late."

"Good. Good. You *certainly* deserve that."

"And I have been sketching again, which has been very nice."

"Good. You were *always* very good."

"And *you*? You are back for a time? How are your business plans going?"

"Good. Good. Very good, actually. Yes, I am back... for a while... or to stay... I am not quite sure..."

I sensed his intense nervousness. I was pretty certain as to what he wanted to lead up to. I was quite surprised at myself that *I* did not feel terribly nervous. I knew that I did not know what I would say if he *did* ask me to marry him... but strangely, somehow, I was managing not to worry about that concern at that moment. I wondered if I should try to help him along, or if I should divert him from his possible intended path. Did I *want* to face the question of marriage right now? No.

"Daisy is a lovely mare." I diverted.

"Oh? My horse... Yes. A good horse. She's a very nice horse."

"Very beautiful."

"Yes. Thank you."

"I love horses... but, I repeat myself."

He faltered in return, "Oh, yes... I love... horses... too."

Oh. dear: love. I should not have said *that* word. I did not quite know what to say now. I was beginning to feel a little nervous. I tried to divert further, "It is a lovely evening."

"Yes."

"Is not that a *lovely* sunset?

"Yes."

"I love sunsets." Oh, dear me, I *kept* saying "lovely" and "love".

"I love sunsets too."

"Well, who would *not*, I suppose. A sunset is like a Heavenly painting each time it happens. And look, we have a full moon tonight. I love clear nights like this when there is a full moon." There. I said the word "love" *again*!

"Yes. I love a full moon on a clear night too."

I truly wanted to divert us from using that *word*, "It is amazing how bright the moon can be, and so nice when the night is not so very dark."

"Yes."

"We'd soon be lost in the dark tonight without the full moon."

"Yes... Fionna... there is something I must say to you..."

"Oh?"

"Yes... I... well... now that you are no longer teaching, what would you think of working in a general store?"

It was not *quite* the something that I thought he would say to me, but it was *much* easier to answer than what I imagined he might say, and so I lightly jumped in, "Oh... Well... of course I would be willing to try it. I think I would enjoy it. It would be quite nice to work in a store."

"If I were to open a store in town, would you be willing to work there... with me?"

"Certainly... I would." I was naively and completely focused on the idea of working: of having a job; of earning my keep.

"Do you think the town could use another shop?"

"I do... think so. The town is growing and, well, I am sure another store would be a good thing there."

"Do you think I would do well?"

"Yes. I do."

Winston stopped and looking intently at me, his eyes almost as large as Daisy's as they both peered at me, "I would not want to open it without... without you working there with me."

Feeling thoroughly silly that I was so terribly unprepared for such, I was initially unable to speak in response. He had broached the subject of working in a shop together before. I had successfully averted the matter then. This was now quite likely... his question... his informal offer... of marriage, to me. Surely he must mean marriage. I had felt that theme of questioning before but now I must consider it, I supposed. There seemed no diverting the direction of the sentiment. I tried to answer without committing myself, "But, you have planned to open a store for so long... and... if I were to stay on the farm instead..."

"If you would not want to work with me in a shop in town... near here... perhaps I would go open a store somewhere else..."

This seemed all very curious. Was he *afraid* to ask me to marry him: afraid my answer might be to decline him? He was surely speaking in a sort of code. Was this his way of testing my possible answer to a question of marriage? Was he not brave enough to ask me outright? I did not know if I wanted to continue speaking in this manner. I did not know what to say now. I did not want to look at him. I looked straight ahead and began slowly walking again, even as I uneasily returned, "Of course you should open a shop wherever you feel it is best for you to do so, but... if it were not near... I would miss you... I would..."

Trying to think clearly, I kept walking, in a slight daze, not truly knowing if Winston was walking with me. Suddenly he stopped me by grabbing my shoulders with both his hands, even with Daisy's reigns in one of them. Daisy jerked a little in fright. He patted her, speaking gentle reassurances to her and then turned again to me, "Fionna. I love you. I want to marry you. Will you marry me?"

I looked away instantaneously. I burst into tears. I did not know *what* had come over me, but I began sobbing even as I was fighting crying. I was flooded with feelings that I could not seem to explain within myself. How could I explain them to Winston? It was as if it *hurt* to hear his declaration of love for me. It pained me to know that I loved him too. The question pained me like I never imagined it could. I wanted to say that I loved him too. I *wanted* to say yes to his proposal. But I was struck dumb... except for my weeping.

I chanced a glance over at him. He looked confused. It was no wonder to me. What could I say now? How could I say anything in the midst of struggling to stop my sobbing? Directly, his confusion turned to compassion and he put an arm around me and asked, "What is *wrong*? Why are you weeping?"

Well, I wept all the more for his kind concern. I loved him all the more. He stood there trying to console me with his arm about me: his hand patting my back gently and slowly. I determined to take hold of myself. I would tell him I loved him too. I did not know about my answer to his question of marriage as yet, but I *could* admit to my feelings for him. He had offered so much, after all, I could venture to offer *that* much. I swallowed hard, over and over. I wiped my tears. I breathed deeply. I finally spoke, "Winston. I love you too."

In one swift motion, he let go of his mare's reigns and picked me up in a swirling embrace, calling out for the full moon to hear, "I love you! I love you!" Daisy retreated a little. It was a wonder that she did not run off in fright! A part of me wanted to run.

He put me down and said with his face shining brightly with delight under the moonlight, "Then I will open that shop in town and we will work side by side in it. I want to be married right away! Can you marry me right away? I do not want to delay... unless... unless you need some time... to prepare?"

I hesitated but had to press, "Yes, Winston... I need... some time..."

"All right... then I will have the store built while I wait. How do you feel about living upstairs above the shop? We could start off cozy like that and then, later... well... I want to build you a big beautiful house later... maybe after we have had a few children... and you are too busy with them to work in the shop... and we would need a bigger home anyway... so I would build you a mansion... everything you truly deserve..."

"Winston..."

"Yes, my love?"

"I... need... some time... to..."

"Yes. I know you want to wait a little to marry... and so I will build you our shop and our little home on top... and then when it is all ready, we will be married!"

He picked me up and twirled me around again. He was ecstatic. He was floating as if on the moon above us. Oh, but I did not want to bring him down to earth. But I simply *had* to. I had to be completely honest with him and so I spoke in a serious and firm tone, "Winston. Winston... I need *time* to..."

He looked confused, "Time to... *what?*"

"I need time to think over the *question* of marriage."

"The *question?* The question of *marriage?* What ever do you mean?"

"Winston, I love you... but..."

He looked completely dashed and entirely confused, *"But?"*

"But I need time to *think* it over."

"What is there to think *over?* We love each other. Is not marriage the *answer* to love rather than a *question?*"

"Well, perhaps to most, but..."

"Fionna. You are *not* making any sense. You said you love me. *Don't* you love me? I love you. I want you to marry me. Don't you want to marry me?"

"I do *not* know." I said, somewhat sadly.

"You do not *know?!*" He looked incredulously at me.

"No... I..."

"You love me... but you don't *know* if you want to marry me?"

"Winston. I *do* love you. I have never come *close* to loving any other man before. It is *you* that I love. I cannot *imagine* loving any other man besides you. I am very happy that you love me. I... I... I so appreciate that you want to marry me... but... I... I don't know if I *ever* want to marry. I am... *afraid* of marriage."

"*Afraid*? Afraid of *marriage*? Why?"

"Because I have seen such *heartbreak*: I have seen the failings of marriages around me. I have seen the unhappiness in *other* marriages. I do not want to end up *unhappy*."

"But, Fionna... do you think you will be happier *alone*?"

"I *might* be."

"You *might* be. But you *might* be happier in *marriage*."

"I know... I don't know."

"Fionna. How can either of us truly know if we would be happier together or apart? All I know is that it feels *right* to me to marry you."

"But I don't know what feels *right* to me. A part of me truly wants to marry you, but the *other* part of me is terrified of marriage altogether and does not want to *ever* marry. Maybe I am simply not *ready* for marriage right now. Maybe I need some time to get ready to face it. I don't know. I do know that I need time. I just can't say yes to marriage *yet*. Can we not be friends for *now*? Can you give me some time to think about it a *little* while?"

He looked quite sad and yet very thoughtful. He paused a long while and then finally spoke, "All right... then... Yes. I will give you some time to ponder the matter over. But... I cannot wait around *forever* while you decide. I can't really wait long around here. I can't go ahead and have a store built if you won't marry me, and work in and live above the shop with me. I can't very well go somewhere else and start my shop only to have you call me back here when you are suddenly ready for marriage... I will tell you what I will do... I will go away again a while. I have more business I can do before I build my store. I will *prepare* some more... and then I will come back and ask you *one* more time. But you need to decide *yes* or no. I cannot wait *forever*."

"But, could you not stay here for a time while I *think* about marriage? We could see each other... maybe get to know each other better... and..."

"Fionna, I cannot be aimlessly waiting for you to decide. I have to be working towards my business in the meantime. Besides, I confess it *hurts* me that you don't know if you *want* to marry me. I would rather leave than stay, for staying would hurt me further."

"Winston... I am *so* sorry... but..."

"Fionna, I love you. I am going away and I hope you will say yes when I return."

"I love you too, Winston. I hope that I can say yes too."

He kissed my forehead: a long and tender kiss, as he held my face tenderly, yet firmly with both his hands. I was sure I saw tears glistening in his eyes when he mounted his mare and rode off. He did not look back. My tears began.

I was very close to home. I wished myself very far away so I would have hours further to walk to get home. How could I enter the house like this? I began to sob, thinking, 'What have I done? What *have* I done? I have thrown it all away! What if he *never* comes back? I *love* him! I *do* want to marry him! Why do I continue to *push* him away? He is the *only* man I would *ever* want to marry. Why can I not simply agree to marry him? I don't *really* want to be alone. He is a *good* man...'

I composed myself enough to get inside and up into my room, where I cried quietly most of the night. I do not know that I slept at all.

For days afterwards, I felt such a mix of emotions. I was dreadfully confused within myself. My soul felt completely downtrodden. I was so incredibly sad that Winston had gone away, that I had pushed him away... again, that I could not seem to say yes to his proposal, and yet I felt a certain joy within me because of what he had declared and proposed. Many moments found me in tears: trying to hide my tears from everyone.

I knew I could not confide in anyone, nor speak to anyone about my dilemma, and I certainly could not seek advice from any person

I knew. I had no doubt that if Mother Jones, my sisters or any friend knew of what had transpired, they would think me thoroughly unwise and indeed *worse* than silly to have declined such a wonderful offer of marriage. I was very sure that if Mother and Victoria knew I had not jumped at the chance to marry the likes of Winston, they would want to scold me if they could. What woman in her right mind would have done what I had done? *Was* I in my right mind?

I spent most of my time pondering the matter over and over in my head. I thought that my fears of marriage were likely unreasonable, mostly unfounded and certainly an emotional problem within me that I must try to conquer: and *before* Winston's return. I wondered if perhaps Winston and a marriage to him might simply be *too* good to be true, or maybe that *providence* had other plans for me. I did not want to make a mistake. I wanted to be *certain* that marrying Winston was the right thing to do. I did not want to follow my romantic side into a wrong choice. I surely must decide which was right for me before Winston came back to ask me again.

Praying on the question seemed a right thing to do and so I did take time here and there: day and night, sending my question up to Heaven above, in the hopes that I might sense the right answer and know what to do. As time passed, I began to feel better and better about taking the risk of marriage with Winston. A certain peace seemed to come over me and *stay* with me. My fears, concerns and worries began to subside. I began to believe that marrying Winston was the right thing for me to do. I eventually became certain that life *with* Winston would be a safe and happy one for me, and indeed I began to ache horribly at the thought of living my life *without* being with him.

Soon I craved the event of Winston's return. I began to watch the road for him. I hoped for word from or about him. I wondered how long it would be before he came back, to ask me to marry him again.

I thought much about what I would say, when I saw him again, and how joy would fill both of us when I gave him my answer. I imagined how he would react. I could picture him in raptures knowing what my feelings now were and that I now wanted nothing but to marry him. I could not help but remember him picking me up and spinning me around, in his delight of thinking that I had said yes to marriage to him. Oh, but I wished I had left him thinking that, instead of admitting my fears of marriage. But now I was sure. I knew I wanted to marry him; and once he was back and knew my answer was yes, any past hurt would be washed away. Anticipation of his homecoming to me and our upcoming marriage kept my spirits high, and I felt as if I was walking on air much of the time.

Within myself, I wished there was someone that I felt I could tell, but I chose to keep it all to myself. If Victoria were here I would surely have told her every detail. I knew she would have understood me as completely as anybody could, and would have shared absolutely in my joy. Perhaps I could have confided in my sisters or Mother Jones, but I simply did not feel as close to them, as I had been to Victoria and so did not feel compelled to share my secret. I decided that nobody need know that I had not instantly accepted Winston's offer after his first declaration of love, for that could remain a secret between us forever, if he so chose. I would wait until Winston had returned and our marriage date was fixed, before telling anyone. I hoped the world would know soon enough. I wished for Winston to come back to me in all haste.

As days and weeks dragged by, I wished with all my heart that Winston had given me an avenue of correspondence with him. I *ached* to write to him to declare my increasing love, and fervent longing to be married as soon as possible. Oh, *why* had he not given me the option of being able to write to him: why had I not thought to ask him where he would be, in case I wished to write him a letter before his return? It was so disconcerting not to be able to write to him. The passing time was torturing me *terribly*. When would Winston come back to me?!

The more time that passed, the more I began to wonder if Winston might not ever come again. Perhaps he had begun to rethink his choice? Maybe his love for me was fading? Did he not love me anymore? Had he met someone else? Did he now love *another*? Had he since declared his love to a woman who instantly responded in kind? Oh, how I tortured myself with anger within for having not been ready to agree to marriage with him. I began to truly fear that I had missed my *only* chance at a happy marriage.

Over time, my spirits truly languished. I tried to hold out hope that Winston would soon return; that his feelings for me would be the same or perhaps even stronger, and that we would soon be married and happily running our shop together: but I was more inclined to believe that Winston had met, fallen in love with and married another and that I would never see him again. I began to believe I would never marry, for if I could not marry Winston, I was certain I would never wish to marry anyone else.

I tried to focus on living. I did my best not to think about Winston, deciding that if he never returned, my life would go on as before and if he did return I would be happily married shortly thereafter. It seemed wisest for me to think on everything *but* Winston. I spent time drawing horses, helping Mother Jones and visiting with my sisters, brothers and others.

33
Singing

A second letter from Charlotte and Elizabeth's husbands finally arrived filled with enough good news so that Mother Jones could go on in good spirits, knowing her sons were doing relatively well. It was always a relief to know Jacob or Joseph, or Clara, Anna and their husbands were well, on their trek into the frontier. I wondered where Clara and Anna were and when we would read from them again. I hoped and prayed that they were well. I also wondered about Benjamin and hoped and prayed for him, although I had long since accepted that we would not be reunited with him in this life. I held onto the belief that we would have a reunion with him in the next life. Perhaps it could be as *if* we had never been parted. My sincerest desire for him was that he was being raised and treated *well*. I knew he could not possibly remember us and so at least he would not suffer feelings of loss, as we *had* and still *did* for him.

It seemed so long since I had seen Winston that I began instinctively not to think of him at all: at *least* I thought of him very little. When I *did* think of him, I exerted my full strength to drive thoughts of him *out* of my mind, for it pained me greatly to think of him. My heart *ached* to be reminded of him. I could not let myself remember him. I decided that I *must* forget him.

Sometimes I wondered if I should go to town to a dance or some other social kind of event, to amuse myself conversing and dancing with young men. Even contemplating such a thought glared at me as folly for *who* would I desire to dance with? Sometimes a part of me hungered for social interactions beyond the farm, and more particularly, beyond what my sisters offered me. There were times my legs ached to take me to town, though, who was there to truly befriend me now? There were acquaintances to be sure, but no intimate friends to converse with. Catherine had been as a sister and a good friend to me, but, she was a busy married woman.

Ah... Catherine. What had become of Catherine? She was likely still angry with me. We had not spoken since that day we quarreled. I had all but almost forgotten. I had not seen her in town and she had not sought me out: she had not come to the farm to see me. I wondered if she was healed and happy in her marriage, and so now did not need me. I *hoped* that was so. I hoped she was happy in her marriage. I hoped she was able to finally feel one and at peace with her husband again.

The next time I went to town I saw her. I tried to speak with her but Catherine was obviously not interested in being amiable with me. I could see that she no longer considered me a friend. Her manner was quite overtly cold towards me. We conversed very little and the only comment she made that I can not help but recall was something to the effect that she wondered why Winston had left town so quickly, when she had been quite certain that he had had plans to stay. Then she finished with an assurance that he was better off where he was now wherever that may be, and that she hoped he had found love. I thought it a cutting, although cloaked, remark against me. I wondered exactly what she thought or might know, but I was sure she was referring to her knowledge of my fears of marriage and not knowing if I could say yes to Winston. I thought it *especially* cruel of her to treat me in that way and it did hurt me to my core, knowing how diligently and gently I had tried to comfort *her* in her many hours of need.

Knowing Catherine could not know how my heart ached to see Winston again and to marry him, I did my utmost to tolerate her ignorance and forgive her for her unkind words to me. It seemed incredulous to me that a friend, whom I had given so much of my heart and time to, could so quickly toss me aside for a few words that I had mistakenly spoken without realizing the possible hurtful effect upon her. I wondered if I should try to obtain some sort of forgiveness and renewal of friendship with Catherine, but I sensed that she needed to walk away from me in order to completely forget what her husband had done to hurt her so deeply. I supposed that in my knowing their painful secret, I might remind her of all her sorrow and suffering relative to her husband's wayward offense. Since she had confided it all only in me, by walking away from my friendship, she was possibly walking away from all reminders of her past hurts.

If putting me aside as a friend helped in her healing and happiness, so be it. Still, it did hurt to know that I had offered and given so much and now was esteemed almost as if an enemy. I did not feel that I deserved such treatment, but no matter: I could let go, forgive, forget and focus on those who were yet my friends. Catherine had her husband and family, and in my heart I wished her well with them.

***

As Charlotte and Elizabeth were so fond of going to town, they had been quite inclined to take charge of the gathering of supplies whenever need be, and had oft taken one of the boys with them. Bertram and Edward had lately become especially fond of going in to town to help their sisters at the general store or wherever their supply hunt took them. I suppose I had not truly noticed, but my brothers were indeed getting older and were beginning to take notice of young ladies.

Suddenly one day, after the boys had been in town with our sisters, Bertram announced to me, "It is high time that you took Edward and I to town dances and since there is one coming up, we should surely go to it."

Without thinking on the matter thoroughly, but pausing on it promptly, I instantly instinctively begged, "But can you not go without me? I do not wish to go to dances."

"Charlotte and Elizabeth should not take us, as they are married with their husbands away. Father and Mother Jones do not wish to go as they prefer to stay home, and they have asked that we not go alone without some sort of chaperone... so you *must* go with us. You are the only one *left* to take us."

Charlotte was nearby and put in (half jesting, I imagined), "Oh, Fionna, must you *persist* in being an old maid? Take the boys to dances, help them begin towards finding wives for themselves and get yourself a husband while you are at it: while you still can!"

If only Charlotte knew of my feelings and thoughts regarding Winston, and my aching heart because he had not come back for me. I did not presently care to find myself another to be my husband. I wondered if Charlotte had put Bertram up to this sudden plan... perhaps a plan to get me to town, to the dances and in the company of any man that would still desire an old maid like me. Well, no matter, at least Bertram and perhaps Edward were more than old enough to begin to think about courting a young lady; and so I gladly complied for my brothers' sakes. I could go to the dances. I did not have to dance. I was not inclined to dance.

When Bertram, Edward and I attended their first dance in town, at first I felt quite awkward, for I felt too old to be there as a single lady; but soon, my old favorite students were reacquainting themselves with me and I enjoyed seeing them very much. I did also especially delight in seeing my brothers dancing after they finally got up the courage to ask the young ladies that interested them. It was clear the young women were only too happy to encourage such attentions.

I thoroughly enjoyed visiting with friends, but more especially I thrilled to watch my brothers delight in dancing and conversing with many lovely young ladies. As I watched their choices, I sincerely hoped that they would be able to make wise matches. I found it interesting that within myself, I worried far more regarding my brothers' choices than I ever had my sisters'. I supposed it was my haunting thoughts about Father and his second and final choice, and other examples I knew such as Ethan and his alternate and concluding choice. I did fear that my brothers might suffer the same fate as Ethan and Father in that they might each choose a wife who was conniving and manipulative, as far too many young ladies and women are sadly apt to be. Of course, I *hoped* not. I hoped and *prayed* that they would each find a sweet girl who would bring out the best in them and be only but good for them.

In the days that followed, I took opportunity to encourage my brothers to entertain thoughts about *many* young ladies that they may learn to observe and *compare* the relative differences between all these young women who were vying for their attentions. I thought that the more they explored the territory of choices that lay before each of them, the better they might do in their *final* preference and selection. I tried to instill in them both that there was no hurry: no need to rush into a marriage. I teased them that even though a woman had the worry of becoming an old maid, this was *no* quandary or challenge for *any* man. A man had *time*: much time for choosing his bride. Time was on his side to be sure.

I advised them each to take a good deal of time in choosing, saying that it was a life-long choice that could make *so* much difference in their happiness and so it was so *incredibly* important to choose wisely. I dared to mention Father and his ill choice of Mildred, pointing out the result of ruination to our family because of that union. My brothers quickly *tired* of my lectures and teased back that I was an old maid, and that of *course* I believed in being terribly careful in choosing a mate, which was why I was not married *still*. What could I *say* to that? Well, I did declare that I would rather be alone in life than to marry the wrong man, and that to settle with the wrong mate was no triumphant settlement.

***

Finally, a letter came from Anna: they were settling in at their final destination. They were at last come to that place they had told us of: the Williamette Valley, in Oregon Country. Anna described it as an extraordinarily lush place with abundantly rich soil. They had staked out their land there already, had constructed humble temporary abodes and were beginning to farm that land. I could see from Anna's words that they were all quite exhausted and had suffered through many challenges along the trail, but they were *still* full of hope and faith for their future in this new land. As *always*, I hoped and prayed, for their sakes, that their hopes would indeed be fulfilled.

Mother Jones was elated for our other sisters and although she did not hear from her sons enough equal to her liking, her faith in their safety, health, success and eventual triumphant return was surely boosted, for Clara and Anna seemed to be doing well despite the hardships inherent in such a bold and lengthy venture. I thought that Mother Jones believed that if Clara, Anna and their husbands could make it to Oregon territory unscathed, and indeed still full of bright hopes for their future out there, *surely* her sons could make it to California territory and do well there too; for California Country was so very near and indeed just south of the Oregon lands.

***

One very still and peacefully wonderful early summer afternoon, I was putting out the laundry to dry, enjoying the sun shining warmly on my shoulders and on the top of my head, my face happily shaded by my bonnet brim, as I sang a favorite song. Thinking myself quite alone, for my brothers were far out in the fields with Father Jones, and Mother Jones had gone into town with my sisters: I sang out quite loudly. In fact, when I heard a voice speak from behind me, it stunned me so much so that I dropped my basket, and the few remaining wet items of clothing in it were tossed out from the fall. I swiftly turned around to see Winston standing there before me.

Surely I was quite a sight: my mouth agape, my face quite suddenly crimson, my basket on the ground with its last contents now strewn round about it and myself unable to speak a word. I could barely think. At first my mind began to rush with thoughts of what I might or *should* say, and then it filled with embarrassing thoughts about being caught singing quite aloud. Finally, I tried to recall what Winston had just said to me. I could not grasp a word of what he had said: all I knew was that I had heard his voice in the midst of my singing.

He spoke again, "I never knew you possessed such a *lovely* singing voice. Why did you never *tell* me? What *other* talents have you been hiding?"

"Oh... I..." I looked down, blushing all the more, "Thank you... I..."

"Well... I am here *again*... and here you *still* are: still *so* beautiful."

I looked at him, deep into his eyes, trying to discern whether or not he still loved me. I thought I could see quite clearly that he did. I wondered if he feared that I might still have the same fears. I wondered if he had been in torture all this time and had finally been able to come back to give me one last chance at his question. I gathered my strength together to answer.

Deciding to act quickly before losing resolve, before torturing him any further, trying to make up for the hurt and the waiting that I had caused by not knowing he was right in the first place, and *perhaps* even accepting his offer before it could be rescinded; I stunned myself by quite blurting out, "Winston! The answer is *yes*! I *do* want to marry you! I *knew* it was right almost *immediately* after you left! Why did you leave right away? Why could you not have given me even a day or two to ponder the matter over? Oh, *why* did you take so dreadfully long to return to me? What *torture* you have put me through. I truly had given up on you coming back to me. Why did you not write me any *letters*? I *feared* you had stopped loving me even as I loved you *all* the more. I was *so* worried you had found love with another."

He did not instantly pick me up and spin me around in ecstatic joy, as I had in the past so often imagined he would do again upon hearing my final happy answer. He did not answer me at all which seemed uncomfortably curious. *Why* was he not overjoyed at my blissful answer to his life-altering question after *all* this time? I could not determine what he might be thinking as he stood in front of me in this curiously still and silent way. I wanted to ask, to speak... to get him to speak... but I could not. I feared to tread further. Had he changed his mind? *Was* there someone else? I waited for him to break the silence. The brief time of intense quiet seemed to last forever. Oh, what torment!

Winston finally ended my agony, "Are you sure... very sure? Are you certain that you *do* want to marry me?"

"Yes... yes! I am *certain*! I *am* sure!"

Winston's hesitance was palpable, "And you won't be changing your mind, then? You are *sure* of marriage now? Sure of *me*?"

I fairly beamed, "I am wonderfully sure of marriage with *you*! Yes, Winston, yes!"

Winston smiled rather bashfully, "Do you want to marry quite soon, or do you want to... wait..."

"As soon as you want to... I want to, my... darling. We need not wait."

Winston hastily pulled me to him, into his arms, embracing me fully. I melted into him. He kissed the top of my head upon my sun-bleached bonnet, and then lifted its brim and pressed a most tender kiss upon my forehead. My heart felt warmer than the sun that day. It was not the extreme blush of embarrassment that Winston had brought out in me so many times before. No, it was a steady heat all at once, of both comfort and intensity. I reached out for his hand and he took mine with his instantly, leading me for a stroll far beyond the house. We walked for what seemed at least miles and hours, saying little, his hand squeezing mine and then mine pressing his, each in our turn; momentarily gazing at each other, smiling broadly and then shyly from time to time.

In our many gentle moments that day, we blissfully planned our future together. Winston would commission and help to build a little store with a home above, for us in town. We would work there side by side until I was too big or busy with our babies, to help him out in the shop as much. We would wait to marry, but only long enough to have our home and business done and ready for us to move into, together. I did secretly take comfort in having a little extra time to fall more and more in love with my man, before walking the bridge over to married life with him. My nervousness was still a little part of me. I knew Winston could ease my concerns and steady me to step into marital life with more confidence in the institution, because of a greater confidence in him.

As the golden sun began to sink along the azure sky, towards a magnificent magenta horizon, Winston stopped to kiss my forehead at luxurious length again, and then scooping his arm around my waist, began to lead me towards the house. Chills ran through me. What ecstasy. How ever could I have *imagined* these heights of feelings before I had my own man? Never did I know such that I was missing. But now, it was mine. He was mine.

When we said goodbye that evening, feelings of contentment and excitement took their turns with me. *Never* had a goodbye been accompanied with such a warmth and security. It was almost as if we could not say goodbye. I did not want to let him *go* and he did not wish to *leave* me. Because we had both agreed on as early a wedding date as realistically possible, this seemed to give us *strength* to part that night. Finally, I as much as pushed him up and onto his horse and waved him off that he might arrive to his home before darkness made the journey difficult (and even possibly dangerous for him, I suddenly considered). My *complete* sense of love and concern for his welfare seemed to overwhelm me.

As he rode off and away, he turned back to look and wave at me: I stood still, waving at him and watching him as his silhouette gradually disappeared into the distance. Could I paint such a picture? One became stored in my mind.

The following morning after breakfast, on a Sunday, everyone was indoors about to prepare to go to church. I was out sweeping up the veranda when I caught a glimpse of Winston riding towards me. I stopped and enjoyed the sight: a glorious scene to behold. As he drew nearer to me, I marveled at how exceedingly attractive my man on his horse *was* to me. I knew not just *any* man could excite these profoundly intense feelings within, although I knew that a man on a horse must be the *most* attractive possibility. Oh, how extremely handsome *my* betrothed looked to me at that moment in time.

I tried to finish sweeping as I enjoyed the magnificent sight of the man I was about to marry, but my broom seemed suspended in my hands as they and the rest of me could not seem to move beyond gazing at *my* beloved in his final approach.

"Whoa!" he said to his fine horse as he prepared to dismount.

I smiled with delight, "Hello!"

"Greetings, fair maiden!" he seemed to tease.

"Are you thirsty? Perhaps you are hungry as well?"

"Yes... how sweet of you to ask me. How did you know, my love?"

"I am only too happy to offer you any refreshment I can find for you in the kitchen. There is still some breakfast to be had."

"So..." he seemed to proclaim as he stepped up next to me on the veranda, grabbing and kissing my hand.

"*So?*"

"Have you told anyone yet?"

"What?"

"That we are to be *married*, of course!" he looked *quite* incredulous to see that I had not instantaneously known exactly what he had meant.

I felt terribly silly that I had not been exactly sure whether he was inquiring regarding our planning on marrying, or also possibly our plans to build a store. I ventured, "Oh... I suppose I am still in a state of astonishment and... I simply was not sure if *that* alone was what you were wondering... if I had revealed our betrothal... or also spoken of our plans to build a store... no... I have not told anyone any thing as yet."

"You are not *ashamed* of me, or afraid to admit to succumbing to a marriage offer, are you?" he winked.

"Of *course* not!" I was playfully shocked.

"Well, *I* have already told *everyone* I know!"

"Oh, my! Then I had better tell everyone *I* know... before they begin to hear *rumors*!"

"Why did you keep it a secret?"

Feeling still in somewhat of a daze from what had transpired the night before, I feared within me a little that all of it had been too good to be true. I did not want to prematurely or unwarrantedly excite myself nor anyone else, about the dream I felt I was in. I could not seem to speak such to him at that instant in time nor try to explain by touching uncomfortably on that main point. Instead, I could only honestly muster, "I was not sure if we were to announce it... as yet. We had not discussed... I knew not your wishes."

"Why ever not?! I wanted to proclaim it aloud all the way home and I thought you would be feeling the *same!*"

"I *felt* the same... but... but I did not know if you wanted me to tell anyone yet... and to own the truth, I *feared* it was all a dream... or... that you might change your mind on your way home... or..."

Winston laughed and kissed my hand repeatedly before speaking, "No... no my sweet... I will never change my mind about you. And you know, maybe my *own* fears that you might change *your* mind prompted me to tell every one, so that you could not easily back out! You have said yes to me... at least I think you have... and I mean to *hold* you to it! At least I *hope* to be able to."

"It *is* settled... and maybe I shall insist you marry me within the next few days... before *you* can back out!" I teased and then, "Come with me... and help me tell everyone."

"You wouldn't rather tell them on your own? They barely know me."

"No. I do not want you to leave me so soon... so you must come *with* me to tell everyone. Besides, you are hungry and thirsty. Remember?"

"All right then, I will help you break the news... and yes, I could certainly use some breakfast."

I thought perhaps that Winston was a little nervous: worrying that everyone would not be overjoyed with him. He feared displeasure with our match, but even more to his pleasant surprise than mine, everyone could not have been more delighted and extremely vocal about it. My sisters were so exceedingly elated as to surprise me *immensely* but what did *not* really surprise me was that Mother Jones was beside herself with abundant joy. Father Jones and my brothers seemed so especially happy for me as well.

It seemed that Winston's good reputation had preceded him, and I wondered if perhaps there had already been rumors that had made their way to Mother Jones' and my sisters' ears, for they did not seem all that surprised at our news. They seemed to know that Winston was in a fine way towards making a good living for us. I suspected that there was a collective sigh of relief that I had finally succumbed to Winston's attentions.

Of course I gave Winston ample nourishment before readying myself for church, and then we all went to town together. Winston and I walked arm in arm into the chapel and sat happily compressed together in one long center pew, alongside the Jones, my two sisters and three brothers. I confess this was perhaps my happiest moment ever in a church. I thrilled at simply sitting beside Winston, knowing I was to be *his* for a lifetime. I began to imagine scenes of our upcoming marriage in this or any other church.

Winston and I secretively and discreetly held hands under the allowed expanse of my skirt fabric close beside him. The warmth of his hand transferred to me as mine surely did to him. I felt an intense euphoric love for this man sitting beside me. My heart leapt and soared in turns. It was a dream-world. I easily ignored those who seemed to whisper about or peer and peek towards us. Winston seemed completely oblivious to them. He regularly glanced down at me. I could not resist glancing up at him each time he instigated such a connection. We could not suppress our smiles for each other. Staring into each others eyes seemed requisite. What was said or sung in that church that day I could not tell you. I might as well have been sitting alone in a field with Winston, for what I could fathom around us.

This was Mother Jones' own chosen church of many years and she outwardly burst with pride and glee to see members of her congregation glancing and gawking our way, to see Winston and me: the new couple. When the meeting was over, Mother Jones seemed flitting everywhere at once, swiftly apprising everyone of my betrothal to Winston and then she could not seem to introduce us to her friends fast enough, as the newly engaged pair. I could not help but delight in Mother Jones' triumph of being first to announce our news to everyone she knew. I felt such joy in knowing that *she* was beaming with joy, knowing I was to finally be wed.

My sisters smilingly twittered with their friends. From not too afar off I could hear snippets of their conversation as they speculated on the decorative details of the happy event on the horizon. I knew Mother Jones and my sisters would hold sway over much of such. Beyond talk of the lace, silk, foods and frills of a wedding, all these young women seemed to say that they each *always* knew that Winston would finally be mine: that I would eventually relent. My sisters seemed to deem themselves the most visionary of the fluttering flock. I would not deny any of them their supposed victories. Too blissful to correct any of their boasts, I simply smiled as I treasured the arm I held fast to.

***

Winston came to the farm and took me to town scores of times in following weeks and we indulged in numerous afternoon or early evening strolls. Delighting in many meals together, our conversations traversed over multiple topics. We shared our ideals and dreams with each other. After completing our initial plans for a shop with our home atop, and the building of the structure being begun, we were sometimes somewhat free to more thoroughly acquaint ourselves with each other. Winston was of course required to spend some time overseeing the construction, and was quite involved in that work to some degree to be sure, but, there was still time in-between his labors, for Winston's unwavering devotions to me. I took full advantage of Winston's moments away from assisting in work on our home and business structure, although I did not wish to hamper the process, for, the more speedily this building finished completion, the sooner Winston and I could be married. Indeed, when Winston was working on our building, I was laboriously working on quilts, curtains and all things imaginable for it. I was increasingly as anxious as Winston was to make our own place ready, so that we could move into it together.

One of our stolen magical hours together was off and away on a quiet wooded path, when and where the sun glistened and glittered through the branches, dancing upon us as our hearts danced, energized by the warmth of both the sunlight and our clasped hands.

"You thought me a *snob* at first," I teased.

He laughed and said, "Yes, I suppose I did... yes, at first."

"I nearly never forgave you for *thinking* such of me." I solemnly pronounced.

"Ah... but... forgiveness is divine... and since *you* are divine... you could not but forgive me."

"At first I was determined *never* to dance with you."

"But you *relented*."

"How could I *resist* your charms?"

"How could I *not* pursue you?"

"Why did you delight in making me blush?"

"You look all the more beautiful in red."

"But any hue of blue is your favorite color." I challenged.

He pouted, "And I was dashed to see you wear that green instead."

"I never promised you I would wear the blue *first*."

"Although you *knew* it was my sincere desire."

"And that is *why* I could not wear it at first."

He sighed, "You would rather tease me?"

I chuckled, "No, but you surely delighted in teasing *me*."

"*Anything* to make you smile."

"It was *you* who smiled incessantly!"

"In your company, I can not imagine *other* than smiling."

"I surely hope we will always smile together, Winston."

"We will, Fionna, I assure you."

He stopped, looking deep into the soul within my eyes, and then embraced me in all gentle tenderness, in a loving moment that as if lasted forever.

382839